THE WHITENESS OF THE WHALE

Previous Books by David Poyer

Tales of the Modern Navy
The Towers
The Crisis
The Weapon
Korea Strait
The Threat
The Command
Black Storm
China Sea
Tomahawk
The Passage
The Circle
The Gulf
The Med

Tiller Galloway
Down to a Sunless Sea
Louisiana Blue
Bahamas Blue
Hatteras Blue

The Civil War at Sea
That Anvil of Our Souls
A Country of Our Own
Fire on the Waters

Hemlock County
Thunder on the Mountain
As the Wolf Loves Winter
Winter in the Heart
The Dead of Winter

Other Books
Happier Than This Day and Time
Ghosting
The Only Thing to Fear
Stepfather Bank
The Return of Philo T. McGiffin
Star Seed
The Shiloh Project
White Continent

C-2

THE WHITENESS OF THE WHALE

DAVID POYER

ST. MARTIN'S PRESS
New York

This is a work of fiction. All of the characters, organizations, and events portrayed in this novel are either products of the author's imagination or are used fictitiously.

www.stmartins.com

Design by Kathryn Parise

ISBN 978-1-250-02056-7 (hardcover)
ISBN 978-1-250-02057-4 (e-book)

St. Martin's Press books may be purchased for educational, business, or promotional use. For information on bulk purchases, please contact Macmillan Corporate and Premium Sales Department at 1-800-221-7945 extension 5442 or write specialmarkets@macmillan.com

First Edition: April 2013

10 9 8 7 6 5 4 3 2 1

For—absurd as it may seem—men are only made to comprehend things which they comprehended before (though but in the embryo, as it were). Things new it is impossible to make them comprehend; in their own hearts they really believe they do comprehend; outwardly look as though they did *comprehend; wag their bushy tails comprehendingly; but for all that, they do not comprehend.*

—Melville, *Pierre; or, The Ambiguities*

THE WHITENESS OF THE WHALE

1

Loomings

Forehead pressing cold scratched plastic, Sara Pollard looked down on melted silver and snowcapped mountains. From those gigantic peaks, reared in some ancient and unimaginably violent collision, glowing fingers of cloud groped toward a shabby jumble of tin roofs and shipping containers faded to the pinks and blues of sea-bleached shells.

The plane shuddered and tilted, lining up on a runway between blasted hills that bulged as if monsters writhed beneath them. Around her the other passengers stirred, speaking in many languages. Bad weather had grounded flights to Tierra del Fuego for a week. Making her barely in time, if one of those tiny specks below was the boat she was bound for.

Ushuaia. The southernmost city in Argentina.

The end is where we start from. Or so T. S. Eliot had said. But starting from the end of the world, what destination could her future possibly hold?

At the foot of a concrete pier a mustached taxi driver heaved her carry-on out into a brisk wind that smelled of ice, mountains, and sea. Hugging herself, she contemplated the craft still bound to the land by red nylon lines thick as her wrists.

Black Anemone was all white fiberglass and curves. A broad stern tapered like a splitting-wedge to a retro-looking bowsprit. Her smooth sides gleamed stark as an iceberg. Along her flank, a stylized logo of a fisted arm curled protectively around a breaching whale. A transparent plastic bubble midships looked out of place on a sailboat. A generator murmured, and a plume of steam or smoke drifted off toward those towering mountains. Sara glimpsed within its murky turbulence a figure bent over the lip of the pier, staring down. Into the water, or at something white beneath it, shimmering as if dissolving in the transparent blue.

The steam whipped away, and through it stepped an unshaven man in a black wool sweater, dark jeans, and deck boots. Deep-set eyes under heavy black brows measured her. Clearing her throat, she extended a hand. "I'm Dr. Pollard."

His grip closed on hers strong as any human grip she'd ever felt. Rough as old leather, hard as rusted iron. She shivered at the memory it evoked of another hand, even more powerful. This man's skin was weathered dark, though he couldn't be much past thirty. His cropped hair was black and his beard stubble was pointed with pewter. Ivory teeth gleamed in a reluctant and quickly erased smile. A tear in his sweater had been stitched with oiled twine. She tried to hold his gaze but hers wavered and fell.

She'd always hated the way she looked. Too tall, too thin, face too pointed, lips too scanty, a sharp New England jaw. Hair a nest of curls. But really, who cared? Hadn't she learned, by now? She averted her eyes from those teeth, that penetrating gaze.

"Dru Perrault," he said. His accent was French, or perhaps French Canadian. "*Anemone*'s captain. We're getting a late start, but I hope to head out before dusk. That your gear?"

"I think I brought everything." She caught his glance at her shoes; added hastily, "I brought sea boots, too. These aren't—"

"What color?"

"Excuse me?"

"What color are the boots?"

"Um, kind of lime green. If that's—"

Perrault frowned. "Green, no. Everyone but *her* will be wearing ship's gear." He swept up the suitcase she'd barely been able to lift and with one hand tossed it over the lifelines, where it disappeared with a thud. "You'll be rooming with Eddi. Up forward."

"Eddie?"

"Skipper!" A bulky man in dirty coveralls swung down from the deck, vaulted a mooring line, and dropped heavily to the concrete. His gaze met hers, then hardened into . . . contempt? His piglike face seemed familiar, though surely they'd never met. She disliked him, instinctively, with no more justification than for love at first sight. "Any sign of 'em?" he asked Perrault.

"Not yet. Oh, this is the whale doctor." The captain nodded her way. "Dr. Pollard; Jamie Quill. First mate."

"Pleased to meet you, Jamie."

"Yeah, same here." But he didn't look pleased. His accent was English or Irish, but not upper-class; almost Cockney-sounding. He scratched in a tangled beard as if hunting for fleas. A pale belly crusted with black hair gaped where buttons were missing. She looked away. He added, slightly less dismissively, "Welcome aboard. We're gonna do some good out there."

"I hope so. But I'm not really a whale specialist. Though I am an ethologist."

"A what?" Quill frowned.

"I study animal behavior."

Perrault's eyebrows contracted, then relaxed. "Well, doesn't matter now. Get your things aboard. We'll sail as soon as *she* arrives. Jamie, lend me a hand up forward."

The scooped-out afterdeck was packed tight with lemon-yellow plastic drums, lashed so intricately she wondered if someone was into bondage. She slid between them and a stainless-steel ship's wheel to reach the companionway down.

Belowdecks, she wove between duffels and backpacks, heavy suits dangling from carabiners, coils of cable, toolboxes, crates. Netted bags of potatoes and onions swayed from overhead hooks. The interior was more spacious than she'd expected. Louvered teak doors led aft. Midships was one great saloon roofed with curved transparent plastic. Unfamiliar smells; oil, acetone? She threaded the control area to emerge into a wedge-walled space with cavelike nooks to either hand, carved from what looked like white ice. As she edged past she glanced through the slit of a partially drawn curtain.

And stopped, blinking.

The woman was nude, her back turned. But the bare skin, the smooth curve of well-muscled flank and buttock—that was not what had riveted her gaze.

The pattern ran from her right shoulder across her back and down to the left buttock, where it curled around her side. At first Sara thought it was a scarf, but her eye swiftly revised this impression into a massive scar. Healed, now, but welted and puckered as if a hot soldering iron had been dragged down the flesh. Looking more closely, she saw that the wound itself, so like a seam in the woman's skin, had been tattooed with an intricately braided design.

Sara frowned, torn between curiosity and shame; finally took a step back.

Some sound as she did so must have reached the woman, who turned. By then Sara was facing away, but she heard quick steps, then a sliding rattle as the curtain twitched closed. Almost immediately it rattled open and the small woman, in blue running pants and a workout tee, stepped out lightly as a dancer.

"I'm sorry. Excuse me. Do you know where Eddie is?" Sara asked her.

"That's me. Eddi. Edwige Auer." A small hand pressed hers. "C'mon in. I took the lower because I'm short. Looks like that'll work out, unless—?"

"No, no, that's fine." Sara hoisted her carry-on into a curved nook with recessed lighting, a small flat pillow, a neatly folded blanket of harsh gray wool. Her new roommate's blond hair was cropped short. Bare muscular shoulders were sleeved with swirling tattoos of intricately intertwined whales and octopi and swordfish. A hard case lay open beside a video camera on her bunk. Sara fingered her glasses, then crossed her arms. "Have you been aboard long?"

"Two days. Been helping stow stores."

"This is quite a boat."

"It's a Dewoitine. Do you sail?"

"A little, when I was a kid. In Nantucket. Where are you from?"

"Most recently, California. Before that, Munich. Dru's a Vendée sailor. He skippered last year. In the lead most of the way, but he didn't finish. Need help with that bag?"

"Just to get it out of the way for now."

"You'll want to change," Auer said, eyeing her shoes the same way the captain had. "You're supposed to wear what I've got on. Look on the table in the salon. You can go a little tight, we'll probably be losing weight. And get boots."

When Sara had everything stuffed into the locker, or at least on her bunk, she went to pick through a sheaf of plastic-filmed packages. She found a women's medium long. In a coffinlike restroom she combed wind tangles out of her hair, cleaned her glasses, and washed away some of the airplane grime. The blue thermal ski gear fit reasonably well, though she wasn't sure why they all had to dress alike. White piping outlined arms and legs, and the same arm-and-whale logo as on the outer hull was embroidered on the left breast.

She found her way topside once more as a delivery van pulled up where Perrault and Quill were working out of a large gray inflatable. The captain signed the clipboard with a flourish, then tossed Sara the package. "On the nav desk, yes?"

She ducked below, then came back up. Watched them work for a time, and finally ventured, "Uh, is there anything I can help out with?"

Perrault gave her a handheld two-way and sent her out to the marina gate. "Watch for a car from the airport. Call as soon as you spot it coming down the road. Then make sure the driver knows exactly where we're moored."

This seemed simple enough and she set out. On the far side of the fence the mountains, vast and tormented, like the frozen waves of an alien sea, accompanied her as she walked.

She waited for two hours, past when the floodlights came on, shivering and watching for a car that never came. Finally she called the boat on the handheld, but no one answered. She trudged back through the dark between long sheds and fishing vessels propped on blocks and abandoned-looking masts and spars piled against a fence. The loose-fitting boots chafed her heels. No one was out on the pier. Nor on deck, though yellow light glowed from the rounded, futuristic dome, like the upper half of a flying saucer. She almost expected to see big-eyed faces, both childlike and infinitely wise, peering out.

She let herself down the companionway into mouthwatering smells of garlic, basil, wine. The others looked up blankly. "Nothing?" Perrault said.

"No cars. I tried to call, on the radio—"

"I must have been up forward. Have some stew. Freeze-dried, but Eddi got us fresh bread out in town."

"There's no meat in this," Auer said. "Just soy protein. All our food's vegetarian on this cruise." Aside from a snort from Quill, the two men didn't say anything, just kept eating.

"For whom are we waiting?" Sara asked. They didn't answer, just glanced at each other. Eddi jacked an eyebrow. Had she said something wrong?

"We have to get under way," Perrault said at last. "Going to be pretty far along in the season, by the time we get out there.—Jamie, where can we stow another drum of fuel?"

When Sara's bowl was empty Eddi got up and returned it rinsed out and filled with preserved pears. Their sweet pale flesh was so delicious she ate a second helping. The men got up and left, leaving everything on the table.

Eddi began to clear, but Sara hesitated. Her waitressing days were long past. Leo'd had his faults, but he'd always cleared at least his own place. Finally she carried her own plate and bowl into the galley.

Eddi left. Through the window Sara caught a frame of her under one of the pier lights, waving a finger as she argued with her cell. The wind was rising. Plastic bags and paper debris scudded along under the cold vibrating greenish light. Beyond the pier lay darkness. The boat jostled and leaned, creaked and sighed and clanked. A gurgle came from beneath, faded, then repeated itself, like some submarine monster attempting to communicate.

Hugging her chest, she walked the length of the boat, peeping into each compartment. The one farthest forward would probably be the lab. Someone had already installed a good deal of electronic equipment. She opened the louvered doors aft and looked in. Larger bunks—no, real beds—quite unlike the narrow shelves she and Eddi occupied. A corridor led to steps down which a faint light burned; the smells of diesel fuel and metal welled up. She considered her own cell, but couldn't think of anyone who'd welcome hearing from her.

Finally she drew the curtain on her nook and undressed. The deck was cold against her bare feet. She shivered again, pulling palms down bare arms. Piloerection: an early mammalian response to fright and cold. She squirmed into her sleeping bag and pulled the blanket over it.

Then couldn't sleep. The slight but never-ending motion, the abrupt, unfamiliar noises, kept startling her awake. She stared at the shifting pattern the light made as it came through the single port high up beside her bunk. It gleamed on the curved white of the bulkhead. Ivory white, white as . . .

. . . As teeth in a jaw ripped clean of flesh.

Terror rose like a cold sheet drawn up over her face, racing her heart, breaking sweat all over her body. She suffered it for a few minutes, then tried to roll out, intending to power up her e-reader. But she couldn't move. She stared into the dark, panting, mind spiraling down into dumb panic.

Each time she saw a face—or even if she glimpsed her own, reflected in a mirrored surface—it came back.

She'd raised Arminius from a baby. Fed him with her own hands, nestled him to her breast in sleep. Taught him sign, and spent endless hours introducing him to the Montessori toys. Even when he'd grown to two hundred pounds, adolescent, tumescent, curious, he'd never shown her the least sign of agonistic behavior: the stretched lips, the bared teeth and fixed stare of the angry primate.

Save for an uncharacteristically grouchy snarl that last morning, as she'd slid his breakfast bowl into his cage.

Had the research assistant somehow angered him? Or had he, so imprinted on humans, become in his rough way enamored? They'd never know. The security guard, confronted by a supine girl, a mass of spattering blood, and the incisor-bared, window-rattling scream of an enraged adult male chimpanzee, had drawn his gun. Sara had heard the shot from her office, and come running.

Too late. For them all.

Someone had to bear the blame. So the university's legal department had said. Better her than the school, her own counsel had advised. Accept responsibility. Move on. But there were memories one could not move past. Like distant mountains they walked with you, looming through veils of cloud on nights that hid gleaming shadows.

A once-lovely twenty-year-old blinded, left without lips or cheeks. The horror of it unveiled in the courtroom for sixty seconds, to stunned silence. Vacant sockets, bereft of sight. The white gleam of eternally bared teeth in what was no longer a face.

The chill shivered her curled-up legs and crawled along her spine. She panted into cupped hands, staring into the dark. Listening to the creak and sway of the boat, the hum of the wind, a distant voice on the pier arguing and arguing out over the ether, she waited helplessly for the dawn.

2

Fin del Mundo

She was on deck the next morning helping Perrault winch the Zodiac up the sloping stern ramp when the taxi rolled in. It didn't stop at the head of the pier, as hers had, but drove right out onto the concrete, braking by the bollards that held *Anemone* fast.

Sara straightened, clamping the steadying line in one gloved hand, clinging to the gunwale with the other. An extremely tall blond young man in jeans hopped out. A worn military-style backpack was slung over his shoulder. From under a ludicrous hat in the shape of a dog's face, long golden hair flickered in the icy sunlight. Startlingly pale blue eyes met hers, crinkling in a smile she couldn't help returning before her gaze dropped.

Behind him, a stockier figure emerged. For a moment it seemed somehow inhuman, and she caught her breath. It swung and thrust its legs out, bending to adjust them. When it straightened, metal and plastic gleamed in the watery sunlight.

This man waved away his companion's hand, braced on the cab's door, and levered himself out. He teetered, then took a hesitant step, as she frowned, hand to her mouth. Then another.

"Ahoy the boat," the blond guy called.

Perrault turned. "Lars? Mick?"

Mick. So he'd be—"Mr. Bodine?" Sara called. "Hi. I'm Dr. Pollard."

The stocky man stood braced against a piling. He didn't answer her. Simply looked the length of the boat, all the way to the bow. Then back to the stern.

She'd pulsed the usual sources for an assistant. But each inquiry had withered on the vine. Word traveled fast in the scientific community, and these days Dr. Sara Pollard might not be the best reference on a curriculum vitae. The only qualified applicant had come through the CPL—the Cetacean Protection League, sponsor of the expedition. Mikhail Bodine was an Afghanistan veteran. His master's thesis had been about how dolphins reacted to confinement. He'd said he had the winter free, and the stipend would pay his plane fare.

But he'd never said anything about being . . . a double amputee.

As she wondered how he'd get around, Bodine stalked stiffly to the gap between pier and deck, bridged by a battered, paint-spattered aluminum gangway. He reached, and massive biceps tensed as he handed himself aboard, moving from handhold to handhold. Almost like . . . she turned away, admiring his adaptation to his handicap even as its resemblance to a great ape's knuckle-walk made her shudder. Behind him the younger man handed across a heavy-looking duffel that clanked as Bodine eased it to the deck with one arm.

"Dr. Pollard?" Turquoise-green eyes, a shade she'd never seen before, locked with hers. "Mick Bodine. We corresponded."

She forced a smile. "We certainly did. Did I say how much I admired your thesis?"

"Did I say how much I liked your book?" He turned to greet Perrault, then Eddi. "This is my good friend Lars Madsen. We did a season together against the Arctic sealers."

They all shook hands. Sara took a deep breath and kept her eyes up, kept herself from backing away. If she did, she'd step off the stern. Lars Madsen's grin was lit from within by a boyish eagerness that made her like him instantly. The hat, made to look like a goofy Saint Bernard, with dangling flaps that were the dog's ears, looked warm, but also said, *I don't take any of this shit too seriously.*

Bodine was another matter. His dark hair was military short and his smile looked even more forced than her own felt. The prostheses, emerging from hiking shorts, looked absurd on a wind-whipped deck, in an open harbor foaming with short choppy whitecaps.

Perrault kept shading his eyes at the clouds, then toward the gate. *She*, he'd said last night. "Right, take it all below," he told the new arrivals. "You two are forward, on the port side. Opposite the girls."

"Got it," Bodine said. He twisted on those incongruous legs and hauled himself down the companionway. The blond, Lars Madsen, began swinging the duffels down to him, to disappear into the dimness.

Madsen crossed the plank several times, passing down more luggage. It must have contained delicate electronics, as he was very careful with it. Finally he paid the driver, who left. Meanwhile she and Eddi had ~~been~~ struggled with the inflatable dinghy. Its engine had snagged as they'd winched it upward. Lars grabbed one of the heavy braided handholds which cornered the rubber mass. "Take that other side—it is Sara?"

"Correct."

"Take that side, and lift when I tell you.—Eddi, yes? Slack us just a tad, let her slide back." His accent was Scandinavian. Madsen, yes, that might be Swedish. Or perhaps Norwegian. The winch clicked reluctantly. "Lift," he grunted, and Sara tugged and something beneath the heavy gray bulk, so like a whale's, popped free. They winched it in until the nose locked into the molded vee at the top of the ramp, and he bent to tie off the lines.

"Thanks," Sara told him.

"Not a problem." With his reddened cheeks, the silly hat, he looked like a boy out playing in the snow. His grin bent itself on her. She noted a complex fold to his eyelids, the beginnings of laugh lines. "Anything else I can help out with?"

Just trying to fit in? Or coming on to her? He *was* attractive, in a tall Nordic way that'd always appealed. And those blue eyes . . . she had to drop her gaze.

"What's the plan?" Bodine's head and shoulders were visible in the companionway.

"It was to get under way yesterday." Perrault snapped a rope's end against the gunwale, frowning. "Season's not that long. We're going to hit a depression if we don't get out there soon."

"Who we waiting on?"

"The principals." The captain turned away.

"Who, or what, are 'the principals'?" Sara asked Eddi. But got only a shrug in return.

Perhaps, like fruit flies, questions bred answers. Within the hour, as she was helping lay out lines, Perrault's radio beeped. Eddi's voice. "*Anemone*, gate: They're here. An airport limo."

She wondered how many limos Ushuaia Airport had. But Perrault was instructing, "Tell the driver exactly how far to the pier. We don't want him making any wrong turns, okay? If he doesn't speak English, draw him a map."

A burst of static, then Eddi's chipper lilt: "*So* on it, Skipper."

Perrault bent to a panel. A whine began and built. When it reached a shriek the captain pressed a button and an engine rumbled into life. He waited, blinking across the bay, then pressed a second button. Another motor started, telegraphing a buzzing tremor through lifelines and shrouds. They sounded extremely powerful.

Perrault stepped up atop the steering dome, shading his eyes. He looked the boat over from masttop to deck, from stem to stern. Sara waited, rubbing her arms. She hadn't worn a sweater this morning, and the Tierra del Fuegan summer was like November in Nantucket. Whitecaps chased each other across the harbor, rocking the boat. Gulls hovered, screaming, and a white fluid spattered down, just missing the boat. Across the pier a fishing trawler gunned its engine, sending a cloud of blue smoke drifting over them. Perrault coughed, looking annoyed. He pointed. "Forward spring. Take the slack out."

"Which one . . . ?"

He coughed again and frowned. "That one, by your foot. Now, when *she* comes aboard, stay out of her way."

Sara nodded, still unclear whom they were referring to. She was about to ask when a black Mercedes turned onto the pier, slowed, and came to a noiseless halt. Behind it were other cars, a motorcade. From these spilled men and women in parkas and sweatshirts. They readied notebooks and serious-looking video cameras, jockeying for vantages. The limo's doors stayed closed. At last the driver came around to open them. He bowed and stepped back.

"Oh my God," Sara whispered.

Leggy, rangy, incredibly slim, the woman posed on the pier, shaking shining long black hair out into the breeze. With her, and a broadly smiling yet uneasy-looking Perrault, an older man, lean, tanned, silver-haired, sunglassed, waved to the cameras. Sara backed slowly away from the gangway, unable to believe her eyes, as the actress placed one boot on it, as if claiming a newly discovered land.

Yes; it was really her. She wore suede jeans that fit like a spray tan and a white parka with faux fox trim. Silk showed bright scarlet at her throat. The gulls darted madly overhead, screeching insults; she laughed, pointing them out to the older man. Past her Sara saw Lars Madsen unloading brass-trimmed butterscotch-leather suitcases from the limo's boot. Then they were all headed for her: Perrault, Dorée, the older guy, in suit and tie and camel topcoat, and two more young women. The last woman onto the gangway turned and grasped both hand-chains, blocking it against the photographers, who promptly spread out along the pier. One focused a telephoto on Sara, who lifted a hand to shield her face. Just as she'd had to do outside the courtroom.

"Our crew, Miss Dorée," Perrault was saying, and Sara started and bent awkwardly before an extended hand. As Dorée patted her shoulder as if knighting her, Sara stared wordless at a face familiar from enormous screens.

She'd often wondered, eyeing the tabloids in the checkout lines, what the celebrities on their covers really looked like. Without makeup and hair and lighting. Just like anyone else, she'd told herself scornfully. But no. This face and lips and chin spoke without speaking, invited without words, as if behind surface beauty lay another, transcendent, ageless, almost alien in its perfection. Tawny streaks gleamed within long black lashes, like the gems called tiger's-eye. The curve of a full-lipped half smile was like the bestowal of a divine blessing.

Before she'd grasped it the moment was past. The actress was turning to Bodine, who'd hoisted himself into the sunlight and was leaning, artificial limbs sheathed in khaki Dockers, against a digital display sited to be visible from the large wheel aft. An identical pat on the shoulder, an identical smile. Behind her Eddi came jogging down the pier. She took in the logjam at the gangway, and stepped on a huge black rubber fender between the boat and the pier and vaulted aboard farther forward.

A horn from the harbor spun them. Five more paparazzi roared past in outboards, cameras pointed. Where had they come from? Did they follow the actress literally to the ends of the earth? Sara felt her own gaze dragged inevitably back, as a lover's to his most beloved, and her heart yearned in exactly the same way. She wanted to stroke that shining hair. Fold, or better yet be folded, within those arms. She shook her head, confused. Was it sexual? It felt deeper, more moving. More like . . . worship?

"Is that really . . . Tehiyah Dorée?" Eddi murmured, flushed, panting, beside her. "Or am I dreaming this?"

"I think it is, Eddi."

"Holy cow. I mean . . . holy *cow*."

Dorée was talking with Perrault. One of the women who'd accompanied her aboard stood an arm's length away. The captain was saying, "Our space is limited, Tehiyah. I can take five pieces of luggage—absolutely no more. Scientific equipment, food, and fuel have to take precedence. And we don't have any extra bunks."

The full lips pouted. "I really need Georgita. She can film, too. So we wouldn't need anyone for that."

"Eddi's already part of the team. She has a lot of experience with whales."

"We have enough whale scientists." Dorée's gaze flicked around, lighted on Sara. Who felt absurdly like genuflecting. She suddenly realized she was grinning in a silly way, and dropped her gaze to her boots. Only to feel it drawn up again, to rest once more on the flushed cheeks, the wind-whipped silken hair. "Are you trying to tell me she can't come?" Dorée added.

The captain cleared his throat. "I'm afraid—well, yes. Sorry."

"You wouldn't have this boat, be taking this voyage, without me. Isn't that right?"

"Without Jules-Louis, that's true."

"Well, I'm sure he doesn't want me to sail all alone. That can't be what you had in mind either. Can it?"

"I wish you'd brought this up before. We have so little space, only so much food—"

"Like I said. Leave someone else ashore." Dorée looked around; noticed Sara. Waved a hand. "Her."

"She's the doctor. The scientist."

"Then someone else. I don't care. Georgita's coming."

Through all this the mild-looking, wan, slightly hunched girl in question had stood unspeaking, not participating beyond a glance down the companionway, then out at the bay. She clutched a wrap close against her chest.

The standing group broke, then re-formed as the silver-haired man in the topcoat bounded up the gangway. Suddenly the actress shrank two or three inches. She relaxed into him, twined an arm around his sleeve, and *became a different woman.* Sara blinked, not crediting what she'd just seen. Dorée looked up into the older man's face with a yearning, dreamy fascination.

He put an arm around her shoulders. "There is a problem? Dru?"

"Monsieur," Perrault said, and saluted. "Welcome back aboard."

"The owner," Eddi whispered. "Dru's boss. He used to race too, years ago. He's loaning his boat to the Protectors."

Perrault began in rapid French, but the older man held up a hand and said pleasantly, "In English, please. For Tehiyah. The new engines? They are not working out?"

"No, they're fine. The problem . . . as you know, space is very limited. I didn't plan on another crew member."

"Well, I understand that. Ty, darling, can you possibly get along without her? I'm sure Dru will do everything he can to make you comfortable."

"I need someone to talk to. We'll be out a long time. It's a girl thing, Jules."

"Well then. There's a woman—*bien sûr.* There's another." The Frenchman smiled at Sara and Eddi. "I'm sure they'd be happy to help with your hair, or—whatever else you might need. Dru's been sailing with me a good many years. He would not say it was inconvenient if this weren't so. And he's right about all that luggage. You really do tend to—"

"'Inconvenient.' Why can't *you* come? Honey?"

"I would very much like to, but there is the commitment in Djibouti. Really, one has to make compromises now and then. This is an adventure, after all."

"I just can't go without her," Dorée said. The pale woman they were discussing never moved, never spoke. Sara wondered if she was mute.

Beside her, Eddi seemed to flinch, then stepped forward. "Really, if it's a question of bunks . . . she can have mine."

Perrault frowned. Before he could say anything Dorée said, "Oh, my, no. We couldn't. Where would *you* go?"

"I don't need much. Any flat place. I can sleep somewhere up forward."

"Then it's settled," the older man said. Sara could see in his eyes what he was thinking: Let the little people deal with it.

"One moment." Perrault ran a hand through his hair; he seemed to be gritting his teeth. "We already have so much extra fuel I'm compromising stability. I can't take any more *mon tabarnak de* luggage—"

"Georgita won't bring much. Will you, Georgie?"

The girl shrugged. The wind changed, blowing exhaust their way from the stern. Perrault coughed into a fist, then sneezed. Jamie Quill came stepping lightly along the deck-edge from forward. Despite his bulk the first mate moved like a cat on a fence, one foot in front of the other despite *Anemone*'s pitching as wakes from the circling paparazzi lifted, then dropped her below the level of the pier. "Dru. We doin' this?"

"Spring lines first. Then the stern."

"Looks like you're ready." The older Frenchman looked aloft, then to where the sea opened. "I wish . . . well, you'll see some sights. Take good care of her, Dru."

"I will, Jules."

They shook hands, and the owner turned to Dorée. They embraced, held it; Sara looked away. Strobes flashed. Then, at some unseen signal, both turned to the cameras, to the raised, extended boom mikes dangling above them. Madsen took off his silly hat and moved up to stand with Dorée and the Frenchman. Perrault, too, turned to face the reporters.

"This is a great moment," the older Frenchman said sonorously, removing his sunglasses. "For the first time, a mission of the Cetacean Protection League sets sail. We wish these courageous sailors the best. I now introduce Lars Madsen, of the CPL."

Madsen said a few words Sara couldn't quite hear. He ended, "And now: Tehiyah Dorée."

The actress lifted her face; blinked up at the sky. Spread her arms; and her voice rang out over the listeners.

"The earth is our responsibility. For too long, we've treated it as our hunting grounds and our trash heap. We sail today to protect the noblest creatures on this watery planet from greed and murder. I thank all our patrons for their great generosity, especially Jules-Louis Vergeigne." Drawing him in by one arm, she turned a brilliant smile to the lenses, eyes glittering with incipient tears. "We sail! Thank you all for your prayers and good wishes. Until we are victorious, we will not return."

With a creak and a sway of the narrow gangway, Vergeigne loped up onto the pier and turned, palm lifted in farewell. Perrault and Madsen braced their shoulders to it, and the brow rolled up onto the pier. "Both springs aboard," Quill yelled from forward.

"Très bien." Perrault bent to uncleat one of the mooring lines. He shook it in some abrupt complex way, and a wave traveled along it and on the pier a loop jumped straight up off its bollard. He hauled it in hand over hand and coiled it down into a locker in the stern. Then pushed past Sara to the wheel, shoving her aside. She stepped out of his way, muttering an apology. The engines dropped to a drone. He rotated a lever up, then circled his index in the air.

Cries from the pier mingled with those of circling gulls. *"Au revoir!"* "Love you, *chérie!*" "You're our favorite, Tehiyah!" "Good-bye! Be careful!"

The engines climbed the scale again. White water shot out with a gushing roar. A gap rocking with dark green miniature maelstroms widened between *Anemone* and the pier. Far down in them Sara glimpsed small fish fleeing frantically in among the pilings. A shiver raveled her spine the way the wave had traveled up the mooring line. Past one of the bollards she caught a squared-off silhouette; another. Dully gleaming, brass-bound butterscotch leather.

Someone on the pier noticed at the same time. "Georgie—Tehiyah's bags!"

"You've forgotten two of Miss Dorée's bags," the pale-haired woman said, answering Sara's doubt that she could speak. Dorée herself had climbed onto the forward deck and was standing at the very bow, posing like a Nike, scarlet scarf fluttering in the rising wind. "We have to go back!"

"C'est bien assez, c'est trop," Perrault muttered. He looked at Sara and the creases deepened around his eyes. "She's got enough luggage. Don't you think?"

"Georgie! *Tehiyah!*" the voices grew fainter as distance expanded, as the boat became a separate world. The pier slowly moved aft, the mountains marching with *Anemone*. Perrault touched the wheel only now and then, avoiding the motorboats that fell in on either side. Stone breakwaters reached out, and *Anemone* rolled between them. Sara lost her balance and almost fell, but caught herself. Pain twisted through her wrist.

Perrault shouted to Dorée to come aft. He bent to the panel, and a pane of heavy, glossy-shining cloth expanded. It stiffened in the wind as it unfurled, and the boat heeled.

Past the breakwaters the motorboats circled them one last time, lurching and pitching in the heavier seas, then headed back. The silver inlet she'd seen from the air stretched out before them, the whitecapped mountains glinting across it. As the sail hardened, *Anemone* dipped and rose. Spray arched in shimmering rainbows. The wind was much colder out here than in Ushuaia. Cold and utterly fresh, as if no human lung had ever taken it in.

The captain depressed a button and a second enormously tall sail complexly woven of some shining fiber hummed upward from within the boom. Sapphire and cream and bronze, covered with aggressively abstract logos and brand names, it burned in the weak sunlight. *Anemone* steadied into its stride like a dressage horse, accelerating swiftly. He shut the engines down and another sail unloomed itself, glittering in gold and bronze, and the big Dewoitine accelerated yet again, lifting from the sea as if creating her own wind.

They sped along a rocky coast, planing over a light chop, a broad bay glittering to starboard. Sara clung to the lifeline, exhilarated both at their unexpected speed and at the barren beauty of the swiftly passing shore. Beside her Eddi breathed, "Oh my cow. Can you believe it?"

Small black shapes—penguins! she thought, thrilled at her first glimpse of them—dotted the snow. Or was that white coating acres of guano? A red and white lighthouse glimmered in the distance, rose, then fell behind. The sail creaked, the boat leaned, the sea rushed and tumbled past.

"Fair winds and a full ship," she murmured.

"What's that, Sara?"

"Oh—just something they used to say where I grew up."

"Dolphins," Madsen yelled, and she followed his pointing glove to silver wheels turning just beneath the sea. They parted as *Anemone* slid past, streamlined, reaching for the wind, full of power and curves and light and spray that blew over their faces from the waves she severed and trod underfoot. The world glittered and shone, and Sara sucked deep breaths of it and laughed aloud for the first time in what felt like longer than forever.

3

The Convergence

Two days later, she gripped a handhold in the galley as *Anemone* launched herself into space for the hundred thousandth time. Pans screeched across the stove's grillwork, setting her teeth on edge. The fumes of stewing ratatouille nauseated her. They were supposed to take turns cooking, but she'd noticed not everyone who was supposed to ended up actually doing it.

Quill said *Anemone* was a good sea boat, but as far as she could see sailing aboard her was as miserable as a stretch in Guantanamo. The interrupted sleep. The cramped quarters. And everyone caged up together, like rats in an underfunded lab. Since they'd left Ushuaia something had gone haywire every day. First the port shaft had started vibrating, leaking through what Perrault and Quill called a "dripless" seal—she couldn't tell if they meant this ironically or not. Then the salon, which was supposed to rotate to counterbalance the heel of the boat, kept jamming, stopped in the wrong position.

Not to mention living with the same eight people always in arm's reach, with no escape, to never be alone even for an hour.

Sara carried the steaming entree out into the salon, where a table gimballed this way and that beneath a ventilation hatch down which fresh wind and blue sky poured. "Lunch!" she yelled.

Madsen and Quill were on deck, where the crew took turns, two at a time: Eddi and Sara, Dorée and Perrault, Lars and Jamie. Even when he wasn't on watch, the captain seemed to be working on something pretty much around the clock. Bodine was exempted, of course, and Georgita was off, too; three hours after they'd passed the red-and-white lighthouse at Fin del Mundo, Norris-Simpson—that was her last name—had staggered whey-faced to her bunk and not been seen since.

"LUNCH!" Sara hollered again, grateful she'd barely felt queasy even the first day at sea, though the sheer unendingness of the motion was wearing her out.

"One minute." Perrault's voice floated up.

She stumbled over a displaced square of decking and looked down. Into the bilge: unfinished raw fiberglass, dirty water, hoses, wires, tools, and in among them his body, cramped into a crooked curl, like a corpse forced into a too-small coffin.

"What're you doing down there . . . uh, Dru?"

"Keel seal's leaking. Go ahead, eat. I'll be right up."

Eddi and Bodine straggled to the table, clinging to handholds like astronauts on a space walk. The door to the aft cabin opened and Dorée groped out. She almost fell into the open void, saved only by Bodine's warning. She made a face and slid onto the banquette next to Auer. "Get some sleep?" Eddi asked her.

"Jesus, everything's leaking," Dorée grumbled. "What *is* this?" She pushed tomatoes and eggplant around on her plate, then shoved it away. "I said vegetarian, not inedible. What else is there?"

"Georgita drink any water?" Bodine asked. "She gets dehydrated, she could be in bad shape."

"I made her drink some this morning, with sugar in it.—That's all I made, Tehiyah," Sara said. Resisting the urge to shove her head down into it.

"Well, I can't eat it. How about some risotto? With a salad?"

Sara made herself count. One. Two. Three. Then said as evenly as she could, "I'm sorry, Tehiyah. I'm an ethologist, not a gourmet chef. As a matter of fact, wasn't it your turn to make lunch?"

Dorée took a small bite. "God," she muttered.

"It's good," Eddi said. "I like it, Sara. Mick?"

"Better than MREs and sand," Bodine said. A stock phrase they got to hear at almost every meal.

The boat soared over a swell, and each diner clutched his or her plate with one hand and the bench seat with the other. When they crashed down the whole craft quivered, and smoking sauce spattered from the bowls. Sara's tailbone ached where she'd already bruised it. Spray rattled topside. From behind the curtain of her sleeping nook Georgita coughed like a dying fawn.

"Tapioca for dessert," Sara said brightly, smiling around.

"God. I hate fucking tapioca."

"Sounds good, Sara."

"Better than MRE cookies."

"I'm sorry if I'm cranky, but I didn't get a wink of sleep. It's colder than an agent's heart," Dorée muttered. "The rest of you out here, at least you have each other's body heat."

"Well, this *is* the Antarctic," Sara observed.

Dorée ignored her. "Perrault? Hey, Dru?"

"*Comment?* What is it?" A hollow voice from below. From offstage, like the ghost in *Hamlet*.

"I'm *freezing.* Can't we turn the heaters on?"

Bodine frowned. "The heaters aft take electricity. But there's only so much capacity in the batteries, unless the engines are running."

"I didn't ask you. I asked the captain."

"He's right," Perrault said from beneath them. "We have oil heaters, too. One aft, one forward. But I'm not turning them on until we truly need them." Blows echoed, as if he were forging iron. Four heavy strokes. A pause. Then four more.

"Fine." Dorée shrugged. "Turn the generator on. Or the engines, or whatever. It'd be different if you hadn't left all my warm stuff on the fucking pier."

"Sorry. An oversight."

"Oversight, my ass! You saw my bags sitting there. My people were yelling. You just kept going."

"There are crew jackets." Eddi pointed a fork at the locker.

"Blue's not my color, honey."

"For Christ's sake," Bodine muttered.

"What? What did you say?"

"I said, you need to suck it up, babe."

"Fuck you. I'm used to roughing it. I filmed in fucking Ghana! I can suck it up fine. What I don't like is freezing my ass off for no reason."

Eddi said, "If you'd rather sleep up forward, you can have my spot."

"Oh, so you want my room? I've seen that dog's bed you made. Foam rubber and rags. Like a street person."

Sara filled her mouth with ratatouille to keep silent. This, after Eddi had given up her own bunk for the useless wraith-woman Dorée had insisted on bringing as a personal servant? "This isn't a pleasure cruise, Tehiyah," she observed.

"Well, no shit! Sure hasn't been so far."

"We're out here to save whales from being slaughtered," Bodine said. "You need to man up and stop whining."

Silence fell, broken only by a worried *hmm* from Eddi. Dorée glared across the table at Bodine. "What . . . did . . . you . . . *say*?"

"We're not here to coddle you." He wolfed another heaped spoonful. "You should listen to yourself. 'Blue's not my color,'" he mimicked. "'The rest of you have body heat.' Why'd you come on this voyage, anyway? Just for a photo op with Free Willy?"

"I believe deeply in this cause," Dorée gritted out, every muscle tensed in her long slender neck. The lovely face changed. Suddenly the eyes of a vengeful demon burned out from a twisted, frightening mask. The others dropped their forks; Sara shivered. "If you think I don't, then ask yourself why I bothered with this expedition. Who secured the funding? Got you this boat? Okay, I feel sorry for you, G.I. Joe. Without legs and all. But I don't overlook rudeness. Jules-Louis will hear about you insulting me."

Eddi broke the silence with, "Tehiyah . . . wasn't that Francine, in *Last Rites*?"

"Ha-ha." The demonic snarl faded. "Absolutely, Eddi. Score one for you."

"Hey! You guys leave us any food?" Madsen appeared at the companionway, the ears of his silly hound cap dangling jesterlike. Sara knew now he wasn't Norwegian or Swedish, as she'd first thought, but Danish. Close, anyway.

"Nah, we ate it all," Bodine yelled back.

"We'd like to get relieved."

Sara sighed, and looked around for her jacket.

Perrault insisted everyone wear what he called "mustang suits" whenever they went topside. The bulky waterproof one-pieces were a tiger-lily red-orange, with harness points and silver reflective tape. They were insulated and had flotation cells. The zippers, which started at the crotch, were supposed to be watertight. Sara's was extremely hard to zip without jamming. She felt like the Michelin Woman as she bent over to tug on heavy dark blue insulated boots over three pair of socks. She was sweating by the time she climbed the companionway.

She blinked, clinging to a coaming as the wind punched and rocked her. It howled each time *Anemone* heaved on immense black seas, then sank to a whisper as the boat dropped. The bellied-out sail was driving them at a tearing speed that threw out great curving sheets of clear water to either side. She'd never have believed a sailboat could rocket along like this. Madsen was back by the wheel, though it was the self-steerer, a windvane that controlled a micro rudder, that was keeping them on course at the moment.

Quill motioned her and Eddi in toward him, then bent so his wart-like nose was only inches from theirs. His black beard stuck out in tufts from the hood, with little eyes staring balefully out above it. "Keep your safety lines secured," he shouted. "Those suits won't save you. Remember, go in the water here, you're helpless in sixty seconds. Dead in five minutes."

She nodded. Not that they needed the warning. One glance at the roaring emptiness all around was enough to make her heart sink. They hadn't spotted another ship or boat since leaving Argentina. Only those incredibly dark seas, gigantic up close, as they were about to break, then smaller and smaller as they marched off to the jagged horizon. The face of each was wrinkled and furrowed like an old woman's. The sun was a refrigerator-bulb gleam through a frosted scrim of cloud. The wind generator was a whining, vibrating blur. A thin glaze of water coated every winch, line, and surface. At least it wasn't frozen. The air was chilly, but not yet cold enough to freeze the moisture in Quill's beard. The sun glittered off the passing waves as from tilted mirrors of black glass.

"Bloody boo'tiful weather," he shouted. "Hardly any seas. We made two hundred and twenty miles noon to noon. You're steering between one twenty and one thirty. One reef in the main. Wind's between twenty-two and twenty-five, gusting thirty. I know we haven't seen anybody for a while, but keep one eye on your radar and the other to weather. If you make a squall bearing down, or fog, or another ship, call Dru. Hear anything on channel sixteen, call Dru. If the boat starts to feel strange, or the steering goes—"

"Call Dru," Eddi chimed in.

Quill eyed her morosely. Just like that, Sara knew why he seemed so familiar. She'd met a tame boar hog once, on Ossabaw Island, Georgia, with that exact expression. The hog had been named Paul Mitchell, for the way his bristles stuck up in unruly spikes. The memory made her smile.

Surprising her, Quill smiled back. "Okay, girls, all yours.—Lars, boy, let's eat."

When they were alone together Eddi hunched into a small seat back by the wheel. Sara balanced an arm's length farther forward, where she could see around the straining sail. Hardly any seas? Right. She kept pressing the lid back down on the panic she'd felt from the moment they'd left land behind. If this was "boo'tiful," what would it be like farther south?

She stood for a time flexing her knees against the leap and crash of the boat, staggering drunkenly when she misjudged. Glad once again not to be seasick. She eyed the colored speckle of the radar screen; glanced aloft to see the little antenna still sweeping around, the French tricolor still flapping angrily. At last she edged aft and wedged in beside Auer. The seats were cramped, with hardly any legroom. A remnant of *Anemone*'s racing pedigree, probably. "We staying on course?"

"Right where Jamie said." Eddi was staring at the self-steering. Her bare hands were burrowed into the pockets of the orange suit; her sailing gloves lay on the deck. "Wish I could figure out how this thing works."

"It's not electrical, anyway."

Eddi grinned. "Yeah, that's good."

The compass swung wildly, but they did seem to be staying more or less on course. Sara cleared her throat. "Those are, you know, great tattoos. D'you get them done in the States?"

"Oh yes. In San Francisco."

"All those sea animals. So beautiful."

"They're all guys I worked with. Each one has a name."

Sara regarded her with surprise. Remembered to check around the horizon; still empty. Then looked back at her watchmate. "Oh, that's right—you were a performer. At Sea Universe, right?"

Auer smiled, but without reproach. "They called us trainers, not performers. There at the end, I was filming with El Tigre."

"Oh really." Then Sara sat up straight. "El Tigre. The uh, the orca?"

"That's right." Eddi hugged herself. Her already-small body seemed to shrink.

"I . . . think I saw something about that on television. Wasn't he the one that . . ."

"Yeah."

"But surely it wasn't you he—"

"That was me," Auer said, looking away.

Sara braced herself against the pitching, flashing on YouTube clips of a huge black-and-white killer whale turning on a petite trainer. The massive orca had whipped the blue pool water into froth. The trainer—this small woman beside her—had tried again and again to escape. Safety divers had tried to distract the beast. It had ignored them, toying with the swimmer like a gigantic cat, gripping and shaking her in its jaws before pulling her beneath the surface. The audience had screamed as the foam turned pink. Somehow, despite her injuries, the swimmer had reached the edge of the pool. But it had caught her again. Dragged her back into the center of the arena and slammed its massive body down on her imploring arms, driving her under. The clip had run for only half a minute, but watching it had seemed to take hours.

"Why—I mean, do you have any idea?"

Auer shrugged. "He loved me. I thought. He could be so sweet. Take your hand in his mouth, lick it with that big soft tongue. Rub up against you like a cat when you were swimming with him.

"But he was weird that day. Like he didn't want to go onstage. I kept signaling, but he'd just flick his tail and stare at me. Then all at once he, like, went bonkers. Just blind rage. If Cokie—another trainer—if he hadn't come in after me, I'd have died. I'm sure of that much." She shook her head. "I've never been so terrified. I was ready to die. Totally helpless."

Sara took a deep breath. "There must've been *something* different that day. Some reason he perceived you as a threat, or as a prey animal—"

"No. There was *nothing different*. They said, after, that it was my ponytail. But I *always* wore a ponytail. They said he had high testosterone. That he wanted to mate with me, which is just ridiculous. They don't attack each other when they mate.

"Tigre knew I wasn't prey, or his girlfriend. He wasn't overworked; he'd just had three days off. He was trying to *kill me*. He had murder in his eyes when he kept coming after me."

Sara tried to slow her breathing. She lifted her head and shaded her gaze around the heaving horizon. Bent to the radar. Nothing. "So you got the tattoos."

"I got the scars first. Then, when they healed, the body art. I don't agree with the people who say we should release all the captive whales. If we did, they'd die. They're not wild anymore. But we shouldn't capture new ones, or keep breeding them. Anyhow, I never got back in the tank with him. Or any of the other killers." She laughed breathlessly. "We weren't allowed to call them that. Just 'orcas.' But we knew it could happen. We were like lion tamers. Like Siegfried and Roy. There's a reason they call them that, you know."

"They're apex predators."

"Like us." Eddi nodded. "Only we're like the apex of the apex. At least, so far. And we treat the ones below us . . . really badly. Don't you think?"

"I do." Sara had no trouble agreeing with that.

Auer's slightly protruding blue eyes were troubled. "And, whatever's in us that, you know, thinks and feels, well—I don't even pretend to know what that is. I'm just somebody who takes pictures. But I see it in a whale's eyes . . . d'you know what I mean?"

"I think so." Sara shook herself, surprised at how deep the conversation had suddenly gone. But she *did* know. Had seen it in Arminius's gaze: a dawning consciousness that had begun to think beyond its immediate needs. An all but human yearning for understanding . . .

"So where'd you say you were from? Sara?"

"Hmm? Oh . . . Nantucket."

"Oh. Right." Auer looked impressed. "So your family's got money."

Sara laughed. "Hardly. My grandfather had a scallop shanty. We all scalloped in the winter." She made a prying motion with her hands. "Open it, flip the guts into the gut bucket, the meat goes in the sell bucket. But the state shut us down. Health regulations. So we lost the shanty, and then our house. . . ."

"So how'd you get to be a doctor? A scientist, I mean."

"Just lucky. I'd be waitressing in a seafood restaurant if it hadn't been for the local science center, and scholarships."

Auer glanced at the companionway. Quill said they had to keep the hatch closed as much as possible, in case of a pitchpole or capsize. Also, of course, to keep what little heat they had down in the cabin. "Man, these fucking suits . . . I've got to pee. Keep an eye on the course?"

"You bet. Going below?"

"No, just gonna peel down and squat back by the ramp." She started to unzip.

"Be careful," Sara said. "Remember, 'If you go in the water here—'"

"'Helpless in sixty seconds.'"

"'Dead in five minutes.'"

They both giggled. Then Sara, looking ahead, sobered. "What's that?" she muttered. Eddi turned and they both stared.

A strange milkiness lay on the sea, a queer shimmer in the air. As *Anemone* drew nearer, nodding over gentling seas, the low haze coalesced into hundreds, thousands of milling specks, like the clouds of mayflies Sara had walked through as a child in the island spring. As the mist rose the sea glowed from deep within.

"Don't know," Auer breathed, stretching out over the gunwale. Lifting her face to the wind. "It's . . . it's getting colder."

"Smells different," Sara said at the same moment. They peered ahead, crouching, wary.

The boat nodded again, rose, and sailed into a broad, roiling band of lighter water. In the space of three hull-lengths the sea turned from black to a turbid, roiling, pearlescent green, with floating scum patches the color of old rust. Sara noted the same iridescent haze lying across the horizon ahead. It loomed like a cliff, yet didn't appear solid. The hairs rose on her nape.

"Hadn't we better call Dru?" Eddi asked.

Sara was still bent over the side, studying the sea. Seabirds rose from its slick-looking surface, dipping and swooping in short arcs around the greater wings of the sails, shrieking down. She frowned, bent farther, and one boot shot out from under her. She grabbed for the gunwale and only just saved herself from sliding over its slick curve.

The rusty patches were thousands of creatures the size of grasshoppers, as if a plague of locusts had fallen from the sky. They looked like tiny pincerless crayfish. And they were all dead. Millions of corpses laid a reddish-brown carpet that heaved gently on the boiling smoky green. They stretched to the horizon, as far as she could see. And there were more below, layer beneath layer sifting down farther and farther beneath the visible surface, until she had no idea or even guess as how far they extended. She found herself straining to imagine this much life.

And this much death.

"Dr. Pollard? You okay?" Perrault said from behind her.

She recoiled from the edge, realizing she'd almost fallen overboard. "Yes. Yes, I am. But—what is this? Some kind of red-tide phenomenon?"

"This?" The captain glanced at the birds, at the sea. He sniffed. "It's the Convergence. Farther south this year. Interesting."

"What's 'the Convergence'?" Eddi said eagerly.

"The cold water—coming off the continent—hits the subtropical ocean up here. Cold water's heavier than warm, yes? You're looking at where they mix. Then it . . . slides underneath the warm water, and keeps flowing north, deep down, out of our sight."

Sara shivered to a wind like an opened morgue refrigerator. The ammoniacal smell of death, rising with the mourning keen of the birds. "Are those krill? There must be billions of them. Thousands of tons."

"The shock of the warm water kills them." Perrault shaded his eyes ahead. "They die; the birds eat. Nature, yes? Feel the chill? It grows steadily colder from here. We'll have fog, and some weather to windward may come down. Call me if you can't see more than a mile ahead. Expect ice from here on. Small bits at first, but even they can punch through our hull if we hit right." He gave them both sharp looks, seemed about to say something else. But at last only nodded, and ducked below.

They shivered through the watch, and lay below gratefully when they were relieved.

The cabin smelled of diesel. Someone had turned the heaters on, and it felt almost warm when she unpeeled the heavy suit. Her sweaty stink welled from clothes she'd worn for days now, rancid and unwashed. Like her brother's dirty socks, in the little apartment in Mid-island they'd moved to after losing everything. She hung it to drip-dry in the swaying, packed-solid wet-gear locker, and cleaned up as best she could in the head. Dragged a comb through oily hair. She'd cut it after Leo had left, trying for a fresh start. And it'd helped; changing your hairstyle did make you feel different somehow.

When she got to the table only a corner was left between Bodine and Eddi to wedge into. Perrault wasn't there, but the bilge access was screwed down. Jamie lurched from the galley cradling a large pot that smelled wonderful. He reeled across the slanting space like a dancing bear, landed the steaming tureen dead center in a boxed-in grill, then toppled. Bodine grabbed his belt to steady him. "Thanks," the mate grunted.

The hot polenta was spicy, cheesy, with canned tomato and generous hunks of soy bacon. Water sprang into her mouth. Her hands began to shake. She ladled a hefty portion. "Damn, this here's good," Bodine said, sopping gravy from his bowl with a torn-off chunk of bread. The others mumbled agreement through full mouths.

"Just the instant shite, tarted up a bit," Quill said, but he was smiling behind the bush of beard.

The companionway hatch banged back; cold air whistled through the cabin. The mate wheeled, annoyed, but all faces went carefully blank as the opening outlined Tehiyah. "That smells so good," she said. "Dru says he's okay up there alone."

Quill slid a filled bowl and a hunk of buttered bread down, which the actress acknowledged with a nod. Sara was struck anew by how beautiful she was, even with frizzled hair and dark circles from lack of sleep. Those high, perfectly regular cheekbones. Perfect butterscotch skin, framed by shining jet-black hair. But the eyes were what stopped you. Larger than any human's had a right to be, and more expressive. They could be a devil's, or an angel's; a goddess's, or those of some fey race more charmed than human.

But beside her Sara became conscious of another face, another set of eyes. A nearly transparent blue, and bent on her. "How about some more?" Lars Madsen's smile was warm and real and not fey at all.

"I—I don't know. Maybe a little. You can have my bacon."

"It's fake. But who cares." He fished a large piece off the top and dropped it into his bowl. Had he stroked the back of her wrist by accident? She caught Eddi's upquirked eyebrow.

"I'll take some of that," Dorée said gaily. She held out her bowl, and after a moment's hesitation Madsen dipped the rest of the imitation meat out of Sara's bowl to enrich the actress's.

Sara caught Bodine's flicked gaze. Did the heat on her cheeks show? She quickly mumbled around a mouthful, "Mick, let's get together up in the lab. After we finish here?"

"Sure, boss."

The boat leaned, bounded. Bowls and plates lifted a few inches, then crashed down. From behind the swaying curtain came a low groan. "She sounds so miserable," Dorée said. "I had no idea, when she insisted on coming, she'd be this much trouble."

"She'll get over it," Quill grunted. "Last call. Anybody for more tuck?"

The actress napkined her lips. "Is there possibly some of that great cocoa? Before I have to go back up."

"I'll make some, Miss Dorée. Coming right up."

"Thanks so much, Jamic. Maybc a mug for thc captain, too?"

Sara was all the way forward, in the cramped low-ceilinged pie wedge they called the "lab." Bodine had been sleeping here, to judge by the camo-patterned mummy bag stuffed into a shelf. Even with the heaters on aft, the air was icy. It smelled of bitter plastic, damp line, preservative chemicals. Clipboards swung from strings. Everything not tied down was in motion. Bodine hunched in a chair bolted in front of racks of equipment, studying a display. Light moved across it, paused, resumed. Headphones swayed on a hook. His shaggy hair hung uncombed. He shaved only occasionally, and the last occasion hadn't been recent. He looked like Russell Crowe, but with even more massive arms. He didn't have his artificial legs strapped on, but seemed content to move about the boat without them.

He pressed keys on a board that unfolded into his lap and the screen changed to a weather chart. "Where are we?" she asked, leaning over his shoulder.

"Here. See the southern tip of del Fuego . . . six hundred miles as the albatross flies from there to the Palmer Peninsula. Where the cruise ships go."

"But we're not headed there."

"Right. We're aimed east. Sea Shepherd's engaging in the grounds south of Australia and New Zealand. But when the Japanese hunt to the west, between Kerguelen and the Weddell Sea, they're out of their range from Sydney. Dorée's idea—actually, her PR firm's—is to shadow and harass them when they come west of zero longitude." He tapped the chart. "Plenty of krill in these waters. And a lot of the upwelling that brings it to the surface."

"We saw that topside. At the Convergence."

"Must be what I've been hearing on the sonar. Well, whales follow krill. So they're here somewhere. The Japanese, I mean."

"We're sailing east—"

"Don't have much of a choice. Down here, south of Argentina and Australia, this is the only stretch of ocean that wraps around the world. No land. The wind blows west to east, uninterrupted. And the fetch builds up these huge swells. That's why they call them the roaring forties, and the screaming fifties."

This was the most lucid explanation she'd yet heard. "So how do we find them?"

"We head for the whaling grounds. Then listen." Bodine pointed to a rack above his head. It was dark, unlit, draped with wires. He waited, as if for more questions. When they didn't come, he reared back. The chair's armrests were wrapped with green duct tape. "I know why *they're* out here. Killing the last great sea creatures on earth. For profit. What I wonder is why you're with us."

The space leaned; she braced herself to avoid sliding into his lap. "I explained that. To study atypical behaviors in population statistical outliers."

"I read what you sent. But I'm not sure I understand it."

"Well." She rubbed her forehead. "I'm primarily interested in agonistic behavior—sudden violence—unprovoked by any apparent threat. The phenomenon occurs in several species."

He knitted his brows. "Rogue elephants?"

"The elephant's a well-known example."

"What's your hypothesis?"

She hesitated, looking at the dark hairs on his forearms, from which he'd turned the sleeves back. She didn't want to discuss this. But he was supposed to be her assistant. The more minds on a problem, the more fruitful the collaboration. Rachel had been a big help when—

Oh God. *Rachel.* She laced her fingers over her face and bent into them. Remembering white bone shining through bright blood. The lacerated, streaming eye sockets.

No. That collaboration hadn't turned out well.

A hand cupped her cheek. "You okay, Doc?"

"Yeah . . . yes." She took a ragged breath and shoved it away. "Please don't touch me."

"Sorry."

"I—I might have a theory. I want to look into a certain large, long brain cells: Von Economo bipolar neurons. They're found in what seem to be the most recent structures to evolve—the fronto-insular cortex and the anterior cingulate cortex."

"Yeah, I read about that," he said. "They're like high-volume digital circuits. Carry a lot of data, fast. But I thought they were supposed to be involved in empathy, reading social situations—"

"The science is murky. You're right, they do seem to be connected in some way with higher-order social cognition—the ability to identify with and interact altruistically with others. I'm wondering if those we perceive as rogue individuals, perhaps even human serial killers, might have a deficiency or deficit of these neurons. Lesions, some disease or trauma—"

"Might trigger violent behavior?"

"Maybe not directly. But it may be worth looking into."

He frowned. "But why whales? I'm not seeing the link."

"Not every mammal has VENs," she said. "So far the only species we see them in are the most intelligent, social ones. Humans, the great apes, elephants . . . and certain whales."

He shrugged. "But there aren't any rogue whales . . . Whoa. Wait a minute." He blinked. "There *was* one, wasn't there?"

"Probably not just one," she told him. "Most likely several that attacked ships in the early nineteenth century, when the populations were much larger. The old whalers conflated them into one legend. Mocha Dick, they called him. Moby Dick, in Melville's novel."

"So how do *we* investigate them? It's the Japs who're cutting them up. You should be on the factory ship with them, not with us."

She shook her head. "I have zero interest in 'cutting up' animals, as you put it. A behaviorist observes live subjects, either in the wild, or in a controlled setting. Plots social interactions, the way Goodall did with gorillas.

"But right now, I'm only speculating. It would be a long time before we could demonstrate that damage to or lack of VENs leads to violent behavior. But that's how science progresses. These neurons were first described in the 1920s. It's taken this long just to start to guess what their function might be."

Bodine was hitching himself up in the chair. Despite herself, her gaze drifted to where his legs would have been. She jerked her eyes up as he said, "Problem with your theory. You're assuming what you're calling 'rogue' behavior is some kind of aberration." He was looking at the slanting, banging coils of cable around them, not at her. "But people fight over territory. Resources. Politics. Even what name to call God. Do we blame that on a short circuit in our neurons?"

"Group defense is different. You can't equate a soldier going ashore at D-Day with a serial killer."

"Okay, but even as an individual—couldn't violence sometimes be a rational response to seeing the world as it really is? A lot of progress has been due to people who didn't play nice with others. John Brown. Joan of Arc. Tom Paine."

"John Wilkes Booth," she countered. "Richard Speck. Lee Harvey Oswald, and Ted Bundy. The ones who really changed humankind for the better—Jesus, Gandhi, King—they weren't men of violence. They were men of peace."

"Uh, what did they change, again?" Bodine said, face harsh in the dim light. "Every one you mentioned—they killed him. And, human kind? There's two words that don't belong next to each other."

Up in the bow the unceasing motion was more extreme than farther aft. She stood, wondering how he could take it cooped up here. Then thought: What choice does he have? "You lost your legs in Afghanistan?" she blurted, surprising herself.

"That's right."

"What happened?"

"A mine." He looked away. "Some old Russian piece of shit they laid years ago."

"I'm sorry."

He shrugged. "Over and done. At least I'm still breathing. Hey—you smell coffee?"

He bent over the keyboard and tapped. The sea really must be turning colder. Condensation was beading on the hull interior—not fiberglass, Quill had said, but some kind of superstrong carbon fiber. Moisture ran down the bulkheads like tears. She hesitated, looking at the coarse hair on Bodine's exposed nape. The rich roasted scent of fresh-brewed from the galley was half tempting, half nauseating. She pushed her hair off her face, trying to decide if she wanted any. "I'll bring us some," she said at last. He nodded, intent on the screen.

In the salon Dorée was sitting close to Perrault. Almost, Sara thought, in his lap. "Brr. It's getting colder and colder," she said. "Can't we turn that heater up, Dru? It's barely above freezing in here."

"We have to conserve fuel, Tehiyah. For when we find the fleet."

"Then run the motor."

"That uses fuel too. Plus, we're not going to slip up on any whales if we do that. You wanted to see whales, remember?"

As she turned to sidle past, Dorée put out a hand. Sara halted. Dorée tugged her head down to whisper into her ear. "We don't need to *compete.* Which one do you want, Sara? Lars, or Dru?"

Sara blinked, brain erased like a whiteboard covered with erroneous equations. Before she could answer, the other woman gave her a catlike, conspiratorial smile and patted her cheek. Sara tried to come up with some joking reply, but failed.

The smell of the coffee soured suddenly in her stomach, or in her vagus nerves. A spring of saliva tided at the back of her throat. She hauled herself from handhold to handhold as the boat rolled and pitched, looking for a place to vomit as acid rose and burned, and she swallowed again and again.

4

Antarctic Sea

Sara clung to the wheel, feeling as close as she ever had to dead as the seas raved and the boat bounded for the four hundredth time since she'd come on watch. There was no dawn, as there'd been no real dark. The sun levitated above the horizon, steel gray and heatless behind thin clouds like iced-over glass. The cold air rushed over her, bleeding life itself away hour by hour. Her feet were dead even within four pairs of socks and heavy boots. Her hands felt nothing inside undergloves, then knitted wool, then waterproof fishermen's gloves. She squinted through ski goggles strapped over a wool balaclava.

"Here it comes," Eddi yelled from forward, where she knelt on the crazily pitching bow, hanging on like a squirrel on a wind-lashed branch. She leaned out with a baseball bat to smash a chip of white ice off the drum of the roller furler, where it had frozen like a dipped string of rock candy.

Sara glanced over a shoulder. A slaty mountain loomed behind her like a landslide. She hunched, clutching the wheel as the stern shot upward. The boat slipped sideways and she hauled the wheel over, panting. The sea peaked behind them and tore past, hissing threats, and the stern sagged again. The sail rustled and flapped, and she spun the wheel hard to starboard. The phosphorescent line on the compass steadied and began to march the other way.

A week out from Ushuaia, and she was wheezing, bone tired, bone cold, but beginning to feel she knew what to do, and might even be equal to it. Quill left her and Eddi in charge topside now, which made an ember of pride glow beneath the fatigue.

Though she'd always known that about herself: she'd work her ass off if anyone offered a little praise. That was the kind of lab rat that college, grad school, doctorate, and research bred. The Good Little Girl. The credulous Work Hard and You Will Be Rewarded fool. She smiled thinly beneath the balaclava. Right.

They didn't stand set watches. A pair would come topside, stay until they simply couldn't anymore, then yell down for relief. Dorée usually lasted half an hour. Sara tried grimly to take it for two. By that metric, she still had another hour to go.

Seven days at sea, and not another sail. Not a single ship. Only the occasional distant circling of an albatross, observing with the aloofness of a clockmaker God *Anemone*'s progress across the hazy wastes. Headed east, the wind at their stern. A course that brought those great rollers down on them again, again, again. Quill had warned against losing concentration even for an instant. "Let her come beam to, and she'll bloody well broach. Roll over on her beam ends, and maybe keep going. I been on boats that went on over. Builder designed her to come back upright, but the sea don't honor guarantees."

The companionway slid back with a thud and Madsen peered out. He was growing his beard out and his cheeks glowed gold in the subdued cold light. Her gaze lingered on the long jaw, the wide brow. Those Arctic-pale irises blinked into the light, then locked on her. "Going okay, Sara?"

"Fine, Lars."

"Where's Eddi?"

"Chipping ice, up on the bow."

"Want company?"

She said sure and presently he reappeared in a heavy sweatshirt and the white-and-brown doggie cap, the flaps that were its floppy ears tied down. He hauled himself into the cockpit and found a place out of the wind behind one of the yellow drums. Looked around the horizon, at the radar. Peered forward at Auer as she wound up for a swing, then back at Sara. Examining her. She kept her own gaze on the downwind path the bow would take. Quill had warned them to watch for ice, drifting logs, anything that might penetrate the hull. "*Anemone*'s fast because she's light," he'd growled. "But she's brittle. We hit something hard, she'll shatter. Be ice any day now. If it's your watch, make fooking bloody sure you spot it before I do. That's why you're on the wheel, not to lollygag around with the self-steerer on like bloody fooking cruise control."

She asked the Dane, "Aren't you freezing in just a sweatshirt?"

"Guess I'm cold-blooded. How long's Eddi been at that?"

"Fifteen minutes. Seems to build up as fast as she chips it off."

"It's the spray. I'd say leave it, but it'll make us top-heavy if we don't keep after it."

"That's what Jamie said." They gazed at each other for a couple of seconds before she had to look to the horizon again. She shivered inside the heavy suit, but maybe not from the cold. A delicious tremor ran up the insides of her legs. No. She wasn't going to think about that.

"Want a break?"

She relinquished the wheel gratefully, flexing cramped frozen fingers inside the mittens. Lars stood with boots planted wide, back straight, head up and chin out. The effort it had taken her to fight the steering looked like nothing to him. The bow rose to the sky as the next sea overtook them. He hardly glanced back, only touching the wheel now and then, yet the stern rose straight up. "How do you do that?" she said.

"Open yourself."

"To what?"

"The rhythm of the sea. She knows the course. All you need to do is let her follow it."

Mystical bullshit, but she didn't want to argue. Relieved of the strain, her arms wanted to float straight up into the clouds. She glanced forward guiltily. "I should help Eddi."

"Stay with me a minute."

She sank back. Silence, broken only by the howl of the wind as they crested once more. Finally she said, "You've done a lot of sailing."

"A lot of steering. Not so much sailing."

"Were you in the navy?"

"Sea Shepherds." Madsen fed the wheel a spoke right. A moment later, the boat lurched left, but by then the correction had taken effect, and the bow guillotined a hole down into the sea on a perfectly straight course.

Sara sat hugging herself. The Sea Shepherds were a splinter group of activists, more militant than Greenpeace. They harassed and boarded whaling ships, threw stink bombs to foul the meat. "How long were you with them?"

"Two seasons."

"Was it fun?" God, how inane. Had she really said that?

"Fun?" He frowned at the radar. "Whales have been here for millions of years. Their brains are larger than ours. But these . . . people turn them into dog food, at so many dollars a ton. That is . . . well, obscene is the only word I know that comes close."

"It's still legal, though. Unfortunately."

He gave her a sharp glance. "It *isn't*. Even the International Whaling Commission recognized populations were declining. They put the Southern Ocean out of bounds. But the Japanese are still killing."

"I'm not sure I understand. If it's illegal—"

"There's a loophole for science. And each country gets to define it. There's nobody down here to enforce the convention. So the Japanese set their own quotas, and call it 'research.'"

"Why did you leave the Shepherds?"

He steered for a time before answering. "At first, when they saw us, the Japanese would turn tail and run. Then they put up antiboarding nets, and spikes, and installed water cannons. Then they started shining lasers, hoping to blind us."

"I think I heard about that."

"If you did, that's unusual—news channels are controlled by the same corporate interests that support the whaling fleet."

"You mean, Japanese stations?"

"I mean *all* news." The more he spoke, the less his accent intruded, or maybe she was getting used to it. "They called us terrorists, even though we were careful never to hurt anyone. Last season we actually started to cut into the fleet's quota. So they decided to take more aggressive countermeasures."

On the bow, Eddi staggered as she took a swing. The bat glanced off the ice and flew out of her hand as if jerked by an invisible string. It caromed off a wave, came up on a long graygreen backswell, then dropped astern. Auer shook a fist and shouted after it, but nothing audible made it aft. She turned and began crawling back.

Sara half stood and cupped hands around her mouth. "Watch out for that ice on deck," she shouted.

"Wet ice, that's not good," Madsen muttered. They watched tensely as she crept aft hand over hand along her safety line. Her braced boots slipped off a stanchion once as the boat leaped, and Sara tensed; but Auer hung on like grim Death itself and at last Sara leaned to pull her bulky-clothed body into the cockpit.

Eddi sagged as if being deflated. "Gee. I feel really dizzy."

"I wonder why. Sit down, you're shaking. Better go below."

". . . on-n-n w-watch." Her chattering teeth cut the words in pieces.

"Lars'll help me."

"Sure, Sara and I have it. Go below. Get warmed up." Madsen bent to haul in the mainsheet, altering the set of the huge sail that strained above, dragging them over the waves. Immediately, *Anemone* picked up speed.

When the hatch slid closed Sara moved aft, to just beside the wheel. Where she could look up into his face. His cheeks were reddening; moisture glistened at the corners of his eyes. His nose was running. The blond stubble accentuated Viking cheekbones. Those ash-blue eyes gazed steadily ahead. Only now and then did he glance back for an oncoming sea, then ease the wheel this way or that. He looked as if he could stand there for weeks, like Ulysses, or maybe Leif Eriksson.

"You said . . . more aggressive countermeasures," she prodded.

He cleared his throat. "We lost steerageway in front of one of their harpoon ships. The killer ships, that chase the pods and fire explosive-laden harpoons. They're fast and maneuverable, with huge bows like axes. They rammed our boat. They called it an accident. But I looked up, just before they hit us, and saw the captain standing out on the bridge. Looking down at me. He yelled an order, and they swerved to hit us. Deliberately. It sank our boat. Two of our guys drowned.

"After that, our higher-ups decided to back off. So the whalers finished their season. Worse; they announced they'd taken even more, to make up the quota they hadn't filled the year before. So we lost all the ground we'd gained, and didn't save a single animal."

She kept silent, looking alternately at the radar and the sea ahead. They were traveling faster, planing from wave to wave. The jolting was like repeated punches to her kidneys. Perrault stuck his head up into the transparent dome forward of the cockpit and searched around the horizon. He nodded to them, then sank out of sight.

"So you don't . . . think they should have backed off?"

"No. We were costing the Japanese millions. Sooner or later, they would have had to stop. But when we started actually taking losses, we just . . . quit."

"But the CPL doesn't seem . . . my understanding was, they're no more, uh, ready to use force than the other groups."

He shrugged. "But we're taking the fight to a different part of the Antarctic. Increasing the pressure. Have you ever seen a whale?"

"Once or twice. From far away, on the beach."

"Once you do, up close, you'll understand. They're so beautiful. Intelligent, but not in our competitive, destructive way. We must save them, Sara. Whatever the cost."

She shaded her eyes. "Hey—sorry to interrupt—"

"No problem, what?"

"Look over there. To starboard. No, farther forward. Do you see something?"

He narrowed his gaze too. After a long while he said, "Better call Dru."

Perrault stood with one arm around the mast for a long while, steadying the binoculars against the surge and roll. Then handed them down without a word. They buzzed in her hand as if filled with bees. When she focused them the dark blur floated above the horizon, shapeless, inchoate, holding no fixed form. It seemed to be upside down. The boat was gyrating, pitching, but somehow whatever was humming inside the binoculars held the image steady, making her instantly seasick. She lowered them hurriedly. "An island?"

"Zavodovski," the captain said, still gazing toward it. "Northernmost of the eleven South Sandwich Islands. A volcanic chain."

She swallowed, trying to recall what solidity felt like underfoot. "Will we land?"

"Nothing there. It's only five miles long. Unpopulated. No harbor. We'll pass to the north, then come south again at about twenty-six west."

She looked again. Even through the powerful binoculars it was only a jagged darkness, with clouds of colorless vapor shrouding its upper reaches. "Have you been on it?"

"Never set foot. The Vendée route's well north of here."

The round-the-world single-handed race he'd sailed in, where, Eddi said, something had happened. But she didn't know what, and the captain didn't seem to welcome personal questions. In fact, he said little that wasn't directly related to the boat's condition, or standing what he called a "rigorous watch." He looked drawn. Black stubble stood out against pallid skin.

"How much farther to the whaling grounds?" Madsen asked in a low voice.

"We could see whales anytime. Or ice. Hope you're staying alert up here."

"We are," Sara said. "Eddi's just below to warm up. Lars is giving her a short break. We're staying on the radar."

"Then why is it off?" the captain asked.

She looked, and sucked a breath. The screen was blank. "Uh, but—it wasn't a few seconds ago." She checked the power switch, but it was already in the on position. "There's no power."

"The breaker," Madsen suggested. "It flipped off on our watch, too."

Perrault said he'd check it out. "Stay on this course." He looked around once more, and slid back down the companionway.

"I'll take that," she said. Lars looked at her, then stepped aside, relinquishing the wheel with a bow.

He took her place huddled between fuel barrels as she resumed wrestling with the helm. "Relax," he said. "Reach for the Force."

"Ha. Not much force left in these arms."

"Think two seconds ahead. Steer from where she's going to be, not from where she is."

"I just don't have it." She glanced at the screen; it was back on, the island a coruscating yellow-and-orange blotch. Why couldn't they at least sail closer? Even if they couldn't land.

"How'd *you* get wrapped up in all this?" he asked, settling back. His windburned flush was fading, replaced with a waxy pallor.

She gave a sanitized version of why she'd left Brown. "I did a position search, but nothing's turned up yet. Primate ethology's a small field. Everybody knows everybody—de Waal, Wrangham, Boesch, Matsuzawa—and there aren't many positions. And my—previous project didn't—didn't work out. The only opportunities were in medical research, which meant animal experimentation. Which I don't care for. I had my 401(k) from the college, so I didn't need a salary, if I could move out of my apartment. Then I saw the CPL wanted someone."

He nodded. Rubbed his cheeks as if to massage circulation into them. His fingers were long even in the mittens, his legs thin; the knees poked up. He murmured, looking toward the distant island, "Anybody waiting for you at home?"

So. She hadn't been imagining it. "Um, just some cousins. Back in Nantucket."

"That's surprising."

"My parents are dead. I was married, but it didn't work out. He said I spent more time with monkeys than with human beings." She hesitated, then added gently, "I'm older than you think, Lars."

He blinked. "How old do you think I am?"

"I don't know. Twenty-four?"

He pulled out the corners of his eyes, erasing the squint lines. Tears skittered in the icy wind. "Now?"

She had to chuckle. "Twenty?" Then sobered. "I don't want to play games. I like you, but there's no room in my life right now for a . . . I don't know, for . . ." Any word she could think of to end that sentence seemed either too trivial or too serious. "Anyway, no room," she said firmly. "So, do you know where we're going? After this island? Dru said south."

He blotted his cheeks with the backs of his gloves. "Want me to take that again?"

"I've got it. But thanks."

"He's going to head south between twenty-six and twenty degrees west. Turn right and aim directly for the coast."

She tried to remember the chart. "Are there more islands?"

"Not after the South Sandwiches. Just ocean. We'll have sailed two thousand miles by the time we get down to where the whales should be. Maybe even cross the Antarctic Circle—depends on how the ice looks this year. And where the fleet is. That'll be the tough part. Finding them."

The radar peeped. The island flashed on the screen. "Proximity alarm," Madsen said, and pushed a button. The beeping stopped.

"That's why Greenpeace and Sea Shepherd spend so long at sea. The whalers are closemouthed about their itinerary. Then they chase the pods. They'll follow one for weeks, vacuuming up each member, one after the other, until they're all dead. But this time we have a secret weapon."

"That's interesting," she said casually. "Where'd it come from?"

"The Protection League."

"Meaning Tehiyah."

"She and Jules-Louis, they're supporters, but not the only ones. Some are former Sea Shepherds. Some, former Greenpeace. Others, PETA. Others, just people who want to see whaling stopped, even if risks have to be taken." He looked at her directly. "I hope you're of the same mind."

"I try not to get emotionally attached. But I don't like seeing an endangered species killed for money, in defiance of international convention.

No." She smiled, then remembered he couldn't see her face beneath the black wool. "I hope that's close enough?"

A head bobbed in the bubble dome. The hatch clacked back and Eddi crawled out. She looked around. "Hey. We're going so fast."

"Just letting her run." The Dane slacked the mainsheet and the boat rolled and seemed to sag back, abruptly more sluggish, no longer the seabird leaping from crest to crest.

Sara breathed a sigh, both relieved and saddened. It had felt dangerous but exhilarating, racing at top speed, sending spray flying with each chop of the bow.

Behind Eddi a dark head emerged. Tehiyah Dorée, followed by the captain. "I'll take it," the actress said, muffled behind a cold-weather mask. Behind them rose a third form, wraithlike, thin, moving very slowly in a much-too-large mustang suit. The face was bare except for ski goggles, pale, expressionless. It took a moment before Sara recognized her.

"Georgita! You're up."

"I feel better," the assistant murmured, not meeting anyone's eyes. An uncertain smile curved bloodless lips. She lowered a black waterproof case to the deck, leaned against a fuel drum, and looked around. "We're really . . . far out here."

"Isn't it beautiful?" the actress said.

"It's scary. I don't know what I . . . what are we supposed to do up here?"

"I'll show you," Dorée said. "You can stand watch with me." Sara glanced at her, taken aback. For a moment, she'd sounded as if she cared.

It wasn't exactly warm below, but they were out of the wind. She struggled out of the heavy suit, hung it and her boots in the mildew-and-salt-rimed wet-gear locker, and padded into the salon in damp socks. A framework had been swung out of the side of the hull. Perrault was bolting supports into place beneath the bubble. The elevated seat was positioned directly beneath the dome. The buckle of a lap belt pendulumed. "This is where we'll stand watch from, when the weather gets heavy," he said to her questioning glance. "When things get really bad, we won't want anybody out on deck."

"It's going to get *worse*?"

"We haven't even hit a storm yet. I got knocked down twice on my first Vendée. Broke my spreaders, tore my mainsail track out."

Again she thought about asking, Is that the time you turned back? Then remembered no, Eddi had said that was last year, and he'd said "my first" not "my last." "Is that likely? Isn't this a bigger boat?"

"Depends on what we hit. But for a green crew, you're doing great. Step up here. You're just about the tallest, except for Lars. I'll adjust it so you have headroom."

She obediently climbed the pegs, swung in, and clicked the belt shut. A crank ratcheted and the seat slowly rose until her hair brushed the apex of the dome. She could see all around the horizon. Twisting to look aft, she spotted a shaky Georgita pointing a camera at Dorée. The actress had taken off her mask and shaken out her hair. It streamed like a black flag as she gripped the wheel. She lifted her chin as the assistant continued to record. The bow began to come left. The stern rose. Sara tensed. If a sea hit now . . . but at the last moment Dorée seemed to realize the danger and hastily steered back.

"Okay, thanks," Perrault said. The boat lurched as she climbed down; his hand cupped her butt, bracing her. "Sorry," he muttered, staring past her up into the dome.

"No problem."

She staggered to her bunk, pulled the curtain, and peeled off the track suit. The smell came up in a sickening wave. For a second she debated going to the head, scrubbing pits and crotch, all you could do with the gallon a day Quill allotted. Then shrugged it off. Too cold to even think about splashing near-freezing water over herself. She stank, so what. They all did. Eddi was smart. She'd brought baby wipes. But Tehiyah had borrowed them, and they hadn't seen them since.

Up forward, on a narrow sole before the equipment void, Auer was a shapeless lump inside her Goofy and Mickey sleeping bag. Sara grabbed the handhold and waited for the boat to take a leap. Then gave a tug and floated up off the deck, twisted, and slotted herself into the thirteen inches between the bunk and the curved white overhead. She groped for the strap and snapped it into place, so she wouldn't roll out. Put her hand between her legs, rubbed once or twice, but couldn't muster the interest to continue. She stretched and sighed. Four or five slow deep breaths, her thudding heart quieting, the world and consciousness constricting with each heartbeat. Then darkness hurtled in.

A hand shaking her in the dim. "You want ta eat, get up," Quill grunted.

Sara blinked and coughed. Every muscle ached. Every tendon twanged. At last she willed herself to grab the handhold and roll out. But was stopped dead, hanging half in and half out, caught between heaven and earth by the bunk strap. She unhooked it and dropped, narrowly missing Georgita as she too crawled out, moaning softly.

When she slid back the curtain Eddi was standing on Goofy's face, her blue bikini underpants sagging. Sweat showed dark on her German army sleeveless tee, and a smear of brownish red—menstrual blood?—lined the crack of her ass. Sara turned away and rooted in the dirty laundry on the deck for her fleece-lined pants.

In the galley Quill had laid out bread and sliced cheese in a fiddleboard. "Last of the fresh," the bearded mate grumbled as they took a bounding pitch. Plastic glasses shivered in the overhead stowage. Dishes rattled in the sink. "Canned or frozen from here on."

If Jamie was here, where was Lars? She craned and saw him ensconced in the dome chair like a fly trapped by a spider. His elbows were braced against the framework; his head was poked up into the bubble as he worked—on some piece of electronics, to judge by the dangling wires. "Where's Mick?" she asked the salon at large.

"Up forward."

"I'll take him a plate." More easily said than done, but she clamped one of the unbreakable dishes over another with the sandwich and felt her way forward.

Past the salon and the berthing area the coachroof slanted down. She was bowing by the time she got to the semicircular hatch leading to the long narrow forward void. She knocked off the dogs with an elbow and backed in. "Mick. Brought you—"

"Close the hatch. Right now!"

She slammed it, nearly losing the sandwich. To find herself in pitch darkness, surrounded by a high-pitched electronic ululation like theremins in a science-fiction film. A buzzing hiss came and went.

Within the tapered tunnel Bodine crouched in front of a screen, face lit green and pink and yellow. He turned a dial in minuscule increments, head cocked like a curious raven. The buzzing hiss sharpened, each repetition ending with a zipping snap. It grew crisp, then faded again into an all-encompassing hiss.

"What's that? What're you picking up?"

"Can you get Dru in here? Or Jamie?" he said, not looking at her. Head still tilted in that listening attitude.

"Not until you tell me what's going on."

He threw a hard glance over his shoulder. "Just *do it*, Sara."

Puzzled, angry—this was her space, the lab—she slammed the dishes down. She called into the berthing area, "Dru? Jamie? *Mick* wants you."

She went back in and perched on one of the equipment cases. The captain came in immediately. He looked at her, then at Bodine. "What is it you have?"

"Two radars, bearing roughly one three zero. Not much angular separation."

"Japanese?"

"Japanese-made. All I can say for sure."

Perrault hung over Bodine's shoulder watching the screen. The hatch creaked open and Madsen came in too. They huddled like husbands at a Super Bowl game. All I need is to put out the chips and beer, she thought.

"Okay, what's going on?" Her words emerged harsher than she'd meant.

They glanced at her. Perrault started to turn back to the screen, then heaved a sigh. "Mick has direction-finding equipment, to home on the fleet's radar transmissions. Up in the sea lanes, it'd be hopeless. Hundreds of radars up there. Even back by the Palmer Peninsula, it might be a cruise ship. But out here, if we hear a signal, it's likely to be them."

"The Japanese. So you can hear them? From how far?"

"Two, three hundred kilometers. Unless they shut their radars down."

"A few other tricks they can use," Bodine muttered. "But until they tumble to how we're tracking them, we've got a lock on their position. So, Dru? Alter course?"

"Not just yet. We might have weather coming up. Can you tell which way they're headed?"

"If we can hold contact, I can get a bearing drift. Maybe work up their course from that."

"Sara?" Eddi's pixie face appeared at the hatch. "You in here? We need to get up on deck."

Already? she thought, and sighed. "Coming."

Her suit was still wringing wet, and plunging dry feet into rubber boots with half an inch of icy water in the bottom dampened her spirits as well as her socks. She climbed the companion ladder as if towing the weight of the world. Not just fatigue, but a visceral unwillingness to go back up. She panted to force oxygen into her bloodstream. Maybe not two hours this time. Maybe she'd give herself a break for once.

Topside the sky was still light. The sea seemed rougher, the wind even colder. Jamie Quill was huddled before the wheel. His little pig eyes peered suspiciously out of a black nest of balaclava from which beard stuck out in tufts. "'Bout time," he grumbled, slapping himself with flailing arms. "Fooking freezing up here. What'd they want Lars for?"

"Mick picked up the whaling fleet. We'll probably be changing course."

"Huh. Okay. But for now, we're still on the same heading. Wind's up to thirty, gusting to thirty-five. Main's double reefed. Jib's halfway out. Auto's keeping us on course, but be ready to grab the wheel if it goes bonkers. Gonna get darker soon. The sun don't go down, but it dips, so remember to check the lights. And keep a close eye on that radar. There'll be ice sooner or later. We want to see it first."

She told him they had it, he could go below. She checked the autopilot—apparently it was all right to use it now—and made sure they were on course. Flicked it off, steered herself for a few minutes, then turned it back on. An anthracite sea built aft until it towered over them. "Hold on," she shouted to Eddi. *Anemone* felt heavier, and didn't rise as quickly as it had that morning. The sea surged up the slanted stern-ramp, over the inflatable, and detonated into a heavy burst of icy spray, soaking the wool over her face and obliterating sight as her glasses flooded even beneath the goggles.

A waterproof intercom connected the cockpit with the salon. She pressed the button and bent her mouth close. "Dru? We're taking a lot of spray up here. And the waves're getting bigger."

"I ballasted aft. It'll be wetter, for sure. Try and stay out of the worst of it. Keep your safety lines tight." A pause, then, "I'll be right up."

She helped him winch the main into its boom and lash it down. They wound the jib in and *Anemone* slowed further. He beckoned her forward, bright tangerine safety lines spinning out behind them like twin spider threads. They snugged everything tight and locked off the furling lines and beat ice off everything they could reach.

By the time they crawled aft again she could barely creep on all fours. While she rested, Perrault got the lines up off the cockpit sole and back into their bags. He looked aft at their trailing line, which led to a fluorescent green torpedo kicking up spray fifty yards astern. If someone fell overboard and his safety line broke, his only chance was to grab that green line, hang on, and hope one of the others slowed the boat and reeled him in before he passed out from hypothermia.

"We're going to move you inside," Dru said at last. "As soon as I get everything ready to stand watch from the dome."

When he went below again she felt twice as lonely. The sea was an infinite corrugation of huge swells. The wind shredded their tops off and blew them along the surface in long straight streamers of spray. Not even an albatross wheeled between them and the dull clouds, low and rain-leaded. She coiled her safety line and joined Eddi in the lee, where they hugged each other for the illusion of body heat as a fine shower began to fall. She sank into a stupor, broken by spasms of shivering.

Some interminable time later Eddi was shaking her. "Get up. Sara. Wake up. There's something ahead."

She opened her eyes into failing light, a low-hanging drizzle. Auer was pointing. Sara sat up and blinked. Obscure in the mist, a massive shape glowed in the falling dusk. *Anemone* was headed for it. A ship? An island? She hit the intercom.

Perrault was topside in seconds, stuffing a heavy plaid wool shirt into waterproof pants. She felt guilty, he looked so obviously yanked from sleep. "Up there," she said, pointing.

"Iceberg. Didn't you see it on the radar?"

"N . . . no. We didn't," Auer said, shamefaced. "Sorry, uh, Captain . . ."

He frowned. "You'll have to be more alert."

"Sorry," they chorused, and he nodded, unsmiling, but not pursuing it. He looked ahead again. "It's a big one. Maybe a mile across."

The word spread. One by one the crew came up and ranged along the coachroof, staring. She gazed, forgetting her misery as they drew closer. Irregular and spiky, with scooped-out sides, the berg reminded her of a modern artist's take on a giant white cake. Even through the pewter mist it glowed cerulean and cream, the sea frothing and seething at its base. Perrault pressed the pedal to release the self-steerer and took the wheel. They skirted it slowly. Deep bays gradually opened to reveal melt-runs like waterslides sloping down to blue pools. She took the binoculars someone handed her and focused on black specks. "Penguins," Eddi murmured.

Anemone rolled to a larger-than-usual wave. Dorée gave a short scream and flung herself into Perrault's arms. He held her, face unreadable, and shouted, "Okay, most of you, below. You can take turns coming up to look, but we can't have everybody up here at once." Sara saw Bodine's shaggy black head cupped by the dome, and wondered how he'd gotten himself up there. Climbed, with those incredibly powerful arms, no doubt.

Quill, who had the wheel now, turned it to sheer away, but Dorée cried, "No! Go closer. I want to film this. Our first iceberg."

They sailed slowly past. The drizzle thickened to an icy sleet, dancing across the deck like steel needles punching up through it. Sara watched the sea bursting against the strangely skirtlike bottom of the berg. Portions were planed flat, tilting this way and that at queer angles. In the subdued light blue shadows shifted as if something were moving about deep within. It must once have been flat on top, but had broken apart and tumbled, then frozen back together. A strange exercise in topology, saddles and valleys, and abrupt peaks stabbing the mist. As they neared, the penguins began sliding down the wash like toddler-sized skateboarders, disappearing into the waves that frothed at the base. The ice cliff reared up many yards taller than *Anemone*'s mast. Another huge wave foamed past, then broke into spattering suds against the berg.

"Farther off, Jamie," Perrault called, waving.

"Oh, just a little closer. Dru, *please*."

Dorée had gone all the way forward. She stood with arms outstretched, hood tossed back, smiling radiantly. For a moment Sara thought she was smiling at her. Then saw the pale assistant crouched on her heels atop the coachroof, aiming the camera.

"Can you see it, Georgita? Get it all in the frame!"

"Not quite, Miss Tehiyah. Wait, hold that . . . I'm filming now."

Dorée half turned and pointed. "There it is! Careful, Captain, not too close!"

"Not quite so shrill," the assistant murmured.

"There it is. Careful, not too close!"

"Better, okay . . . one more take."

"There it is, Dru. Careful! Not too close!"

"Good. Good."

"Now get the sea behind me. Those white pieces bobbing around. Can you pan along with the penguins jumping out of the water between them? That's a great shot. Higher, Georgie. Can you get a little higher, and shoot down? And get them, behind me?"

"I'll try." The assistant lurched to her feet and crept to the peak of the roof, then hauled herself one-armed up onto the boom. She stood swaying, one white-knuckled hand gripping the mast, the other aiming the camera.

"Careful," Sara called.

"Hey! You! Get down!" Quill barked.

Sara turned and saw the wave bearing down. "Get down!" she called, and started forward along the sleet-slicked deck.

Georgie looked frightened. She crouched, cradling the camera to her breast like a baby. The boat rose, rose, then sank away. She teetered, but held on.

The wave burst against the berg, and the backwash rolled toward *Anemone*. Georgita, on the boom, had one foot extended to the coach-roof when the boat leaned out from beneath her. Her boot slipped, and shot out into space.

She went down hard, rolled, and slid down the slanted roof toward the lifeline. Her right arm still cradled the camera. Her left caught the stanchion, but awkwardly, and as the weight of her tobogganing body hit it there was a loud crack like a breaking tree limb.

An instant later both Madsen and Quill had their fists embedded in her suit and were dragging her back over the gunwale. Georgita hadn't actually gone into the slowly passing sea, but her left arm dangled and her face had gone white as the bobbing chunks, the size of basketballs, that drifted past.

Eddi put an arm carefully around her. "God, Georgie, you all right?"

Her face was pale ivory around the nose and lips. "I—I slipped."

"I told her not to get up there," Dorée snapped.

Sara said, "Let us through. Let's get her below."

"Oh, my. It hurts."

"We'll take a look. Give me the camera." Sara handed it to Madsen and together she and Eddi got the girl, tears and snot glazing her chin, down the companionway and onto the salon table, where they peeled off the mustang suit, then the blue fleece.

The arm didn't look quite right, but there was no jagged bone breaking the skin, and no blood. The injured girl stared up into the light, pupils dilated.

Bodine staggered out of his sanctum on plastic and titanium. "She hurt?"

"Broken arm, looks like," Sara told him.

"Fracture? Usually pretty easy to deal with."

"You have training?"

"Battlefield medic. Want me to check her out?"

"Please." She turned to Eddi. "We could use a blanket."

Perrault came down as Bodine was manipulating Georgita's arm. "Proximal humerus," he told the captain. "Looks a little crooked, but it doesn't seem grossly displaced."

"Lucky it wasn't her pelvis or hip, the way she went down." The captain stroked her shoulder. "Georgie, do you need a shot? I have morphine in the aid kit."

She groaned, but didn't speak.

"I'd rather wait a little. I want her to be able to talk," Bodine said, tickling the tips of Georgita's fingers. "Can you feel this? Georgie-girl?"

"No." She spoke into the light, not looking at their faces. Shivers racked her. Eddi came back with the blanket, spread it and tucked it in. "Thanks," she whispered.

"I'm going to have to do something now that'll hurt. But I'll get it over fast as I can." Without waiting for an answer, Bodine turned the arm and began pressing strong fingers deep into it. A reddish-purple blush bloomed under the skin. His fingers probed behind it, paused, moved on. Came back and pressed harder. The girl stiffened and cried out.

"Displaced?" Sara muttered.

"Can't really tell without X-rays. But I think I can get it back where it belongs. Or close. Got to do this now, before it swells. Dru, get her feet. Eddi, take her shoulders." Auer, freckles standing out, took her place at the head of the table, biting her lip. "Sara, I need downward tension. When I say so, pull on her arm."

"How hard?"

"Hard as you can, but pull steadily, don't yank at it. The biceps is starting to knot. Get braced—ready—*now*."

A full-throated scream burst from the woman on the table. Auer grabbed for her free arm, but took a whack across the face as Georgita thrashed. A flailing boot caught Perrault in the mouth before he pinned it. Sara kept her attention on Bodine as she maintained tension on the arm. His fingers pressed deep into the purpling flesh, expression abstracted, remote, as he probed. Then he shifted his thumbs and leaned into them. Georgita screamed again, a burst of agony that filled the salon.

"Okay, the ends are lined up. You can let go. . . . All done, kiddo. We'll get you fixed up, then give you something to help you sleep."

Sara was wringing with sweat despite the chill air by the time they were done. Helped by Perrault, Bodine sawed a spare antenna into seven-inch sections, then splinted them around the break with an elastic bandage. He dosed her with morphine and Aleve and sent Eddi topside for ice to make a pack. "The less swelling, the less she'll hurt," he explained. "You can sit up now, Georgie. Cradle that arm with your other one. I'm going to make you a sling."

When he'd folded and pinned a canvas reefing strap into place, Sara and Eddi stood on either side as the girl swung her legs down off the table. She said in a shaky voice, "I think I'm going to v-vomit."

"Into the bathroom . . . oops. Never mind. We'll clean that up. Let's just get you into your bunk."

Some time later Sara told Perrault, who was sitting in the elevated chair beneath the dome, "She's resting."

"Strapped in?"

"Yes. I wedged her in good." She hesitated. "We're heading back, right?"

He didn't look at her. "Heading back? Why?"

"Well, I mean . . . her arm . . ."

"I've sailed single-handed with a broken arm. She'll be fine."

She blinked. "Are we still expecting bad weather?"

"Well, I'm hoping to avoid it," the captain said, pressing keys on a dashboard beneath the dome. A pump hummed aft. "But we need to get ready, just in case. There's a big low-pressure system headed our way. Weather marches west to east down here. Fifty-knot winds, gusting to fifty-five or sixty. In open sea, that means thirty-foot waves. Maybe more. Plus snow. We've been casual up to now. About stowage, and . . . other things. Now we have to get serious."

"I'm ready to help prepare. Whatever we need—"

"See Jamie. He'll put you to work." He studied a screen. "I'm glad you're aboard, Sara. You're a . . . steadying influence."

"Thanks."

"Sorry we haven't been able to further your research."

She smiled. "Maybe we'll find some pods."

"*Oui.* If we locate the fleet, we'll find your whales."

She nodded. He looked haggard. The hoar in his beard seemed to have spread, like advancing frost. He didn't look down at her. Nor at anything below. Just squinted ahead, chin held low, the leaden light circling him like an ominous halo.

5

Force Eight

Over the next day, though, the weather stayed the same; a varying wind, steel overcast, the sea rough, but nowhere near what they'd feared. She and Eddi and Lars started at the nook of the bow, where spare sails and lines lay bagged and tagged, and worked aft. Everything had to be lashed down, Quill said. So firmly stowed that even if *Anemone* turned turtle, it would stay in place. The mate followed them, tugging on each knot they made and kicking gear to make sure it wouldn't move.

Between spells of work Sara stood watch. Sometimes on deck for brief periods, but more often, as the temperature fell, strapped into the interior steering station. She had to admit, the dome was surprisingly comfortable. The radar and other instruments were laid out at waist level. The control lines from the sails came through rubber-sealed tubes, so you only occasionally got a blast of cold air. The clear plastic gave a view around the horizon, except for directly forward, which was masked by the jib. Up here the boat seemed to rotate around her when it pitched, making the violent gyrations when a sea twisted *Anemone*'s tail easier to bear. Or perhaps she was just getting used to it.

She was up there, staying alert for the ice that lay scattered across the sea, when Bodine stuck his head out of the forward compartment. "Lars! Where's—?"

"Here." Madsen stepped out of the galley holding an apple.

"We lost the signal."

The Dane's face went stony. He ducked inside. Not long after, he came out again, and went in search of the captain.

Sara tried not to let it distract her. The lumps of ice varied from the size of refrigerators to that of tractor-trailers. Quill said these "bergie bits" came off icebergs. Only a little showed above the surface, but each could weigh tons. More than enough to crash through *Anemone*'s eggshell hull. The swells were running high, so the radar didn't help, and you couldn't see them until you were almost on top of them. So she was sailing under a heavily reefed main and foresail, keeping their speed down, and altering course left and right ten degrees every few minutes to see around the canvas. There was only room for one under the dome, so she and Eddi took turns, swapping out every half hour. The break helped, but it was still nerve-racking.

Perrault came out and stood swaying in the salon. He kneaded his mouth. Quill turned from his seat at the navigation station. "Dru? You okay?"

"We lost the radar."

"It's down?"

"I mean, theirs. All at once, like it was turned off."

Quill clawed in his beard. He'd been braiding it, until he looked like Blackbeard. Then he scratched his ass. "Maybe for the best. D'you see the prognostic?"

They went to the nav station, and she heard nothing for a time. Then Perrault murmured something involving millibars, and more words she couldn't quite make out.

Quill grunted, "North'd be safer."

"They're not headed north. If we stay on this course, we can pick them up when they turn their radars back on."

"Sure we're looking at the same low here? This bitch's as big as New Zealand. Check out those winds."

Another murmured exchange. Then Quill said, "You're the skipper, but that projected track? It's really going to fooking blow. We get on the wrong side of it, we'll have the wind on our nose, and seas like Paddy's barn. It's not coming so fast we can't turn and—"

"That's right. I'm the skipper," Perrault snapped. Then added in a calmer tone, "We knew there'd be rough weather. And we're ready. Right?"

The mate's muscle-packed shoulders slumped. Perrault turned away. His gaze locked with Sara's, dropped, then lifted again. He came over to grip her ankle. "Speed?"

"Twelve, by the knotmeter. A little more by the chartplotter."

"The GPS will give you a higher reading because the surface water's being driven by the wind. More ice or less?"

"About the same. But there's, like, a fog building up. If it gets worse . . ."

He stood swaying with the pitch. *Anemone* was heeled to starboard. She felt different under reduced sail. As if relaxing into the sea's arms, rather than agile, avid, as when she tore along on a plane. "How far down are you reefed?"

"Main, all the way. Plus the fore."

"Can you handle it?"

She nodded and he stood there a bit longer, then turned away. The door to the engine compartment banged open, then closed.

"Hear that?" Eddi said. "About the storm?"

Sara sighed. "He knows what he's doing, Eddi. No point worrying."

The videographer sighed, too, and fell silent. Sara peered ahead, caught a speck of white lifted on a grayblue sea. Turned the wheel and watched it slide past, spinning slowly, a bluewhite chunk of destruction, stained with a greenish smear of algae.

She hoped she was right, about Perrault.

When their watch was over she bunked out with her e-reader, trying to make progress on a book about beaked whales. Since they didn't linger on the surface, the way humpbacks did, only recently had they even been noticed by science. New species were still being discovered. A team out of Seattle had put a transponder on one and tracked it diving to almost three thousand feet. They sang complex, lengthy songs. No human knew what they meant, although researchers said they were definitely carrying information of some type.

She cradled the reader, blinking at the underside of the deck above. Imagining a creature that hunted in complete darkness half a mile under the sea. A world of sound, not sight. Of crushing pressure and utter cold. No one knew much about whale social behavior. Which made sense; you could observe chimps and bonobos in the wild, house them in a habitat and test them. But a creature that came to the surface for a breath only once an hour, that spent most of its time where only a submarine could follow? About all you could do was kill them and weigh them. That gave you a sense of their ecological niche, but not much about their lives. How much could you guess about Einstein by examining his stomach contents?

Not that she thought whales were geniuses, no matter what Madsen said. They might have large brains, but comparing brain mass to body weight, humans came out ahead of most whales. But there was still plainly much to learn.

She was rubbing her face, wondering why she had such a headache, when a heavy voice—Quill's—shouted, "Everyone on deck." She flinched, debated leaving her curtain drawn. Then swung out and started pulling on gear.

Topside the wind was much stronger. It bit through the balaclava, numbing her lips and freezing the moisture on her glasses. She pulled her goggles down, panting in short breaths that chilled her tongue. The air tasted like the icicles she'd used to pull off the eaves of their house in Nantucket. She touched the back of a glove to her lips. It came away bloodstained. The repeated exposure was cracking her lips. She crouched behind the drawn-up, shuddering bulk of the Zodiac, squinting as a sea came in from aft. The swells were bigger than ever, and the wind had taken on a near-supersonic shriek. White spray tore off the crests as they broke around the stern, blowing downwind in long roiling streaks. She clung as the boat pitched. The low sky was the same almost-black cinder-gray as a thunderhead. Under that storm-light the sea was a strange hue; neither green nor blue nor gray, yet all of these together; and it seethed under the lash of the wind as if alive, resentful, capable of taking on any and all forms, given time and energy.

Quill had a locker open and was pulling out the metal bats. Sara squatted as *Anemone* soared, teetered on the back of a great silver sea, then plunged. The staysail snapped and cracked, blowing off a metallic-looking halo of spray and ice that rattled across the foredeck. Two red-orange figures, slow as moonwalking astronauts, had ventured out between mast and satellite-antenna dome. They clutched the lifeline with one hand as the bats rose and fell in the other. The whacking thuds came aft only faintly, as if the wind blew away all sound. She coughed. Beside her a bulky figure muttered, "Does he really expect us to go up there?"

"Tehiyah? That you?"

"This is ridiculous. We're risking our lives out here." She turned and Sara saw she didn't have a face covering on. Silvery rime frosted dark lashes. Her perfect teeth were astonishingly white. They *had* to be capped. Sara glanced quickly away as something in her brain reset them into a lower jaw grinning with shining enamel and bloody bone. No, she told herself. Not now.

Dorée yelled, "Is it my imagination, or is it blowing harder?"

"They were talking about a storm."

"Oh, just fucking peachy." She put her arm around Sara, who stiffened. "How are you and Lars getting along?"

"If you mean is anything going on, it isn't." She blinked, wondering where Dorée came from when she did this girlfriend thing. The idea someone like her could see Sara Pollard as some sort of competitor was ludicrous. Unless she was paranoid as hell.

"Too bad. You're not that horrible-looking. Unlike that deformed bitch Angelina. I know an image consultant—"

Quill shouted, "You two, cut the quiffing. Get up there and knock some of that ice off. We need to be light aloft when this thing hits. Clip to the jacklines—the blue lines I ran fore and aft on each side. Don't clip to the lifelines, or the stanchions! If you go overboard at this speed, that lifeline'll break."

Fighting a profound unwillingness, she took a deep breath and forced her shivering, cowardly carcass forward. The wind clawed at her, flapping the hood around her head as if ravens were attacking her. The boat seemed to choose these times to leap into the air and shower her with freezing spray, or slide her crazily across the wet icy deck until she crashed into the deckhouse or bubble or satellite dome. She was going to be covered with bruises, but of more concern at the moment was the livid sea that foamed and heaved only a few feet below. She didn't want to slide off into that cauldron. Halfway forward another bulkily suited figure passed her a baseball bat as it crawled aft. She tucked it into her armpit and pressed on.

At last she and Dorée reached the bow. They huddled there and began flailing. Ice coated the forestay in white tubes. It layered the deck with white sheets greasy with seawater. It loosened its grip reluctantly, only gradually lacing with lucent cracks, like flaws in diamonds, as she whaled at it, then suddenly bursting. Each whack jolted pain up her wrist into the elbow. On the other side of the pulpit Dorée was smashing away, sliding around with each pitch of the deck, grunting like a hog with each blow. A shower of spray submerged them; Sara came up gasping, only to howl as a hammer blow struck her buttock. "That's my fucking *ass*," she roared.

"Sorry," came the answering scream, faint against the whine of the wind, the creak and snap of the storm-sail burning fluorescent orange above them. The sky reeled. A sea humped its back and spat stinging foam. Freezing air sawed in and out of Sara's throat. She hacked and hacked at a lump that wouldn't yield.

Then Dorée whacked her again, this time across the back of the thighs. She twisted, suddenly enraged, and cracked the other woman across her bent back. The actress arched her face to the sky and howled like a dog. "You hit me!"

"Well, you fucking hit me twice!"

"This fucking ice. And these fucking *bats*." Dorée reared and hurled hers whirling like a majorette's baton across the waves. It vanished instantly, rolled over by a huge turbulent locomotive that raced alongside for a hundred yards before breaking in a thunder of rolling foam and needling spray.

Sara's terror buckled and they collapsed in a storm of giggles like fourteen-year-olds, Dorée hugging her as they slid back and forth like pigs on ice. They ended up pinned between the forestay, which trembled as the swollen, balloon-taut fabric barely contained the immense force of the wind, and the bow pulpit, an arrangement of curved stainless tubes that looked like it belonged on a kids' playground.

Another dousing in freezing seawater sobered them both. They crawled aft, separating at the satellite antenna to creep past the lookout dome down the port and starboard walkways. They tumbled into the cockpit as a scowling Quill looked on. And from there, after dripping dry for a few minutes, down the companionway to mugs of hot strong tea cheered with a dollop of rum.

The wind kept rising as the sky darkened all that afternoon. Its keen climbed to a shriek, then to a register almost too high to hear. Quill and Perrault took turns in the chair. The word went around: They were in for hurricane-force winds. Everyone without a reason to be up should weathercloth himself into his bunk.

Before Sara did so, she looked in on Georgita. The assistant was a slight hump under a damp wool blanket. Sara smelled urine, but when she asked the assistant if she needed to go, all she got was a shake of the head. "I prefer not to," Norris-Simpson whispered. Her limpid, unfocused gaze followed as Sara checked the splint, tucked the blanket back in, and tried to feed her a cookie. It too met with the same whispered refusal.

Sara swallowed a handful of dry-roasted peanuts and Aleve, rubbed Vaseline on her cracking lips, climbed into the cupped sleeping shelf, and lashed herself in. But there was no way to sleep while being thrown against the overhead or the bunk strap every few seconds. Not to mention the thump and whoosh against the hull, like trying to nap with your ear pressed against a flushing toilet. So she just lay there with her e-reader, but turned it off too after a while and just lay in the near darkness listening to *Anemone* fight the sea. Ominous creaks and pops came from forward as the hull flexed. The bilge pump cut on, hummed, cut off.

A dull animal terror made it impossible to entertain consecutive thoughts. Water crashed on the coachroof and flooded over the viewport. Cracking noises began to come from aft each time they heaved. Each time she thought it couldn't be worse, an even more extreme sea a few minutes later shook the boat even more violently. The cracking grew louder. She wondered what it was, but no way she was unstrapping and going to look. Her wrists burned. Her back ached. Rain drummed, then tapered off.

When she woke again the cabin was nearly dark. Only the pearly luminosity of Antarctic twilight glowed through the portlights. Something had changed, but she wasn't sure what. She leaned out and parted the curtain.

Perrault was in the dome. Strapped in, leaning forward, head twisted to look astern. His hands never paused on the wheel, exerting so much force they quivered. Beyond a certain point they had to turn off the autopilot. Only a human eye and skill could cope with waves so massive, such an uproarious sea. The captain's lips sagged. He squeezed his eyes closed briefly each time a crest freight-trained past and *Anemone* floated airborne for a few seconds, arching at the top of her parabola as gear rose off the deck and Sara's body surged against the straps. Then it all smashed down, the flat bottom crashing into hard sea like a van dropped from twenty feet onto concrete. Everything vibrated, and that fearsome cracking came again, as if something incredibly strong but not infinitely flexible was snapping fiber by fiber toward ultimate failure. Between these leaps they canted to starboard, and each time this happened tools and cutlery and parts fell clattering and tinkling out of their stowages, shoaling up along the starboard side of the salon.

Sara lay there as long as she could. Then, at one of the lulls between leaps, climbed down over a motionless Georgita, who stank even more strongly now, and hand-over-handed herself up the slanted deck into the salon.

Perrault spared her a glance. “Sixty knots in the gusts.”

“How much worse will it get? What’s the forecast?”

“Forecasts aren’t much good down here.” He squinted ahead. “We just have to hang on until it blows over.”

“Georgita’s not well. I’m getting worried.”

“Is she strapped in?”

“Yes, but she’s not eating, and I don’t think she’s getting out of the bunk to . . . go to the bathroom.”

“Maybe not a bad choice right now, with a broken arm. Can you clean her up?”

She swallowed. Bad memories of taking care of her mother, as she’d died. In terrible pain, with a doctor too frightened of the law to prescribe anything powerful.

“It would be good of you,” he said. “Get Tehiyah to help.”

“Tehiyah?”

“Georgie’s her assistant. Why shouldn’t she help?”

Sara thought this unlikely, but a crazy lean so far to starboard she was lying on the bulkhead interrupted her. *Anemone* hung canted for long seconds, then staggered back. “All right,” she muttered.

“I just don’t think it’s something Georgie’d want one of the men doing.”

A convenient excuse, she thought. The captain twisted to look off to port, then spun the wheel. A wave crashed into the side, toppling them again, though not quite as far.

“We’re rolling a lot harder.”

“It’s veering on us as this low passes. I had to come right, but that’s not good either. Thing is . . .” he glanced back again, corrected, not looking at her. “I can’t build up speed because I have to watch for ice. And in these seas, all this spray, I can’t see more than a hundred yards. At the bottom of the trough there’s no wind, but we have to have speed to maneuver. Then at the crest we get hit with the full force.”

“Are we in danger? Should you, I don’t know, start the engine?”

“We’ll need every drop of fuel when we catch up to the Japanese. And lack of power’s not exactly my problem.”

She nodded, not really understanding, her mind moving to the task ahead. But instead of getting to it she felt her way aft, handhold to handhold, avoiding wet patches on the deck. Finally she reached the after cabin. Rapped on the teak door. "Tehiyah?"

A startled yip. "What?"

"I need help."

"What do you mean?"

"We need to get Georgita cleaned up."

"Can't you take care of it?"

"I could use some help."

Silence was the only response. Sara took a deep breath and lifted a hand to knock again. Then let it drop. She should have known better than to ask.

She was in the galley gathering paper towels and vinegar when the boat toppled again, slowly, deliberately. She clung like a spider, waiting for it to come back, but it hung for as long as she might take to draw a breath.

Then another wave crashed into them, and they went over. Vinegar and towels went flying. Her whole body stiffened, tree-dweller reflex flinging out her arms and crimping her hands against whatever they struck first.

She'd been leaning against the sink; now she was bent backward over it, looking straight up at the galley door, which had swung open and hung straight down. From forward and aft came crashes and screams. Above her a piece of radio gear tore out of a rack, dangled for a moment by its cables, then dropped straight down as if aimed for her. She lay pinned, helpless; all she could do was throw an arm up. At the last possible second the boat staggered and the heavy assembly smashed into the jamb instead, cracking the wood like a hydraulic logsplitter. It spun on its axis, tumbled past her, and demolished the spice cabinet.

The boat sounded as if it was coming apart around them, piece by piece, with every maul-blow of the waves. Lying on her side, *Anemone* was taking each new sea full on her exposed, flat bottom. Each impact smashed her sideways. Sara clung to the sink, waiting for them to turn completely over. If they did, maybe the little semienclosed galley was the safest place just now, to judge by the gear and metal flying around in the main salon. A hollow booming came from forward, then a crash and howled curses in Bodine's voice. A deep strumming echoed from all around, as if they were trapped inside a broken guitar being kicked around on bricks.

Suddenly she had to get out. The wet-gear locker. Her mustang suit. Maybe she wasn't thinking clearly, but staying in here waiting for something to crush her or for the hull to split apart—no. She reached for the jamb where it wasn't splintered. Waited until the world staggered partially upright again, and jumped and caught it and folded herself around as if kipping on a bar. She hung, gasping, then scrambled over into an apelike crouch.

Ahead and above her the captain hung half out of his chair, fighting the wheel savagely. Quill was with him, both straining to force the helm over. The boat started to come back, then shuddered as another huge sea burst over them. Turbulent green covered the plastic dome above the struggling men, then vanished as wind tore it into white froth and whipped it away. The roar and clattering all around made thought impossible. She clung helpless, forgetting where she'd been going. With a hoarse shout a body fell like a shot duck from the portside cubby; Madsen, dropping free across yards of space to crash into the starboard bulkhead with a sickening thump.

She started to fight her way aft, then froze. "What in fuck's name am I doing," she whispered. Hesitated, looking yearningly toward the companionway; then turned back and crept on hands and knees over pots and pans and broken crockery toward where Madsen lay curled like a fried eel, moaning. "Lars, you all right?"

"My head, hit my head. *Pis og lort.*"

"Let me see.—Dru! He's bleeding! You've got to get us back upright!"

"*Tabernac!* What d' hell you think I'm—"

"Jamie—"

"Downwind, Dru, you've got to let her run. Yeah, that's away from the Japs. But it's the only way we're going to recover."

#1 12-07-2018 10:28AM
Item(s) checked out to TYLER, LOUISE R.

TITLE: Tailspin
BARCODE: 35394016830289
DUE DATE: 12-28-18

TITLE: Shell game
BARCODE: 35394017235249
DUE DATE: 12-28-18

TITLE: The whiteness of the whale
BARCODE: 35394012266009
DUE DATE: 12-28-18

TITLE: Tipping point : the war with Chin
BARCODE: 35394014307926
DUE DATE: 12-28-18

TITLE: Madison Avenue shoot
BARCODE: 35394009680196
DUE DATE: 12-28-18

Renew items online at WWW.DPLS.US
or call our automated system at 312-5208

"These seas'll swamp us. Break in the companionway."

"It's our only chance. If that keel snaps, we're never coming back up. We can't keep this course. *Dru!*"

Sara glanced up. She'd thought Quill was trying to help Perrault, but now made out in the dim light that both men, lips drawn into rictuses of effort, were straining *against* each other beneath the dome. She stared, appalled.

Then, all at once, the captain lifted his hands from the helm, raising them like a priest addressing Heaven, and Quill wrenched it over. Now both were working together, one steering, the other hauling madly on the control lines. *Anemone* surged, tried to rise, but failed. She rode up and down again, and more gear tore loose up forward in a cascade of heavy thuds.

At last she gave a drugged lurch and rolled drunkenly upright. She pointed her bow in a great woozy circle, as if feeling her way through a dark tunnel; then staggered into forward motion again. Gradually she straightened still further, as if relieved of some immense burden. She lifted her tail, arching like a cat in heat; then once again resumed that long, violent pitching.

Sara realized she was sitting in wet cloth, cradling Madsen's bloody head on her lap. They were both looking up at the piloting station. Perrault and Quill were steering with heads lifted, as if listening for something astern. "Not swamping us yet," the mate ventured.

"We lost something." The captain passed a hand over a ragged face. "I heard it. A spreader, or a shroud."

"I'll go topside and check."

"No, Jamie. Wait until morning."

"If it's a shroud, the mast'll be gone by then."

Perrault shook his head, lips compressed. "Stay here."

The minutes stretched out, and Sara crouched, still terrified. At last she took a deep breath and looked around. Georgita? No—forget Georgita. She'd see to her in the morning. If they made it to morning. If something else didn't break, and doom them, here in this immense lonely waste.

She stretched out beside Madsen, feeling him gather her in his arms. After a moment she put hers around him, too. But there was no heat in the embrace. They simply lay in the cracking, pitching dark, fingers digging into each other desperately, both of them shuddering, as cold as ice.

6

The Whale

Two days later she climbed the companionway by sheer will. Her arms vibrated like tuning forks. Every muscle had passed through aching into the dull numbness of a dead tooth.

She topped the ladder and shaded her eyes, blinking in the dazzle of a low sun that flashed polished brass off five-foot seas with jade-green flames in their hearts as they rose and heaved and passed on. Offering *Anemone* to the sky, then lowering her to whisper on. The huge golden-and-bronze jib bulged each time she rose, then wrinkled and shrank as she declined. The brightness brought tears to Sara's eyes, and she fumbled at her pockets.

Through polarized sunglasses the sea took on a deeper blue, beyond indigo. Surreal hues oiled waves with the colors of shattered glass found on a deserted beach. A few cotton-puff clouds sailed high above, miles between each and the next. The sky was a dark sapphire cupola above the whirling cups of the masttop windvane. It deepened to lavender, then russet as her gaze dropped to the horizon.

She turned in a complete circle, gripping the companionway coaming as Dorée pushed past into the cockpit. No other sail marred the great circle of the sea. No ice, either, which was reassuring, but made her wonder where it had all gone. They were much farther south than when they'd first encountered the bergies.

"It's almost warm," Eddi said wonderingly.

Sara turned; the videographer squatted atop a yellow drum, lowering the camera. Had she been filming her as she gaped? Fleece ski pants covered the tattoos that snaked down Eddi's legs. She was naked from the waist up, small sallow breasts innocent, brown nipples erect with the cold. Beside her on the drum was spread that same grimy German army sleeveless tee, the black wings of the stylized eagle echoing the riot of animal designs that ran down her arms. She wore fingerless thin black leather gloves.

"Good grief, Eddi. Aren't you freezing?"

A crooked smile. "The sun feels good. Anyway, we've got to get used to being cold."

"I don't seem to be getting used to anything out here." Sara tugged her zipper tighter, shuddering. Sunny it might be, but the air was still glacial. The wild sea was lovely, but she couldn't ease the bone terror learned over the last few days. She eased out a quivering breath. A swaying bundle drew her eye upward again. Perrault, dangling high in a canvas sling. Her gaze traced the hoisting line down to where it wrapped a winch, then rested tautly in Quill's big gloved hand, the mate's boot braced against the coach house as he alternately looked aloft and aft, leering at Auer.

Little eyes squinted redly at Sara; the black braided beard nodded. "See you're up and on deck."

"Good morning to you too, Jamie. What's the damage?"

"Broken spreader."

Dorée snickered. "I know a few actors with that problem."

Sara suppressed a sigh. "That's the horizontal pole up there? That holds the uh . . . the shroud away from the mast?"

"Guess you could say that. Bloody fooking lucky we've that double spreader rig. And that 'twas the starboard one that busted."

She shaded her eyes again, and spotted a dangling length of aluminum or maybe some kind of gleaming carbon. The captain's face was bent to where this connected to the mast. A tool glittered; a repetitive clang drifted down. "What would have happened if . . ."

Quill's gaze kept sliding past her to the half-naked woman in the cockpit. "If the port 'un broke? We'd have lost the buggerin' mast." His free hand slid inside his coveralls. "Eh, you strippin' down too? We can make a party of it."

"No, thank you," she said drily.

A shout from aloft. Quill raised his head and shifted his boots. The winch ratcheted. The wheel rotated tenantless. Who was steering? Then she caught white and brown, the goofy, wide-open cartoon eyes of Madsen's hound-dog hat in the plastic dome.

Which reminded her, she hadn't seen Bodine at all during the storm. "Has anyone seen Mick?"

"I did," Auer said. "He's fine."

"Wonder if he'd like to come up." She waited, but no one said anything.

He did eventually, an hour later, a bundle wadded under his armpit. He balanced on metal and plastic, looking up to where Perrault was pinning a new spreader into place. The old one lay in the cockpit, twisted crystalline gray at the fracture point. "Anywhere up here to hang out wet stuff?"

"Good idea, let's peg out the oilies," Quill said. He picked up the broken metal, examined it critically, and flipped it end over end over the side. It struck with a splash, sinking fast as it dropped astern, visible beneath the water for only a few seconds before it melted into the wavering green. "Long's we got sun. Anywhere on the windward lifeline. There's small stuff in the locker if you want to lash it."

She went below to gather her own clothes. Georgita was awake, staring up at the underside of Sara's bunk. Her reddened eyes did not blink. "You okay, Georgie?" Sara asked her.

"All right."

"Want me to help you to the toilet? To wash up?"

"That's all right. I was just listening."

"Um . . . listening?"

"Can't you hear them? They're all around us."

"Who? Who's all around us?"

"I'm not sure. But I can feel them. So beautiful. Like angels."

What *was* she talking about? Sara frowned. She'd sponged her down during the storm, and Eddi had cleaned her up again the night before. She wouldn't have minded, if the woman had really been ill. But something else was wrong, something more fundamental and systemic than a broken arm. What sane adult seemed perfectly content to soil her sheets? "You ought to get up, Georgie. You can't stay in your bunk forever."

"My arm hurts."

"Let's see." She knelt and peeled the blanket aside. The splints were in place. The arm looked puffy, but not alarmingly so. Yet the girl seemed unable to manage the slightest effort. "You can't stay in bed," she said again, more sternly. "It's nice topside. The sun's out."

"I don't really want to. Thanks." She turned her face to the hull and her eyelids sank closed. Sara hesitated, kneeling. Then thought: Fine. Whatever. She got up and began pulling dirty underclothes out of her laundry bag, wincing at the fermented stench.

Presently the lifeline flapped with socks, underwear, and inside-out mustang suits. Walking the length of the deck, balancing against the roll, but enjoying the opportunity to move around, she doubted they'd dry completely—not soaked with salt water—but there was no fresh to rinse with. The air might be a degree or two above freezing. Auer had put her fleece top back on. The sun was an orange Necco Wafer on the horizon. Below the Circle, it never set, only spiraled, gradually rising each day, until it reached its apex at the height of the Antarctic summer; then slowly declined. She hugged herself, still worrying about Georgita. Bodine could set a bone, but she couldn't shake the feeling something else was wrong. It wasn't natural to lie in your own . . .

"Don't stare at it," Quill warned, hustling past with a heavy-looking bag of red sailcloth. Up forward Perrault and Madsen were dropping the jib, gathering in great flapping folds as it slid to the deck. "And if you stay up much longer, put on sunscreen."

She heaved a sigh. This seemed overprotective, after they'd barely survived a gale, but she just nodded.

"Want some of mine?" Dorée held out a tube.

Surprised, Sara took it. The product was labeled in French and looked expensive. "You sure?"

"Keep it, I have plenty. One of Jules's companies makes it. How's Georgie?"

"I'm worried." She explained. "Now she won't get up at all."

The actress frowned. "Want me to have a look?"

"Actually, Tehiyah, Eddi and I could've used your help cleaning her up."

"I'm no good at that type of thing, I'm afraid. Maybe it was a mistake, letting her come."

Sara stared. Could Dorée have *forgotten* she'd browbeaten the girl into coming? That smooth lovely face gave no clue. The actress massaged her cheeks where the sunscreen emollient glistened. Then her forehead, taking her time, as if working cream polish into a rich leather saddle. Catching Sara's examination she smiled, full dark lips bending into a lovely curve that expressed far more than a simple smile should.

"Do you want me?" she murmured.

Sara started. "I . . . excuse me—?"

Dorée put three fingers on Sara's wrist. Those lips parted, ready to speak, as Sara stopped breathing, unable even to think, much less guess or anticipate what she'd say next.

"Whale ho!" Perrault called from aloft.

She turned as the others scrambled to their feet, staring out to where the captain's outstretched arm pointed. Quill and Madsen stood on the coachroof, shading their eyes. Dorée pushed past to clamber up with them. Auer stared, frozen; then scrambled toward where she'd wedged the camera. Sara started to climb atop a fuel barrel, then remembered what had happened to Georgita. She searched the locker and found the binocular case. Unsnapped it and hastily wiped the lenses clear of crystallized salt.

"There she blows," Dorée called gaily.

Sara shuddered. Surely Tehiyah couldn't mean what she'd inferred. Or could she? But why was she so surprised? Was it that she didn't believe Tehiyah Dorée could go both ways? Or that she could be interested in *her*?

To hell with that. Whales! She jammed the glasses to her face and focused on distant white feathers amid slaty blue, blossoming across many degrees of horizon. Quill went back to the helm. *Anemone* came around and he trimmed the sails on a course to intercept.

The expanse of slowly heaving sea between them and the pod gradually narrowed. Everyone was topside now except for Bodine and Georgita. Madsen hung from a shroud, rather unnecessarily daringly, Sara thought, watching through a small pair of binoculars and carrying on a running commentary. "Five . . . six . . . eight. See the tail? There's a flipper. Pretty sure they're humpbacks. They spend summers here and head north for the winter. Two more! Mick'll be picking up their songs, down below. Wait a minute . . . another group behind the first. To the left. Maybe a dozen more. Smaller."

"Minkes?" Quill said.

"'Piked whales,' Jamie. We don't call whales after their killers. They're both baleen feeders, the pikes and the humpbacks."

She clung to the shroud, unable to look away. The giant flippers of the humpbacks wheeled and crashed with flat smacks and splashes that rolled across the sea like the clash of a distant battle. The pikes were smaller, more streamlined. Their rostrums—the points of their upper jaws—were sharper, their dorsals hooked and set farther back. The second pod stayed clear of the first, the groups not quite intermingling. She started for the companionway, to go down to Bodine and listen, but couldn't leave the spectacle. *Anemone* was sailing nearly parallel to the pod now. They were clearly on the move, although the whales gave the impression of ambling, rather than hurrying.

"Another," Eddi yelled. "One whale. Off to starboard."

Sara snapped round, searching where the videographer pointed. She expected more humpbacks, or more pikes. They were the most common species, since the great whales had been winnowed from the oceans. But this spout was lower and bent to one side. She put a hand on Madsen's shoulder. "What's that?"

He shaded his eyes. "Sperm whale."

"Physeter macrocephalus."

"I can't believe it! All this time at sea and not a single sighting. Now we've got three different species in view at once."

"How it goes," Quill rumbled. "Either too much, or not enough. Like wind."

Remarkable. But then, if they were in an area of rich food resources, not all that strange. The question was, where were the whalers? She studied the distant splashes. Madsen was telling her the pods were mainly females and young. "The males only join them for about three months, to mate. Otherwise they're loners."

"Interesting." The males of many species spent most of their time alone, meeting others only to breed or to defend territory. "You've spent a lot of time whale watching?"

"We all did, whenever we could. It was inspiring. To see the animals we were there to protect."

"I can imagine. All you whale-huggers." She smiled to show she was joking. "Were there scientists on your cruises?"

He hesitated. "Not really. The Japanese claim they're conducting 'research.' Which was why I thought it was strange you were coming. It's a loaded word, in our community." He smiled too. "Us *whale-huggers*. A good one, Sara. I'll remember that."

The humpback pod was closing in on them now. Lifting the glasses, she watched the great heads shoving the water to either side. A blow jetted up every few minutes. Beside some of the larger whales swam smaller copies. Cries rose from the other side of the boat. She turned; one of the humpbacks had come in close and was twisting beneath the water, the white patches of its undersides and flippers a lighter blue in the deep topaz jade. Gulls dipped low, screaming as they plummeted into the froth churned up by great tails. A humpback rolled onto its side, curious eye upturned. Such a small orb to supply view to such an enormous creature. But then, the percentage of brain volume devoted to sight, the visual cortex, was much smaller than in a human being.

She turned back to see the lone sperm had altered its course, maintaining its distance. She raised the glasses. The huge creature looked like a reef in a storm. As it plowed into each wave it shattered it, tossing up violent bursts of spray the wind trailed off in twisting veils.

Then, for just a moment, she saw it clearly. Glimpsed a massive lump of head in the trough between two seas, filling it with heaving green water and foam like beaten eggwhites. She squinted into the eyepieces. Not black, like the others. She couldn't really label its color. Quartz veined with iron, perhaps. Or perhaps that was just the sheen of water on its skin reflecting sky and spume. Its blow jetted sideways in a sudden burst of mist like steam from an old-fashioned factory whistle. It rolled and heaved, far apart from the others. Then the tail levered up slowly, and the sea surged empty once again.

She should get to work. She stowed the glasses carefully, as Quill had taught them, and went below. Her fatigue had backed off. She slid down the companionway and lurch-walked forward as the boat rolled around her like the rotating tunnel in a fun fair. Only now her hands went out of their own accord to grasp and steady, and her boots knew exactly where to step to anticipate the next lean of the deck.

Bodine was in his chair, seatbelt swinging loose, bulky earphones clamped to his big head. His detached legs swung weirdly from a makeshift hook in the overhead. He glanced at her with unfocused eyes. The screen traced colored lines that vibrated. When he actually noticed her he flinched, as if recalled from a dream.

When he turned a knob a long, hissing note, flutelike, yet far more complexly modulated, filled the swaying forepeak. It went up and down the scale in chirps and grunts and fartlike repetitive clicks, going on and on but sounding anything but random.

"The humpbacks?"

"Right. A typical song. This unit downshifts the sound; what they're actually putting out can go way above the highest freq we can hear." He cranked a dial and aligned a needle with a shimmering spoke. "This one's broad on the port beam. From the intensity, four, five hundred yards away."

"About where the pod is." And lifting her head, she could hear them through the hull even without the earphones. Though no doubt she wasn't getting the full range, the way he was.

"It's mainly the males who sing, and they don't usually stick with the pod. But it's not unheard-of." He rooted in a plastic milk crate and came up with a file folder. He flipped to a printout and flicked it over to her.

It was a monograph on the acoustic analysis of humpback songs. She nodded. "You're recording these?"

"Well, I was planning to. Then we got knocked down, and all my zip ties broke and the workstation took a dive out of the rack." He jerked a thumb at a disassembled computer. "Until I get that working again, and our satcom comes back up, I'm not digitizing squat."

That explained the crashes and curses during the storm. She found a perch on a crate of batteries. "Mick . . . what exactly did you do in Afghanistan?"

He showed teeth. "What they told me to."

"Electronics?"

"Sort of a mix of that, and intelligence."

It didn't sound like a way to lose your legs, but he didn't meet her gaze or seem eager to add any specifics. She tried again. "How'd you get hooked up with Sea Shepherd? That's where you met Lars, right?"

He rolled his head as if his neck ached, and she half reached out. Her hand paused, then returned to her lap. For a moment she'd wanted to rub his nape . . . but fortunately he hadn't seen it. "I had my military disability," he said. "Didn't have to work. But after a while I started to feel, like, shit. Sitting at home posting crap on my blog . . . going to grad school . . . I was drinking. Giving my wife a hard time. Ex-wife, now. Classes bored me. Going head-to-head with whalers sounded like it might get the old burn going again."

"Did it?"

"Up to a point. But the Shepherds have these very strict rules of engagement. What they can't or won't do. So it was easy for the whalers to escalate. Then the insurance people and the lawyers got involved and the ship was impounded. Lars and I stayed in touch, though."

He tensed, fixing like a spaniel as a new spoke glimmered into a coruscating fan. Frequency waves raced up and down. "Sperm. Big one."

"There's one up there. Magnificent creature."

"Uh-huh." He flipped switches and keyboarded, then stared at a screen filled with what looked like fuzz. "I was checking for radars. But I suspect they've turned them off."

She was lost for a moment, then realized he'd shifted topic from whales to whalers. "Can they hunt without radar?"

"Not for long, not in ice. But the open sea extends farther south this year. Which may not be good news for the whales. At least, the baleen feeders."

"Why not?"

"The krill eat sea growth on the bottoms of the ice. Less ice, less krill; less krill, fewer whales." He grimaced. "So there's both the Japanese killing them, and less food to go round. I'm not a fanatic, like Lars. But we don't *need* to wipe out species with brains bigger than ours, that sing songs so complex that even after decades of study, we have no idea what they're communicating."

He rubbed the back of his neck. Again she started to lift a hand; again, dropped it. You can't do that, Sara, she told herself. Can't rub your assistant's neck. No matter how harmless it might seem. She stood abruptly, hitting her head on a dangling plastic-and-metal foot. "Oh—sorry. I'm going back topside. Shall I ask Dru to stay with one of the pods?"

"He wants to keep pushing east. But if we could run with the humpies for a few more hours, I might be able to get something recorded. If the hard drive hasn't totally crashed."

Topside everyone was still hanging over the lines, passing binoculars back and forth. Eddi had lashed herself to the mast to free both hands for the camera. The captain listened to Sara's request without expression. Before he could say anything Madsen put in, "We're not out here to watch whales. We're here to stop the slaughter. Right, Dru?"

"The owner's orders are to locate and pursue the fleet," the captain said, gaze fixed above them both.

She said, persuasively as she could without sounding coy, "I understand that, Lars. Dru. But I *am* here to observe. So if we could get just a bit closer?"

Perrault pursed his lips in a fine Gallic expression that held absolutely no possibility of English translation. "I'll stay with them for a couple of hours. But if Mick picks up emissions, I'm heading after the fleet." He took a breath, released it; then put the wheel over. Hauled the mainsheet in hand over hand so quickly the line blurred, and jerked it up into the stainless jaws of the block. *Anemone* heeled as she came around, sails luffing, then snapping back into full draw as she steadied on the new course.

The humpbacks did not seem to mind their company. They continued to spout. The younger ones ventured closer, then were sheepdogged away by vigilant . . . parents? Aunts? She hung over the side, wishing there was some way to make out the sex of these giants.

"Bubble herding," Madsen called down. "See those four off the bow, swimming in a circle? They surround a school, leaving trails of bubbles. The prey moves away from the bubbles, and from the white patches on the whales' fins."

Sara gasped as the sea bulged from beneath. One after the other, the whales came up within the boiling mass of encircled prey, gaping mouths the size of hotel swimming pools, the grooved skin of their lower jaws expanding to take in many tons of seawater and food. Tiny silverine fish leaped within those rapidly shrinking ponds, frantically trying to escape what was already certain destruction. She clung to a shroud, entranced. The whales were cooperating. Using tools to hunt. As clearly as a chimp using a stalk of grass to raid a termite nest.

Another calf ventured their way, but this time its larger guardian hung back. Sara shaded her eyes as it wallowed closer. Hard to call something that huge *cute*, but . . .

Auer called from her perch, "Bend down a little, Sara. As if you're talking to it. That's right." She looked up to see the lens pointed at her.

Dorée came around the coach house and stood watching as Eddi kept asking Sara to turn this way and that. Sara grew annoyed. Had she asked to be filmed? Finally she straightened. "Eddi, I don't really—"

"Oh, a *mother and calf*," the actress said brightly, with a lilting, ardent inflection that turned every head on deck.

Sara blinked. A heavy sweater was unzipped to showcase cleavage. Tehiyah's shaken-out hair streamed in the wind like a dark banner. Her eyes, no longer narrowed at Sara, sparkled. Somehow she'd seized center stage, as if the open deck of the slowly slipping sailboat were the boards of a theater. Those eyes! Sara couldn't pull her gaze from them. Those great tawny pools welcomed the universe, beaming love. Dorée circled the coach house to emerge on the foredeck, where the lines of the swelling sail intersected. As if magnetized, Auer's lens followed. "Can you hear?" Dorée called. "A mother, singing a lullaby to her child."

Sara didn't hear anything but the wind. But every face on deck followed the actress, drawn like sunflowers to the rays of morning. She stopped at the bow and bent; thoughtful; attentive. Beneath the water a cerulean blue flickered, slowly faded, then rose again.

The whales surfaced without haste, the smaller first, closest to the dipping and rising prow. Snapping her attention back from the actress, Sara noted the protuberances of modified hair follicles, the limpish sag of a black dorsal.

She leaned forward, concentrating on the massive beasts that arched and flexed a few arm's lengths away, bathed and cradled by the sea. The massive backs were crosshatched with circular marks, like the scars of many whippings.

"Oh, gosh," Eddi whispered.

White spray burst up, then rained down, the mist drifting for many yards until it swept over them, wild with a dank rankness of fish paste and animal breath. A slitted double nostril gaped, inhaling, one aperture much wider than the other; then snapped closed as a wave washed over it.

The young whale rolled onto its back, flinging out its fins to expose the white underside, long grooves running along it as precisely as if machined. A tight slit perhaps two feet long came into view, surrounded by puckered flesh. "Female," Madsen noted. "Two, three years old."

Dorée pulled her hair back with a graceful motion to reveal a grave, transfigured expression. She spoke to the lens. "These wonderful creatures are being slaughtered by the hundreds each Antarctic summer. A new Holocaust, perpetuated through the ignorance and greed of a few, and the apathy of the rest of us. Only the Cetacean Protectors are here to intervene, at the very bottom of the world.—Pan down to them, Eddi, then close-up on me.—But we will protect these gentle giants. Find their murderers, and the killing will stop."

Auer cleared her throat. "Tehiyah? I didn't come up here to—"

"Back to the whales, Eddi. Then . . . *cut*. Let's do another take. I *love* the baby."

Sara remembered her own Canon, and pulled it from her pocket. There had to be millions of pictures of humpbacks online. These same whales wintered in the Hawaiian Islands. Maybe an opening slide for a presentation. If she ever got invited to another academic conference, which was an open question.

The massive mother blew, an explosive *pffoootsch* that rained down over the sea. She arched her back, an expanse of wet black rubber large enough to play tennis on. Sara snapped off shots as the flukes lifted in a black rainbow, executed a complex flourish, showing the maculated cream-white underside for several seconds. Then the female slipped slowly under.

"Fantastic," Eddi said. "They do put on a terrific show."

"They're not circus animals," Madsen snapped. When Sara looked his jaw was set. "They are not here for our *entertainment*."

"Looking doesn't hurt them, Lars," Eddi said mildly.

"That's what the tour operators say. Then they chase and harass them for hours. We don't just destroy their habitat, slaughter them, make them into meat. We have to make them exhibits, too."

"Look, they're coming back."

They turned to the gigantic animals now rising again, blowing, on the other side. Dorée trotted across the foredeck, calling, "Okay, let's do it again."

"Sorry, Tehiyah. You have your assistant for that."

"And she's fucking useless, so you're my cinematographer now. Get down here. Shoot upward, into my face."

Instead Auer's lip came out. She stuffed the camera back into its case. "Fuck you. I'm not taking orders from you."

"Eddi," Perrault said from the helm. "Control yourself. Your job—"

She whirled, and Sara recoiled from the sudden passion in her voice. "My *job*? Nobody here's paying me! I paid my own airfare down. Anything I film is mine!"

"Anything you film is *ours*," Dorée said.

"That's not the agreement I made."

"Why else would you be along? I assure you, if you don't do your job, you won't work in film again. Or anywhere else in entertainment—aquatic or otherwise."

Sara put her hand on the small woman's arm. Auer was shaking. "Eddi, calm down. Let's discuss this. I'm sure they'll pay you for the footage—"

Dorée said, "We're feeding her and transporting her. She's an *employee*."

"Fuck all of you. I made my arrangements with the CPL office. I'm a *filmmaker*—"

Perrault said, voice iron, "Shut up. Everyone, just *shut up*."

The captain nodded to Quill, who stepped into his place at the wheel, and walked forward, furious gaze jumping from one face to the next. "We will not have screaming matches on my boat. We are shipmates in a dangerous sea. We will behave with courtesy to each other. Is that clear to everyone?"

"We need a photographer—"

"That's *enough*, Tehiyah. The two of you will clean the heads tonight. After dinner, which you will prepare together. If you can't cooperate voluntarily, I must teach you to. *C'est clair?*"

Dorée flushed. She grabbed the lifeline as *Anemone* pitched. Sara noticed the whales had moved off, as if sensing the outbreak of hostilities aboard their big new friend. "*I'm* not cleaning any *toilets*—"

"Yes you are. Or you won't use them. Would you rather hang over the stern? You will all get along. Or you'll regret it."

"I'd take that warning aboard, if I were you people," Quill put in from the helm. He looked quite jolly now. "The captain's word is law. Especially under the *French* maritime code."

Dorée started to speak, then closed her mouth. Her eyes blazed. She turned away and glared seaward.

"Eddi? Understand?"

Auer nodded, lips set. "Yeah."

"Very good." Perrault's gaze met Sara's. Did the crinkles around his eyes deepen? If so, she didn't understand the message. He turned away and hiked back to the wheel, bending en route to repin a flapping sock that was threatening to blow overboard.

Sara eased a breath out and looked for the humpbacks again. They were half a mile distant now. Milky spouts jetted up here and there amid the crests. The minkes, if that's what they'd been, were far away over the curved bluegreen.

"Hey, here's Cappuccino," Auer said, voice trying for lightness.

"Cappuccino?" Madsen said. He spat over the side.

"That's what color it is. Or maybe a mocha latte. But he sure is a venti."

Sara followed Eddi's finger to gaze at a lighter patch glimmering many fathoms down through the green sea. She stared for a moment, puzzled, as it slipped aft, silent, shimmering, seeming to hang motionless down there. Then her eye suddenly assembled it into reality, existence, into something she recognized.

It was the same sperm she'd seen far off, but this time nearly directly below the boat. It shimmered through the jade membrane between them as she leaned over the gunwale, camera dangling forgotten, trying to make it out. Its color . . . a light coffee, as Auer had just said? Or even lighter, the hue of tanned human skin? The surface was veined with lighter creases, like an old handbag or boot. Its size stunned her. It was longer than *Anemone*. Yet its shape did not make sense. Then she realized the squared-off head, larger than a shipping container, was turned on its side, the tiny dark eye gazing up. Did it glimpse them, too, or only the swell of hull? It blinked slowly. Did it understand them as sentient beings? Or comprehend only bits of color in a world of blue? Behind that staring eye the creases became prunelike furrows fissuring away to the vast body.

Then it rolled again, wheeling with enormous ease and gracefulness despite its immense size. To her astonishment, as it passed through the falling slanted rays of the sun it glittered, glimmered, flashed, deep down there in the jade, the fissures veined like some immense mine with yellow metal. “It’s *golden*,” she murmured, hardly able to credit what she was seeing. “But how can—”

“Diatoms,” Madsen said. “They swim through them, and pick up the color.”

The whale’s bulk shrank, dropping away, parting, all that immensity fading slowly through deep green into infinite blue, and vanished in a complexly braided swirl of refracting sea.

Auer chuckled uncertainly. After a moment Sara joined in. Madsen only looked sour. Quill and Perrault, by the wheel, didn’t even glance their way. Dorée, alone on the bow, clung to the stay as she gazed down into the sea. As if each one of them, only an arm’s length distant from the others, was really alone.

7

Secrets

She was losing track of time. It was the eternal half-light, like a perpetual late afternoon. Each day seemed dimmer, not really dusk, for you could see the solar disc, orange or russet or carmine depending on its altitude above the horizon. But never fully day. A ghostly twilight fit for neither sleep nor waking, as if they hovered between one world and the next.

The night after spotting the whales, she'd passed the little closet that served as toilet up forward—there was another, more luxurious one in the owner's cabin aft—to see Auer on her knees, rump pushed up, scrubbing in silence. She blinked. Beside her, Georgita squatted on an overturned plastic bucket, hugging her splinted arm. Her breath steamed in the chill air. "Where's Tehiyah?" Sara asked.

Auer silently sprayed and scrubbed. "She said she'd do the after head. Not this one," Georgita said.

"She's the only one who uses that one."

"Right." The videographer straightened and dragged a sleeve across her face. "So . . . how's that?"

"Much better," Georgita said. "Look, sorry I was so sick for so long."

"Don't worry about it," Sara and Eddi said together. They looked at each other and laughed.

"Sara," Bodine's voice echoed from up forward.

She excused herself and stepped that way, very carefully. She ducked through the little hatch into the always-claustrophobic forward space with its swaying lines, its banks of equipment. Bodine half smiled at her from his chair. She wondered if he slept in it. "Yes, Mick?"

"Do something for me?"

"Sure. What?"

"See if Jamie's in the engine room. Ask if he has some acid—muriatic, sulfuric, whatever. I need to clean these corroded contacts."

She nodded and headed aft. Through the salon, past the dome, down the passageway. Halfway there she heard a groan and stopped. Oriented, in the dim corridor, toward one of the doors. It eased open, then closed again with the boat's pitch. She reached for, almost touched it. Then *Anemone* rolled and it parted another inch, just enough to cut her a narrow slice of what lay within.

On the wide master bed a white rump worked between splayed knees. The legs were darker-complected than the narrow rump, which was fair-skinned. The groan came again. No, a moan, of sexual ecstasy, real or simulated she could not tell. The other answered in kind. Human mating vocalizations, some corner of her mind noted.

"Like that?" Madsen's voice. Then a hand slid down across his back. The rump paused.

"Who's there?" Dorée said sharply.

Sara took a slow breath and backed away, fingers still extended. A step back. Another. Then, when the stiles touched the jamb again, turned and half ran to the ladder down.

When she came back up the passageway, oh-so-carefully balancing a vial of clear acid, the door was firmly closed.

Topside the next morning she blinked into a white nothingness. The temperature had dropped again, and the fog was back big-time. Enough light to see by, but no more. Quill had insisted over and over that they wear a safety line whenever one crew member was topside alone. She snapped her carabiner to the jackline, clambered out of the cockpit, and walked forward.

Anemone moved steadily through the sea, the featureless fog driving along only a little faster in the same direction. Heeling slightly, she overtook each crest and surfed with it for several seconds, bow wave rolling out to either side, before sinking into the trough and beginning to overtake the next.

Sara stripped off a glove. The mist's cold breath flowed over her extended hand like the exhalation of some icy-temperatured animal. A shiver thrilled up her spine. The queer no-color muffled the boom's clank, the cutwater's rush. The sails trapped it and turned it to water. It ran down the taut fabrics as if they were weeping, pattering on the deck in a rhythm she found familiar, though she couldn't say how. Then she did: the tap of a gentle rain on a porch roof. A skin of ice gleamed where the drops fell.

She clung to thc lifeline, wondering if they should be going so fast. Bits of ice the size and texture of snowballs bobbed as they passed, then slid smoothly astern, spinning and rocking in the broad path *Anemone* smoothed on obsidian water. They reminded her of a white body against another, darker one. Apparently Dorée had chosen her sleepover buddy for the voyage.

She frowned and lifted her head, closing her eyes. Sniffing a dank, sharp, somehow black—if black could be a smell—odor. Like the inside of a squirt gun had smelled, when you were a child.

Iceberg? Like the one they'd passed days before, upset and distorted like a fever dream? She went back to the cockpit and examined the radar. The waves sparkled all around, in every direction, but she couldn't tell what was ice and what wasn't. She cracked the companionway hatch. "Dru?"

He glanced up from the navigation nook, eyebrows lifted.

"I think I smell ice."

"Wouldn't be surprising." He bent to examine the display at the nav station, which would be identical to that in the cockpit and the dome. He glanced at Eddi, up in the steering station, but didn't say anything.

"Shouldn't we slow down? We can't see."

"Nothing on the screen. There's been very little ice so far."

"I still smell something."

He sighed. "Be right up."

As he bent beside her to sheet out, the freezing mist flowed past them like a white river. They lost way at once and skated to port before Eddi corrected, the sails slatting and drooping, the long but insubstantial hull rapidly losing impetus. He frowned at the radar screen, then searched ahead. Muttered something in French. Then bent to a rubberized button she hadn't noticed before. A deep drone boomed out, sustained for seconds as he kept the button depressed.

He let up and straightened, facing forward, curved blade of a nose searching the wind. The mist blew past faster now that they'd slowed. His eyelids sank closed. She examined the graying stubble at the point of his chin, then closed her eyes and listened too.

"Anything?"

She shivered. Icy tendrils of fog crept down her collar. ". . . no."

"Neither do I."

"But you do smell it?"

He cocked his head. "*Non.* You are quite sure?"

"Well . . . maybe it's just the fog."

"It is below freezing. Perhaps that's what you smell. I want to keep making easting."

"The fleet?"

"No sign yet, but it must lie somewhere. Still, I will reduce our speed. Until visibility improves." He seized the coaming, started to lower his head, then lifted it again. "Sara. You know . . . you strike me as a person worthy of trust."

An awkward pause. What was he trying to say? "Thanks," she said at last, unsure where to look.

He glanced at her, then away. Seemed to want to add something, but finally said only, "Well, there it is. So you did right to call me. Whenever you suspect danger, you must let me know. *C'est clair?*"

She said quietly that she understood. He told her to stay on deck and sound the horn every two minutes. Then swung below again, releasing himself a few feet above the deck sole and landing lightly, knees bent. There was a balletic grace to the way he moved about the boat. His boat; the one he'd designed, Eddi had said.

Not for the first time, she wondered what had happened on his last round-the-world race. It obviously preyed on his mind. But there'd never seemed a good time to ask, and probing someone else's failures . . . she wouldn't like it if he started interrogating her about her research at Brown. No more than Bodine seemed to want to talk about whatever mistake or mischance had cost him his legs and his military career.

Now that she thought about it, each one aboard seemed to have a reserve, some part of him- or herself kept apart and private. The captain and his lost race. Dorée shared nothing; well, except for her sexual favors. Georgita was utterly passive. Lars was friendly enough, but only enthusiastic when the subject was whales, or what was being done to them by humans. Only little Edwige Auer seemed to meet everyone openly. She too had been grievously wounded. Her very body had been torn apart. Yet instead of denying her scars, she'd made them part of herself; acknowledged them with art.

Had it been two minutes? She gave it another thirty seconds, counting, and bent to press the cold hard black rubber. Held it down, one thousand, two thousand; then let up and straightened, head throbbing with the basso drone, listening with all her attention for echoes from that all-obliterating whiteness that writhed and thickened all around.

An hour later Lars came up. The fog was just as thick. By then she was chilled and shaking, fantasizing unsettling shapes in the flitting whiteness. She thought of asking if he'd enjoyed his time in the aft cabin, but didn't. It wasn't her business, and there was no way she wouldn't come off sounding jealous. She climbed below gratefully and made a steaming mug of Eddi's brown-rice green tea, listening to the every-so-often drone of the foghorn.

On impulse, she made a second mug. But Perrault wasn't in the salon, nor in the engine room. She hesitated, knuckles lifted to knock, outside his stateroom aft. The captain's was next to the master's cabin, but smaller. In the few times she'd been in it, almost cenobitic: plain varnished wood, a vertical locker, a bunk not much larger than hers. A fold-down desk with computer and repeater. She imagined him asleep in it. No . . . wait . . . what was she doing? She dropped her fist and trudged back to the salon.

Eddi was still slumped in the steering chair, one booted leg dangling, the other propped on the dashboard-cum-instrument panel. "Want me to take a turn?" Sara asked.

"Thanks, Sara-oh. I'm fine. Might as well sit around up here as down there."

"What's it doing?"

"Wind's up to . . . twenty-five. Still super foggy."

"Want some green tea? I made some hot."

"Thanks. And a sandwich, if you wouldn't mind making one."

Right, it was lunchtime. But no one else had been in the galley. She checked the Sharpie'd duty list on the fridge.

"Tehiyah!" She pounded on the door, scowling.

A stirring inside; then, "What?"

"Your turn to make lunch. It's already past noon!"

A muffled laugh from within. Echoed, after a moment, by a male chuckle.

Fury ran through her like flame. She had a fist raised again, ready to charge in and make a scene, when something crunched beneath her feet.

A much larger fist than her own, only invisible, grabbed her and slammed her into the bulkhead so hard she couldn't suppress a scream. The boat jarred around them, and a deep grinding came from beneath.

Perrault's door slammed open. "Suits," he yelled. "Everyone into suits, *now*." He scrambled past, not even glancing at her, and ran for the companionway in stockinged feet. Only steps behind, Quill erupted from the engine room and pounded after.

She picked herself up, laboring to catch her breath. Terror caught in her throat, making her so dizzy she had to lean on the bulkhead as *Anemone* rolled. A new noise, a clanking grate, came from below each time the boat pitched.

By the time she'd pulled on the orange suit, heavy and musty-smelling despite the airing a few days before, and gone topside, the others were gathered on the foredeck. Someone had furled the foresail and quick-dropped the main, which lay in roughly bundled folds. Fine powdery snow blew steadily past, and the seas surged them up and down, huge and rough, like big brothers tossing an infant sister back and forth. Or maybe with less care. The world was a circle fifty yards in every direction. Beyond that was only the blurry dim, out of which the waves took shape, surged past, faded again. No birds. Nothing above but the nodding mast and more blank whiteness.

She shivered, wrapping herself with crossed arms, exchanging glances with Georgita, who sat alone in the cockpit, looking frightened. She looked for a safety line, but they all led up forward. In use. She hesitated—not leaving the cockpit without harness and line was second nature now—but finally forced herself to pick her way forward. Very carefully; the deck was snow-slick, and each step threatened to send her overboard into that leaden, sluggish, somehow oily-looking sea.

"Bloody hell sounds like ice," Quill was saying, leaning far out over the bow, one arm anchoring him to the stay. The others stood around looking worried. The forward hatch was open, and Bodine stood in it, elbows braced. "But damn it all—where is it?"

"Ice floats," Dorée said.

Perrault was looking over the side aft of where Quill stared. Sara knelt on the snow-crust and looked down. The sea rolled and pitched them, and slaty brine so cold it stopped her heart slapped her face, instantly numbing it.

The captain cleared his throat. "Okay, we will not see anything up here. Jamie, check below. Lars, get the emergency beacons out. Eddi, bring the abandon-ship bags up. Sara, Tehiyah, get the Zodiac ready to put into the sea."

"Me?" said Bodine.

"Get our position and prepare an emergency transmission. Do not send it yet, but get it ready. Now everybody, move."

Sara found herself opposite Tehiyah, fumbling with the lashings on the inflatable. They were caked over with inches of solid ice, transparent as cast glass but nowhere near as fragile. "Shit, this isn't going to untie," the actress panted from the far side.

Sara opened the cockpit locker, looking for something they could bang it off with. "Tehiyah? Here, try this." She craned around the rubber bulk and handed over one of the winch handles. Then started flailing away at her side with the other. Ice chips stung her face. At the next blow, something sharp flew unerringly up under the lens of her glasses into her bare eye. She gasped at the sudden pain, but closed that eye and struck again. And again, until the ice cracked and whitened and tumbled apart, disclosing layer after layer like a cut pearl.

"Don't launch yet," Madsen yelled from below. "Skipper says just get it ready. Until we see if there's any damage."

That took some of the pressure off, but she still had to try to control her racing heart. From the looks of it, Dorée was just as terrified. Panting, wheezing clouds of white smoke, they finally got all six of the tie-downs chipped loose and ready to let go.

Perrault's face, in the companionway well. "Only taking a little water. Looks like no major hull penetration."

"That's good," Sara muttered. "What, uh, what'd we hit? Ice?"

"No one saw any. The hull doesn't seem damaged."

"But we heard it."

"Yes, we hit quite hard. I suspect it was the keel that actually struck." Perrault squinted. "Is that blood in your eye?"

"An ice chip."

"We will look at it. In a few minutes. But thanks to you, we were not going faster."

"Well—"

"So that was a good call on your part. We will take care of the eye as soon as I see how much damage we have below." He looked from her to Tehiyah, then at the dinghy. "Can the two of you turn that over? Are you strong enough?"

"We'll try."

"On second thought, don't. I'll send Lars and Jamie if we have to get it in the water. You can come below."

Dorée crawled around the dinghy, and Sara saw she didn't have a harness on either, though she'd been working down on the slanted stern. Thin translucent sheets of ice cracked and fell off her suit as she crawled. White ice rimed her eyebrows, and her normally tanned complexion was more like a dove gray. She started to slip backward and Sara got a grip on a line and extended one glove. The actress reached for it and powered herself back up the incline with a gasp just as a sea broke, showering them both with bitter-cold saltwater. They tumbled over each other and landed in the cockpit, Dorée on top.

"There's blood on your cheek. Did you know?"

"I got something in my eye." It was starting to hurt in earnest now. Shit.

Madsen and Eddi climbed into the cockpit, stepping over and wriggling past. "Got to get the main back up," the Dane explained. "Might be better if you went back below."

When they let themselves down the companionway ladder, which heaved as if to buck them off, Quill was head-down in the bilge well. Its covers lay stacked against the table. His boots stuck up, kicking as he struggled. *Anemone* pitched and he grunted. His shoulders bunched as he heaved at something. Beside him the captain squatted on his heels, a prybar across his knees, scratching the back of his head. Sara wanted to ask what was going on, but Perrault didn't look as if he wanted any interruptions.

A hand on her shoulder. "Let's look at that cut," Dorée said. "Come in the galley."

"I'd rather have Mick do it."

A pretty grimace, a roll of those tawny eyes. "Okay, whatever. I'll go get him."

She lay back against the oven, boots braced against a roll rail, as Bodine, shuffling awkwardly around on his artificial legs, got himself braced too. He sent Dorée for the first-aid kit. When she came back she started turning on lights, one after another, until Sara had to squint. "We actually just need that one right above her," he said. "All the rest can go off. Okay, good. Sara, tilt your head back. Look up into that light."

She winced and tensed as something metal grabbed her eyelid and turned it inside out. The light glared. She clutched her thighs with shaking hands, fighting the urge to freak out, jerk away, scream. "Follow my finger. Okay, keep your eyeball right there . . . see it?"

"That dark thing?" Dorée said.

"It's ice," Sara mumbled, trying with all her might not to blink. Each time she did, something cut her eyelid. She wanted it out, *out.*

"It's not ice. Looks like metal. It's embedded in the eyeball. I'm going to have to pull it out."

"Oh. This is really starting to hurt. . . ."

"Tehiyah, know what a hemostat looks like?"

A snort. "Didn't you see me on *Crossing Jordan*?"

"Thanks.—Okay, Sara, now don't blink and don't move. I'll try to make this quick—"

Before she could recoil or protest the instrument crossed her field of vision, gleamed, and twisted. Something stabbed her eyeball so sharply she cried out.

"Got it," Bodine said.

"That *is* nasty looking."

Something warm was running down her cheek. "We'll let that bleed out," he murmured. "I don't want to put anything on it. There are natural antibiotics in the eye fluid.—Close your eye, Sara. I'm going to put this bandage on." She forced trembling arms to relax as darkness descended over half of the world, and strong fingers sealed the edges of the bandage. "There, we're done. Thanks, Tehiyah."

"Thanks," Sara murmured, exhaling in a shaky puff. Regaining her feet, but still trembling.

Perrault raised his voice in the salon, and she followed the others there. "She taken care of? Okay. Here's what we've got.

"We don't know what we hit. Something pretty massive. Not ice, I don't think, but we have no idea what it was.

"The damage. No hole in the hull, which is good. But the keel pins are bent. Jamie inspected them. You all know we have a canting keel, not a fixed one?"

Sara said, "It's leaking?"

"Well, not much," Quill said, sitting down in the bilge well again. "Maybe a couple gallons a minute. The designer left keyways, slots we can wedge dunnage into. They probably originally worked loose in the knockdown. But then we hit this thing, whatever it was, and that really fooked it up."

Bodine said, "So the leak's not actually the problem?"

"Not so much. No."

"But if these pins—?"

Quill shook his head. "This is a heavy piece of merchandise. More like a three-inch-diameter bolt than a pin. It's probably not *bent*. Begging your pardon, Captain. But it's working its way out of the composite. Each time we pitch, it tears out a little more."

"And when it tears free?" Bodine bored in.

Perrault said quietly, "The keel will most likely drop off. We will capsize and probably sink."

They stood around the salon, digesting that. Finally Dorée said, "So what's the plan? Turn back?"

Mate and captain traded glances. "Others have kept sailing with problems like this," Perrault said.

Dorée said, "What did they do? Just sit around and hope it didn't tear off?"

"Not at all. As sailors do, we fashion a rig." The captain looked at Quill again. "We brace the keel with a spare stay. Heavy wire, from the bowsprit down to circle the keel. Another brace aft, to circle the keel as it comes through the hull."

Sara fingered her eyepatch, not sure she understood. Perrault seized a tissue box and clicked a pen. As he drew, it became clear. The wire would keep the keel from moving either forward or back. But Bodine frowned. "How do we get this cable around the keel?"

"We will need to work from the inflatable. Lead the end aft, then around, then back forward." Perrault illustrated with gestures. "Attach it to a turnbuckle, then winch it tight. Lapatine did this three years ago. Sailed eight thousand miles after hitting an unmarked reef off Auckland Island." He looked around, then nodded stiffly. "Jamie, get the wire ready. I'll help the girls with the dinghy."

Sara looked from face to face. Would a wire, even a heavy one, keep the keel from working out of its mountings? Wouldn't it just slip through the loops, and plunge to the bottom? She had confidence in Perrault, but no clue whether what he was proposing was risky or routine. Dorée was frowning. Their eyes met; perhaps the same thoughts were running through her mind. Madsen looked blank; Eddi, agreeable as usual. Georgita seemed to have retreated into apathy again.

Then Quill was climbing out of the bilge well, water dripping from his pants, brusquely barking orders, and the moment of doubt was past.

The next few hours had to count as the hardest physical toil she'd done since clamming with her grandfather, as a kid. Even when they'd lifted the latches holding the restraining straps, the raft had refused to budge. Finally Edwige had realized it was frozen to the slipway. After nearly an hour of (extremely careful) chipping of ice and pouring of hot water, they'd gotten it free, flipped over, and bobbing at the end of its tow. Then the outboard had to be lowered into it while both dinghy and *Anemone* were going up and down, a nerve-racking feat of strength and balance that nearly pulled a red-faced, cursing Madsen over the side after a footloose motor. Finally Quill had reached up, grabbed the engine, and pulled it down onto himself as he collapsed into the deck boards of the dink.

They'd passed down gas tank, paddles, and a bag with radio and strobes, just in case they got separated in the snow, which came down all this time, millions of tiny flakes driving horizontally along the tops of the shark-gray waves before they met and melted into them. The heavily reefed main kept their nose into the wind, but did little to steady the bronco-like plunging.

At each rear and plummet, Sara could hear the keel pins grinding in their sockets like loose teeth. The cracking during the storm: that had been them working loose. The recurrent crunching lent the whole exercise the air of a ticking bomb. Would they get it secured before it dropped free, and the next wave turned them turtle? Meanwhile Perrault, apparently with that contingency in mind, had moved their abandon-ship gear to the foot of the companionway, along with emergency beacons, spare batteries, food, and water. Bodine sent a shortwave message to the home office in Monaco via an amateur radio operator in South Africa. He promised to forward their position to Greenpeace, the International Maritime Authority, and the Argentine navy if they suddenly stopped transmitting. Bodine was sending updates every fifteen minutes, to reassure the ham operator they were still afloat.

"Start, you motherfucker!" Quill reared, baring teeth amid a snow-crusted tangle of beard, and gave the starter cord a yank that would have curbed a mammoth. To everyone's astonishment, it fired. Madsen straightened in the Zodiac's bow, giving those at the lifeline a wide-eyed jaw-dropped silent-film mimicry of astonishment. No one laughed, though. Perrault, at the wheel, spun his hand over his head and pointed forward. The mate twisted the throttle, and the dink buzzed out from behind *Anemone* and began fighting its way into the waves.

Sara paid out the already ice-coated wire hand over hand as the dinghy slowly forged ahead, tossing and surging, the tops of the seas blowing off over the two men in showers of icy spray. Both had safety harnesses, but she couldn't help remembering what Quill had told them over and over. *Dead in five minutes.* The spray froze as it hit the deck, the winches, forming crystal carapaces. She shuddered. So much extra weight. If the keel went, it would throw everyone topside into the water. The cable ran through her gloves and then there was no more wire, only rope. Perrault shouted, "Not so fast. Keep tension on it. Don't let it all go," and she closed her gloves and the dinghy hit a wave and the pull would have yanked her through the lifelines if Eddi and Tehiyah hadn't tackled her and dragged her back.

The inflatable buzzed into the snow until it was only a shadow. It angled left to cross their bow, then headed back. Circled, coming down their port side. She anticipated another heart-stopping moment, but Madsen had the cable lashed to a boat hook and handed it over smooth as glass as they passed the cockpit.

Perrault said, "Take the wheel, Sara. Keep her into the wind." He looped braided metal over one of the winches, and it ratcheted like the tin rattlers kids spun on Halloween.

He straightened, bearded face flushed. "That is one completed," he told her, and went forward to take a second bundle of wire Bodine heaved up from below through the forward hatch.

After four hours of struggling with the wire, then more fighting to get the dinghy back aboard and lashed down, they staggered below like zombies. She leaned against a reeling bulkhead, disoriented, nauseated. It seemed like it should be night, but the same dim no-light half lit the salon. She gagged but only a teaspoon of acid came up, which she spat into her glove. Bodine sat at the table, dispensing hot tea with dollops of rum, but she couldn't even think about drinking anything. Every muscle ached except for dead-numb fingers and feet. Under the bandage her eye felt as if someone were probing it with an ice pick. She got her top unzipped, then sagged back against the bulkhead.

Someone bumped her and she opened one eye to see Perrault beside her. "Sorry," she said.

He didn't move aside, though. "The eye. It will be all right?"

"Mick says so."

"He sewed it up for you?"

"I didn't need stitches. Just to take out a metal splinter. I guess from one of the winch handles we were beating the ice off with."

He smiled. "So now you are a pirate. With the eyepatch."

As she forced a twitch of the lips he added, "It was good to have someone on the wheel I could depend on."

"I just kept her into the wind. Like you said."

"But you don't fear. Like some of the others."

"Oh really?" That was rich. "I'm as afraid as anyone here, Dru."

"Then you don't show it." He put an arm up beside her. Leaned in so close she could scent him. Wet wool, perspiration . . . tobacco? She'd never seen him smoke. And he could smell her too, of course. Which might not be so pleasant right now.

"In fact, I am becoming quite an admirer of yours," he murmured, evading her gaze, as if not quite proud of what he was saying.

If this was a pass, and she was growing uncomfortably aware it probably was, at least it was a low-key, gentlemanly one. She couldn't back away, since he had her against the bulkhead, but she tilted her head away. Said as politely as nausea would permit, "Um, Dru, if you're heading where I think you are, I need to make something clear. I'm not really interested in getting involved with anyone on this . . . cruise."

"I understand. I am the older man."

She shook her head, uneasily admitting that if they were ashore, and guaranteed to never see each other again, she might well lock her fingers in that coarse black hair and pull that beaky nose and those taut wind-chapped lips down to hers, cracked and painful though they were. "You're not *that* much older. And it's not you, believe me. I have a lot of—a lot of baggage that comes along with me. It wouldn't be fair to you."

He still looked hopeful. "Often, what happens at sea stays there."

"Thank you," she said firmly. "But if you need it in words of one syllable, the answer's no." She lifted his arm and slipped under it, and he stepped back and let her go.

The settee was crammed with wet, tired bodies. The air stank of mildew and diesel and old brine and moldy rubber. She was heading for her bunk, but faded halfway across the salon and just sagged to the damp carpet. No one said anything. Just sat swaying, heads nodding with the motion. "Bring her back to base course," Perrault told Madsen, who'd climbed back up into the steering station. Then no one said anything else for quite a long time.

At last Tehiyah cleared her throat. "How long will this repair hold, Dru?"

The Frenchman raised an eyebrow where he sat at the table, cupping a mug. "We'll keep an eye on it, Miss Dorée."

"Will it be calmer? Once this storm passes?"

"Storm? This is no storm. Just a low. We might see a high-pressure cell behind it. But just as likely, another blow. In these latitudes."

"Jamie?" she asked Quill.

"Captain's right," the mate said. "You know what they used to say: Below fifty degrees latitude, there's no law. Below sixty, there's no God."

"Where are we now?" Eddi said, kicking her boots so the heels thumped against the hollow base of the settee.

"Sixty-seven thirty south, nineteen degrees, fifty-two west," Madsen called down. Following the conversation from his perch, and reading off the GPS.

Dorée said, "What I'm getting at is, is it safe to keep on? Now we're damaged?"

"Racers often sail damaged," the captain murmured into the steam drifting off his mug.

"We're not in a race. Is it safe for *us* to keep on?"

He lowered the mug. "If we sail conservatively, I think so. If anything, there will be less strain on the keel running before the wind, than trying to beat back against it."

"Well, I think we need to discuss this," the actress said.

Quill said nothing. Just looked back and forth between woman and skipper, heavy lips pursed. A smile played deep in his braided beard like a rat in a blackberry bramble. The boat rolled and creaked. Sara kept listening for the grinding, but it didn't come, even when they pitched hard. Maybe the braces were holding.

Dorée seemed to gather herself. She leaned across the table. "Maybe it's okay for the moment, but it's still leaking, right? And we still don't know where the Japanese are. Do we? Mick?"

Bodine shook his head. Once.

"I think we should go back to Argentina," Dorée finished, sitting back. "We can try again, once the keel's properly fixed. In a shipyard, or whatever. But now, it's too dangerous. I don't know what you're trying to make up for, Dru. But this isn't the place, or the time, to risk our lives doing it."

Perrault said, very quietly, "We're going on."

"I don't think you heard me. I represent your owner—"

"Dru's the captain," Quill said. As if he enjoyed pointing this out.

"But this isn't his boat. It's Jules-Louis's." She looked from face to face, and her own hardened. She said sharply, "Okay, let's make it a vote. Do we keep on? Or turn back? A show of hands. Lars? Did you hear? We're voting."

She was peering up into the steering station. Madsen's feet shifted, but he didn't answer. She eyed Georgita next, who coughed nervously and half raised a hand.

"Unfortunately, this isn't a democracy," Perrault said. "It is more like a small Third World dictatorship. My orders are to find the whaling fleet. As my owner instructed me. And the CPL office, my charterers on this voyage, expect. I deeply respect you, Miss Dorée, but you do not have the power to alter my instructions."

Dorée's cheeks glowed. She pushed back from the table. Looked around. No one met her eyes. Georgita coughed again, and her hand sank back into her lap. The actress slammed her palms on the table, and pushed herself up. "I don't *believe* this. That isn't the last word. I'm sending a message."

"Mick, give Miss Dorée every facility for transmitting it," Perrault said gravely. "But there is no more to be said. We press on. That is my watchword: *press on*. It has taken me through many storms. So, I will take the first watch. And the rest of you had better try to get some shut-eyes."

His calm gaze met Sara's. She blinked and glanced away; glanced up, at one of the portlights, though which the everlasting hoary light glowed through inches of rime. And one by one, the others rose and stumbled away.

8

Whalesong

Through the rest of that day and into the next the snow continued to fall. They headed southeast under reefed sails. Perrault stayed on deck, backing up whoever was in the bubble. Sara put in four hours on watch, slept for six, then reluctantly took another four in the helmsman's seat when Dorée said she had a migraine and could only see black dots and whirling patterns. Her own eye hurt, but Bodine gave her drops for the pain.

The ice came in all sizes and shapes and colors, aquamarine and old-copper green and pearly white, from flat floes up to the icebergs they'd passed before. Not solid pack, but interspersed with stretches of black sea miles across. The bergs weren't really the danger. They showed up clearly on radar, and the horn echoed from them when Perrault sounded it, a prolonged, mournful drone that seemed to fit perfectly with the seascape. The dangerous ice was the pieces the size of refrigerators or trucks that had splintered off the bigger bergs.

These were so low in the water the radar didn't pick them up. They loomed suddenly out of the twilit fog, coalescing out of the furry opaqueness a hundred, two hundred yards ahead. Which meant she had ten or fifteen seconds to alter course before *Anemone*'s delicate hull would impact. Usually she saw them and put the wheel over, steering downwind when she could, upwind when she couldn't. But sometimes she didn't see them in time. Then the captain would yell over the intercom, rumbling like a French James Earl Jones inside the cold-mask he wore, and she'd startle out of whatever twilight she'd gone to and shiver and put the helm over. Then watch as the slowly heaving masses, sometimes opalescent, sometimes stained with emerald or ocher, populated with raucous seabirds or curiously staring penguins, like retirees watching the world go by from a bench in a small-town hardware store, and once even a somnolent and solitary bull walrus who groggily lifted his shaggy head, slid slowly past. Sometimes, only yards away.

When she climbed down again she could barely move. The cold struck through the thin transparent plastic of the dome. Freed of the support of the padded bucket seat, lap and shoulder belts, she reeled as *Anemone* lunged and banged over jagged seas.

Madsen wriggled up past her through the framework and settled both hands on the wheel. His ridiculous cap pressed against the top of the dome; the floppy earflaps danced and dangled. "Do we know where we're going?" he muttered.

She couldn't meet his eyes. The memory of his pale skinny ass pistoning in the master cabin was too vivid. "I just steer the course, Lars. An hour ago we came left. Zero nine four."

"Yeah, I know. But d'you know why?" He must have caught something on her face because he added hastily, "Mick picked up radars again."

"Uh-huh. Well, the ice comes up on you quick. We're making fifteen knots. Steer downwind of it when you can—"

"I know all that."

"Then you don't need any advice from me," she snapped. Ignoring whatever he muttered behind her, she groped her way to the galley. Hands shaking, she sliced hard waxy slabs off a chunk of Gruyère, squirted mustard on it from the bright yellow French's container, and fitted crackers around it.

She ate four cracker-and-cheese sandwiches, washing them down with cold coffee, followed by a Cadbury raisin-and-nut bar. She thought briefly about what the Dane had said: that they'd picked up the fleet again. Then dismissed it.

Georgita was snoring in the lower berth. Sara chimpanzeed up to her own bunk. She wound like a silkworm into musty blankets, buckled in, and stared up. Above her face swollen droplets of condensation rolled back and forth. They hung, elongated, then pattered to the deck. Black skeins of mold webbed the once-immaculate overhead, creeping over curving white plastic. She stared at them, mind vacant. Then, closing her good eye, submerged without seam into the utter blackness of complete fatigue.

A rough hand was shaking her awake. "I did two tricks," she muttered. "Almost back to back."

"Dinner, Sara. Tofu jambalaya."

An inner debate ended with unbuckling the strap, turning counterclockwise three times to loosen the blankets, and crawling out. She poured bottled water into a washcloth, rubbed her face, touched the eyepatch gently, rinsed her mouth. Her clothes stank, but nothing could be done about that. Georgita's bunk was empty. She rattled the curtain open and stepped through.

Perrault, Tehiyah, Georgita, Lars, and Mick sat round the table, clinging to handholds as the boat jolted. The wind seemed to have come up; the illuminated meter on the bulkhead showed they were making eighteen knots. A spicy-hot smell brought her nose up as Eddi weaved out of the galley, a steaming pan extended gingerly in front of her. Their gazes tracked it anxiously, one or another flinching out of the way as it approached. When it clanged to a landing they were all on it, spooning spicy masses of yellow rice and red sauce into bowls. For a few minutes the only sounds were the whine of the wind, the crash of the sea, and the chomp and smack of mastication. "More, who wants it," Auer yelled from the galley. "I saved some for Jamie when he comes off watch too."

"This is the best stuff I ever ate," Madsen moaned.

"It's very good," Georgita murmured, sniffling.

"*Hell* of a lot better than MREs."

"Yeah, this is great, Eddi," Sara said. "Drives the cold right out of your head."

"You're a great chef, Eddi," Dorée said, holding her bowl up for more as the videographer navigated to the table again. "We should just make you the cook. We'd eat like this all the time."

No one said anything to this. Perrault murmured, "Sara, how is your eye? Any better?"

"It itches."

"Probably a good sign. Healing," Bodine said.

The captain asked, "Mick, how are those radars looking? Anything new?"

"I have two now."

"Any clue as to range? Distance?"

"That's why I wanted to go in at an angle."

"That would take longer to close."

"Right, but it'd've given us a bearing change. I could estimate range from that. But since we're headed directly for them, all I have's a guess. Curvature of the earth, masthead height—could be a hundred miles away. Or closer."

Dorée had been busy with a second bowl of jambalaya. "By the way. I need to use that bow compartment for a couple of hours."

"What for?" Bodine and Sara both said together. They glanced at each other, then back at the actress.

She said into her bowl, "You've got all that room up there, and the dryer isn't working—"

"What dryer?" Auer said, behind her. Sara's ears pricked up too.

"You know, the clothes dryer in the master suite. Georgie did some things for me, but they're not drying right. We need to hang them up. You've got all that room up forward."

"That's our work space," Bodine said. "My equipment. And Sara's whale charts."

Sara sat rigid, suddenly furious. Her spoon rattled against the bowl.

"Wait a minute. You had a *dryer*? While we were going around in moldy clothes, wet all the time?"

Dorée said loftily, "Well, it's in the master suite. Like I said."

"That means there's a washer, too?"

"A very small one. There isn't enough water to take care of everybody. But it's broken now. As I said. The washer-dryer. So there's no point crying over it. But Georgie still has these clothes to deal with. It won't be in your way, Mick. It'll be way above your head. We can string a line—"

"Not in my lab space," Sara said.

"I have to stand with Sara on this one," Bodine said. She hesitated, then nodded thanks. He slowly closed one eye, as if to say: *Gotta stick together.*

Perrault slid his bowl away. He leaned forward, gaze sharpening, but saying nothing as the two women faced off. And before Sara's eyes Dorée made some mysterious transition from *one of them* into *something beyond them*. "I don't like to have to say this. But there's a reason I'm in the master suite."

"We know perfectly well why," Eddi said.

"And who's in there with you," Sara said. She was instantly sorry—whatever privacy any of them had, he or she had a right to—but it was out. Madsen flushed, gaze nailed to the bowl he was fondling.

"Perhaps a liqueur, to finish such a fine meal," said Perrault. "I think we've earned a stimulant."

"There wouldn't be an expedition without me," Dorée said past him. "So it's not out of the ordinary to ask for some small conveniences."

"Why should you get better treatment than the rest of us? Eddi's a videographer. Mick's a handicapped vet. And I'm here to do research," Sara said, hating what she was saying at the same time she took great pleasure in it. Wielding words like a broken bottle in a bar fight, to slash and spray blood. "What do you do? You don't take your turn in the galley, don't clean up, don't even stand watch anymore—"

"I had a migraine. You don't want someone up there who can't see." She turned to the captain, showing perfect white teeth. "Do I really have to put up with these attacks?"

"No. No, you don't." Perrault sucked a breath. Spread long fingers, then tented them. "We all have to pull together here—"

"Obviously not all of us," Auer said, darting a glare at Dorée.

"There has to be a distinction drawn," the actress said. "Between principals and . . . staff."

"We're all shipmates," Perrault said.

"Some more matey than others," Sara said.

Dorée leaned forward. Sara felt the sting on her cheek before she realized what had just happened. A full-handed, resounding slap. "Mind your place," Dorée hissed. "We all know who you are. The unemployed scientist. The one who got her assistant's face torn off, because she fucked up with a wild animal."

"No, Sara. No," said Bodine, and she realized the hands holding her back on that side were his, and that Madsen was gripping her just as tightly. Which was just as well, maybe, because she was going over the table to ruin that perfect face.

Dorée leaned back. "This is so unfair," she choked out. She was crying. Though of course, who knew how authentic *her* tears would be. Sara's rage doubled as she saw the men's expressions soften. "You have no idea whose—how many asses I had to kiss. You think my life's so privileged? I was on stage at ten. I had to—you don't know what I've had to do."

"We've all had to do things to survive," Georgita murmured. "That's certainly true."

"Shut up, Georgie. You're not in this discussion. It all started with you breaking the dryer, anyway."

"I'm sorry, Tehiyah."

"I want everyone to just calm down," Perrault shouted. It was the first time he'd raised his voice to them; a shocked silence fell. "Sara. Tehiyah. You will apologize now to each other."

"I won't. Fuck her, she's fired," Dorée said. Sara just stared, too enraged to get a coherent word out.

"No one's being fired. You will apologize, or I will punish you both."

"You already tried that," Sara said bitterly. "She never touched a scrub brush."

"I still have wet laundry," Dorée stated.

The companionway hatch slid back, and a gust of snowflakes whirled into the salon. Quill's head poked in, masked in black wool and platinum rime. "The hell's going on down here? Sounds like a fooking catfight."

"This is too much. It's cold all the time. Jules said there were heaters. He promised I'd be warm."

"In *Antarctica*?" Sara drawled.

"Shut *up*, Pollard!"

"You didn't like the diesel smell, Tehiyah. And we can't spare fuel to keep it like toast. Now, I've had enough of this. I'm warning you both," Perrault said. He rose, eyed Bodine and Madsen. "Let her go," he said, and Sara felt them uncrimp her arms. He waited to see how she'd react. She hunched her shoulders, but kept her fists in her lap. He nodded, and went into the galley.

When he came out he carried a dark bottle. "I want us to drink together, and remember where we are. In these latitudes, the sea is more dangerous than anywhere else on earth. And any help? It is too far away to matter. There is no room for"—he eyed the women distastefully—"screaming fights. Slapping. Or insults. Once again, I demand an apology."

Dorée smiled through tears like a rainbow emerging through a summer shower. "I *truly* am sorry, Sara dear. We're all so on edge, you know. I didn't mean what I said. About you being a total failure as a scientist, I mean."

"And I didn't mean what I said, about your being so lazy and useless," Sara said, and they glared at each other across the slanting cabin, smiling hard.

She lay huddled in her bunk for some interminable time, curled around the flickering spice-warmth in her belly, and at last drowsed off.

A scrape and jingle as if Marley's Ghost were dragging his chains past her ear woke her. She lay listening, but it trailed away aft and didn't come again. The light through her porthole was dimmer. Evening, though there was no night. The boat was careening from sea to sea with shrugs and bangs that threw her against the straps. She lay listening for ice and fighting the need to pee.

At last she gave in to the inevitable. She unlashed herself and climbed down. Her breath steamed. A stagger of the boat as she stepped to the deck planted her foot square on Georgita's chest, narrowly missing the splinted arm.

"*Oof.* Sara . . . what'd you . . ."

"Sorry, Georgie. I'm so sorry. Go back to sleep."

Shadows loomed in the salon. It was cold as an ice cave. The table gleamed with moisture. Their exhaled breaths, condensing. It pattered down from the curved overhead with each lurch and slam. Black skeins of mildew ran down from the portlights, closing her throat when she got too close. From the dark narrow cave to which the open hatch led echoed the erratic staccato of Bodine's snoring. When she peered forward he was melted into his chair, head back, mouth agape.

The head was flooded. Turds and paper sloshed to and fro in the bowl of the high-tech vacuum toilet. When she pressed the button nothing happened. She wiped the lid down with damp tissue and perched, lifting her feet to avoid the tide each time the boat heeled. A scraping began forward and passed down the port side, followed by something bumping the hull. When she went to wash her hands the faucet hissed ominously, but gave no water.

Quill was in the bubble, ass sagging over the too-small seat. Pouched eyes lined with scarlet inflammation blinked down at her, then back at the sea. His tangled beard was red as blood. After a moment's horrified puzzlement she realized it was only the remains of the jambalaya.

"The toilet doesn't work," she murmured. "And I think the freshwater system's frozen."

"Plunger's in the locker under the sink."

Great. "Where's the captain?"

"Topside."

"I hear ice. And isn't it getting rougher?"

"It's little stuff. Brash. And the fog's closing in. Shitty weather, actually." He leaned into the plastic, tensing, and cranked the wheel hard left. He worked the sheeting mechanism, then twisted in his seat, grimacing. "Fooking cramps in me spine . . . can you take it for a few minutes?"

"Isn't anybody else up?"

"Just you, I guess."

She wavered, liking neither more hours in the seat nor the alternative. Finally she muttered, "I'll see if I can fix the toilet."

Each time they pitched, the bowl's contents sloshed over the sides. She kept dragging her sleeve across her face, breathing through her mouth. At last she got the bowl cleared of solids, the circuit breaker reset, and the clog of soggy paper out of the vacuum line. When she pressed the button the flipper at the bottom opened and with a choking, explosive suck everything vanished, pulled down into oblivion. What happened to it after that she cared not. She found an unopened pack of Wet Wipes, peeled off her top, and cleaned herself as best she could, armpits and neck and face, the too-strong fruit-flowery fragrance for once welcome.

When she weaved back out into the salon Bodine was at the table, prosthetics sticking out stiffly. Perrault and Quill were with him. Mugs steamed and slid. The long jean-clad limbs and sea boots dangling from the bubble must be Madsen's. The captain nodded at her. "Coffee is hot. If you would like some. Jamie says you fixed the WC."

"I guess the doctorate wasn't wasted."

A frown; the irony seemed lost on him. "Go on," he said to Bodine.

"They're mike clicks, all right. You can hear those farther than you can make out speech transmissions. And they're on the channel they use for communications with the kill ships."

The Frenchman exchanged glances with Quill, then faced Bodine again. "The radars?"

"Getting stronger. May be a third, more distant. On almost the same bearing. But masked by the others."

Anemone pitched hard, creaking. The chains rattled again, dragging along the hull. Something thudded and Sara tensed. "Getting heavier,"

Quill observed. "Went through a field an hour ago was almost solid. We get trapped, it'll turn ugly."

"Speed, Lars?" Perrault called.

"Ten."

"*Bien.* Here is what we are going to do." The captain tapped the table with a long index. "Mick: Shortwave *Esperanza.* Let Greenpeace know we have a fix on the fleet. Jamie, take in the main. That will give us more time to avoid floating ice, and less damage if we hit."

Bodine scratched black stubble. "If anyone's listening?"

"What do you mean?"

"If we transmit, the Japanese can pick us up."

"He's right," Madsen said, voice hollowed by the dome, as if he were a sibyl speaking from within a rock-walled cave.

"We must share information. We could box the fleet in between us."

"They won't cooperate," Madsen snorted. "I say leave them out of whatever we do."

Perrault weaved his head in a peculiar snakelike motion. "I hear you both. Well, let me think more about it.

"Meanwhile . . . Sara, would you get the others out here? Eddi and Georgie and Tehiyah? Jamie, another pot of coffee might be in order."

She went aft first, taking particular pleasure in jabbing Dorée hard in the side as she snored sleep-masked and earplugged in the big master bed. Soon everyone was either at the table or, since there wasn't room, hanging from handholds or clinging to the strutwork that supported the steering chair. Water fell in fat heavy drops from the overhead, as if they were deep beneath the sea. *Anemone* careened even more heavily as their speed ebbed. The wind shrieked and whistled.

"All right," the captain began, rubbing his chin. "We are not far from the whaling fleet, we believe. After all this time. Lars?"

"I've sailed against these people before," Madsen said, invisible from the waist up. His boots kicked idly. "They're good seamen, and they react violently to being interfered with. One man's particularly dangerous. We call him 'Captain Crunch' because he rammed a boat two years ago. Two of the crew drowned."

Quill said, "Remember, if you go in the water here—"

"You're bloody well dead in five," they chorused. Georgie giggled.

Perrault said, "I will review our assignments, for if and when we finally encounter those I can only describe as our enemies. In charge of inflatable launch: Mr. Quill, assisted by Ms. Dorée and Ms. Norris-Simpson. In the inflatable: Mr. Madsen, in charge; Mr. Bodine, and Ms. Auer. Their mission is to harass, damage equipment, and place themselves, physically if necessary, between the whalers and their prey. On *Anemone*'s helm: Ms. Pollard. On deck after launch, to recover the boat and respond to orders as necessary: Ms. Dorée and Ms. Norris-Simpson."

He looked around the table. "When in contact with the Japanese, all hands above or below decks will wear exposure suits and life jackets. Anyone topside will also wear safety harnesses. The life raft will be at the foot of the companionway, stocked with radios, batteries, food, water. Jamie, overhaul it today."

"Aye, Skipper."

"Remember what Lars told you. If we seriously hinder their operations, and they see a chance to run us down, this Crunch has proven he will do exactly that. We must be ready to sustain a collision, abandon ship, and survive until we reach land or are rescued.

"Well, that is about all I have to say. Any questions?" He held out his mug and Quill poured it full again. Then he looked down as Dorée covered his hand with hers.

"Why's *she* on the helm?" Tehiyah squinted at Sara. "I told you *I* wanted to do something important. Somewhere I can make a difference."

Perrault cleared his throat, still looking at the fingers resting on his wrist. His eyes flicked up toward Madsen, but the Dane's face wasn't visible. From the angle, though, Sara was pretty sure he could see what was going on. The boots had ceased kicking idly; they braced against a support. Perrault circled her wrist with two fingers and set it aside. "Sara has proven herself on the helm. And launching and recovering the inflatable will be important, once we are in contact. It will also put you out on deck, where Georgie can film you. . . . Any other questions? No? Then one more thing. I wish to have this boat cleaned, very thoroughly. We have let conditions go too far."

Dorée seemed about to protest again, but subsided. Quill showed big yellow teeth in a simian grin. Sara thought he looked more like Hagrid of Hogwarts than ever.

They ran east. She put in another few hours on the wheel while the rest, chivied by Quill, began at the bow. The smells of disinfectant, detergent, and bleach penetrated the chill air, the mildew stink. She smiled down at Dorée's bent back as the actress pushed a mop along the deck. She glanced up, as if feeling Sara's gaze. They regarded each other for a moment; then Dorée, without the slightest change in expression, went back to mopping.

"Inside the bubble, dashboard, everywhere you can reach," the mate said, handing up bucket, sponge, and spray bottle. "But don't let it distract you from the ice."

So far on this watch, though, she hadn't seen any. Stretches of heaving water, black as coal. Shoals of birds. But the snow had stopped. The fog was thinning, visibility opening out, though the dim light made it hard to see far even with the heavy night binoculars that hung by the wheel.

No night, and no day. But the light was ebbing again as she nursed a mug of tepid tea on the salon settee. The boat creaked and swayed. *Anemone* was cutting through the waves with a hiss like sled runners, given her head now that the danger of ice seemed to have receded. Quill's boots now dangled from the steering position. When Sara looked forward the rolling tunnel of the long hull rotated like a funhouse ride. Through the open hatch she could make out the glowing dials and screens that illuminated Bodine's constricted kingdom.

She microwaved another mugful and took it forward, stepping carefully. Past the sounds of sleeping men and women. The washer-dryer had been repaired and all the curtains taken down, laundered, and rehung, and everyone had been issued fresh towels. The newly cleaned bulkheads gleamed, reflecting her in distorted versions as she passed. She corkscrewed through the hatch, caught a handhold, and stepped over and between the green duffels and boxes of stores and reels of heavy line that covered the deck. She couldn't fully straighten, and the overhead came down and the deck up with each step so that by the time she reached where the ex-soldier sat in his taped-up, lashed-down armchair she was crouched in a space barely adequate to breathe in.

"Earl Grey?"

"Hey. Thanks." He removed his eyes from the screen and focused fuzzily on her. Stubble coated his cheeks like black soot. He wore green coveralls with the sleeves pushed back and chest bare at the throat except for a loosely twisted cloth with a reticulated pattern in desert tan. His rumpled hair grew down the back of his neck untrimmed.

"Thanks for sticking up for me. About the—the laundry."

"Not a problem. We don't draw a line in the sand, she'll take the whole boat over." He patted a sailbag. "Grab a perch."

She wriggled down on the crackly bag, her bottom sinking into stiff yet yielding folds within. Her knees stuck up and her back was rammed against a coil of thick yellow line studded with hard round things.

He returned his attention to the screen, which jumped with vertical bars of light. He took off the earphones and turned them toward her. A sizzling static backed by a steady hum pulsed against the swish of water. It occurred to her then that Bodine, alone up here, crippled, with all that gear swaying between him and the hatch, would be trapped if they hit ice. How must he feel when it thumped and banged against the thin fiberglass? She shuddered and hugged herself. It was much colder up here too, far from even the scanty warmth of the heaters.

The man beside her fitted the headphones to his skull once more. He turned switches, and another screen powered above the first. He pulled the keyboard down and typed in a gunfire rattle. Listened, head cocked. Then slid the phones off again and turned up a speaker.

Another sound filtered into the rushing sea and tapping gear and the thump of her heart in her ears. A distant lonely wail, trembling with ethereal beauty. Music from the depths of space. Notes intertwining, playing off one another in ghostly counterpoint. A chant in a cathedral as huge as the ocean itself.

"Humpbacks?" she murmured. "How far?"

"No telling. There's a sound channel that takes it hundreds of miles."

They listened as the eerie music echoed from the deep. Each vocalization began with a trill, then meandered through several phrases before ending on an upward flourish. After several minutes he murmured, "The males come up with a new routine, a new song, every spring. It originates east of New Guinea and gets passed from one pod to another. The North Pacific. The North Atlantic. Antarctica."

She'd read that in the literature, but it was different hearing it. He eased a dial around and the tones became sharper, more piercing. Again, each utterance ended with that upward pitch. She murmured, "It's like a human being asking a question. Can it be they're talking? Rather than singing?"

"Anything's possible. They could be debating their version of Aristotle." His face was entranced, shut off. He seemed to be gazing through the side of the boat, into the chill lightless sea hundreds of fathoms down. The whales gave bubbling trills and gulps that sounded like birdsong processed through an upset stomach. "They use tools—those bubble nets we saw them weave, to fish. I read a paper by some Scottish researchers, about sperm whales. It said they have individual names."

"Actual *names* . . . ?"

"They analyzed a five-click call they make at the beginning of their vocalizations. It's called 5R. Everybody always thought it was the same for every whale. Like every blue jay's call is the same as every other. But when these guys looked at the click timing, they could tell which whale was transmitting. And so, obviously, could the other whales. Which makes sense, when you think about it. We don't typically open our conversations with our names. When we make a radio call, though, we start 'This is *Anemone*.'" His gaze met hers. "Or am I getting too . . . anthropocentric?"

"They don't need to be smart to communicate. Or as smart as we are."

He half smiled. "You consider *us* intelligent?"

"Have to have a benchmark. But I know what you're saying."

"What am I saying?"

She grimaced. Spread her hands. "Individually, we do all right. But as a species, we don't act intelligently. Crime. Greed. War."

"Overpopulation. Destroying the environment we have to live in."

"Apes defecate where they live. When it gets bad, they move. But we—"

"Right," he said. Responding not to what she'd voiced, but to the next step in her reasoning. Which, she had to admit, she liked.

The whales kept calling, echoed now and then by others, fainter, incomparably farther off. No one had realized elephants used ground-conducted subsonics until Katharine Payne at Cornell had discovered their seismic communication. Someday someone would discover just what these "songs" were. She doubted it would be her—better minds had tried—but there could be no doubt the phenomenon carried some freight of meaning. If only to mark territory, or identify a pod. But then why would the songs *change*?

"You're deep in thought."

She half grinned. Conscious, suddenly, of his warmth only inches away. Her eyes drifted to his lap, then to where the legs of the coveralls were neatly rolled and clamped with binder clips. He was damaged, sometimes unpredictable, but she had to admire his determination. He stayed at his post. He hauled himself around the boat using those massive shoulders almost, if not quite, as nimbly as those who still had legs. She'd never heard him complain, though who knew how much it hurt. She cleared her throat. "Are you—comfortable?"

He looked confused. "What?"

"I mean—your injuries. Do they give you pain?"

He looked taken aback, but only shrugged. Seemed to go somewhere else, though he didn't shift in the chair. "Not so much these days," he said, looking away. "Your eye? How's that doing?"

"Better. Not itching as much."

He reared back, stretching. Those powerful shoulders bunched, those big hands worked at his neck. He said through his teeth, "But it does get old, sitting in the same position."

She said, "Turn away."

His hands stopped. "Turn what?"

"Away from me. Bend forward. Yes. Like that."

Under her hands his muscles were hard as resined carbon. So taut it was painful to feel. Her own fingers, stronger than they'd probably ever been after weeks fighting the wheel, barely sank in. He kept leaning away, head bent, and as she worked up and then down his spine he relaxed. "Better?" she murmured.

"You got strong hands."

"Mm-hm." She worked on, until he winced and straightened.

Something rolled off his work surface and fell into her lap. She picked it up, started to replace it, then turned it over in her fingers. At first she'd thought it a spool of green thread. It was a wooden spool, yes, but wrapped with something thicker than thread, so dull and shineless it was almost invisible. "What's this?"

He squinted in the screenlight. "Trip wire."

"*Trip wire?* It looks like what you'd use to . . . strangle someone."

He chuckled. "Not hardly. Breaking strength on that's only about fifty pounds. But it comes in useful more often than you'd think. That and hundred-mile-an-hour tape, you can fix almost anything."

She was still holding it when he gently removed her glasses and took her face in his hands. She stopped thinking. When his mouth found hers in the darkness she seemed to stop feeling. Or felt all too much, as her arms rose to pull him close.

When his hand found her neck and followed its curve down into her pullover she broke away, breathing hard. He tensed. "Sorry . . . am I going too fast?"

She glanced at the open oval of the access. "I don't know. But I'd better close that."

When she came back she stood bent, breathing fast and shallow as he kissed her again. Those rough hands seemed to know in advance every curve they encountered, every zipper. Her top came off and she sank back again on the duffel, unable to muster objections as his fingers found her nipples. She closed her eyes and sighed.

"Feel good?"

"Very."

His mouth sought hers again. The scratchy stubble of bristly beard. Rough warm lips that somehow evoked pleasure down her whole body.

Then his hand slipped lower, and she gasped. Started to push it away, but her arm had lost the power to do so. Enervated by the waves of pleasure that made her hips jerk as his fingers found exactly what she wanted them to. She lay back, eyes still closed, conscious of cold air on her naked skin, throat to belly, but intent above all else on the focused warmth that pulsed and grew. Her hips moved again, and she bit her lip to stifle the noises she wanted to make. Above them the whales still called, trilling and reverberating in haunting refrains that forever hovered at the edge of meaning.

"Such a lovely woman," he murmured, breath hot against her skin.

Astonishment penetrated. Could she really be doing this? Falling for a legless veteran, a man she barely knew? Or were they all so sealed in, so hermetically isolated, she didn't know what she was feeling? Some uninvolved corner of her mind whispered: This is not smart. You're not eighteen anymore, messing around in a car on 'Sconsett Bluff.

His fingers paused. She opened her single eye to his face, hovering. "Still okay?"

"I . . . guess."

"Having doubts?"

"A little."

His lips traced from hers to her neck. And downward. The sea whispered past, hissing and surging. She stiffened, fingers digging into the duffel on which she lay. "—hurt you?" he murmured.

"Uh-uh. Oh. *Oh.*" Shamed, yet still wanting more, she laid her arm over her face. Bit her wrist.

He shifted, grunted deep in his throat, and she heard the chair creak and felt his weight come onto the duffel too. Heard the sloughing of cloth and another exhalation as he shifted again. She lay with legs spread, the air icy between them, and didn't care. She arched her back to shift something hard out from beneath it and lifted her knees. Her shoulders drew back, bracing. A wave gathered between her legs, rising in throbs of something almost like anguish.

When she opened her eye again he hung close above her, bare chest hairy, a steel chain hanging from a dark nest. His neck looked strangely vulnerable, his nostrils like caverns. His hand left her and took his weight to one side as he half rolled, working the last of his clothing down his trunk.

Despite herself, she glanced down.

The cloth pushed free from his crotch and his penis sprang free. But her gaze traveled past it, to where there was . . . nothing. Save blunt appendages seamed with wormtracings of stitching and scar tissue.

She suddenly realized what he intended, and her acquiescence turned inside out. He wore no protection. She had none either. Since Leo had left she hadn't bothered. Hadn't thought it would be necessary. But that wasn't it. She didn't want this, even if he'd worn something, or if she'd brought her pills. They were co-workers. Unprofessional. Stupid. Sara, what are you doing?

"What are you doing?" she said. Her hand came up to shield her nakedness. Her legs straightened, pushing her upright even as his weight eased down on her. She felt his penis probing, rigid, engorged, seeking. "*What are you doing?*"

He went tense too, suddenly suspending motion. Said nothing, though he bent his head back, trying to look down into her face. But her gaze slid aside. She got a hand up and locked an elbow over her breasts.

"What's wrong?"

"This whole thing. That's what's wrong."

"It feels right to me."

"Well, it's not going where you want it to go." She realized as she said this that it was a double entendre, and almost smiled, but still felt intimidated. He was so much stronger, and heavier, and he was right above her. If he wanted to he could keep on, and she'd be helpless, unless she screamed. Which she didn't want to. Above all, she didn't want the others to see her like this.

But instead of pushing her arms aside, he cleared his throat and rolled away, letting in a smell of damp hemp. "I get it," he said, voice altered, cold, ten thousand miles distant.

She fought to sit up and pull her clothes back over her. "Get it . . . get what?"

"I guess it's a turnoff, all right. A shock."

"What are you talking about? I didn't . . ." Her voice trailed off as she realized what he thought. "I . . . I didn't see all that much. But that's not it. Believe me, Mick. Not at all."

"It's got to be pretty *unaesthetic*. To suddenly see those, those stumps, when you're expecting something else."

"No!" She struggled to sit up, appalled. "Mick . . . you have to believe me. That had nothing to do with it. We're co-workers. This boat's too small for us to just . . . hook up, or whatever."

"You don't have to explain. Make excuses."

She suddenly felt guilty. She reached for him. "Let me do something else, then."

"Forget it." His voice had a rough edge that could have been anger or something else. His face was turned to the darkness. "Just get out."

"I told you, it's not what you think. I just don't want to . . . but I'll take care of you." She worked moisture up in her mouth, licked her hand. "Turn this way—"

"I said *get out*."

She backed away. Rearranged her clothes as he hoisted with both arms, poised against the roll of the hull, then lowered himself back into the seat. When he clamped the earphones back on, his shadow, thrown by the dim light against the overhead, seemed to have grown horns, like a bull's. Not looking at her he rasped, again, finally, "Go on. Get out."

She looked back to see him still turned away, deep in the cavelike dim, as the songs of the whales echoed against the hoarse never-ending whisper of the sea.

9

First Encounter

So, d'we have ourselves a little fun last night?"

Sara lifted her attention from Rice Chex and ultrapasteurized milk to Eddi Auer's protuberant blue eyes. They were alone in the galley. "What?"

"I saw you coming back, you know. From up forward."

She pushed hair off her face. "Oh, for . . . *Nothing happened*, Eddi."

"Oh, of course not. Of *course* not."

Why was she so angry? Sara glanced up again. "Wait a minute. *You're* not sweet on him, are you?"

"None of your damn business."

She took the other woman's arm. "Okay, I'll level: I almost gave way. But at the last minute, I decided it wouldn't be smart. Okay? The field's still open. If he's who you want."

Auer wavered, glancing at her and then away. Finally she grinned. Punched Sara's arm. "You whore dog. You really are, you know. All right, forget it. Water over the dam."

Whore dog? "I just wanted you to know—"

"If you got some, good for you. About time somebody did. Besides *her*."

The companionway banged open. Quill's bearded visage hung upside down. "All hands on deck. Get 'em up! Mustang suits and life preservers."

She and Eddi tore their gazes from each other. As they shook people awake a long-unfamiliar rumble began aft, built, then dropped to a steady hum. The engines! Her heart beat faster. They'd caught up with their quarry at last.

When she lumbered topside, bulky and clumsy in heavy gear and face mask and insulated gloves and goggles, Quill and Perrault and Madsen were in the cockpit. The wind was an icy blade in her throat. She gasped, coughing, as she squinted around. The sea surged past in six-foot piles of blue-black ink, tops shredded into long manes of frothy spray. Scattered clouds galloped across a bright sky like spooked horses. Then she remembered. Duh, Sara; you aren't supposed to be up here. She turned to climb back down, but the captain caught her arm. "Where are you going?"

"You wanted me to steer."

"Not in the bubble. From where you can hear my commands." He jerked a thumb at where Madsen stood. "Steer one two five."

The steel tubing of the wheel felt frigid even through padded gloves. She wrestled it, boots slipping on the ice that coated the cockpit sole, and got the lubber's line back on 125. Then lifted her head and squinted.

A distant gray pricking amid scattered mountains of ice. The bergs glowed in the sky, glittered in the pale low sun. A jeweled rampart, white and blue and emerald, sent colored beams searching the majestically sailing clouds. Brightness below, brightness above; and in the distance, a colorless speck irritating the sclera of the vast horizon.

"All the way," Perrault yelled. Quill bent and the big bronze-and-gold genoa flapped and slammed as it fed out of the furler. *Anemone* dipped, then rose, a racehorse leaving the starting gate, and began to accelerate. Sara concentrated on the course, which she saw led almost directly to the gray thing, and on avoiding any brash in their path. Perrault too was searching ahead, binoculars poised on the tips of his gloves. The bow rose, peeling curving foils of transparent sea off to both sides, then leaving them behind to a gathering roar. The genoa cracked and bellied, then snapped full, ripples chasing each other over its turgid surface. The wheel strained against her arm and leg muscles. She spun on left trim and the pull lessened, but she still had to brace herself.

Madsen had binoculars too. He lay out along the coach house aiming them. Then yelled, "It's a kill ship."

"Can you make out a number?"

"Not till we get closer."

She crouched, squinting into the spray that blew over them from windward. The gray speck had become a ship, with black funnel and white pilothouse and a curved, almost sickle-like bow. It was headed away, seemingly oblivious to their presence, but they were catching up. She dropped her gaze; in that second's glimpse she'd gone five degrees off course. She got them back on just in time for Perrault to shout, "Aim for her stern."

"That's me?" she yelled.

"Yes! You must pay attention. And respond instantly. Aim for her stern! We'll pass close aboard, to her port side.—Lars, get ready."

"Inflatable in the water?"

"Not just yet. Let's do a close pass and see what we can see. Maybe get something on their decks, at least."

Madsen pushed back down into the cockpit as Eddi and Georgita and Tehiyah came up the companionway, one after the other, in exposure suits, muffled and goggled. Quill followed. A brief confusion ensued before those who wanted up got up and those who wanted down got down. The women started flailing at the ice and undoing straps on the inflatable. "Don't cast loose yet," Perrault ordered. "Just make sure everything's free and ready." Looking past him, Sara saw the forward hatch come open and a moment later a black head bob up. Bodine, shoulders crowding the coaming, peering under the taut swell of the foresail toward the ship ahead.

Madsen pushed up the companionway again with a wooden box slung over one shoulder. Quill, behind him, toted thick coils of straw-colored plastic line. They clipped safety lanyards and edged forward with their burdens, boots sliding on the slick white crust that frosted the deck.

A translucent carapace stood inches thick on every shroud and winch. With each dash of spray, it seemed to grow. *Anemone* bowed, then surged up as if to attack the very clouds, following the massively swelling genoa, the unreefed main, eager, alive, avid. If a boat could be said to be joyful, Sara thought, puffing freezing air as she made minuscule corrections, then this one was. She too felt like shouting aloud after groping through so many days of overcast and misery. Ahead lay one of the ships they'd pursued for so many weeks, over thousands of miles. She might not share the dedication of some of the CPL members, but she couldn't disagree that whaling in an internationally declared sanctuary had to merit at least a protest.

When she looked up again they were half a mile away. The other ship had come right and she made out again that queerly curved bow. Perrault, back behind binoculars, told her to pass to starboard, not port, as close as she could and still have room to steer clear if the ship turned into them.

"This may well be Nakame."

"Who?"

"The one we told you about," Madsen called back. He was crouched at the lifeline, prying the cover off the wooden crate with a screwdriver. "The guy they call Captain Crunch."

"We have a number yet?" asked Quill. No one answered. He was flaking out the heavy line along *Anemone*'s side. The one she'd been lying against the night before, in Bodine's lair. The hard things that had dug into her back were round plastic floats, knotted into a heavy pale-yellow polyethylene braid every couple of arm's lengths. She flashed back for a fraction of a second as her face heated. "Whore dog." On her back, legs parted—

"Farther right," Perrault snapped. She bit her lip under the knitted mask and concentrated. The boat charged across the waves, barely pitching now. Sails pulling, engines pushing, she left behind a flattened track of green sea flecked with foam, a dash of spray, a curl of exhaust. A patch of sea seethed ahead: krill, or millions of small fish. Gulls parted before the onrushing predator; then whirled up into the bright hard sky, protesting in a harsh clattering cacophony as *Anemone* slashed across the writhing sea, arrow-straight, incredibly fast, finally up on full plane as she drove toward the ship that slowly came around to meet her, lengthening, exposing more and more of herself to sight.

Madsen called, "Something alongside."

Quill, at the same instant: "Whales!"

She lifted her eyes from the compass to a flurry of spume close by the gray hull. At the same moment Perrault yelled, "Left, come left. Pass up her starboard side." She must have responded too slowly, because he grabbed the wheel and wrestled it around, then relinquished it again.

All at once they plunged into a smell that made her throat close. A sulfurous, thick, nauseating stink of rotten meat and decaying blood so dense *Anemone* seemed to slow. Dorée gasped, sealing a glove over her nose. Georgita gagged.

Men in red helmets and yellow parkas moved about the decks of the still slowly turning ship, or stood at the life rails with eyes shaded, watching. Less than a hundred yards away now, Sara made out what thrashed and blew, racing desperately beside the pursuing hull. Two of them. Their raked dorsals proclaimed them minkes. A thick clot of smoke chuffed off the stack, and white foam boiled at the stern. A lone slickered figure stood forward, one hand on the lowered barrel of a harpoon gun, watching the racing whales.

"Stand by the float line," Perrault yelled, and she jerked her attention back. The whales were angling right, away from their pursuer, whose ability to turn after them was blocked now by *Anemone*, coming up astern. Dru was putting them between the hunters and their quarry.

They were close beneath the hull now. A row of ideographs marched across the bow. Beneath it Roman letters read *SIRYU No.* 3. Madsen cupped his hands and shouted at the men who stared down, "Stop your illegal poaching! Stop killing innocent whales!" The Japanese, all in identical yellow slickers, looked down without expression, as if at a not very entertaining performance. One or two X'd their fore arms, a gesture she couldn't interpret. The gunner on the harpoon frowned and swung it toward them. Then, in response to a shout that echoed across the water, aimed it away.

"Closer," Perrault yelled. She took her lip hard in her teeth again and steered so that the gap ahead, already narrow, became disappearingly thin. Madsen pushed the opened crate to Bodine, who seized it. The Dane skidded over the ice to seize the flemished-out line as the mate grabbed the after end. Together, heaving at the mass of polyethylene, they lifted it over the lifeline, festooning it in drooping catenaries just above the rushing sea.

Madsen straightened, pulling a dull gray can with a red stripe from inside his suit. He weighed it in his glove, staring up at the steel wall that rose far above their heads. The sea bulged like a tensed muscle between the hulls. "No closer, she will suck you in," Perrault shouted. "Steady now. Steady. *Throw!*"

Bodine's and Madsen's arms whipped upward simultaneously, and two gray cans lofted, rifled, spinning. One hurtled over the ship's rail; the other crashed against a bow anchor, bounced off, smoking, and dropped into the water.

A searing-hot scent suddenly cut the stink of rotten meat. Another can snapped upward, an overhand by Quill that shattered a window in the other's pilothouse. "Oh, nice pitch," Madsen shouted. "Damn, that was sweet. They won't like that!"

"What's that they're throwing?" Eddi coughed from beneath her glove. Sara shook her head.

The prow of the killer wavered, as if whoever was at the helm had a moment of indecision. Sara eyed it as they drew abreast, then exhaled as *Anemone* forged ahead, into clear sea. She shaded her eyes to see the whales making their escape, pushing white waves, then vanishing as they sounded.

Madsen scampered aft, cradling another can. He gripped the shroud and cocked an arm, head lifted to judge the range; wound up, and threw. This one fell onto the other ship's forecastle, and a silvery smoke burst up around the harpooner. He staggered back, and his screams as he flailed at his eyes rose over the roar of the bow wave.

"What *is* that?" Auer gasped. Sara shook her head, her own eyes and mucous membranes starting to burn in earnest, holding her breath to keep whatever it was from searing her nasal passages. She'd thought they'd be throwing stink bombs, or maybe red paint. Perhaps even blood—something symbolic. But the doused harpooner was hanging over the rail, vomiting and beating at his face.

She was jerked from puzzlement by Perrault cuffing her. "I said, *cross her bow*," the captain yelled. Then pushed her aside. She stumbled back and fell over the inflatable. Dorée and Georgita caught her, and the three women leaned together. "What *is* that stuff?" she muttered. "In the cans they're throwing?"

"You don't know?"

"No, Georgie, I don't," she snapped. "Do you?"

"You didn't smell it? It's tear gas, or pepper spray or something."

"Good God," she muttered.

"Heave," Quill roared. She blinked tears from her vision to see the captain had cut left, directly in front of the racing killer.

Madsen and the mate straightened, each heaving at a loop, and the heavy urine-colored plastic fell into the sea, thrashing and writhing like something alive. It disappeared below the surface, then bobbed up in their wake, borne up by the spherical pods, streamed at the end of a lighter line that uncoiled swiftly aft. The looming prow swung away, roaring out a steady bow wave.

She looked along the other craft's length, now boiling with yellow slickers. The orange floats reached toward the racing bow, then vanished beneath it to a ringing whoop from Bodine and a high-stepping jig from Madsen. She tensed, clutching the helm stand, while Perrault gazed hard aft too. But the enemy, silver smoke still rising from here and there along its decks, kept turning.

With a spurt of foam the floats spat from beneath her counter, dancing along the waves. Perrault's shoulders sagged. Madsen stopped his jig, staring aft. "Fuck," he muttered. A shift in the wind brought the acrid burning again. A sudden pain in her sinuses, a searing irritation in her throat. Dorée doubled, coughing uncontrollably.

Now the other was swinging back. Smoke jetted from the stack, black against blue, and the hammer of her engines came across the water.

A white stream jetted out, swinging this way and that before the wind tattered it into smoking spray. "Hoses," Tehiyah yelled. "They're going to turn fire hoses on us."

"Hold on," Perrault said between clenched teeth. He eyed the telltales on the sail, looked over his shoulder, and suddenly cut hard right. *Aenemone* heeled, swaying far over. The sails sagged for a moment before a leaping Quill was on the winches, elbows blurring as he spun them taut again.

A muffled roar built, like a dragon inhaling before breathing flame. Bodine cried a warning from the forward hatch. She didn't catch the words, but heard the mortal admonition in his tone. Perrault faked a turn to port, then came right again. Past him she saw a berg rolling in the sea, three tour buses long. Waves broke on it in leaping cascades of glowing spray.

She turned, gripping a strap on the inflatable to avoid being bucked overboard as the killer's bow wave surged under them, and found herself looking directly up through the shattered window of its pilothouse into the broad face of a middle-aged Asian. His reddened, pouchy eyes streamed with tears. Above stubbled cheeks, below a brush haircut streaked with gray, she met his harsh, condemning gaze. He mopped his face with a sleeve, then turned to shout at someone out of sight. The helmsman, she guessed, because the bow veered right, toward them, closer and closer as it gathered speed. Now that towering recurved bow was a gray guillotine, peeling the sea apart as it remorselessly tracked them, slashing apart the green turbulent water of their fleeing wake.

The pursued had become the pursuer. The killer of whales, now something even more ominous. "He's going to ram us," she breathed.

"What?" said Eddi. She sounded frightened, crouching on the far side of the inflatable's swelling bulk, cradling her camera. A thin glaze of ice had formed on her upwind flank, and white rime coated the mouth-hole where she breathed through her mask.

"Dru," Dorée screamed shrilly. "He's going to run us down!"

Perrault didn't answer. Looking forward, Sara saw his spine a tense line, his attention pinned to the swiftly narrowing gap between *Anemo-*

ne's outthrust sprit and the surging breakers that marked the berg ahead. He tossed a glance back over one shoulder, then faced forward again.

Something heavy and incredibly powerful slammed her down onto the icy deck. She screamed as it shook her body and filled her mouth. She emerged choking and shaking as the heavy solid jet moved forward, splintering on the cockpit lockers and fuel drums into a white gush of saltwater that blew handles overboard off the winches and slammed the locker covers up and wrenched them off their hinges. The hose-jets blocked Perrault against the wheel, pinning him there for seconds before lifting and moving on to pour their combined streams through the open companionway. One caught Quill as he struggled aft, swept his feet out from under him, and rolled him forward all flailing arms and legs until he fetched up in the bow pulpit. When the spray blew off she saw with a squeeze of the heart the berg, now surging and rolling mere yards ahead. The waves were blasting themselves apart against it with terrific force.

Perrault rose, flinging water off like a wet Labrador. He staggered, then shifted his grip on the wheel he'd never released, even when the fire hoses had fixed him to it. He shouted to Quill in a thick voice, "Jibing!"

"Jibing, aye. All hands, heads down." The bearlike mate was staggering aft, bent over his belly, which he clutched with both hands. When he reached the coach house he rolled over it like a child in the snow, landing on the starboard side. He reeled, almost went overboard, but yanked the safety line taut to brake his frictionless slide. He spun lightly as a ballerina and his wrists blurred as he slacked the genoa.

"Helm's over," Perrault yelled, bending to spin the wheel so fast the spokes became invisible, just as the massive blade of the oncoming ship passed through the space where their stern had been a moment before.

The heavy aluminum boom hesitated, then slammed from one side to the other as a curve passed from the trailing edge of the great mainsail up toward the masttop, twisting, then yanking the sail over as the wind shifted from one side to the other. The women shouted and slid, grabbing at each other and at the lifeline that was all that barriered them from the roaring sea. *Anemone* kept heeling, port lifeline submerged in the freezing froth, a clamor as of a collapsing mine coming from below as everything not lashed down freed itself and made for the downhill side. Quill remained bent over the winch, elbows pumping as he cranked. As *Anemone*'s stern passed through the wind the captain, hanging like Ixion to the wheel, advanced the throttle. The engines howled. Sea the color of limes shot from beneath the stern. Quill scrambled to the mainsheet and hauled in hand over hand. The boom quivered as it drew slowly toward centerline.

Sara shuddered, looking aft. Her soaked clothing was stiff, freezing on her. Their bubbled wake formed a bright green hairpin turn in the darker jostling waves. The whaler had started to follow them around, but its captain must have seen he couldn't turn sharply enough to avoid the berg. Instead she steamed on, leaving a rolling mass of spume and white ice between her and the sailboat. Faces lined the rail, staring down at them, deadpan as robots.

Then one hand lifted, farther aft. Sara squinted. A single figure aft of the smokestack was giving them a slow, cautious wave. She couldn't make out his face—too far away—but she too lifted a hand.

Quill rose from his kneel by the mainsheet. Then slumped, gripping his belly again. When he lifted a glove Sara saw the bright crimson smear. "Jamie! Jamie's hurt," she yelled.

"Take the wheel," Perrault snapped. She halted short, and obeyed. The captain dropped to his knees. "Jamie. You all right?"

"Something sharp," the mate grunted, chewing his beard. He lifted the other hand, which was bloody too. "That fire hose tumbled me ass over teacups. Poked me right in the fooking gut."

"Can you walk? Best get below, if you can. Have Bodine take a look."

Quill hesitated, cradling his midriff. Then lumbered up, wincing, and staggered to the companionway. "Watch those wet steps," Georgie called after him.

Eyeing their much larger opponent, Perrault spun the wheel again as soon as they cleared the berg. This put the wind on their beam and they gathered velocity once more as the kill ship came right too. Only its track now led far wide of theirs. He shaded his eyes to where round yellow floats bobbed on a dark olive sea. "Mick, Sara: grab the boat hooks. Let's pick up that line and try again."

"Fuck that! They almost ran us down," Dorée shouted, crouched beside the inflatable. She got up and felt her way forward, plumped down in the cockpit. Ice crackled off her suit. She tore off her mask, exposing flushed hectic cheeks. "Do we really want to try that again?"

He ignored her. Sara, after a moment's glance back, went forward as ordered. She clipped her safety line midships and grabbed the boat hook.

Before they could pick the float line up, though, the whaler came about. It headed off past the berg, bounding ahead like a whistled-up collie. Away from them. Perrault cursed and looked from it to the floats. "Headed for the factory ship?" Madsen said.

"Possibly. Possibly."

"We found the fleet. Can't lose them now."

Perrault glanced upwind again, then nodded. *Anemone* hauled around again and steadied several points off the wind. Madsen bent to the winch; the captain, to the mainsheets. The boat climbed up on plane again, scalpeling smoothly through the seas. Sara crouched as a sheet of spray doused her, freezing another layer on her suit like another skin on an onion. The salt trickled down under her eyepatch, itching and burning, and she couldn't help rubbing it.

"What're we doing? Chasing them? How about picking up the float line?"

"We'll have to let it go," Madsen said. "We've got to stick with the fleet." He grinned at her. "Isn't this great? Did you see those whales swimming away, free? That pitch Jamie made?"

"But I saw him get hurt, too. And I saw us almost get run down, Lars."

"That's just a scrape. He'll be back on deck in a minute." The Dane chafed his gloves together briskly. "And now they're running. Not a bad day's work, I'd say. What're we logging, Dru?"

"Nineteen." The captain was hunched over the wheel, frowning ahead. They were catching up to the whaler. Slowly, overtaking from behind, but gaining, surging over bigger seas, slicing through the smaller ones.

"This was worth everything. All we went through." Madsen seized her shoulder. "The storm. *Everything.* We spoiled their hunt. Saved whales. We've got them on the run!"

Sara studied him, wiping tears from her weeping eye. He looked manic, and she felt suddenly afraid. She pulled free. "Lars, that's all great. But we almost got killed, too. That asshole captain tried to crowd us into that berg. And those water cannons—they could've knocked someone overboard."

"We have to take risks, Sara. Understand? You accept danger, in battle. This is our war, for the whales." He hammered a gloved fist on the cockpit coaming.

"You are *so* committed, Lars," Dorée purred, sliding both arms around his waist from behind. She smiled at Sara over his shoulder. "It's what I love about you."

"I'm going below," Georgita said, and pushed past, cradling her arm. Sara almost asked if she'd hurt it again, but one look at the assistant's closed face stopped her question dead.

"What's with her?" Dorée shrugged dismissively. "Better yet, who cares.—Eddi. Eddi! Did you get all that? Were you filming?"

Auer crawled from behind the inflatable, still clutching her camera. She half rose, then sank back. "My gosh—I don't think we've ever gone this fast before."

Sara realized she was gripping a stanchion so tightly her hand was cramping. *Anemone* was trembling all along her length, as if approaching some transition speed where she would leap free of the sea entirely, like a flying fish, and take to the air. How much power the wind had. Enough to lift whole icebergs. Frightened, exhilarated, she opened her mouth wide to the gale and laughed.

"Sara," Perrault said, craning around. "Oh, there you are. Take the wheel while I check on Jamie. Aim for her stern. Watch for ice. I shall not be long."

"Aye aye, Captain." She dashed him a mock salute and untangled herself from the stanchion. From the salt spray and maybe the fire hoses too the sole was nearly free of ice now, though chunks of crust still made the footing treacherous. She braced her boots and fought the helm with all her strength as the boat took great leaps across the sea. The stern of the whaler rose ahead, trailing a smoke of birds. Brown exhaust stained the blue sky. She could just make out a lone figure in yellow slicker and red helmet, gazing back from the stern rail.

But something was wrong. Something was changing. She could see the Japanese ship's bow again. She glanced at the compass, then back at the whaler.

"Dru! Captain! He's turning."

Perrault's hawklike face reappeared at the bottom of the companionway. "What?"

"The whaler—it's turning."

"Which way?"

"Right. To starboard."

"Into the wind? *Caulisse.*" He climbed the ladder. Braced himself and stared forward, then bent to the mainsheet again, hauling it in until the boom was nearly centered. *Anemone* faltered. Sara brought her back on course, but the compass kept ticking over. The boat's head sought the wind, wavered, then fell away.

"Can't keep my course," she shouted.

"He's trying to shake us off." Madsen lowered binoculars. "Speeded up, and turned into the wind."

The sails flapped as the racer coasted forward ever more slowly. Perrault cursed and reached for the throttle. He yelled to Madsen to furl the genoa. Sara made as if to step away, but he grunted, "Stay there. You're doing fine."

Meter by meter, the flapping expanse of high-tech fabric twisted itself into its housing. The engines rose to a howl, to an ear-stabbing whine. "Turbine superchargers," the Frenchman muttered. He rubbed his mouth with the back of a hand and looked from the instrument panel to the ship ahead. Hesitated, then pushed the twin levers all the way forward.

Anemone snarled. Water blasted from her stern, and she shot ahead, skipping across the waves like an eighty-foot Jet Ski. "We're catching up again," Eddi yelled.

They craned forward, squinting in the port-wine rays of the low sun. The distant bergs were scarlet and pink and ruby and gold. A soft-drink can bobbed past jauntily in the clean cold water, spinning to show a colorful manga schoolgirl with skirt flying up to reveal white panties. Madsen spat over the side.

For several minutes it did seem they would overtake. But more smoke shot from the killer's stack. The distance held for five minutes. Ten. Then Perrault straightened from the radar, and shook his head. "She has found another knot somewhere. I think we could overtake downwind. Or on a beam reach." He glanced whalerward, defeat shadowing his eyes. "We thought *Anemone* would be fast. And she is. But that killer . . . he's just the littlest bit faster."

"Ice ahead," Dorée screeched. Perrault flinched and shaded his eyes, then snapped orders. The stern skated around, but the dark-green-stained chunk, so low in the water no one else had seen it, approached inexorably. Sara grabbed for a handhold, flashing on the thin taut wires that alone kept the keel from parting company with the hull. Envisioning them snapping, the boat going end over end . . . but they skated past mere yards from the sullen, slowly rolling menace.

"Launch the inflatable?" Lars shouted.

The captain shook his head. "Too rough. You'll never catch her."

"I'm willing to take a chance."

"So am I," Dorée said, but Perrault shook his head again, firmly.

The gray ship shrank. Perrault pulled the throttles back. The whine dropped to a murmur. He shut the engines down and tacked away, still heading in the general direction of the kill ship, but at an angle that let the wind resume driving them.

Madsen came to stand behind him, expression grim. "We can't lose them."

The captain said, "We won't. They cannot maintain that speed for long. They have fuel limits too. He'll get out of sight, then reduce power. And go back to hunting. We must just . . . press on."

The Dane tipped his mask back, and Sara traced the bitter set of his lips. Then they quirked upward, and he threw her a chapped smile.

"Well . . . we saved whales today. Anyway. Those minkes . . . I mean, piked whales. Alive. Free. Because of us."

"That's right. *We* did that," Dorée agreed. She rubbed her eyes, and looked around. "Eddi?"

"I got some good footage," Auer called from up forward. "When we were alongside."

"While they were trying to run us down?"

"Yes, Tehiyah," Eddi said patiently. "I got it all. Wide angle. It's going to be terrific."

Sara sagged against the steering pedestal and tugged off her mask. Her eye still burned from the gas, as if she'd rubbed pepper into it. Eddi peered down at her. "Uh, Sara? Your nose is all white."

"My *nose*?" She put her fingers over it. It felt like rubbing a stone.

"Oh my God," said Dorée. "Here, let me."

Tehiyah leaned close. Her lips parted, and suddenly warmth engulfed Sara's face. She went rigid, blinking. After thirty seconds the actress straightened, wiping her mouth. "It's frostbite. Had to warm it up." Eyes veined with tawny gold twinkled down at her. "Better? Put your mask back on. Right now. Hear?"

She couldn't think of a thing to say, other than to mutter, "Thanks."

"Okay, let's get below," the captain said. "Next time, we'll do even better. I am proud of everyone."

They were standing at the companionway, in line to go below, when Sara happened to glance forward. The departing whaler had changed course to avoid another berg. Just as it turned back, though, a spot of bright color hung suspended for a moment from the stern, then dropped into the wake.

She blinked, hardly believing what she'd just seen, and pointed. "On the ship. I think . . . I think I just saw someone fall overboard."

"Probably just dumping trash," Madsen said, but reached for the binoculars.

Perrault frowned, shading his eyes. "Yes, perhaps it is someone overboard," he said slowly. "In the water, to the left."

"Oh my God," Dorée said.

Dru snapped to Lars, "We're coming about. Tend the sheets." He brought the prow around smartly. The sails snapped, then filled again. *Anemone* leaped forward, making up on a bright yellow object that floated, spinning slowly, in the jade-foamed wake of the killer. It had vanished behind the berg, only pilothouse and stack and antennas visible now, and continuing to shrink.

"Is it a man?" Georgita whispered from the companionway.

Madsen held the binoculars for several seconds. "Yeah."

"Sara, boat hook, to starboard. Tehiyah, Eddi, hand me that sheet." The captain spun the wheel lock on, and with a complex motion of both hands dropped a knotted loop into Dorée's gloves. "Use this. Sara will get it around him, with the boat hook. And all four of you will pull him aboard. *C'est clair?*"

It seemed clear enough. She went forward and clipped her safety line and reeved the slack out of it. She braced her boots and aimed the boat hook over the side like a lance. The others ranged themselves behind her. The man was now clearly visible a hundred yards ahead. He floated low in the sea, heaved upward and then down by the swells. A sallow oval yearned toward them. Dark hair crowned a bullet head. An arm lifted, waved weakly, then sank back.

"One pass," Perrault called. "One chance. If we must take time to come around again, he will be dead."

Sara kicked ice overboard. She didn't want to slip at the crucial moment. The captain said something to Madsen, who bent to the sheets. *Anemone* began to slow, the big mainsail luffing and cracking above them. When she glanced aft the captain was the picture of concentration, gloves welded to the wheel.

"Now," he shouted, and *Anemone* headed up into the wind, shedding speed, her sharp prow swinging toward the castaway. He stared helplessly up, then sank back into what she saw was a life preserver, eyelids sagging closed.

"Now," Perrault shouted. Sara scampered forward, lowered the pole, and for a heart-stopping moment thought she'd missed him. But at the second jab the curved hook snagged a strap and she gaffed him in. A surge of the boat nearly dragged the hook from her hands, but she held on grimly and a loop sailed out and over the floating man's head.

He stirred, but didn't open his eyes. "Pull," Georgie yelled, at the same time Madsen shouted, "Don't! It's not under his arms yet." She braced herself as the boat continued forward. Then suddenly was pinned against the lifeline, the body dragging through green water at the end of her boat hook, her shoulders nearly dislocated from their sockets each time a wave rolled past.

Then Madsen was beside her, strong arms joined hers on the wooden pole, and hand over hand they hoisted the resistless and lolling weight up to where the others, reaching under the lifeline, were able to get gloves on slicker and arms and life vest. "All together, *heave*," Dorée grunted, and the body, smaller than she'd expected, though sodden-heavy, emerged from the green and was pulled over the hastily-dropped lifelines onto the deck.

Sara cradled his head in her lap. He was young, full-cheeked, with dark lashes and close-cropped black hair. His skin was oyster-flesh pale, and when she laid her palm against a cheek it was icy.

"Below, get those clothes off him," Perrault snapped. "Blankets. Something hot to drink. And somebody, bundle up with him."

Eddi said she would; they were about the same size. Sara wasn't sure what that had to do with it, but didn't object. She and Madsen and Dorée improvised a makeshift carry. They maneuvered him into the cockpit, then lowered him, very carefully, into Auer's upstretched arms. Perrault, meanwhile, was speaking urgently into the VHF remote. "*Siryu Maru Number Three*, *Siryu Maru Number Three*. This is Cetacean Protection League ship *Black Anemone*. I have recovered a man overboard from your crew. Please respond, *Siryu Maru Number Three*. Over." The radio crackled, clicked with what might have been a microphone triggering, but did not reply.

Sara leaned against the coach house, shaking, breathing hard. She stared to where the whaler had disappeared behind the tabular iceberg. But the ship was out of sight, out of mind, and did not answer them. All that remained was her smoke, the faintest stain of tea on a horizon of fading rose.

10

New Faces

Perrault kept them a point or two off the wind, enough to stay headed west. He left Madsen topside and went below with the others.

In the salon, Auer had the castaway hoisted onto the table. The heavy slicker lay like a shed skin on deck, streaming water. A padded jacket lay beside it, and Eddi was struggling with a tartan-patterned pullover. "Just cut it off," Bodine said. He lurch-walked forward and with a click the black blade of a combat-style knife flicked out. "Is he still breathing?"

"Shallow, but it's there," Perrault said.

"Careful," Sara couldn't help saying. Bodine's glance met hers for just a second, affectless, remote. As if he orbited at such times beyond human feelings. He pulled the wet cloth taut, and the serrated blade slid through with barely a whisper. White waffled underclothing came into view. He sliced this off too.

"He's not shivering," Dorée observed.

"Because he's in hypothermic shock. Roll him over. Gently! You two, on that side. One, two, *heave*. Towels, and blankets. Lift that right leg. Knee up—yeah, like that. I'll get a core temperature. Then we'll put him in Georgie's bunk."

Bodine lifted the upper buttock and carefully worked a thermometer into the unconscious man's rectum. Sara couldn't take her eyes from the smooth hairless chest, the husk of maleness at the groin. Short curly hair. A helplessly curled, uncircumcised penis. Chubby cheeks and closed eyes made the slack face look very young. As Georgita tugged the ruins of clothing from beneath him something clicked to the deck. She rose with a pair of gold-framed glasses. "These must be his. I'll keep them for him."

Bodine was searching through the ribboned fabric of khaki trousers. His face changed as he came up with transparent plastic. He unzipped it and took out a billfold and a maroon-backed passport. He flipped the wallet open. "In Japanese. Of course. Here's a license of some kind. And . . . this is interesting. An ID from Tokyo University." He looked at Sara. "What's a guy from a university doing on a whaling ship?"

She frowned. "I don't know. But isn't the first thing to get him warmed up?"

Bodine extracted the thermometer and straightened the boy's legs. He examined it, then wiped it on his pants. "Ninety-three Fahrenheit. He ought to be okay, but it might take a while. Sara, get his legs. Dru, under the shoulders. Eddi, ready to be his snuggle bunny?"

"It won't be that hard."

"Ha-ha," said Dorée. "Maybe we can *make* it hard. If we both snuggle in, one on each side."

"Enough." Perrault laid a palm on the pale forehead. "Mick? I have Calvados."

"No alcohol. That actually reduces core temperature. Heat up some rice or oatmeal. Use it for hot packs. Ready? All together—lift."

When he was settled in one of the bunks Eddi stripped off to sports bra and panties. The tattoos writhed over her shoulders, down her back, as she stretched and sighed. Then turned back the blankets and crawled in. She embraced the seaman, wrapping him with arms and legs. Kissed his forehead. "Life," she murmured, as if invoking a spirit. "Life."

The others looked on for a while. Then drifted out.

Sara microwaved two makeshift hot packs and took them in to Eddi. Then went aft to see how Quill was doing.

She hadn't been in the mate's quarters before. She was surprised at how small the space was. Barely more than a cupboard, next to the captain's cabin. He was doubled in an uncomfortable-looking half-sitting position, holding a towel to his belly and staring up into his reading light. Following his gaze, she was confronted with the wide-open crotch of a foldout nude taped to the bulkhead. She cleared her throat. "How you doing, Jamie? Anything I can get for you?"

"I'm all right. Just a nick."

"We picked up a man overboard from the whaler. After you got hurt. We're not really sure yet how he got in the water. Fell off the stern, we think."

"That right?" He didn't seem especially interested. "There's one lucky bugger, for sure."

"One funny thing. His wallet and passport were wrapped in plastic. When we took them out of his pants, they were still dry."

"Then he didn't fall. He jumped. If he wrapped his shite waterproof before he went."

"That's what I was thinking."

"What's he got to say for himself, then?"

"He's hypothermic. Unconscious. Eddi's warming him up."

"Send her in here next. Unless you got a free minute."

"Uh, right . . . Well, thanks for keeping me from going over. When that fire hose hit us."

Quill shrugged. Looked back at the pinup, then at her. Not her face, but at her chest. She sighed. "I'll look in again. Sure there's nothing you need? Juice? Something to eat?"

"Old Mick says I'm not to eat for a while. Gave me some antibiotic pills. But thanks."

"Okay then." She waited a moment more, then backed out and clicked the door closed.

She made potato soup for lunch, or whatever meal it was—the time of day seemed to matter less and less when dark and light did not alternate. The potatoes all had eyes, which she carefully cut out. Knowing, as a scientist, that it was a waste of effort, but her mother had told her when she was little, back on the island, that the dark nubs were poison. She caught her eyepatched reflection in the stainless steel of the stove. Did she still need that? She lifted it and peered out. The world leaped into 3-D. She took it off. Her eye smarted, but seemed better.

She cut up and sautéed onions and the last green pepper and thickened the soup with corn starch. She laid out crackers and canned butter and made coffee. They were finished and getting up from the littered table when Eddi wandered in. "He's awake," she said.

Bodine lurched to his feet. He walked stiffly to the curtain and drew it back. "Hey there. You with us, amigo?"

"He's Japanese, not Mexican," Dorée said, smoothing back her hair. A rash or some skin eruption showed blotchy at her neckline. "The word for friend is *tomodachi*. The reason I know that—"

"Doing okay, buddy? Speak any English? Doesn't respond. Well, takes a while to come back from a hypothermic episode," Bodine said. "See if he wants coffee. Put a lot of sugar in it."

"I've got it." Sara poured a mug and pushed the curtain aside. And was embarrassed at the dangling bras she'd hung to dry after handwashing in the sink. Was her underwear the first thing he'd seen when he woke?

He was sitting up, wrapped in blankets. Heavy eyelids, but bright black eyes peered out from under them. His skin tone was darker, less waxy. But he still looked very young. "Hello," she said, enunciating very clearly. "My name is Sara. Would you like some coffee?"

"Thank you." He blinked slowly, looking around. "I am on your boat?"

"That's right." She held the mug to his lips. He sipped slowly, then greedily, lashes fluttering. Finally he lay back, sighing.

The curtain rattled again. Perrault and Bodine, with Dorée close behind. "He's awake," she told them. "Took some coffee."

"*Parlez français?*" the captain said.

"*Nein,*" the man in the bunk said. A smile dawned. "But a . . . little English. Thank you for, for, handling me."

"For picking you up? Not a problem." Bodine took his wrist. "Good pulse. How you feeling?"

"Hungry?"

"I've got more soup," she said. "It's okay for him to have it?"

Bodine said it was, and she left, pushing through the crowd.

When she came back they'd all managed to fit themselves into her cubicle, Dorée, Bodine, Georgita, Perrault, and Eddi. "He says his name's Kimura," Auer whispered.

"So what're you doing here with us, Kimura?"

"It is Hideyashi, first name. To you Hideyashi Kimura. I worked on the ship."

"Okay, Hideyashi. What did you do on the ship?"

"They used me as translator, but I am a PhD candidate."

That explained the academic ID. "What discipline?" Sara asked him.

"Neurobiology."

"Really." The others looked at her; she picked up the thread of the questioning. "Of whales, I take it?"

"Whales, yes, that's right." He sipped more coffee; he seemed to be growing more responsive by the minute. "I was . . . hired as part for the research team. But I quickly realize it is not real research."

"It's slaughter," Bodine said.

"You are very right, sir. They do not even weigh stomachs like they say. Only when cameras watch." His gaze came back to Sara. "You are scientist too?"

"A behaviorist. Specializing in . . . primates. At least, I was."

"*So desu ka.* Do you know Dr. Tetsuro Matsuzawa?"

"Of the Inuyama Primate Research Institute? I heard him present in Chicago." She straightened, nodded at the others. As if to say, *He's real.*

"So you didn't fall overboard," Perrault said. "By the way, I'm the captain. Dru Perrault."

Kimura took his hand gravely, then struggled to sit up. "Captain? Thank you so much. Thank you. No. I did not fall. I jump. I see your small boat try to stop the killing. So very brave. So I am ashamed. And I try to swim to you. But the water, so cold I cannot move. Then sleepy. I wake up here with"—he examined their faces, nodded at Eddi—"that one, no-clothing with me. Very pretty lady. I see her *irezumi*—I do not know the word—like *yakuza*."

"My tattoos." Eddi reached out to rub his head. "So you didn't mind me sprawling all over you."

"Is very nice." He looked hopeful. "You do more now?"

They all laughed. "Not *right* now," she said, but it didn't sound like an unequivocal refusal.

Bodine hoisted himself with his arms, and Sara saw how the Japanese's eyes widened as they noted his prosthetics. "We're glad to have you with us, Hideyashi, but we better let you rest. Sara'll get you some hot soup. And give him carbs—chocolate or honey. You're okay otherwise? Do you take any medicine, Hideyashi?"

"Only aspirin. When head aching." He hesitated, then said in a rush, "Captain. Is it possible I radio my family? Tell them I am all right? I do not wish them to worry. It was risk, yes. But worth dying, to be off that evil ship. I want to stay with you. Help stop this horrible slaughter. This very dreadful impurity."

Perrault patted his shoulder. "We can get a shortwave message off to our shore office. Maybe in two hours? We have a scheduled contact then."

"Thank you, Captain. Thank you, everyone."

"Okay then. Let him rest." Bodine shooed them out and slid the curtain closed.

Back in the salon, he frowned. "What do you think?" he murmured.

"What do you mean?" Sara said.

Perrault made a hushing gesture. "Let's go to the engine room," he suggested. "You, me, and Sara. Or—just a moment. Let me look at the sky, and get Eddi to relieve Lars. I will meet you down there."

Heat still radiated off the massive hulks of steel, though they were shut down. She found a perch between the starboard engine block and a large piece of metal and rubber ductwork, and enjoyed the toasting until the door opened and Perrault stepped down, followed by Bodine and Madsen. The Dane looked taken aback at seeing her there. Bodine just glanced over, then away.

Perrault waited until they all found places to lean, then took off his watch cap and ruffled his hair. Was it her imagination, or was it grayer than when they'd left Ushuaia? "All right, what does everybody think?"

"I've been topside," Madsen interjected.

Bodine brought him up to date in a few sentences. He finished, "He says he's a neurobiologist. Sara?"

"Well—a doctoral candidate. Probably working on his thesis."

"Is he what he says?"

She lifted her eyebrows. "He knew a prominent primate researcher."

"He knew his *name*," Bodine corrected. "Which he could have been primed with."

"Primed with for what?" She frowned.

"To make us accept him," Madsen said.

She understood suddenly. "You think he's been, what—*sent* here?"

"It'd make sense." Bodine absently scratched a prosthesis as if it were a real limb. "Look at it from their point of view. They know Greenpeace. They know Sea Shepherds. But they don't know CPL. We've tried to keep everything low-key. Funded with private donations, not public appeals. No press releases. An unknown quantity. Faced with that, any commander would want intel."

"By having one of his men jump overboard?" She shook her head. "If I hadn't seen him, he'd have died. If Dru hadn't gotten to him in time, he'd be a floating popsicle. He's some kind of spy? I don't think so."

"Or worse," Madsen put in darkly. "That was Captain Crunch on that bridge. Same guy who killed two protesters a couple seasons ago. I can see him sending somebody aboard with orders to make trouble. Maybe even scuttle us."

Sara remembered a middle-aged Japanese, a swarthy, hard face glaring down at them. Then turning away, to snap an order that was tantamount to murder. But what the boy had said had the ring of truth to her. "Oh, for heaven's sake. *Scuttle* us? He'd go down too."

"Why not?" But he sounded defensive. Perrault looked doubtful too.

She said, "I just don't see it, Mick. I think he, Hideyashi, is either brave as hell, or maybe, slightly nutty. In a harmless way, I think. But I don't think he's what you're suggesting."

The captain said, "What about this radio message he wants us to send?"

"It's to his *parents*, for God's sake. The whaler will report him lost at sea."

The Frenchman sighed and dug something out from between his teeth. "I'm worried about Jamie, too."

"I think he'll be okay," Bodine said. "If he doesn't get an infection. That's the big hurdle there."

"So you think he's what he says he is? Sara?"

"It'll be easy to tell if he's actually got a background in mammalian neuroscience. Nobody's going to be able to fake that at short notice."

"I'd keep a close eye on him," Madsen said. "Keep him tied to his bunk."

The captain looked at the overhead. "Sara will test him. But I'm not tying him to the bunk. For one thing, we don't have enough beds to start tying people into them. He's going to have to share anyway. At least until we give him back."

Sara frowned. "Give him back? But—"

"There may be legal issues involved. Right now, I don't know. I radioed *Maru Number 3* that we recovered a man overboard. That much we owe them, in case they're searching for him. I also notified our home office, so the legal people can do the research. Meanwhile, he needs to share someone's bunk. Lars?"

Madsen drew back. "I don't want him."

"You could keep a better eye on him."

"How? He'd be up when I was asleep. And vice versa."

"Just do it," the captain said. The Dane looked sullen, but nodded curtly.

The door opened and they turned. It was Eddi, and she looked scared, hugging herself, eyes wide. "What is it?" Perrault said.

"Mick? I think you better come. There's something bad wrong with Jamie."

Sara stood in the doorway while Bodine and the captain crouched next to the bunk. It was shaking. Quaking so hard it squeaked. The mate was conscious, but his whole body was spasming so violently it was a wonder he didn't buck out onto the deck. Bodine had his thermometer out, was about to thrust it into Jamie's mouth, when Perrault said, "Mick."

"What?"

"The thermometer."

A blank look; then comprehension. "Gotcha." He bent and from a small locker under the mate's sink extracted a liter bottle. Popov. Wiped down with vodka, flicked dry again, the instrument went under the mate's tongue. "Don't bite through it," Bodine warned. "We don't have a spare."

" 'Ry not oo." Quill tried to haul himself upright, but shook so badly he slid down flat on the bunk again. He blinked above the thermometer, which presently commenced a shrill electronic peeping like a tiny truck backing up. Bodine whipped it out and examined it. But didn't immediately speak.

"Well?"

"It's high."

"How high," Sara prompted.

"Hundred and four," Bodine said reluctantly. "How you feel, Jamie?"

"Not too bad, except for this fucking shaking."

"Chills? Feel cold?"

"Yeah. Course, that's nothing new." He forced a grin through his beard, but was beginning to look apprehensive. "What've I got, sawbones?"

"Might have a bug," Bodine said.

"Thought you already gave me some shite for that."

"Yeah, well, we're gonna give you more. Be right back." To Sara he said, "Better get him another blanket."

She followed him out while the captain drew a chair up beside the bunk. Down the corridor, past the master suite, she said in a low voice, "What's he got?"

"It's not good. Something sharp perforated his stomach. We never did figure out what. Probably a piece of stray wire, something like that."

"His stomach . . . his intestines?"

On into the salon, continuing forward. Bodine kept all his medical supplies up in the forward tunnel. He muttered, "Couldn't tell. No X-ray equipment. I cleaned it out with Betadine and bandaged it. Gave him a thousand milligrams of ciprofloxacin. A wide-spectrum antibiotic. I've seen some pretty serious gut wounds pull through on cipro."

"Yeah, but they were operated on afterward—right?"

He didn't answer, just ducked through the hatch. She didn't pursue him, just stood there in the cold. Then recollected: blanket. She ducked behind her curtain. Kimura quickly covered himself and smiled. "Can you spare one of these?" she asked him.

"Oh, oh sure. I can spare."

Bodine came back through the salon and she dogged after him. "So what's he got, then? Jamie, I mean?"

"Chills and fever." He stopped opposite the kitchen, and frank worry filled his eyes instead of the barrier that had been there before. "Bacteremia. What used to be called septicemia. And before that, blood poisoning."

"But you gave him antibiotics."

"Enough for a horse. Trouble is, whatever's in his bloodstream is resistant to cipro. Obviously. I'll give him more, but unfortunately, that's the only antibiotic we have."

"If it doesn't work?"

He shrugged. "His organs will shut down, and he'll die."

"But . . ." She struggled briefly with the logic. "Then we have to go back. Get him to a hospital. At least, someplace with different antibiotics."

"Where? He'll be dead long before we reach Ushuaia, or anywhere else with a doctor. He's strong. But that may not be enough." He held her gaze for a second, then turned back for the mate's cabin. Leaving her standing in the passageway, hugging herself.

Their new guest was sitting at the table in blue CPL ski pants, a blanket over his shoulders. His breath plumed in the still air, and he looked rather green. Eddi Auer was fussing across the salon, setting up a videocamera on a tripod, a light. *Anemone* rolled, and she snapped a bungee around the tripod as it teetered. "This boat moves a great deal more than ours," the Japanese said. Made a hesitant gesture. "You are—?"

"Dr. Sara Pollard."

"That is right. Dr. Pollard. I will remember next time." He rubbed his head, looking lost.

"What are you doing?" she asked Eddi, who told her Perrault wanted a recorded statement from the new arrival testifying that he was being well treated. "For publicity, or to avoid any legal problems—I'm not exactly sure," she added. Sara hesitated, then took a seat beside him. Close up he smelled of saltwater and some kind of liniment or alcohol rub.

Eddi had just turned on the light when Dorée came forward. She was in a skintight black sweater, hair pulled tight to her skull in a French braid. She wore full makeup, eyeliner, everything. She sat down on Kimura's other side as Eddi began, reading from a card, "This is an interview aboard the French-flagged Cetacean Protection League vessel *Black Anemone*, with a castaway picked up earlier today. Sir, please state your name and nationality."

"I am Hideyashi Kimura, graduate student at Tokyo University. I live in Chiyoda, Japan. I am a Japanese citizen."

Dorée said, "I have a lot of fans in Japan."

Kimura looked confused. He half turned to her. "I am sorry?"

"I have a lot of followers in Tokyo. A huge fan club."

"*So desu ka*. You are . . . ?"

She smiled. "You must not have heard. Of course not; you were so frozen. I'm Tehiyah Dorée. You've seen my films."

She held out a hand and Kimura took it hesitantly. He looked from Dorée to Auer. "You both make films?"

Sara found herself suddenly choking. She caught Eddi's ironic glance and had to turn away not to laugh out loud. Dorée bit her lip. "Never mind." She glared from one woman to the other. "Do your fucking interview, then. I'll be in my cabin. And be sure to edit that out."

"I'll do that, Tehiyah."

When she left they both burst out laughing. Their guest looked puzzled. Finally Eddi asked what ship he'd been on, whether he'd gone overboard on purpose, and if he wanted to be returned. To the last question he said firmly, "No. I leave for ethical reasons. I do not wish to be returned against my will. I send respect to my father, mother, and family. I am being treated well here and wish to stay."

"Anything else?" Eddi asked him, and he shook his head. She shut off the lights. "I'll get this uploaded," she said, and took the camera off the stand and went forward.

Leaving Sara with him. Okay, she thought. Dru wants to know if he's really a neurobiologist. She opened with, "So how did you meet Dr. Matsuzawa? You said you knew him."

"Yes. My adviser, I think that is the word, was one of his students. He came to Tokyo University to give a lecture."

"What on?"

"Well, he began with computer modeling of visual neuroscience. How to reduce . . . no, *replicate* in silicon the synaptic structures underlying primate vision. He had a model he ran on a computer. The results—very impressive. We could see how information became abstracted, passed up the chain toward the conscious level."

"Tell me more."

Kimura hunched forward, smiling, apparently forgetting his seasickness. Or trying to ignore it. "Of course. He described a model of how neural networks transmit. And at the same time, interpolate . . . no, *interpret* information an organism may perceive as important to its survival. Food. Sexual objects. Threats. Sensory transduction in a molecular cascade. How the brain, uh, short-circuits responses to stimuli it thinks might be life-threatening. Then he spoke about ethical challenges in working with advanced, uh, species. Such as primates and whales." Kimura smiled sheepishly. "Actually I asked that question, at the end."

"I see. What's your thesis on, Hideyashi?"

He hesitated; but apparently was only trying to reformulate Japanese to English. "It centers on the analogy between what I am calling the 4, K area of the generic whale brain and the amygdala in primate brain. You know the role of the amygdala in anxiety and social disorders?"

"The *suspected* role."

"Oh, I think it is confirmed by PET-scan studies. Most of them, of humans with selective bilateral damage. But there are so few. Mostly war victims. So Dr. Matsuzawa was employing chimpanzee subjects. They live in highly structured groups with hierarchical relationships. Thus they require to do a great deal of interpretation of social communication. The chimps, that is. He ablated—is that the word? Yes?—areas of the amygdala and observed the resultant psychopathology."

She was so interested now she almost forgot the purpose of the interrogation. "What were his results?"

"He described how the amygdala operates to inhibit threat response in social situations. This slows cascading transduction and allows time for evaluation on the preconscious level. He also thinks human, what you call, social phobia or—we call it *taijin kyofusho*—is it, body dysmorphic disorder? To reflect a dysregulation of this discriminative procedure." He flushed. "I am sorry, my English is not good—these are complex matters—"

"Your English is excellent. Don't worry about that. Did you happen to hear him mention Von Economo neurons?"

"These are also called the spindle neurons, correct?" She nodded and he went on. "Yes, they too are involved in social interactions, in the mirroring function. You know, when you see someone dancing and your legs twitch."

"That's not all they do. There are Von Economos that have nothing to do with visual processing—"

"Perhaps I don't understand that so well. I do know spindle neurons, though. I have dissected one hundred and forty-four humpback brains since this cruise began. I have preserved and stained over a thousand slides."

Eddi came back from forward, but stopped dead on hearing that. "*A hundred and forty-four* humpbacks?"

He bit his lip. "Yes, miss."

Sara kept a firm grip on the conversation. "Tell me more about your own research."

Kimura reached for a napkin and began sketching. A strange, irregular outline, like a broccoli chopped in half. "Well, as I said, he found damage to amygdala caused dysfunction in social relationships. I am trying to establish what structure in whale brain corresponds to human and primate amygdala. A study at Emory University located a limbic-like structure in the brains of *Orcinus orca* with MRI imaging. Here, where I circle? It elucidated the gross morphology and described extensive cortical gyrification and sulcation. The cortical map is different from that of humans. No one agrees which structures mediate which behaviors. However, they described a cortical limbic lobe, here, and what appears to be a well-developed amygdala. For killer whales, as I said. I attempted to map the corresponding structures in the humpback—"

"This is sickening," Auer said. "You cut up a hundred and forty-four whales for their *brains*?"

"Eddi," Sara said.

"What? I just asked him—"

Anemone rocked and shuddered like an oxcart rolling over rubble. Perrault came staggering forward, rubbing his chin. When he saw Sara he raised his eyebrows. Under the table, where the man she was interviewing could not see, she pointed a thumb up. The captain nodded. "Sara, can I see you up forward?"

In the long forepeak gear stirred uneasily in the shadows. Bodine's worn chair was empty; he was probably still aft with Quill. Perrault eased the door shut and murmured, "Well?"

"How's he doing?"

"Jamie? He is strong. We'll just have to wait and see. The Japanese?"

"He's the real thing, Dru. A neuroanatomist, not a behaviorist like me. But he knows his way around the whale brain."

Perrault considered this. "What's he say about why he jumped ship?"

"We haven't gotten to that yet."

"Okay, let's find out."

Back in the salon, the captain ranged long arms and legs in a chair and sighed. "Sara tells me you're a brain researcher," he began.

Kimura nodded politely and folded his hands. "That is accurate, Captain."

"Cut up a lot of whales, over there?"

"A hundred and forty-four," Auer put in, scowling.

"Eddi, do me a favor. Go relieve Lars, on deck. He needs to be in on this."

"I was going to give him a—"

"Just for a little while. Please. I believe we are in an ice-free area, but keep a sharp lookout all the same."

When she was gone they waited in silence until Madsen staggered down the companionway, shedding snow and water off his mustang suit, cursing. He began stripping off the gear, leaving puddles as he walked toward them, his boots squelching.

"How's the visibility up there?"

"Not so bad." He half turned as Bodine limped out of the passageway, and the two men, each trying to get out of the other's way, collided clumsily. "Sorry."

"My fault." Bodine looked at Perrault. "He's resting. I gave him double the dose of cipro. All I could think of to do."

"Will he pull through?"

"I don't know, Sara. We'll just have to wait and see."

"Thank you," Perrault said. Bodine limped on forward, disappeared into his space, and closed the door.

The captain said, "Lars, we were about to get into why Hideyashi jumped ship."

"Okay." Madsen threw himself on the settee and stretched out an arm. Glanced at Sara, then back at the Japanese. "I'm listening."

"You cut up a lot of whales," the captain repeated.

"Yes." Kimura sighed, looking at his hands. "But they were already dead, of course."

"You're part of their *research* effort?" Madsen said, straightening again.

"I was. Yes."

"He's a bona fide neuroanatomist. I've established that," Sara put in.

"All right, then. Why'd you jump ship?"

"I am not only a scientist," Kimura said. "I am also the son of a priest at the Yasukuni shrine."

Madsen tilted his head. "What is that, exactly?"

"The principal Shinto shrine in Chiyoda—in Tokyo."

"What's that got to do with jumping overboard?"

"I have explained some of this to Dr. Pollard. When I applied for permission to do research, the executives of the institute—"

"That's the Institute of Cetacean Research?" Madsen said.

"Correct. They were very welcoming. They promised a laboratory assistant, a dedicated space, and a budget of seven hundred thirty thousand yen."

Sara said, "Didn't they come through?"

"Oh yes. They provided the grant, the lab, and the assistant. What they did not say was that I was expected to lie."

Madsen leaned forward. "Lie about what?"

"To receive the grant, I had to also agree to act as the scientific observer for the—they call it an 'expedition.' But of course it is not. As I quickly came to understand."

"All right," said Sara. "What did they want you to do—certify false results?"

He shook his head. "My results were my own. No one cared what I was doing, anyway. They just cut out the brains and carried them up to me in buckets. What they wanted me to certify—to lie about—was the kill figures."

"The quotas." Madsen still leaned forward, intent. "The Japanese government sets them. Nine hundred beaked whales—"

Kimura frowned. "Nine hundred what?"

The Dane hesitated. "Sometimes called minkes."

"Oh yes, minkes. We call them 'cockroaches' on the ship. That is right. Nine hundred minkes, one hundred humpbacks, and one hundred fin whales."

"But you said earlier you dissected one hundred forty-four humpback brains," Sara said. Feeling sick as she remembered the eerie beauty of a symphony in the deep.

"So they're taking more whales than the quota permits," Madsen bored in.

Kimura nodded. "When it was made plain I would have to certify that only the quota had been taken, I pointed out a problem. I had over that number of samples. Publication of my paper would make obvious the quota had been exceeded. I was then ordered to destroy forty-four of my sample sets."

"And you refused," Sara guessed.

He twisted his fingers. "Of course! I could not do otherwise. They tried to reason with me. Then said I would lose my grant, and not receive my doctorate. I still would not cooperate."

"Then what?"

"One morning I went to my laboratory to find that all my samples had been thrown overboard, and my data deleted from my computer. Because I had talked to others in the crew, they removed me from the processing ship and put me to work on *Number 3* cleaning toilets. It was then I realized that this was *kigare*, that I had brought it down on myself. True research must be carried out in the spirit of truth."

Perrault said, "What was that word you used?"

"*Kigare?* It is like karma. The *kami*—the spirits—ensure that one pays for what one does. Unless one expiates wrong actions, this accumulation of evil determines fate. I became convinced I was taking part in wrong, in killing these great creatures. When a man realizes this, it is his duty to cease the action and purify himself. The usual ritual involves water." He smiled. "So you see why jumping overboard seemed appropriate."

Sara sat back, uncertain how to take this. A student with scientific training, believing in spirits, karma? "And you feel this . . . ritual . . . purified you?"

Kimura chuckled. "I see your mind, Dr. Pollard. You are saying, to yourself, How can a scientist think like this? I know, it will seem not quite rational. But you forget, I am Japanese."

"And the son of a priest."

"Exactly so. I know there is nothing to these feelings. But the feelings themselves have objective reality. And I truly have come to believe killing animals with brains that show structures consistent with a capability for intelligent thought—well, you see where I am going." He shrugged. "No doubt you feel the same way. Or you would not be trying to stop us."

She felt uneasy at that assumption, but didn't contradict him. Kimura sat back and adjusted his blanket. He looked around and shivered. "It is really very cold in this ship."

"*We* don't burn whale oil for heat," Madsen said harshly. "So, you jumped ship to purify yourself. Like Sara asked: Are you purified?"

Kimura gave a slight shrug. "That is for the *kami* to say. The spirits of nature. Not me."

Perrault said, "What do you expect us to do with you?"

"I will assist in whatever way I can that does not involve hurting people."

Madsen said, "Even if they're doing evil?"

The Japanese said in a modest voice, "That is difficult to say."

Lars threw Sara a glance she found difficult to read. Suspicion, though, was definitely part of it.

The forward hatch creaked open. Bodine stood framed by darkness. "Captain? Answer to your message."

Perrault rose. "Which one?"

"To *Maru Number* 3." He waved a scrap of paper.

"Read it."

"Captain Nakame demands the return of the junior research employee Kimura Hideyashi, who was restricted to his quarters pending trial in Japan for drunkenness, disobeying orders, fighting with crew members, and destroying scientific equipment. He will steam to meet us. He requests our position."

Perrault swayed as the deck pitched. "No response from the home office?"

"Not yet."

"You will not return me," a soft voice said. "Please? If you do, I will only jump again. And this time you may not be there."

They waited as Perrault swayed, shadows beneath his eyes. The captain finally drew a breath and muttered, "I won't return you. No."

"Good decision," Madsen said.

Perrault looked at his watch. "I'll want you back at the wheel, Sara. With those sharp eyes. Keep Eddi up there as your ice lookout."

"Yes, sir." She rose.

"Mick, send the following: 'Message received.' Give them coordinates one hundred miles southwest of our current position. Then shut down. Turn off our radar and running lights. Sara, head north. Away from the ice."

"But you're giving up the fleet," Madsen said. "Heading away from them. That's not—"

"Until we get a legal opinion," Perrault said. "If anyone has a problem with that decision, I will be in my cabin." He started back, then turned. "Or, no. I will be in Mr. Quill's room."

When he'd left they sat or stood for a moment in the near dark. Then silently scattered, each to his or her assigned task.

11

The Corvette

She steered for hours, locked in the queer fishbowl world under the dome; within the boat, yet not. In all that time the seas rolled huge and empty under chasing clouds that only occasionally parted for a low sun the ominous reddish black of a rotting tomato. Each sea built off *Anemone*'s quarter, loomed, then burst against her side, seething the smooth composite with harshly hissing foam. Sara's mind wandered, but her attention did not slip from the one hundred to four hundred yards in front of the dipping, tossing prow.

Then something seized her thigh and she flinched, only belatedly recalling she had a body that was not the boat's, tendons other than shrouds, a consciousness not bounded by a saw-toothed horizon. It was Perrault. He clambered up to relieve her, their bodies twisting around each other like in an interpretive dance, or a party game designed to be played drunk. When she climbed down she staggered. Fell to her knees. Then groped erect again, and felt her way to her bunk.

"Breakfast," Eddi sang.

Sara woke from a sleep akin to death. Found herself shuddering, bare of blankets. Nosing her own dank animal reek. Was this what she smelled like to the others? Of too much perfume over underwear stink and old sweat? She shivered and reached for the damp sweater that swayed from a hook. Grabbed the handhold and waited for the roll and swung herself down.

Dorée stood braced in the galley, hair hanging over her face, pushing something around on the stove to the accompaniment of a popping sizzle. Plates slid this way and that, corraled by the wooden grid that kept them from flying off. Sara got coffee and joined Auer, Bodine, and Georgie. Kimura sat a few feet off, cocooned in blankets but still shivering. His face was lemony gray, and his gaze was locked to a fire extinguisher bracketed to the bulkhead. A glance upward told her Lars was steering. She murmured a good-morning that only Georgie returned. "How's Jamie doing?" she asked Bodine. He shook his head, squinting as if the light hurt his eyes. Their exhaled breaths mingled, white, vaporous, like visible ghosts.

Dorée lurched from the galley like a hermit crab venturing from its shell, caught herself on a stanchion, then slapped a platter down in front of them. Sara noticed that the rash, or whatever it was, extended up her neck now. The digits sticking out of teal gloves with the fingers snipped short were white and red with chilblains.

"Thank you, Tehiyah."

A sour glance. "I never cook. Remember?"

"Well, I see I was wrong." The eggs were partially charred, rubber at the edges. The toast, cremated. Shriveled, turdlike objects turned out to be soy sausages. Sara forced herself to chew one. Swallowed. There. Another bite.

From nowhere a distant voice whispered. Distorted, incomprehensible, but in distinct words. She lifted her head. The others looked up too, some quickly, others slowly. We're all getting stupid, she thought.

Norris-Simpson frowned. "D' I just hear something?"

"Shut up," said Bodine. They listened. The voice spoke again, low and crackling. Sara pushed back her plate and rose. It seemed to be coming from back by the nav station.

"VHF call," Madsen's shout echoed down. "Get the captain."

Sara crammed the last sausage into her mouth and lurched up, rising off her feet as the deck slanted away, then coming down so hard pain shot through her knees. She gasped, and scurried aft.

Perrault was a long hump under a pile of covers. She shook his shoulder and he bolted upright, striking his head on a fold-down bookshelf. He rolled out, rubbing his forehead but looking unsurprised, as if this happened often. He followed her out without a word.

When they emerged Madsen's voice was echoing in the bubble. The others were gathered around the tubing that supported his chair. All except the Japanese, who still sat tented and shivering on the settee. They parted to let Perrault through. He said roughly, "What is it?"

"Someone calling for us. Sounds like Spanish."

"Anyone here speak Spanish?" Perrault looked around, then snorted. "Okay, give me the mike. You haven't answered yet?"

"No. I figured it was one of the whalers, trying to get us to transmit."

"Good thinking. It's—"

He cut himself short as the radio spoke again. Madsen had turned the gain all the way up. "*Black Anemone, Black Anemone. Estamosla corbeta Argentina Guerrico. Black Anemone, Black Anemone.*"

The voice was definitely Spanish-accented. They all looked at Perrault, who scowled, scraping his chin with his fingernails. He sighed. "*Corbeta argentina*—what do you think, Lars?"

"Can Mick get us a bearing?"

"Three five five," Bodine yelled from up forward. "Just about due north."

"We last saw the whalers to the east," Madsen added.

"We last saw *one kill ship* to the east," Perrault corrected.

"True."

"You're our official CPL representative," the captain reminded him. "This is properly your decision as much as mine."

Sara blinked. This was the first time she'd heard Lars had any kind of official status.

"Hey. Hideyashi," Lars yelled. The Japanese flinched. "C'mon over here. Listen to this. Tell me if this guy's Japanese, pretending to speak Spanish."

"Black Anemone, Black Anemone. Esta corbeta Argentina Guerrico. Over."

Kimura shook his head. "That is not a Japanese speaker."

"You're sure?" Perrault said. "You understand, if it is, they could demand your return. And I might not be able to refuse them. Not if the alternative is being run down."

Kimura nodded, looking glum. "Absolutely. No possibility otherwise."

The voice took on new sharpness, as if it could hear them discussing it. *"Corbeta Guerrico. Te vemos hacia el sur a una distancia de quince kilómetros. Por favor, responda!"*

Perrault took another breath. "Well?" he said. Madsen shrugged and spread his hands.

The captain raised the mike to his lips like an unwelcome chalice.

The ship was three times their length and its sides towered like a gray iceberg. She heaved several hundred yards away, all sharp angles and slants. Riding, like *Anemone*, several points off the wind. A sea crested against her side and broke in trailing bridal veils. A single cannon on her bow pointed backward at a lofty pilothouse with square windows. The number 32 was painted in white angular symbols a third of the way back from her stem. Red and yellow and white flags snapped in the wind, and a sparse brown smoke stripped off the stack. At the mast whipped the same blue-and-white flag that had welcomed them at Ushuaia.

Perrault was on deck, supervising as the women heaved at the Zodiac. It tore free at last and slid down its ramp, the line uncoiling, and spooled out behind them, tossing higher than their heads, then sinking away. A larger inflatable dangled from the corvette, swaying and bouncing off the hull as the ship rolled. Men tumbled into it, and a davit rotated. Before long it was surging across the waves toward them.

"Keep her steady, now," the captain told Sara. She bit a fold of her sweatshirt pulled up from under her suit and concentrated on the compass. "We'll transfer one by one. Into the dinghy first. From there, to their boat. Be very careful. *Comprenez?*"

"Who's going?"

"Me, Lars, and you. They're bringing a medical officer to look at Jamie."

"I'm not?" Dorée said, beside them.

"I'm sorry, Tehiyah," the captain said. "I don't really want to risk—"

"No. I'm going."

Perrault sighed. Started to turn away, but the actress seized his arm. "Yes, Tehiyah," he said. "You are going. Tell Mick he's in charge. I want Eddi on the wheel."

Dorée went below. Sara concentrated on steering a straight course through the mountainous waves. Seas, she reflected, that would have had her moaning in terror not long before. She still feared them, but now understood how to slip around their blows and tap their immense power to lift the planing hull beneath her and surf at dizzying speeds for hundreds of feet before they sank back.

Not that she was doing that now. Not with the Argentine navy boat coming up astern. It disappeared for seconds in the troughs, but each time bobbed up closer. The crew stood black-suited, black-hooded, holding grip rails on the center console. The next time she glanced back they were reaching for *Anemone*'s inflatable. In a minute or two voices rose. A rubber-suited figure crawled past and down the companionway, a waterproof bag stenciled with a red cross slung over one shoulder. She glanced back again to see Perrault spidering into the inflatable. He slid in cautiously, hung to the line by one arm, then let go. The boat skated aft on the smoothed water behind the stern.

She faced forward again. Until Madsen said into her ear, "Okay, I got the wheel. In the inflatable, then over to their boat. Keep your hands and feet out from between them, and do *not* let go."

Getting into the dink was fairly easy, but as the boat from the warship roared in again she felt real fear. If she slipped, or missed, trying to make the transfer, they'd never find her in these seas. Not in time. Water surged back and forth in the bottom of the inflatable. She got her boots braced and rose, clinging to rope handholds as the other craft soared above her, then dropped nearly to her level. She launched herself and hands grabbed her arms. She stumbled and fell against legs, then something hard slammed her mouth so violently she felt a tooth loosen. Fuck, she thought. A front one, too.

Then the hands hauled her up and fastened her fingers to handgrips. The big swollen-looking outboards roared, and she clung like a shaken monkey watching *Anemone*, her world for so many weeks, shrink amid the rolling waste, the dashing spray, the clouds that pressed down. The whole world was black and gray and white. Monochrome, like in an old adventure film.

A wetshining wall so high it looked unclimbable. A sling came down, and she slipped it over her arms. It steadied her as she climbed a rope-and-batten ladder, straight up, until more arms reached down and pulled her the last few feet up and over.

She staggered crazily across a strange deck, stared blinking into strange faces. A sense of another life, another planet, another race. The weird sensation of another ship under her feet.

When they took them below her glasses fogged instantly. She took them off and was led through white-painted passageways that smelled impossibly clean and glowed impossibly bright to a huge space of vast tables set with white china with blue rims. Smiling stewards in starched white jackets served salads, chops, lima beans, carrots, whipped potatoes, fresh milk, apple cobbler. The food was the best she'd ever tasted and despite feeling queasy from the long, slow heave and roll, so different from *Anemone*'s, she ate until she could hold no more. Then came coffee, black and richly flavorful, and fruit, and packages of cigarettes, and small wrapped peppermints.

When they could eat no more, a young officer rose and led them through more passageways, or maybe the same passageways, and up a ladder until they filed one by one into a spacious teak-paneled room. Only then, looking about, did she realize they'd left Tehiyah back in the dining area.

A dark-complected officer introduced himself as Capitán Simon Giordano and another, taller, younger man as Teniente Ferrero. Giordano tried Spanish, got blank stares, and shifted to a heavily accented but passable English. "Please, you will sit? This sofa is very comfortable. You had a good lunch, yes? I would have eaten with you, but a report had to be made. Which is Captain Perrault? You, sir. Welcome. Sit, please, ladies. Where is the famous Tehiyah Dorée?"

"I think she's finishing her coffee."

"Perhaps I can meet her later." He bent to Sara's hand. "And you, miss?"

"Dr. Sara Pollard."

"I am sorry, I understood there was no doctor aboard."

"Not a medical doctor. A behaviorist."

"*Sí, claro,* a scientist—I understand. We supply our country's science outposts in Antarctica. Will you smoke? Do you mind?" They didn't and he and Perrault lit up, which surprised her. She'd never seen him with a cigarette, but he exhaled the sweet smoke of the Argentine tobacco with pleasure and what looked like haggard relief. Giordano leaned back in a leather chair. "So, you are comfortable? I imagine it is a change from your sailboat."

"We're at your disposal," Perrault said. "But I did want to thank you for sending your doctor."

"That is all right, we are all men of the sea." He waved the cigarette dismissively. "He will report shortly to me. Now, forgive, shall we get down to business? I must begin by asking officially, what is your intention in our fishery and economic zone off Argentine Antarctica?"

Perrault said, "Lars?"

Madsen said, "Captain, we are operating under United Nations charter. The World Charter for Nature authorizes private bodies to help monitor and enforce international conservation laws." He produced a slip of paper sleeved in plastic and read from it. "'Article 24. Each person has a duty to act in accordance with the provisions of the present Charter; acting individually, in association with others or through participation in the political process, each person shall strive to ensure that the objectives and requirements of the present Charter are met.'"

Giordano nodded as if he'd heard it before. "Yes, yes. But specifically, no? What are your aims here?"

"Commercial whaling was banned in 1986. Japan continues to kill, process, and sell whale products illegally. Not only that, they do it within an internationally declared sanctuary surrounding Antarctica. Argentina, by the way, signed these conventions. So you see, we're on the same side, Captain."

The Argentinian nodded. "But if Argentina should undertake whaling here ourselves, or mining, or test a nuclear weapon—you would support us in that as well? Yes, or no?"

Madsen shrugged.

"Captain Perrault?"

"Mr. Madsen has stated our case."

"Very well." Giordano took a last drag, stubbed his cigarette out, and opened a folder. "The Japanese have entered a formal protest to my government, that you interfere with their fishing operations and endanger safety of navigation. I would just as soon have nothing to do with this. I am not fond of the Japanese treating our waters as their own. But here I am on fisheries patrol and so the matter comes to me. They also allege you refuse to return a crewman who fell overboard."

"A student researcher who jumped ship," Perrault said. He finished his own cigarette and stubbed it out with evident regret. "He left voluntarily and does not wish to return. I am treating him as a refugee."

"They say he is a drunk and mutineer who fled to escape punishment."

"He has convinced us otherwise. In any case, to return him—a civilian—involuntarily is to place him in the condition of a slave."

The navy captain lit another cigarette, gaze neutral. Offered the pack to Perrault, who shook his head no. No one said anything for a while. Finally Giordano said, "And the charge of interfering with navigation?"

Madsen said, "We observed the kill ship *Maru Number* 3 chasing a mother-calf pair, which is illegal under International Whaling Commission regulations. We placed ourselves between the ship and the threatened animals."

Sara frowned. She'd seen two whales, but mother and calf? She held her tongue, though, as Giordano exchanged murmurs in Spanish with the other officer.

Finally he said, "This is a delicate matter. Here is what I will do. I will send my second in command to take an official statement from your refugee. I will not remove him from your ship, if he says he wants to stay. If Japan wishes him extradited, they will have to proceed against him when he reaches land. However, these other accusations I cannot ignore. I have prepared for you an official warning about illegal actions and endangering other vessels in Argentine waters. I will require a signature on this document."

"Perfectly willing," Madsen put in. "As long as you issue the same document to Captain Nakame, warning him about illegally taking whales, and endangering *our* navigation in Argentine waters."

Giordano looked from him to Perrault, then nodded and reached for a sideboard. "Perrault. You are, I think, from France?"

"Provence, by way of Quebec."

"Ah! Provence, the true wine country. Have you ever tasted Malbec? We have been out some time, so this is my last bottle. Lars, the lovely Sara—you will help me finish it?"

"Happy to," said Perrault. "Then we can discuss perhaps obtaining some fuel and steel wire, and other stores, for which we will be glad to pay."

The wine was sharp and deep and sparkled with sunlight, and she was savoring it with her eyes closed when a burst of laughter and music came from somewhere. The captain frowned, and spoke angrily to the younger officer. Ferrero swiftly left. A moment later Giordano stood too. "If you will accompany me," he said stiffly.

When they followed him to the bridge it was filled with sailors. One was strumming a guitar; others were eagerly focusing cameras on the helm. Where, Sara saw, a radiant Tehiyah Dorée was posing with dark hair shaken free over her shoulders, blouse unbuttoned to the navel. She held a plastic rose in her teeth and was dancing a flamenco—actually, with great skill and extreme vivacity. Sara suddenly recognized the dance from *Juan Gallardo*, the Steven Spielberg remake of *Blood and Sand*. Dorée had played Ina, Carmen's hot-blooded and sadistic sister. A supporting role, but she'd shone. Especially in Ina's final scene, where, trapped in a burning stable, overtaken by madness and despair, she'd danced until the roof fell in.

The crewmen swayed and clapped, hooting and whistling. Even Giordano stood rooted. Cigarette ash drooped, fell, and showered his jacket. He cursed and beat at the sparks. The sailor with the guitar played faster, then faster still. Dorée kept pace, hair flying, feet stamping, a whirlwind, a dervish. The sailors clapped harder, shouting, joining in a roar of song as the guitar hammered.

Then suddenly the dancer stretched out a hand, and Sara was shaking her head no, no, but being pulled out nevertheless into the center of the pilothouse. Dorée faced her, snapping fingers over her head, stamping her feet. She tried desperately to back away, but the sailors thrust her forward again, shouting.

"No. I can't," she said, and lowered her hands. The flame in Dorée's tawny eyes died. Then it rekindled as a short dark sailor stripped off his blouse and stepped out to the cheers of his mates.

The guitar became a storm, a passion of music that whirled the two figures at its core. Giordano leaned on the radar, grinning. A junior officer stood rooted beside him, binoculars fixed directly ahead. Past him Sara saw *Anemone* lifted on a sea, genoa rippling as she rolled. Her decks were stained and faded. She looked very small from up here.

A hoarse chorus urged the dancers on. Sweat spray flew from Dorée's dark maelstrom of hair. Her heels beat a tattoo on the steel deck. She flitted from man to man, reclining in one's arms, caressing another's brow, staring deep as a mesmerist into each sailor's eyes, leaving him dizzy and shaken when, at last, he reached out, and she spun instantly away.

She moved back to the center, and the guitar climaxed, strings a flashing blur. The small man circled her like a stalking lion, one hand on his hip, the other snapping fingers as his head whipped this way and that, flinging off sweat that glowed in the pearly light. The clapping and stamping had merged, synchronized. The sailors swayed; even the roll of the ship seemed part of the dance as Tehiyah Dorée's flying feet stamped out the flames that seemed to writhe almost visibly around her. And then the strings snapped; she clutched her throat; the scorching smoke overcame her. She slumped, arms and legs outstretched in a lovely mockery of death.

A moment of absolute quiet. Then pandemonium broke, and they mobbed her, hoisting her, shouting. She floated above them, radiant, streaming with perspiration, ecstatic in a way she'd not appeared since Sara had first seen her on the pier in Ushuaia.

Then the young officer lifted his ear from his radio. He beckoned to Perrault. Sara walked over in time to hear, "I'm afraid I have some bad news for you, *Capitán*."

The wind was even more incredibly cold after the steam-heated warmth of the ship. She clung as the whaleboat swayed and pitched, thumping and yawing its way across. A tightly lashed coil of braided wire, drums of fuel, and crates of fruit and food lifted from the floorboards and crashed down again. *Anemone* grew steadily, but still looked so small.

Guerrico's medical officer had said Quill's liver was failing. His kidney functions were compromised. To combat advanced bacteremia, they needed to run an IV. So Jamie had to go with them, first to the scientific station they were resupplying, then back to Argentina. They'd take the mate back to the corvette in this same whaleboat, but the weather was threatening to worsen, to the point they might not be able to make the transfer. So its crew had to return to *Anemone* now.

Sara hunkered as freezing spray blew over them. Back to our own cooking, she thought. A hundred yards ahead a tiny figure that must be Georgita was paying out the line on the inflatable. The whaleboat hung back until it streamed astern. Then the outboards roared again, and she took fast breaths, looking at the shrinking strip of deadly sea, preparing herself for the transfer once again.

The salon now seemed cramped, dirty, and bitterly cold. The musty air stank of old socks and mold. They'd cleaned up only days ago; how had all this black stuff grown back so swiftly? She stripped off her suit as two Argentines emerged from the aft passageway, banging a litter against one bulkhead, then the other, as the boat rolled around them.

On it Quill's face lolled, and she gasped. All the fat had melted from his cheeks. Above the beard his skin was jaundiced parchment and his closed eyes made him look as if he were already a corpse. She reached for his hand, but his arms were lashed to the litter and a blanket was strapped over them. She contented herself with patting his chest. "Get well, Jamie."

His eyelids fluttered, but didn't open. She patted him again, tears stinging, and went back to see if there was anything she could do.

In the mate's cabin Perrault was contemplating a *BraBuster* magazine. He stuffed it hastily into Quill's carry bag as she entered and began jamming in clothing on top of it.

"Will he be back, Dru?"

"With us? No. I just hope they can get the infection under control." He groped around the headboard until he came up with a red passport. This too went in the bag, which he zipped and shouldered. "Need to get past you."

She followed him to the salon, where the navymen were feeding the litter up the companionway headfirst. It slid up and out into wind and gray light. Flakes of snow whirled down.

"All right," said one of the black-clad sailors, whom Sara recognized as the medical officer. "We will leave now. Señor Kimura? You are coming with us?"

"I am staying with these friends, to help defend the whales," Hideyashi said, but he rubbed his lips with the back of his hand, almost as if to recall the words. His gaze grazed Sara's, then dropped.

"Just a minute," said an uncertain voice. Sara turned to see Georgita with a hand lifted, like a child pleading for a bathroom break. "Sir?"

"What is it? We must leave. Strong wind is coming."

"Sir, I would like to go, too."

They all twisted to look at her, even the sailors. Dorée said, "Georgie? What are you saying?"

"I want to go home, Tehiyah." Then she seemed to muster her courage; added, "I think you should too. This is not turning out to be . . . I've had enough. I'm just scared all the time."

Tehiyah laid a glove on the girl's arm. "Dear Georgie. But I've grown to depend on you."

She shook her head violently, staring at the deck. "You don't need me."

"Believe me, I do."

A brief light blazed in the washed-out face. "Maybe to clean your toilet, and iron your panties. But—"

Dorée's smile took on a definite stiffening. "But *what,* Georgie dear?"

"Nothing. Nothing." She ducked her head. "Sorry I said that. I was upset. And scared. Like I said."

"So you'll stay. That's my girl."

Norris-Simpson hesitated, gulped, then said, with a quick glance at the now-open companionway, "No. No! I'm not a fool." She took a step toward the gray light, then turned. Tears brimmed, then streamed down her cheeks. She reached out. "Come with me. Please. These people are all going to die."

"Don't say that," Perrault snapped.

"Really," Dorée said. "Georgie. Please." But her tone wavered.

"Tehiyah. *I'm begging you!*"

"Casting off," came a shout from above.

Georgita bolted. She pushed past them and seized the companionway handrails. At the top she turned and screamed back down, "Tehiyah! *Come with me! Now!*"

Perrault said, "If you want to leave, Miss Dorée, this would be the time." His voice was respectful, unjudging. Madsen stood behind him, pale, but saying nothing.

The celebrity activist stood irresolute, one enameled nail picking at the rash on her neck. "Well, then," she drawled. "Just let me get my things." She stood scratching a moment longer, then strolled aft.

"Hold the boat," Perrault shouted. "Eddi! Tell them: One more passenger. Tehiyah Dorée."

"And good fucking riddance," Sara heard Bodine growl, behind her.

She climbed the ladder and poked her head out. The wind was stronger, all right. The seas were building, turning dark as the clouds passed between them and the low sun. Another storm? Her innards shrank. How many more could they take? Maybe she should climb into the tossing whaleboat with Jamie and Georgie and Tehiyah. Then she smiled grimly. And go back to . . . what? No job, no life, no one to love?

She'd stay. But it would be an altered dynamic without the flirtatious superstar and her flaccid ghost-servant. A better one, she was willing to bet. It was *almost* worth losing Jamie as well. She just hoped he'd recover. By the sound of it, he was even sicker than they'd thought.

The stuttering drone of a ship's horn. "Tehiyah?" Georgie's whine, over the roar of the wind. "They want to go. *Tehiyah!*"

Sara held up a finger—one minute—and looked below. Dorée stood in the center of the salon, a carry bag and a hanging bag slumped at her feet.

"The boat's waiting," Sara called. She came down a few steps, to help hand up the luggage.

Instead, the actress shuddered. Dark eyes streaked with gold blinked up at her. "Sara. Am I really going—or staying here? With the whales? And you, and Dru, and Lars?"

"Well—*I* thought you were leaving."

"So did I." She shook her head. "But I don't think I am." She called up, "Dru, I'm staying."

"*Tehiyah!*" Norris-Simpson wailed.

"Georgie's calling you," Sara said.

"Tell her thanks for sticking with me," Dorée said bitterly. Then turned and carried her things aft, back to her cabin.

Sara stared after her, astonished. Then clambered back up and stood waving as the boat cast off and grew smaller, lifting and vanishing among enormous leaden seas, the snow flurrying down, harder and harder, until at last she could no longer see it or the distant ship at all.

12

Second Encounter

They zigzagged through fog and snow through a long nightless evening. In the morning Perrault called a meeting and rejuggled the berthing. Madsen, Bodine, Tehiyah, and Eddi stayed put, but Hideyashi got his own bunk. To Sara's surprise, the captain wanted her to move aft. "Take Jamie's cabin," he said. "A little more room for your computer, no?"

She moved with some reluctance. Her once-loathed curtained alcove had become a snug home. But Eddi helped and they pitched in with spray bottles and sponges to clean up the mess in the mate's cabin. More tattered, much-handled porn magazines went into the trash. They turned up their noses and made jokes as they disposed of dozens of beef jerky wrappers and even less-savory remnants of the mate's bachelor existence. They cleaned so hard Sara actually began to feel warm, and Eddi took off her jacket and worked in her German army tee with the black eagle on the front. But finally the cabin was habitable and when she plugged in her laptop on a fold-down desk and hung her clothes in the louvered teak vertical locker instead of stuffing them into a bag to mildew she felt as if she'd moved into the Trump Towers. "I'll miss smelling Georgita's pee," she told Eddi.

"Yeah, same here." They both snickered.

"If you want to do laundry, guess I get washing machine privileges now."

"Yeah, you've risen in the world." The videographer looked up. "Hey. Is it getting calmer?"

"Seems to be pitching less. Maybe we're behind an iceberg or something." Sara sat on the bunk and lowered her voice, not sure how much would get through the walls. The captain's and the master suites were next door. "I was surprised *she* stayed."

"I was hoping she wouldn't. Then at the last minute—bam." Auer shrugged and the octopus draped across her shoulder writhed. She cocked a biceps and smiled down at an open-mawed green moray as if they shared a secret. "So. Well, what the fuck."

"Maybe she's not like we thought. Or at least, not totally."

"Maybe." Auer's lips twitched. She straightened and heaved a sigh. "I got to take the wheel for a while. Can you do it after that?"

Sara said she would, and Eddi left. She looked around the bunk again. Then slowly, slowly, lay down. Eased her eyes shut. And drifted away.

Back in the bubble she steered for hours through scattered chunks of ice varied by larger bergs that oozed past on the horizon, when there was a horizon the snow and fog didn't shut down. The knotmeter read between eight and ten, not terrific, but the wind was barely ruffling the waves and there didn't seem to be any reason to go any faster. All that time the sun glowed remotely, coldly, never quite visible, a mere pretense of illumination. Then Dorée squeezed her ankle and said she'd take a turn. Sara could eat; Madsen had made spaghetti.

"Fresh peppers, Lars?" she said, finding a seat at the salon table.

"From the corvette. Hold your plate up. The sauce is out of a can."

Eddi said, "It's really getting calm. Calm and foggy. Spooky, after all that wind."

"I thought we were in for another storm," Sara said.

"It missed us." Perrault held out his plate for more. "Well, this is not bad. And our supplies will last longer now." He slurped noodles. "I feel much better, having Jamie with them. I know you were doing your best, Mick, but I was very much afraid he was not going to make it."

"Me too." Bodine looked as if he wasn't getting as much sleep as he needed. His stubble was solid beard along throat and jawline. Sara almost met his eyes, but he still wouldn't look directly at her. Ever since their near-close encounter. He reached for a mug of juice. "Look, Dru, what exactly're we doing right now? Far's as I can tell, we're heading away from the fleet."

"I'm protecting Hideyashi."

The Japanese smiled, not looking at anyone. He was very cautiously winding spaghetti around his fork, as if he'd never done such a thing before.

Lars said, "If we wanted to protect him, we should have offshipped him to the Argentines."

"He didn't want to go."

"Then you should've made him. We're down here to shut down whalers. Avoiding them isn't the way to do it."

He and the captain eyed each other across the table. After a moment the Dane added, "That's still our mission. Isn't it?"

"It is."

"Then we need to refocus. Mick, do you still have their signals?"

"Lost 'em some time ago. But I have a pretty good idea where we should head to reacquire."

"Captain?" Madsen eyed Perrault. Letting the question hang.

Instead of answering, the Frenchman unfolded from his seat and strolled toward the companionway. He paused there, wiping his face on a paper napkin, which he tucked into a pocket. Then swung up the ladderway and disappeared into the opal light revealed at the top for a moment like the snap of a shutter, before cutting off again.

"Our skipper hath spoken," Bodine said. "Or not."

"I'll have a word with him." Madsen threw down his napkin.

Sara hadn't cooked, so the rule was she had to either clear or wash up. "Can you give me a hand with this?" she asked Kimura. He got up quickly, grabbed plates, and followed her into the galley. "Do you wash dishes?"

"Why would you think I do not wash dishes?"

"I've heard about Japanese men."

He seized a sponge. "I can wash dishes with the best. If you will stay and talk to me."

She leaned back, folding her arms. If she turned her head she could see out the portlight. Fog hugged a black sea. *Anemone* rose and fell with a long croon, only an occasional clank or groan attesting that they were at sea at all and not anchored in some sheltered cove. It didn't look as if they were making even the eight knots they'd averaged on her watch.

She shivered, a random chill rippling up her spinal cord, and turned her attention back within the galley. Kimura was swilling out the pasta pot, banging metal, making a big production, the way some men seemed to feel they had to when doing what they considered women's work. "So, you decided to stay with us."

"You rescued me."

"But you didn't have to stay."

He worked for a time, then said, "That Tehiyah Dorée. She is a very nice lady."

She started. "You didn't stay because of—"

"No. No! But she's inspiring. Very warm. She really cares for the natural—for the natural world. You can see that. She is so famous. But she gives that all up to come out here." He swayed, smiling as he scrubbed. "You are so lucky, to be her friend."

She almost had to pinch her lips with her fingers. "I'm sure you can be her friend too, Hideyashi," she said, hoping she didn't sound *too* sarcastic. "It's very easy. Just do exactly what she wants, as soon as she wants it."

It went right past him. "You, for example, you are researching. Yes? Your theory of spindle neuron deficiency triggering rogue behavior. Very interesting." He glanced at her and gave a strange intaking hiss. "But I get the feeling you are not really interested in whales. Not as the others are."

"Well, you're wrong there, Hideyashi."

"They called me Hy in my English classes."

"Oh yeah? All right . . . Hy. I admit I wasn't much of an activist when I signed on. And maybe I'm still not as . . . dyed-in-the-wool as Mick or Lars. Or Eddi. But I'm not about to say, I support killing whales for food. Don't we have enough pigs and cattle?"

"Well, I agree," Kimura said.

"And just for the record, I didn't actually say, spindle—Von Economo—neuron *deficiency*. My hypothesis is a bit more subtle."

He rinsed, shuddering. She understood; the water in the tanks was icy cold, only a few degrees above freezing. There wasn't electricity to heat it, and sometimes she wondered why it didn't freeze solid. "What is your hypothesis?"

"Well, it involves the role of these neurons in slowing down the cascading of transductions in evaluating threats. I think you used the phrase short-circuiting, when we talked before."

Kimura squinted, a bowl motionless in his hands. "*So desu ka.* That would occur in what I am calling the 4, K area."

She frowned. "I'm not familiar with that localization nomenclature."

"I invented it. Usually, when we discuss neurological function, we talk about human structure. We say, 'in the limbic system' or 'in Broca's area.' But when we talk about whales, that may lead to false conclusions. Cetacean brains display many features associated with sophisticated cognition. But if it's not some organic lesion or deficiency, what you are describing is also involving what we call the developmental HPA axis—hypothalamic-pituitary-adrenal."

"Well, I'm not as keyed to structure as you are. I'm the behaviorist, remember?"

"Maybe if you put the two of us together, we would have one neuroethologist," Kimura said.

"Very funny."

"Well, I know whales. You know primates. All we would need is someone who knew elephants and we would—I think you say, corner the market?"

"You really do speak excellent English, Hy. Want to hand me that?"

"What?"

"That bowl you're waving around."

He looked at it, surprised, and handed it over to be dried. Reached for another. "So, expand on your hypothesis."

"Well, basically, that either physical or infectious trauma, or possibly social disruption, impairs the regulation function of these neurons. You say they're short-circuited; I say, they fail to regulate. Either way, the result's massive social dysfunction, and unexplained, sudden violent behavior."

She glanced away, all at once feeling her face heat. As if she were standing inches from a red-hot metal surface. *Gleaming teeth. White bone.* A sense of imminent doom speeded her breathing. Her heart throbbed oddly, and she had to take a deep breath. Another. The bowl clattered as she forced it into its rack.

"You are disturbed. Something I said?"

"No. No, something that happened to me."

She glanced behind them. The salon was empty. Snoring came from behind one of the curtains, she wasn't sure whose. Still, she lowered her voice. "One of my chimpanzees, at Brown. He went—out of control."

"Wait a moment." His brow furrowed. "I read of this event. A young woman. You?"

"No—unfortunately." She kept forcing herself to breathe. The words were hard to say. She had to fight to make her mouth articulate them. "A lab assistant. She lost most of her face, and her . . . sight."

A hand gripped her shoulder. "This is most unfortunate. But you could not be to blame."

She covered her face. Ashamed of the tears, yet unable to stop them. "She was new to the project. I should have been the one he turned on."

"What happened to the subject?"

"I told you. She—"

"I am sorry. I mean the animal. What happened to it?"

"Shot by a security guard."

"Was there an examination? An autopsy?"

"I tried to arrange one. The college said no. On the lawyers' advice. They said if I accepted responsibility, the school would pay a settlement. If I didn't, there'd be a trial. I don't have that kind of money. If it went to a civil trial, and I lost, there'd be nothing for the woman who was injured." She shrugged. "I said it was my fault, for not putting in enough safeguards, giving her enough training."

He squeezed her arm again. She sniffled, hating herself for crying, and wiped her face with a paper towel. Finally he said, "So that is why you are interested in the rogue phenomenon."

"Well. Yes." She blew her nose. Barked a short laugh. "Though there was another one, a very famous one, early in our family's history."

"Oh yes," he said. "Pollard."

"You know?"

"I put it together. You said you were from Nantucket. I have read the literature. About Captain George Pollard, from Nantucket, and how his ship was attacked by a sperm whale." He leaned to look out the portlight. "I thought that was why you were out here."

"Not quite so direct a relationship. But it did cross my mind, when I was invited on this expedition."

"Your great-grandfather?"

"Oh, much further back than that. And I don't know if old George was actually a direct ancestor. But there weren't that many families on the island. We're all related, the Starbucks and the Coffins and the Folgers and the Pollards. And then there were the—the circumstances of what happened after. After his ship sank, I mean."

"That I did not read of. What happened?"

She looked away, both ashamed and astonished that such ancient history could still affect her. "Well. After the *Essex* went down—that was the ship the whale attacked—he and his crew were adrift in the Pacific for months. This was in 1820. There weren't that many places they could land. It's a long story. Some say one thing, some another. But eventually they ran out of food. So they picked straws, and Captain Pollard's young cousin lost."

"And then the book was written."

"That's it, though they say Melville only met Captain Pollard after it was published."

"That was a long time ago, Sara. No need to conceal it."

"I didn't *conceal* it," she flared, then caught herself. "Well, I don't exactly tell everyone about it either."

"I understand, believe me. We all have not so happy things in our family history." He squinted again, not at her, and she got the impression he too was thinking of something personal and specific. But he didn't share it.

They finished the washing up and she made coffee and they moved out to the salon, where Madsen, smelling the fresh brew, slid back his curtain and joined them.

They sat for a while around the table before the Dane said, out of the blue, "So, you saw whaling up close."

"All too close—closely—I am afraid. It is not pretty, the business." He waved toward the galley, for what reason Sara didn't quite see. "And it *is* a business. Each whale, twenty million yen."

"About a quarter million dollars, I heard," Madsen said.

"That is about the same. As there are fewer whales, each is worth more." Kimura snickered. "Like tigers to Chinese. A very impure business."

"An interesting word," Lars said. "I'd use 'cruel,' or maybe 'bloody.'"

"Maybe 'corrupt' is the word I want. 'Impure' I think has the religious meaning?"

They nodded, Sara thinking how much better his command of the language was when he was discussing neurobiology. "Few Japanese eat whale meat. The ruling party gives subsidies. Gives children whale meat in school. But the fleet is under pressure, too. The commanders of the kill ships, they are driven men. For them, it is a share system. If they do not kill enough, they are not paid; their men lose money too. That is why they hate you."

"Hate us? Good," Madsen said. "Do you know Captain Nakame?"

Hideyashi tucked his chin, surprised. "Of course. He is captain of *Maru Number 3*. The ship they sent me to, after they wrecked my lab."

"He's the one who rammed our boat season before last."

"I heard the crew talking of it. You call him 'Captain Crunch.' Is that not so?"

Madsen grinned. "Yeah. We do." He sobered. "Slavery was profitable once, too. But whaling . . . we've got to stop it. Some whales—sperms, for example—have the largest brains that have ever existed on earth. The other groups just want to stop the hunting. But the Cetacean Protection League believes whales and certain other species—great apes, chimpanzees—should have some special status. Maybe like corporations—nonhuman persons, with rights and legal representation. Until they do, even if we stop harpooning them, we'll keep destroying their environment. The end will be slower, but the same."

Sara was pondering this when Dorée suddenly appeared, hanging upside down in the companionway. "Come up, come up!" she yelled. Her voice was so high it broke. They stopped talking instantly, and set their mugs aside.

The first thing she noticed was that the wind had died away altogether. For the first time, as far as she could recall, since they'd left Ushuaia. Its absence seemed unnatural. The second was that the sky was, not exactly clear, but brighter than it had been in days. Now and then the sun was even visible, as if through a worn wrapping of old gauze, glowing a cold, strange saffron, as if it had been replaced by some alien star.

Dorée was pointing ahead, to where that sallow light glimmered on a distorted city of pinnacles and towers, top-heavy bulging minarets with flattened tops. With the naked eye they seemed real, but when Sara put binoculars to her eyes they dissolved into wavering blurs. *Anemone* slid silently over a soundless sea, slow, languorous, and somehow oppressive, rippling its gently heaving yet dully mirrorlike surface in her passing. Sara shivered, gazing at the distant bergs that glittered and shone sapphire and aquamarine, topaz and carnelian.

"Over there," Tehiyah cried in a queer hushed voice. The helm creaked as she put the wheel over, and *Anemone*, silently obedient as some mystically animated conveyance, imperceptibly marched her bow around the horizon.

Toward two tabular bergs whose outstretched arms sheltered an embayment, a patch of open water that, unlike the mirror around the boat, seethed and glittered in the ominous light of that never-setting sun. Bits of berg gleamed redly between their prow and the distant sparkle. *Anemone* passed one at the length of a bow-shot. Penguins stood like patient commuters on a platform, watching them ghost past. The sail shivered as if taking a chill, fell limp, swelled again. She couldn't feel any wind, but it was still breathing them onward, as if the boat slid on slightly undulating, frictionless ice. Like skating on the frozen cranberry bogs, in the Nantucket winter . . . Perrault stood with one arm wrapped around the forestay, binoculars in the other hand. The rest came up from below behind her, and the forward hatch slid open to the seal-like hump of Bodine's head. Yet no one spoke; as if the distant city, the play and glitter of carmine light, were a Tír na nÓg, beyond any map, not to be prattled of, or its spell would be shattered.

"How lovely," Dorée breathed.

"If you'll move a little to the left," Eddi suggested.

The actress flinched and glanced back, as if, Sara thought, she'd forgotten for once cameras existed. She arched her spine and pasted on a smile. "How's this?"

"Great."

"Deep in the Antarctic, we relax during a rare break in the heavy weather. When it's calm, the sea is incredibly beautiful. I can look deep down into it, and watch our shadow moving with us. Ahead, over my shoulder, you can see two large tabular icebergs. Is that something moving, over there? Captain?"

"Whales," Perrault called back. Auer shifted the lens to him, but he didn't take the binoculars from his eyes. Far ahead, a tail lifted from the water, flourished, then slid gracefully under.

"Humpbacks, I think," Madsen added from his perch on the coach house.

"Really." Kimura wriggled up the companionway. He shivered—he was in just the poly-cotton blue pullover jacket and pants, and a pair of Eddi's Dacca shoes, made out of recycled plastic bags—but kept climbing, until he stood in the crimson sunlight. When he put out a hand to steady himself it landed on Sara's thigh. She stepped away, but he didn't seem to notice, just groped again and this time got a winch. "Humpbacks? A pod?"

"Doesn't sound like it," Bodine called back. She saw why his head looked deformed: earphones were clamped to it. He lifted one side. "I'm not sure what it is."

"I'm heading for them," Dorée called, and the captain, without turning, nodded.

The twin bergs slowly rose, the sky golden-white as French vanilla above them. Turquoise shadows shifted at their bases. Petrels and whalebirds darted across the fissured faces. At their base the slow swell, almost imperceptible in the open, exploded with a sullen roar. Sara clung to the lifeline. It was still the Antarctic, but the lack of wind made it seem almost warm.

"They're not humpbacks," Madsen called. "I'm not sure what they are."

"Killers?"

"No, they're all black. And they're bigger."

They rounded a point of ice, and there they lay. Blowing, rolling on their backs, tossing out their flippers. Here and there one breached, thrusting its massive body free of the liquid element that buoyed it, then crashing back in a burst of spray. Up forward Madsen was in an excited discussion with the captain. At last Perrault nodded, and the Dane shouted back, "They're right whales!"

"Rights?" Kimura and Auer both echoed.

"*Eubalaena.* I've never seen them before! Let's bring in the genoa. Then drop the main. We can watch, but we're not going any closer."

Anemone slid past another massive wedding-cake furrowed and seamed and spotted with lichen like old rust, or old blood. The sails hummed down and she drifted sedately to a halt and began rolling as her crew gathered on the port side, each with binoculars or camera or video recorder.

Auer and Madsen both fed Dorée sentences, with the camera off; then the actress talked excitedly into the lens about how huge these whales were, how endangered, how they'd gotten the name "right whale." "They were rich in oil, easy to harpoon, and they floated after they were dead. That made them the 'right' whales to kill. They've been protected since 1937. The species may be slowly recovering, but is still quite rare."

They seemed to be feeding, but in a leisurely way. The sea had taken on a strawberry-jam tinge, and looking down into it Sara noted streams of krill moving past. A current? Or could they swim? She just didn't know enough about this ecosystem. She lifted her binoculars, trying to pick out an individual, but in the flurry of feeding and play she couldn't be sure where any given right surfaced or blew again. They'd need to tag them with sonar transducers. Plot their movements with GPS. Any serious study would require more boats, more researchers, and far more time and money than she'd ever be able to assemble.

For the first time the whalers' contention made a brutal sense. The only way to extract actual data from whales was to kill them. But as Hideyashi had pointed out, that yielded only the grossest information. Like trying to study theology by autopsying a dead bishop.

She lowered the glasses, then raised them again. A whale blew, sunlight sparkling through the spray in a caressing rainbow. Calves roamed the pod, venturing away from their mothers. "Dolphins with them," Kimura said beside her. "Between that one that just sounded, and the floe?"

"I don't—I don't see them."

"Hourglasses, I think. The little black-and-white ones. We often saw them together." She realized he meant *we* as he and the other whalers.

Bodine poked his head up again. "Got something weird here."

"What, Mick?"

"Remember the 5R call? The five-click names? I'm picking that up here. Loud and clear."

For a moment she was confused, then remembered. "So there are sperm whales here too?"

"I'm only picking up one. And not in the pod, I don't think. Somewhere off to the west."

"Keep the tapes running," she called back. "Maybe we can get a specific call and localize it to a visual sighting." He nodded and disappeared again into the forepeak.

They lay to, marveling, for some time. Gradually the rights, wary at first, moved closer. Led, as both Lars and Hideyashi said was usual, by the calves. They were much bigger than humpbacks, their fins shorter, almost blunt, with a notch that reminded her of the leaf of a shamrock. At one point an adult sniffed within a hundred yards, close enough to make out the blanched callosities on its head. Kimura said these were small colonies in their own right, of whale lice, barnacles, worms, a whole ecosystem that lived on the leftovers of the whale's feeding.

"Is that enough?" Dorée said at last, tossing her hair over a shoulder.

Eddi lowered the camera. "If you think so, Tehiyah."

"There's got to be something there we can use. I'm so cold! I'll come back up later." She shivered dramatically, and let herself down the companionway.

The cinematographer set the camera carefully in its case, arranged lenses and memory chips, snapped it closed. She straightened and gazed at the whales. Said, tentatively, "It's been a long time since I've been in the water."

"Good grief, Eddi. It's got to be beyond freezing."

"We have wet suits. Lars? Wouldn't you like to swim with them?"

Madsen rubbed a dirty blond beard. "Uh . . . maybe. I don't see any leopard seals or killers. Really think we could?"

"We'll probably never have another chance." She fiddled with the case. "I have a waterproof housing for this. But I don't want to go in alone . . . Sara?"

"You're crazy." Sara laughed. "You're not getting *me* in there."

She teetered uncertainly where the stern ramp dropped to the water. The inflatable bobbed astern. The swim platform Perrault had rigged shifted under her weight as she struggled the fins on over heavy booties. Her whole body was sausaged into thick rubber. Under that was thermal underwear and a wool sweater, but her skin was still goose-pimpling in advance. Eddi kept saying it would be cold at first, then warm as the water next to her skin heated. What she didn't say was how warm "warm" was, and Sara was getting the feeling her own standards of comfort and those of the ex-trainer might be different. Above her Madsen swung a leg over the side. Below, Auer was finning her way to the inflatable. When she reached it she grabbed a line and turned. Hooked an arm and aimed the camera, now in a plastic housing. "Come on, Sara. Soon as you get in the water, it'll feel a lot nicer."

"Oh shit," she muttered, already regretting she'd caved in. Sailing to Antarctica was crazy enough. But splashing around in freezing water with whales—she had to admit, though, Eddi was right. She'd probably never have the chance to do this again.

"Waiting for you, Sara-o," Lars called from above. She muttered, "Shit," pressed the mask to her face with one hand, as Eddi had, and took a long stride out.

Blue light. Incredible, stabbing cold. She gasped and fought her way to the surface. The suit made that easy; in fact, it would have been hard to stay down. She bobbed, gasping and hacking, fighting to get air through the snorkel even as her whole inside seemed to recoil away from her skin, which was rapidly being coated in liquid ice from the neck down. The cold was so intense that after the initial burn, which felt like being plunged into hot grease, it numbed within seconds.

Beside her a crash, a burst of foam, as the Dane plunged in a few feet away. "Swim," Auer called. "Kick, Sara. It'll warm you up."

Shitshitshit. Sara, you idiot. She kicked. Reached for the line and followed it. More sea came down the snorkel and she coughed it out, nearly retching. Oh yes, this was fun.

"Get on the line. On this side. Lars, you on the other . . . Dru, you can cast us off. All right, everybody, kick."

She got the snorkel cleared and sucked a cold lungful. Activity did seem to drive the numbness back, so she kicked, hard, hanging off the Zodiac. The idea seemed to be to use its dull bulk for support and, maybe, camouflage as they approached the pod. They couldn't fire up the motor, of course. She kept flailing and kicking. Chills shuddered down her flanks. A stitch twisted a needle between her ribs.

She relaxed her death grip on the line, and her mask sank through the surface. She jerked it up, then realized she could still breathe. The harsh hollow rush rasped in her ears. She blinked, fighting terror, and looked down.

Into an immense blue depth. Save for strands of some brownish-red substance it was perfectly clear, as if she were floating in blueberry Kool-Aid. Except for the rusty drifting skeins the water was perfectly transparent; she could see every bubble-laced flick of Lars's fins. When she bobbed up again they were heading off away from the whales. *Kick* . . . she swam harder and they straightened out.

Gradually she noticed muffled clicks and a high-pitched wheezing. A grinding, like tectonic plates colliding. The cold retreated, though her face still prickled with icy pins. She lifted her head. The spouts seemed barely closer.

They came to packed ice and had to detour. Eddi swam ahead to reconnoiter a lead. A lifted arm beckoned them forward, and she kicked again, getting tired now, breath ragged, limbs lagging.

Then they were through, and the embayment opened. Above, a wrinkled, gently warping surface, intensely blue. To left and right masses of ice reached down, grown over with shaggy submarine meadows of bluish-green algae. She looked down into infinity, following red-gold rays that descended into the dimness until lost in a powdered midnight blue-black.

Through those searching beams coursed huge *things* of such power and slow deliberate grace her breath froze in the plastic tube that contained it. Like locomotives gliding past, but locomotives so perfectly streamlined, so minutely controlled, that the tiniest flick of a massive fluke altered their courses. As one passed she traced the slowly rising and falling tail, the seemingly infinite flexibility of the whole aft three-quarters of the animal. The queer distorted mouth, lower jaw so huge it seemed as if the face were upside down. Buff and white callosities dotted the nose and head, and a school of small fish accompanied it as it slowly passed. She couldn't locate the eye, but the sea was filled with clicking and grunting. They were definitely being examined. And possibly, discussed.

She let go, thrust herself under the raft, and finned after the creature, pulse suddenly lumbering with such huge slow beats her vision throbbed. But it moved on, away, unhurried, as if its internal watch ticked in aeons. The great broad tail slowly swept up and down as its outlines blurred into haze. Then it was gone, and she had to rise, lungs aching, and there was the raft, and the outlines of her friends . . . she surfaced strangling and blowing, and spat out the mouthpiece. "Did you see it? Did you?"

"We saw," Madsen said from the far side. "There's another off to our left. Come on, we'll swim in among them."

She hung on the handropes, panting, catching her breath. Hadn't he been the one excoriating whale tourists earlier? "Are you joking?"

"Come on." He let go, and swam forward.

She hesitated, looking all around for some dimly dreaded threat. The blue was empty, but it still echoed and groaned. And underneath everything lay that queer low grinding, which had to be ice, but sounded like giant wheels crushing basalt to dust. Dozens of white-and-black torpedoes undulated by at the edge of vision. She goggled, throat closing, before they snapped into scale; penguins, zagging with just as much grace as their vast competitors, but much more rapidly. She let go, retucked the snorkel, and swam after Lars, the pounding of her heart making things tremble in the corner of her vision. She glanced back to see if Eddi was coming, and caught an old-gold flash off a lens pointed her way.

She finned on, approaching a pulsating, fuzzy ocher cloud that at the edges fizzed apart into tiny creatures. She waved a hand slowly, trying to catch one, but they sensed the motion and evaded her.

She kicked on into the brown fog and her faceplate was blanked out by a darting, perking soup of tiny beings, so many the sea grew dark. The animals that drew the birds, the whales, the penguins.

Beautiful as it looked, this blue-and-scarlet world was a battle zone of death and feeding. She suddenly remembered, with a thrill of fear, how the humpbacks had circled, drawing their airy nets around these swarms; then suddenly surged up, enormous mouths agape. But surely all these clicks and buzzings meant they knew she was here. They could sense the trembling, pulsating bubbles of her lungs. Couldn't they? She looked over one shoulder, thinking to ask Eddi, but she wasn't in sight.

Lars jackknifed and sank, driving himself downward. She finned slowly to where he'd dropped away. She was deathly afraid, yet also queerly fearless. As if she too were one of these colossal creatures, masters of an icy universe roofed with undulating sun, floored with forever violet. But what was he doing? Hovering a few feet down, staring into the haze—

Out of which was taking shape—

The gigantic right coalesced out of the hazy blue, head-on. The huge curved mouth grinned as it swam, tail pumping up and down every four seconds. Bubbles trailed from its back, forming a silvery stream. They slowly lofted, rocking and glittering like rose pearls. The whale grew, passing just below them, and she saw Madsen had positioned them so. The fissured skin slid by beneath her like a passing asteroid. She reached down and closed her glove on the edge of its dorsal.

And almost had her arm jerked out of its socket. The current pressed her mask into her cheeks and made the useless snorkel flutter and snap against her ear. She rode for endless seconds, the massive beast undulating beneath her, the surface shimmering above, her whole body flapping like a flag in a high wind; until the whale rose, and she turned her face up and laughed aloud, being towed along in the open air. Then suddenly was all but deafened as a rubbery orifice snapped open and a blast of compressed air and funky water blew her mask askew. She let go and tumbled, and thought for a moment fearfully *the tail* but the massive slab of black flesh tilted and she was gently lifted, then slid off into the water again. Where she bobbed and spun, rocked by the massive backwash as her living chariot moved serenely off, trailing a vee-shaped train lined with a rocking slip of foam.

She hoisted into the raft and sat shaking as she looked around for Eddi. Her teeth chattered. No sign of the videographer. At last she spotted her, far back toward the boat, sitting atop one of the unstable-looking floes. She lifted a hand, and Auer waved back.

A splash, a blowing like a porpoise, and Lars surfaced. When he pushed his mask back his face was a livid purplish blue. "We need to get w-warmed up," she told him.

"Isn't this great?" The Dane looked higher than Sara had ever seen him. "This . . . out here, it's still Eden. Know what I'm saying?"

"Oh, yes—it's fantastic. Incredible. But I'm *freezing*, Lars. And your face—you look like a Smurf."

He made a disgusted moue but hauled himself in, rolling over the gunwale. They paddled back toward the ice. As they neared, Eddi slid down a chute and breaststroked to meet them.

"Why didn't you come with us?" Sara asked her, then wished she hadn't.

"Oh, I was just . . . I didn't want to."

"Those are baleens," Madsen said. "Not toothed whales, Eddi."

Sara felt like punching him. It was perfectly obvious why Auer had spooked. If she'd gotten nearly killed, sustained hideous injuries, she'd have had second thoughts herself. Different whales, true. Rights, not killers. But your mind could tell you one thing, and your fears something quite different. She said quickly, "You were probably right to get out of the water. We're f-frozen through."

No one was on deck as they made up on *Anemone*. They shouted up, with no response. Not until Lars tapped the hull with a paddle was there an answering call from inside.

Dorée stuck her head out of the companionway. Her hair was tousled and she wore a conspiratorial grin. "Sorry, Dru and I were . . . busy. How was it, Lars?"

Madsen's face went blank. He turned away abruptly and busied himself with the line. It uncoiled in the air, nearly striking Dorée. She ducked, still smiling. Then Perrault was there, zipping his jacket, grabbing the line, bending it to a winch. Sara and Eddi scrambled into the cockpit; Lars stayed in the inflatable as Perrault cranked it up the ramp. When the captain straightened, Dorée twined her fingers into his hand. He took it reluctantly, looking trapped.

"So what's the plan?" the Dane said tightly, throwing the paddles into a locker with a clatter. "We need to get after the fleet again."

"Hard to go anywhere without wind."

"You got fuel from the corvette—"

"We'll see wind soon," the captain said. Dorée stroked his hair and he looked pained. Took a step away. "But if we don't, sure. We could burn some fuel. Head east. Maybe find the processing ship this time. Press on, and see what happens."

Madsen stepped out of the inflatable. Without looking at either of them, he brushed past Dorée and the captain, and slammed his way below.

13

White Labyrinth

They stayed near the embayment for the rest of that day and through the Antarctic dusk. Waiting for wind, and for Bodine to come up with a direction to search. Madsen had withdrawn, as much as one could aboard a seventy-eight-foot boat; his answers were short, and when he made chowder that "night" it was barely edible. Bodine, too, looked upset, though Sara could assign less reason. Eddi seemed subdued; Perrault, by turns apologetic and brusque, as if reminding them he was in charge, no matter whom he was sleeping with. Dorée, on the other hand, bubbled, telling animated stories about her rise in pictures, about her first movie lead—in a college-zombies-from-another-planet semi-spoof called *Got Brains?*—and the practical jokes she and the other actors had played on Wes Craven.

Sara hit her bunk early and lay there, still shuddering though she was wearing every piece of warm clothing she owned. She stared at the overhead, noticing a spot they'd missed when cleaning the mate's cabin.

She closed her eyes, returning to the blue, surrounded once more by the giant creatures they were here to save. She wanted to engrave those moments into her memory, to replay whenever she was downhearted or doubted what she was doing here.

When they'd left Ushuaia she'd been an agnostic about this voyage (though of course she'd said the right things to the interviewer). But face-to-face, so to speak, with the great animals, she had to admit it: she was converted. To kill one would be nothing less than murder.

She looked around the table at her shipmates. She'd seen the flaws of each; yet each had also something noble. Dorée was a classic narcissist, but she'd refused the chance to desert. Perrault seemed more sailor than savior, but as such, he'd kept them at sea through storm and breakdown. Eddi was fighting her own demons, that was clear; but she *was* fighting. Mick and Lars were the hard core, the most dedicated. But each in his way was here to defend something beyond himself, and willing to sacrifice to do it.

And their newest crew member? Lars and Mick still seemed not to fully trust him, but that was ridiculous. It'd only been the sheerest luck she'd caught sight of his fall; Hy could easily have died in that freezing water. Remembering just how cold now, she shivered so hard the bunk squeaked.

She rolled over, enjoying the extra space, but missing her little portlight. The mate's cubby had none. A voice murmured next door. Perrault's? Dorée's? *Anemone* creaked lazily. The last thought that passed through her mind, before unconsciousness succeeded it, was: The wind must be coming up at last.

But when she went topside next morning the breeze barely cooled her cheek. It chased ripples across the water between the ice, but those leads were smaller. The rights were gone, though penguins still wandered the bergs like lost tourists. Then she noticed those bergs had drifted closer, and that a grinding groan almost too low to hear was coming from all around.

"It's packing up," Perrault said, lowering his binoculars. He looked worried. "I hope we can get out."

"Is that the noise? You mean we could be trapped?"

"Not for long. This hull won't stand much pressure. We'd break up and go down." He scratched his chin, which Sara noticed was freshly shaven for a change. "We need to find our way back to the open sea. Let's shake that genoa out and see if we can make steerageway."

"Don't we have a really big sail? A spinnaker? I thought—"

"We do, but this lull's not going to last. Trim in that port sheet . . . that's good, make it off there."

The grind of the winch and the thump of activity on deck brought Eddi up, then the others. Perrault took the wheel, looking from compass, to sail, to the ice around them. The boat gathered speed, but he kept her sheeted out to slow her. Which made sense, given the narrowness of the leads between the floes. If that was the right name for a tortured jumble of ragged blocks, some white, some blue, others stained all the hues of the rainbow. The sea lapped and broke, lifting the lighter chunks, rising and falling on the flanks of the larger. The huge tabular formations fell slowly behind, but if anything the ice cover increased. They picked their way through a wilderness: pieces large as containers, as ferryboats, down to bits that bobbed past smaller than doghouses, but still capable of punching a hole if a spur reached out. She hugged herself, looking down apprehensively as they slid past a low chunk whose submerged wings spread far out to either side, the lighter ice a brilliant turquoise just below the rippled surface.

"Tricky," Bodine said. The first time he'd addressed her directly, begun a conversation, since their encounter in the forepeak. He was propped where the cockpit coaming curved into the deck house, limbs splayed out. "This ice."

"It seems to be getting heavier."

"Driven together by the current, I guess. What was it like, yesterday? Swimming with them?"

"Unforgettable, Mick. It seems like a dream now, but I'll remember it forever."

"All rights, correct? You didn't see any sperms?"

"No. Would you find a sperm in a right whale pod?"

"You wouldn't think so. But I'm sure I heard one."

She remembered: the five-click signal. "Just the rights, and the dolphins. And penguins, of course."

"Calves?"

"Uh, you could ask Lars."

"If the rights can come back, so can the blues. So can all of them." He squinted off toward where jagged shards clashed slowly as they rose and fell on the long breathing swell. "People are coming around to our way of thinking. Every piece of research that proves their intelligence makes the case stronger. We've just got to buy time."

"I'm starting to feel the importance, Mick."

That sea-green gaze sought hers. "You didn't before?"

"Let's just say I didn't have the emotional commitment."

"Fair enough. Sometimes you have to see things . . . threatened before you realize how important they are." He looked away. "Wonder how Jamie's making out. I wish we'd hear from them. Or from Monaco."

"Sara. Mick. I could use some help," Perrault called.

He wanted her up on the mast with binoculars, scoping for a channel out of what was looking more and more like a maze. He warned her to keep a safety line fastened, and to come down if she got dizzy. She snapped a halyard to her harness, slung the glasses, and climbed the riveted bent metal steps hand over hand. When she looked down again the deck had shrunk alarmingly. She sucked a cold breath and quickly looked upward. The masttop was far as Heaven. Below forty, no God. She ran out of gumption at the second set of crosstrees and snapped the carabiners, locking herself on, and fumbled the binocs out.

The lead they followed was a dark blue crack through rough country. She yelled down, "This dead-ends half a mile ahead."

"*Crisse de caulisse de cave de tabarnak,*" Perrault swore. "Any that lead east?"

"I'm looking. . . . We need to backtrack, then take that opening to the left. To port, I mean."

From this vantage she could see order in what appeared chaos from on deck. Like shattered glass on a kitchen floor, the ice lay scattered randomly; but this floor undulated, grinding each bit against another. The wind was driving the loose pack into the tabular bergs to the southeast, but they weren't moving at the same rate, or in the same direction. The ice was shoaling up, packing, and in an immense game of chess *Anemone* was slowly being checkmated by the massive pieces that drifted and collided in unsettling roars. The engines coughed, then whined, sounding strange from up here. The genoa shrank, winding in as Perrault shifted into reverse.

The next lead extended a mile before it too was pinched off between two slowly rolling masses of dirty corrosion whose one flat surface attested they'd once been part of a tabular berg. The rest was seamed yellow and green like aged Stilton. Perrault hung back as Sara searched anxiously for a path. Finally the house-sized masses eased apart, and he nudged between them. They crunched as the hull slid past, and spun slowly in the plaited wake.

Bodine kept feeding the captain recommendations from the radar; Sara climbed a few more feet, snapped on again, and spotted a debris field that seemed to have a darker patch beyond it. She yelled that down, and Mick confirmed the radar showed open water in that direction.

To get there, though, they'd have to transit a zone of larger bergs about a mile wide. Perrault hesitated for a long time as *Anemone* rolled, picking up the rhythm of the swells, the engine puttering. Then put her in gear again and eased forward.

A slam and a lurch threw Sara against the mast. A boot slipped and she gasped, dropping several heart-stopping inches before the harness brought her up with a jerk. "Careful," Eddi called up. "Want me to spell you?"

"No, s'okay. My foot slipped."

"Warm enough up there?"

"I'm *okay*, I said." She'd spoken angrily, and felt sorry at once; but pushed it aside and concentrated again. The patch ahead was nearly solid with battered ice in every imaginable shape. A faint, almost mechanical grinding, like a factory floor, underlay the purr of the motor. Gray birds with white heads wheeled above an open pool a hundred yards away, dipping and rising as they fed. Penguins stood about on a slant-topped berg like construction spectators, watching them pass. She wondered briefly what they made of such a bristling apparition, then focused again. "Looks like a lead, about thirty degrees to the right," she called down.

"I see it." Perrault spun the wheel dexterously and the boat fitted her prow into the gap, no more than twenty yards wide, with needle-threading precision.

She yelled down, "Three, four hundred yards clear. Then a dogleg, but I can't see past that orangish berg."

Anemone purred to the end of the channel and angled left. Past the Creamsicle-colored berg a mass of smaller debris jostled as they rose and fell. Perrault put the prow against one and applied power. It bulldozed aside with a slow crushing noise. Sara felt the tremor all the way up the mast, and the shrouds vibrated like plucked strings. She sucked air and blew out. All it would take was one sharp punch through the half-inch composite.

Perrault must have come to the same conclusion, because he slowed the engine. *Anemone* coasted to a halt amid rocking SUV- and bus-sized masses. "I'm going to put the Zodiac in," he called up. "Sara, can you take the wheel? Eddi, relieve her as lookout."

An hour later they'd cleared the debris, working through with the skipper and Madsen in the inflatable up ahead, the outboard purring as they set blunt rubber against rotting ice and applied power. The wake foamed, the motor buzzed, and slowly, so gradually as to be almost imperceptible, a lead would widen. Sara would advance the throttle a few rpm, noodge the rudder, and nose into the gap. Dru had told her to be extremely cautious going forward, and not to back down at all until she'd checked that there was no ice near the screws. Some risk was unavoidable, but they couldn't afford mistakes. Tehiyah stood on the foredeck, filming the process with Eddi's videocamera and adding dramatic commentary about what would happen if submerged ice raked their hull. Commentary none of them really wanted to hear, but then again, one of the aims of the voyage was to get video the CPL could use for Web crowd funding and possibly a cable special.

"He says come a little to starboard," Eddi called down from the masthead. When the Zodiac was directly on the bow, Sara couldn't make out Perrault's hand signals. She brought the wheel right, leaning far out over the gunwale to see where she was going. The water was intensely blue-black between the bergs and she couldn't suppress a shudder, looking down. She had no desire to be stranded on this restless ice. Even if they got a message off before they went down, there might not be a ship within a thousand miles. She didn't want to think about their chances if that happened.

"Tea?" Kimura's serious face appeared like the rising moon, framed by the companionway hatch. Without waiting for an answer, he set a steaming mug on the cockpit seat. She balanced on one foot to reach for it, then sipped, keeping her attention forward. The hot sweet brew warmed all the way down. "Thanks, Hy," she murmured.

"A little left . . . slower," drifted from the masthead. She nudged the throttle back.

"Are we making any headway?"

"Creeping along, but we're getting there."

"We are chasing the fleet?"

"I guess we'll be trying to find it again. Once we get out of this friggin' ice."

"I would be happy to help. In any way I can." He looked away. "I feel you are all part of something. And I am not. Not yet. But I would very much like to be."

"Just let it happen, Hy. Don't worry. I'm glad you're here."

"Thank you, Sara." He sipped from his own mug, his exhaled breath an uneasy ghost. "The captain depends on you. I wish I could steer."

"I'm sure you have other talents."

"Do you want to talk about your theory? About spindle neurons."

"Uh, not just now, Hy. Got to keep my head on this. No offense—"

He said quietly that he understood, he'd see about making lunch.

"There are smoked 'kippers' in cans. Are those . . . fish? I can make *onigiri*—"

"Yes, kippers are small fish. You can make what?"

"Sticky rice balls, with the fish inside. You can eat them with one hand. Good for while you work."

She said that would be great. His head bobbed, vanished, and she craned to see over the deck house as a craggy, violet-seamed overhang loomed along the port side. The outboard whined, echoing in a sudden quiet as the wind died away again. Very slowly, the lead widened, and she advanced another couple of boat's lengths toward the distant flat sootiness she hoped was open sea.

They weren't that far from that longed-for haven when it happened. She was still on the helm as *Anemone* nosed into a narrow gap between three large, slowly heaving masses of chocolate-seamed ice, made a few yards, then slid to a halt with a crackling reverberation. Bodine popped up from the forepeak, yelling "The hull's bending in!" Sweat trickling down her ribs under the exposure suit, she checked that the stern was clear, eased into reverse, and advanced the throttle. The engines growled, then whined as the turbochargers cut in. The whole stern vibrated. But the boat didn't move. Not an inch. Just shivered like a whipped horse, and began very slowly to heel to starboard. She remembered the wire bracing the keel. What was happening below the waterline? She eased the throttle back, disengaged the gears, and walked forward, leaving the engines idling.

Perrault stood in the stern of the inflatable. "No luck," she reported.

"Shift the rudder back and forth. Race the engine. See if you can pry her out backward."

"I'll try, but I was at full power. She didn't budge."

The captain braced himself on the center console and peered up at the largest chunk, which rose twenty feet over his head. Roughly pyramidal, it surged with massive slowness, and *Anemone* moved in perfect synchronization. Madsen probed the black water with a bow hook. "There's an underwater shelf," he said at last. "That's what we're hung up on. Probably, by the wire brace. If we can free that, we could slide by. I think."

"We need to K-Y this bitch?" Bodine contributed, from the forward hatch.

They regarded him stonily. Perrault shook his head. "That's open water ahead. Let's see if we can open this gap up just a little.—Or no; wait; the boat's got much more power than this outboard. Sara, put your rudder full left. Your right engine, full ahead. The port engine, back down. That will twist you into this piece, and I'll push at the same time. If something gives, put both engines ahead and try to bull through. But if you hear more of that shuddering, back off."

"Got it." She turned and walked aft, bootsoles crunching on crushed ice that had fallen on deck as they'd squeezed past overhanging bergs. She was ready to get out of here, to revel in what felt now like the safety of open ocean. She set up the gears and advanced the throttles. The engines hummed, then roared. From up ahead the outboard rose to a whine as well.

For perhaps a minute nothing happened. Then, with a violent lurch, the boat sagged, coming free of whatever had snagged it—though it actually felt as if something holding it up had snapped away, suddenly subsiding under them. She craned over the deckhouse. Perrault, still standing, was circling a finger above his head, telling her *full power.* She hesitated, then advanced the throttles again, both together, smoothly, just as he'd taught her.

The boat lurched again and shouldered forward. But at the same moment the massive wall of ice to their left began to tilt toward them. To her disbelieving gaze, it inclined farther.

For a moment she didn't understand. Then a mass of greenish-yellow, creamy ice came thrusting up out of the sea on the far side of the boat, surging violently to the surface as if just released from bondage far below.

Her hands froze on the throttles as the whole immense frozen mass to port began to roll. With the underwater shelf on their side snapped off by *Anemone*'s weight, it was capsizing. Revolving, its towering upperworks coming down in front of the boat. Coming down right where the inflatable rode—

Oh God. She pushed both throttles all the way forward, instinctively trying to interpose the boat between the rotating hundreds or thousands of tons of ice and the bobbing Zodiac, but though the engines whined and the bowsprit grated, boring icy chunks out of its slowly rotating flank like a drill bit, she could not move forward at all.

From the mast, Eddi screamed.

Sara slammed both throttles to idle and the shift to neutral. Grabbing a throwable life preserver, she ran forward, slipping and sliding on the ice littering the deck. The massive berg kept rotating, with the low, rough grumbling of a giant gravel crusher. Half-melted angles reared up dripping into view, coated with shaggy masses of bluegreen algae. Crablike crustaceans scuttled over them in mad terror at the sudden exposure to air and sunlight, and the fulmars began wheeling and dipping with abrupt shrieks.

Each step seemed to take an age. By the time she got to the bow Eddi was right behind her, having unclipped her harness, wrapped her legs around the mast, and slid down fireman-style. The mass of ice was still teetering, sloshing the water in the lead back and forth like some superpowered wave machine as it settled to a new stability. They stared down into a welter of small ice, green froth, bubbles, masses of algae.

The inflatable burst through the surface, nose up like a broaching whale. It leapt halfway out of the sea, then settled back, capsized. "Oh God," Auer breathed, hand to her mouth. "Lars—Dru—"

"What happened?" Dorée shouted, behind them. They didn't answer.

A head broke the surface, and flung the sea from its hair in a golden wheel. Madsen. Sara aimed and pitched. The preserver rotated in the air and hit five feet from him. He took two easy strokes, grabbed it, and floated, craning around. Then yelled up, "D'you see Dru?"

"No! We don't see him!"

Madsen nodded. He looked around again, then jackknifed under. The water was so turbid he disappeared the instant he submerged.

Eddi swung a leg over the bow pulpit. "Stay here. I'll help him look."

"Be careful. Don't dive—there could be more ice down there. Please, Eddi—"

She poised on the gunwale and sprang off in a graceful dive, entering the water at a shallow angle with barely a splash.

Sara turned. Dorée stood struck dumb atop the deckhouse. "Tehiyah! We need more flotation. Life preservers. And we'll need blankets, when they come out—"

"What happened?"

"A berg capsized on the inflatable."

"But . . . Dru?"

"He hasn't come up yet." She turned back, wanting to do more, but knowing someone had to stay with the boat. Perrault and Quill had drilled that into them. And she'd been on the wheel when it happened.

Lars and Eddi surfaced together. They consulted briefly in the still-murky water, then dove again in opposite directions. The inflatable rotated slowly, bobbing in the choppy pool. To one side floated what must have been the shelf *Anemone*'s weight had sheared free. Snapped off the berg, it had reduced its buoyancy on one side. And the much larger mass had capsized, seeking a new equilibrium. The same process must have happened over and over to the misshapen, melted-looking forms all around them. No wonder Perrault had been so tense, threading his way through this white labyrinth.

She shook herself and lifted her head, noting that the lead was narrowing. The massive floes were still pressing in. Slowly barring their escape. She leaned over the bow and when the pair in the water surfaced again shouted down, "Do you see him?"

"No sign," Lars shouted up. His face was blue like a Smurf again. "He might be—he might be pretty far under that berg. The way it is now. Farther than I can swim."

"Look under the inflatable."

"I did. He's not. . . . I don't know where he is. He might have just . . . gone down."

Auer came up and floated on her back. Looking up at the sky. "Anything?" Madsen called. She shook her head.

"You both need to get out of the water," Sara shouted down. Flinching at its cruelty, she added, "He can't be alive now. And we have to keep moving. The ice is closing in on us."

"I know," Madsen called.

"What are you saying?" Dorée snapped, behind her. She had an armful of life preservers, which she held over the bow and dropped one by one into the slowly gentling currents. "Did you find him?"

"I'm afraid he's gone, Tehiyah."

"Gone," repeated Kimura dully. He'd come up on deck and stood shivering, arms wrapped around his chest, looking bewildered.

"Move up in the lead," Madsen called up, side stroking toward the inflatable. "Sound the horn. Maybe he came up on the far side, and can't see us to swim back."

Sara walked aft, the ice crunching again, and sounded several long, very loud blasts. They died in thousands of echoes, pealing out and away, answered only by the sullen rumble of ice. She sounded it again, then looked ahead. The lead was even narrower. She put the boat in gear with the engine still in idle. *Anemone* floated forward, almost too slowly to be perceived, and edged past the still-rolling berg with no more than a slight scrape, a nearly imperceptible quiver.

"Where *is* he?" Tehiyah breathed. "Oh my God, my God—"

"I'm afraid, still down there," Sara told her.

"No." She stood stock-still, palms clapped over her face. Hideyashi hesitated, then put an arm around her, but she shook it off. "He was my . . . we were soul mates. Oh my God."

"Help them aboard, Tehiyah. Hy. Snap out of it! We've got to keep going." Through her disbelief and shock Sara felt heartless, a monster. But regardless of what had happened, the ice was still closing in. If they didn't escape now, the lead would vanish. *Anemone* would be crushed, and none of them would get out alive.

"'Keep going'? What are you talking about? We have to look for him. He's out there somewhere."

"Tehiyah, it's been too long. Dru died trying to save us. Don't waste it, all right? We'll cry in a few minutes, when we get out of the ice. Okay?"

The actress wavered, then broke. She stumbled aft, weeping and screaming that tragedy followed her, that whenever she found love it fled. Kimura lowered lines to the Zodiac. When they had it turned right side up and in tow, with Lars and Eddi shivering but safe aboard, Sara pointed the prow into the next twist in the lead. The path from there was twice as wide and in a hundred yards the pack began to loosen, the sea-gaps growing larger and larger.

When next she looked over her shoulder, the berg that had capsized was difficult to locate among the others. At the next, as the open horizon yawned and she pressed the button to unfurl the sails, it had become merely another nameless and indistinguishable atom in the immense, slowly undulating mass of white, like a field of huge, blanched bones, that slowly dwindled astern.

14

Council of War

The sky clouded over and the wind picked up that afternoon. By dusk it was blowing at thirty knots, raising heavy short seas through which *Anemone*, heading east, rode with a violent pitching stagger, boom and stays groaning. After canned cheese ravioli hastily heated, they gathered in the salon. Now there were seats for everyone, at least once Lars asked Hideyashi if he'd mind steering. He said he didn't know how, which meant a twenty-minute postponement for lessons. When they reconvened Eddi poured more tea and they sat in the swaying light, grabbing for holds when Kimura misjudged a sea.

And then, they did not seem to know where to begin.

Finally Bodine cleared his throat and hitched forward. "Nobody wants to, but let's get down to it. Dru's gone. We all miss him, but he's fucking gone. So we got a decision to make. Where we go from here. What we do next."

Madsen said, "We sailed under the CPL flag, to defend whales. That's still the mission."

"It's still the mission, but now we don't have a captain or even a mate," Eddi said, then doubled over and coughed. She had on her blue track suit, a sweater over that, and a brown towel wrapped cravat-style around her neck, and wore gloves and a wool cap jammed low over her hair. Yet her face was still pale as a snowman's and she still shuddered so deeply now and again that her fingernails rattled on the table.

"Eddi, that cough doesn't sound good."

"I'll be okay, Sara.—We lost Jamie. Lost Dru. We can't stay out without them. So I think the only question is, where do we head to get back?"

Sara said, "Well, we all know the wind blows from the west. So going back to Argentina would be too rough and take too long. If we went north, that would take us to South Africa. Northeast would be Australia." She looked at Bodine. "Right, Mick?"

"Kind of. In a gross sense."

"Then it's not? If it isn't, let's talk about it now." Her tone was sharper than she'd meant, but then, his hadn't been so pleasant either. As if just by speaking out, she'd contradicted him. "How about food? Fuel? Any idea how much longer we can stay at sea?"

"We burned up what was in the drums on deck, but we haven't used much out of the main tanks yet," Madsen said. His eye sockets looked hollow; his face, shadowed. "As to food, we stocked for seven people for three months. Georgie made eight, but she's gone too. We've got five mouths now. So we should be okay for quite a while yet."

"Six," said Eddi. "You forgot Hy."

"Oh yeah. Sorry. But we've still got plenty."

"How long would it take to get to South Africa?" Eddi murmured into the slanting air. No one answered, so Sara got up and went to the navigating station. She rummaged and found a chart. They pored over it.

"Five thousand miles to Capetown," Eddi whispered. Then added longingly, "It'll be warm there. Summer."

"We'd be sailing crosswind the whole way," Bodine pointed out. "A rough trip."

"We went through a lot of bad weather to get down here," Eddi said. "Why can't we go through a little more?"

"If we did decide to abort, it'd be easier to keep going east," Bodine pointed out. "The way we're headed now. Then at about this longitude"—he tapped the chart with a blunt, blackened, nail-chewed forefinger—"head off to the north for Sydney."

"Sydney in the summer," Dorée murmured. "That sounds good too."

"Mick, do you know where the whaling fleet is?" Madsen asked.

"I get flashes of their emissions. Weak, but I'd call it southeast."

Hideyashi called down, "I know where they are."

They twisted in their seats. "You do?" Bodine said.

"They will be where the whales are: at the edge of the pack. You have seen this. Haven't you? Find the krill and you find the whales. Find the edge of the pack and you find the krill. I can tell you where that latitude will be."

"That gives us a cross-bearing," Bodine said. "Thanks, Hy."

"You are welcome."

The Dane said, turning back to the table, "Here's my opinion. We're still seaworthy. We have plenty of food and fuel. Losing Dru . . . no question, that's a major setback. But he taught us a lot. Not just how to sail, but how to always keep pushing. 'Press on'—remember what he always said? If this was the start of the cruise, I'd say, we couldn't go on. Especially since Quill's gone too—our two experienced sailors.

"But now we're all experienced. And the League sent us out here to do a job. Track the whalers. Get between them and the whales. Jam their screws, cut their lines, frustrate their efforts. So far we haven't done much, except make them look stupid over Hy. That's a publicity coup, but not a big payoff from all the planning that went into this. As the CPL representative, I think—"

"As the what?" Dorée said. "I beg your pardon, but I'm one of the people who're actually funding this."

"You helped fund this cruise, Tehiyah, yes. And we are grateful. But I'm actually on the board of directors. So since this is a League charter, and the captain is—deceased"—the others stirred, and he looked around the table, squinting inflamed-looking eyes—"I'm left in charge. That's how I see it."

"A ship needs a captain," Bodine said. "I don't think there's going to be any argument about that. And Lars's been out on Greenpeace ships. He's got more experience at sea than any of the rest of us—right?" Madsen nodded. "I think I'm going with Lars."

"No fucking way," Dorée said. "Jules-Louis made it clear to me there was a limit. He loves this boat. He helped design it. 'Bring her back safe,' he told me, 'and bring yourself back safe too, Tehiyah.' What about the keel? Dru knew how to fix things like that. Do we?"

"We can keep her sailing," Bodine said.

Another pause, then an appalling bang and racket from above. *Anemone* slewed, lurching over. Everyone at the table seized a handhold as the deck tilted thirty, forty-five, fifty degrees, until Sara stared nearly straight down into Bodine's eyes. Which turned away, blinking. He couldn't still hold their encounter against her, could he? She'd thought that'd blown over. "I don't know what to do," Kimura shouted from the steering dome, voice high. "Help. *Help!*"

"He's jibed," Eddi said. She let go of the table and scrambled like a spider monkey up the support structure. "Watch the wind indicator. Don't let it get too close to the stern, or that boom will go over again. That puts strain on the rigging. It might break. Especially when the wind's real high, like this. Okay? Understand now?" A murmur from the Japanese. "I know. I know! But we all had to learn. You got to have confidence steering," she added firmly.

"Okay, where were we?" Lars resumed when she climbed back down.

"I was saying, we're risking too much." Dorée smoothed long black hair that Sara suddenly noticed was lank and dull with dirt. The rashy pimples were even bigger, and spreading up that long slender neck. "There's a limit to what we can do with six people."

Madsen said, "I'd say, there's no limit to what six people can do. If they're truly dedicated."

"Hear, hear." Mick lifted a mug.

"We're all *dedicated*," Eddi said. "That's not the question. The question is, at what point is it too dangerous to keep going. With a damaged boat and all. I'm not saying you wouldn't be a good captain, Lars. But do you have Dru's sailing experience? Can you navigate, like he could? I think we should call this off and go home. Get another crew, see if Jamie's well enough to come back. Get the keel repaired. Then try again."

"We couldn't do that before the summer's over. We'd lose a whole season," Bodine pointed out. "Meanwhile, they're killing more whales. More even than we thought, according to Hy.

"As far as navigation goes, it's not like in the old days, with a fucking sextant. I can use GPS as well as Dru, and triangulate radio stations, too. We know where the fleet is. Or at least which way to sail to intercept them again. Now that we're down here, we should stay. As long as we possibly can. Okay, sure—it's risky. We knew that when we signed up."

The discussion guttered out. They stared at one another. Finally Sara said, "Well, let's vote. Is that fair?"

"What do we have to vote on?" Bodine said, not looking at her. "Lars's the captain. We do what the captain says."

"You aren't in the army anymore, Mick," Dorée said. "And neither are we. And Lars is *not* the captain, until we say he is. Eddi?"

A nod. "Sure. Let's vote."

"On what?" Bodine said again. Madsen leaned back, looking angry, but saying nothing.

"First, on what we're going to do." Sara tried for a tentative tone; suggesting, not advocating. "Once we decide that, we vote on who's captain."

"That's ass-backward." Bodine was openly antagonistic now. "What's the point of having a captain if he doesn't make the decisions?"

Tehiyah shook her head. "Dru didn't decide where to go. You're confusing the owner and the captain. The captain, I don't know how else to say this, isn't a—a principal—he's staff. He does what he's told, just like anyone else you hire."

Sara crossed her arms and sat back, letting them argue. They were coming at it from different directions. Bodine had a military mind-set. The man in charge had to be obeyed. Madsen seemed more intent on saving the whales than anything else. Dorée seemed to think of the captain as just another hireling, to be fired at will.

Finally Eddi burst out, "I don't get it. I won't even talk about how miserable we all are. Always cold. Always wet. Our clothes stink. *We* stink."

She coughed, a raw tearing rasp that made Sara wince. "But Jamie got hurt. Dru *died*. Doesn't anybody understand how dangerous this is? We need to go back before someone else gets killed. Or before *all* of us do." She half turned and called up, "Hy, you listening? Do you have anything to say?"

"I am not really one of you. I will do whatever is decided."

"Thanks for that," Auer muttered.

Bodine slammed his hands down. "Okay, if we got to, let's vote. Go back, or stay out. For going back?"

"Me." Eddi's hand shot up. Sara gave it a moment, then added her own. Looked around the table. At Dorée, who smiled at her, but made no move to raise a hand.

"Two for—for Australia? Right. Okay, all for continuing to chase the fleet." He lifted his own hand, and Madsen immediately did too.

They all looked at Dorée again, but she still hadn't moved. "Tehiyah?" Eddi said. "You didn't vote."

"There are good arguments for both sides." She tossed her hair back, enjoying the attention. Good grief, Sara thought. The actress stretched languorously, playing the slow move for all it was worth. "It's very dangerous. We all know that. Especially me. Considering what I've lost . . . *who* I've lost. The one I loved. The only one who understood me." She covered her face. "I can't . . . No. I can't go on."

Eddi patted her shoulder. "Poor honey. You've given up more than any of us. To come down here, and go through so much." She rolled her eyes at Sara.

"I know." She sobbed for a moment, then gazed up through shining tears. "But when you care about something, so much, that's—that's really when you can't stop to count the cost."

"Tehiyah?"

"Yes, Lars?"

"Dru gave his life for this. Are you going to say he gave it for nothing? If we turn back, that's what it means."

"No it doesn't," Sara said. "You can't say what he'd have done, Lars."

"Tehiyah, you're the swing vote," Eddi told her. "You have to decide."

She looked slowly around, lower lip caught in flawless teeth. Very slowly, she raised one hand. "All right then. I vote . . ."

They all waited, Sara feeling like she was going to scream. In another moment, she would. She promised herself that. Dorée's gaze sought the overhead, calling on Heaven itself to witness this moment.

"I vote yes," she said.

"For what?" "Which way?" "How?"

"I vote . . . we keep on." She half smiled through tears. "If Lars thinks that's what we should do."

Sara hammered the table so hard her wrist hurt. "You want to *stay out here*?"

"That's how she just voted," Bodine observed.

"But she hasn't—"

"Three to two," Madsen said coldly. "So we press on."

"For how long?" Sara was trying hard not to sound desperate, or weepy. "We really don't even know how to sail. And the engines, how do we—"

"We know enough." Bodine cut in. "That's what we came here for. So let's do it."

"Sara, enough. It's settled," Dorée murmured.

She vibrated, angry, frightened too. Then forced herself to sink back into her chair. *Anemone* chose that moment to launch herself into the sky, so she ended up floating, gripping the table edge, before the boat crashed down again, stabbing pain up her backbone.

"And Lars takes over as captain," Bodine pressed. Madsen looked from face to face, but no one objected this time.

"So what about—about what Sara just asked? When *do* we go back, Lars?" Eddi asked him. "After somebody else gets hurt, or dies? Or what? I just want to know."

"We don't leave until we've done what we came so far to do."

"And what is that, Lars? Exactly?" Sara asked him. "If you're the captain, we ought to know."

He looked away then, and the pale blue eyes seemed to see far beyond the hull. "You want to know what I think? Seriously? Okay. We're in a war. But a different kind than people used to fight."

Across from them, Bodine smiled grimly.

"A war," Eddi said. "Against who?"

Madsen took a breath and lifted his head. He looked from gaze to gaze, and those pale blue eyes widened. "I think . . . no . . . this is something new. People used to have to fight just to survive. Darwin, and all that. Then they fought each other. For land, and gold and stuff. But now we don't have to. Or else, it's just too dangerous—we'd destroy the world, if we really got going."

"So we're in a war for the whales?" Sara asked him.

"It's bigger than that. There's so many of us, and we've got so much power. Like, you saw the krill. The penguins, the killers, the sea lions. That whole struggle-for-existence thing. We came out of that. But we came out on top.

"So that makes us . . . responsible, now. We could kill every whale and lion and elephant, but what would it prove?" The boat staggered, and he and Bodine, beside him, gripped each other to keep from falling backward. "They used to think God was in charge, or Nature. Well, we killed God, and we're working on Nature. We can keep murdering, until there's nothing left. Or else start acting like we know what we're doing.

"That's what we're down here for. To strike a blow. And we can't go back before we do."

Sara took a deep breath, feeling even less reassured than before he'd explained. The two men sat close together, legs crossed the same way, body language echoing each other's. "What *kind* of a blow, Lars? How hard? We just want to know when we can say, we're done."

"We'll know. Don't worry about that," Bodine said.

Madsen looked around again, then hoisted himself. Clinging to the table, then the support beams as he made his way to the steering station. He called up, "Hy? Bring her around to starboard. Course, about one one five. —That about right, Mick?"

"It'll get us to the vicinity," Bodine said. "I'll plot what Hy gives us, for the pack edge, and cross-check that against my bearings."

As the steering creaked and *Anemone* heeled under them Dorée got to her feet too. She wiped her eyes and smiled brightly. "So, all together now? No more arguing? Then I have something for everybody. Finish your tea. Eddi, would you please—the camera? To get this, for the special?"

She slugged back what was left in her white-and-blue-striped *Anemone* mug, and poured it full from a square dark bottle. Rum, Sara saw. "All for one," Tehiyah said, lifting the brimming mug, and the dark liquid topped its rim and spattered the table as the very air staggered. "To fight to the end, like Lars says. Drink, and pass."

"Absolutely," said Madsen, and Bodine murmured something Sara didn't catch. The actress tilted it back for a long swallow, then handed it to Eddi. Who set the camera aside, hesitated, then took it. Her throat worked. Then she doubled, coughing. "Leave some for us," Bodine said, and Lars chuckled. They drank next.

The mug came to Sara. She looked down into the black fluid. What they were celebrating, or ratifying, she wasn't sure. But the vote had been taken. She raised it to her lips. The hot vaporish sweetness opened her sinuses. Her throat, her stomach, craved its warmth, its lethean forgetfulness.

Instead she lowered it without tasting. Saying nothing, just passing it on to Tehiyah. Who threw her a glance sharp as shattered glass. She lifted it in both hands, and set it down empty, exhaling, her eyes closed.

"Thanks for the vote of confidence, everyone," Lars said. "I'm not Dru Perrault. But I'll try to do a good job."

"You'll do fine," Dorée said, opening those tawny eyes to look directly into the camera. Smiling into the unwinking ruby, as *Anemone* moaned and crackled around her, whispering through the endless swells.

15

The Holocaust

The wind gusted and ebbed, but gradually blew harder, until they had to run under mere scraps of sail. Madsen held a southeast course as Bodine, secluded in the forepeak, kept at the search. The self-steerer had shown long before that it could not handle such enormous and unpredictable forces. They couldn't steer from the dome: the ice lay too low to spot. Human eyes had to blink into the wind to find it, human minds had to anticipate the next rolling crest, human muscles had to strain to evade the frigid mountains that toppled and fell with the thunder of avalanches. The days dissolved into an endless round of watches and miserable, half-awake bunk time. Sara and Eddi and Lars and Hy took turn and turn about as the gusts came hard and the granite seas grew out of the fog behind them, towered, and then collapsed, shooting forward in violent topplings that sometimes submerged the watchstanders beneath murky, bubble-lined green. Sometimes they could manage only half an hour before sagging exhausted, arms screaming, minds blasted numb. But always *Anemone* shook off the sea's claws, rolled upright, and breached again to the cinder-dim sky under hurtling clouds.

Two days after the conference Sara twisted as Eddi slid past her to the helm. The smaller woman's arms bulged to take the strain Sara released. Without thought, from habit, ritual, their hands sought each other, and she felt or at least imagined through wool and rubber the disappearing-faint heat of live flesh in the midst of immense cold. Then released it as the smaller woman concentrated on the compass. Sara crumpled, nearly falling, unlocking her attention from the gray wool-skeins that blew low over the wave-tops, the writhing, troubling figures that after anguished staring had begun to haunt the banks of fog.

She picked her way down to the salon and collapsed in a weak-kneed heap on the wet deck. Water surged back and forth. No one had time to clean now. Black strands spidered across white composite, and a choking smell permeated the freezing air. A sea thundered overhead, hammering the hull so hard it flexed, cracking and popping as it bent and sprang back. How many times, she wondered, before resin fatigued. How long before carbon composite and stainless steel gave way, the mast toppled, the keel pin snapped. Nothing endured forever.

Nothing save stubborn resolve. The Dane hunched at the nav table hour after hour, the screen of the chartplotter glowing multicolored in the dim. From time to time Bodine would drag aft, metal and plastic clattering against stanchion and settee, and the two would confer over a printout. Only now and then could they pick up the electronic murmurs of their quarry. Bodine said darkly that the Japanese must be minimizing their transmissions. Kimura sat with them over the charts, all three reeling, eyes red-rimmed, lips slack. And gradually the emissions grew louder. Closer. They spread across a narrow arc of bearing Bodine said indicated they were closing in on a fleet that moved now not as a colony but as a single organism.

The clicks on the radio expanded into the burble of distant conversation, then discernible speech. Kimura huddled, eavesdropping. Bearings and longitudes went onto the chart and lines were drawn and the limits of the ice were debated. *Anemone* plunged and rose through the olivine seas. And those who ministered to her slept and rose and fought, and tried to sleep again, lying awake as the freezing waves tried to crush her under. And failed. And failed. And failed again.

But someday, Sara thought, nursing a mug of reheated cocoa without cream or sugar, something would go bang, or someone would misjudge one of those racing mountains, and over she'd topple. End over end, snapping spreaders and sheets and the long bones of those within. Or perhaps simply cut into one of these gigantic waves at a deeper angle than usual, and never emerge.

Her lids drifted closed. The boat lurched; she snapped awake as the overturned mug cascaded chocolate dark as blood over the tabletop, running first toward her, then hesitating, pausing, recoiling as the bow surged upward. She snatched a damp towel.

Bodine, at the opening of the forepeak. Hanging by long arms, legless, brachiopoid. He stared with eyes like burned-out holes. "Lars up here?"

"Haven't seen him. Probably aft." The Dane had taken Perrault's cabin without comment, simply moved his sleeping bag in.

"Mind getting him up? I'm picking up sonar."

"Sonar? Not radar?"

"You heard what I said." He turned his gaze away, still hanging there as the boat romped. Kimura peered sleepily out from behind blue cloth, gaze unfocused; then the curtain twitched closed again.

She blinked and rubbed her face with the towel, wincing at the rancid mildew stink. Then reached her way aft, hunched to keep her center of gravity low.

Madsen was snoring. She shook him awake and told him what Bodine wanted. He stared blinking, lids crusted with brown matter, blond beard stained dark. His look was sunk away, as if she stared down at him through many fathoms of seething brit. He unzipped the dirty flap of his sleeping bag and worked chilblained feet into sea boots. "Be right out," he mumbled.

When she followed him into the forepeak, only gradually could she make out the veteran in his accustomed seat. "What you got?" Madsen asked. Triggering a keep-silent, warding-off gesture as the bent figure glared down unblinking at the screen.

Finally it straightened. "Sonar. Close-range, high-frequency pings. Some low subsonics, too," he muttered.

"What kind? What do you mean?"

"The kind ice makes. That full-spectrum grinding. And a funny clicking . . . not really sure what that is."

Sara rubbed her face, remembering the colliding chaos that had all but swallowed *Anemone*; that even yet held their captain's body. If the creatures of sea and sky had not yet picked his skeleton clean. Bodine oozed a knob around, spiraling in on a flickering spoke that danced, danced, slowly solidifying. "Can't be far off. Not getting it this loud."

"How far? How many?"

"All I can say is, more than one. We'll see them today, we hold this speed. So best get ready, figure out what we're going to do."

Madsen nodded slowly.

Preparations took several hours, including a long time just trying to get the engines running. They started, but shut down after two or three minutes. Finally, crawling and worming through the engine room, she and Bodine discovered why. The strainers that filtered their cooling water were frozen into bronze-jacketed popsicles. As he chipped at them, and she carried boiling water from the galley, Madsen was supervising preparations on deck.

They heard the detonations from far off in the fog. Low-pitched booms, spaced minutes apart. By then they were on deck, the sail reefed hard as they slid between spaced swells. Sara balanced gripping the forestay as *Anemone* dipped and rose, scanning the sea as it emerged like rippled lavender silk from low-hanging fog. Madsen had rigged a black wire along the stay's leading edge, running all the way to the masthead. He'd cautioned them to keep their hands away from it.

"Ice," she shouted, and threw a glance back to make sure Lars, at the wheel now, heard. He lifted a hand. They hissed past a corroded, slowly rolling wedge of seamed malachite and ultramarine as it heaved, surrounded by a mass of greenish foam and smaller bobbing bits. A thin transparent slick rolled to and fro beneath her boots, mixed with ice fallen from the rigging. Her heart hammered in her throat. Her fingers clutched and loosened on the icy stay as another detonation boomed out, closer, though she could see nothing.

The fog thinned. They slid past another slowly heaving raft of ice to emerge into air not clear, yet not completely impenetrable.

The fog seemed to rise, to stream upward, revealing like an ascending stage curtain a scene miles across, littered with floating bergies, backdropped with the icy rampart of a great flat-topped floe. It shone like pink quartz in the reddish radiance of a low-burning sun layered with thin strips of cloud like wrappings on an infected wound. In the foreground, dozens of dark shapes huddled low in the water, herded together and facing outward, as around and among them sliced the swift hulls of the kill craft. Far off to the south, a ghostly castle rose above the fog that hung close to the sea in that quarter: the many-storied upperworks of a much larger ship than any they'd seen thus far.

"Oh my God," Tehiyah said, from a few feet aft. Sara gazed without speaking, frozen to the stay. As they watched a *thing* darted from the bow of one of the killers, and a thin instantaneous line drew itself across air and sea. The boom echoed away into the fog. The speedily extended line arrested with a second, muted detonation, piercing a shining-black mass that instantly recoiled, flukes and tail lashing dark water into a welter that within seconds was tinged pink. Behind and beyond it a second killer rotated in swift tight circles, fastened by a second line to something beneath. That line vibrated, churning white where it met black sea, yet showing nothing of that which fought for its life below.

"Get set," Madsen called from aft. Both women flinched and half turned. Sara wanted to look away, but couldn't.

Half a mile distant the flurry where the line led down turned saffron, then bloody. The minke emerged, its slim sharp shape queerly small to the eye after the more massive rights and humpbacks. Still fighting, but obviously weakening. The ship ranged up to it, towering above it. A tiny figure bent over the gunwale, aiming down. The distant pop of a rifle, negligible, almost comic after the deeper detonation of the harpoon gun, snapped over the water. Then another.

She let go a shuddering breath and took another, deep, trying to steady herself as with a rustling clatter the main shook out its reefings and the deck beneath her heeled, picking up speed. Across the nearly flat water, lee'd by the masses of ice that half ringed it, were scattered smaller bits that were nonetheless large enough to punch through *Anemone*'s hull.

Behind her the remaining crew were taking their positions. They wore hard hats and flotation vests, exposure suits and safety harnesses. Eddi snapped a carabiner to lash herself to the mast, cameras dangling like cavalry pistols on fluorescent lanyards. Hy and Tehiyah were laying out hanks of mooring line. In the forward hatch Bodine weighed tear gas grenades, one in each hand. Their gazes met. He called, "*Maru Number 1*, off to port. Another killer to starboard. Can't see who yet. That big one off by the berg, that's the factory ship. *Ishinomaki Maru*." He hefted one of the gray canisters. "Know how to use these?"

"No."

"Pull this pin and throw. Fast and hard. Get it up on their deck, as close to the pilothouse as you can."

"You throw, Mick. I have to watch for ice."

"Hold on, we're coming around," Eddi called, apparently relaying word from aft. Sara braced her boots. *Anemone* heeled. With a hoarse cough the engines began to hum, and she accelerated in earnest. Sara sank to her knees, clutching the rail of the bow pulpit, bracing her knees against the deck as it tilted farther and farther, trying to cant her off into the greenblack sea that rushed past faster and faster only a few feet below. She scrabbled and only barely caught herself before she slid over.

When she looked up again the whale was almost on them. Dead, or perhaps still dying; rolling, with the sea breaking over its bloody, blown-open back. The harpoon had penetrated only shallowly before exploding, scooping a hole the size of a wheelbarrow. Blubber and flesh was peeled back, layers beneath layers, raw red and yellow beneath graphite, revealing deep within the pumping bellows of blue-veined lungs. A spring of blood welled up in pulses and lapped like a pool and ran down its sides, turning the water around the dying creature a dull red through which sinuous shapes maneuvered and twisted, bathing in scarlet slantwise prisms of sunlight that searched the green depths. Half turned on its side, pointed head parallel to the boat's course, the animal's tiny eye blinked up as *Anemone* rippled past, pressed by a cloud of blue and bronze and white. When she looked back Eddi had the camera on it. "You'll be the last one to die," Madsen yelled as they left it in their wake.

Ahead, other minkes cut from right to left, breaching to breathe in quick snorts that left puffs of vapor shredding into the mist. She caught their scent, heavy, fishy, with something else all of itself, a rich smell like fresh-turned earth that once sensed could never be forgotten.

Behind and above her the main refilled with a shuddering snap and *Anemone* leaned in the opposite direction. The engines were whining now. Another detonation rolled across the uneasy sea, and she lifted her eyes to see one of the kill ships lined fast to yet another writhing victim. Its grayblue hull and white pilothouse and black stack jarred into recognition with a physical shock that quivered in her stomach like nausea. She called back, "Is that *Number* 3?"

Eddi yelled from the mast, "They're just killing them and leaving them to float. One after the other . . ." Glancing back, Sara saw tears were freezing on her cheeks, the camera shaking as she tried to focus on a struggling animal. It was biting at the line as other whales surged alongside, nuzzling at it as if trying to help dislodge the cruel needle lodged in its flesh. Then Madsen yelled something incoherent, or maybe the words were just blown away by the wind and the thunder of the sail and the whine of the turbochargers. Auer yelled, passing it on, "Sara! Lars wants you back aft. He's going in."

She bent and scrambled along the lifeline, past Bodine in the open hatch, past Eddi, past the coach house and the winch heads like miniature castle keeps protruding from caked snow-ice, and tumbled into the cockpit with a *whoof* as she slammed into the lid of an open locker. She crouched, catching her breath and sorting out impressions coming almost too fast to process. Then they snapped into a coherent whole.

Madsen was steering for the line that stretched between the newly harpooned minke and *Siryu Maru Number* 3. The whale, which was streaming a red trail but did not seem to yet be mortally injured, and the kill ship were at full speed, tossing up foam as they plowed together over the furrowed surface. *Anemone*, on a broad reach with the main drawing hard and engines whining at full power, was planing like a skipping stone, rapidly overtaking. Madsen stood at the wheel, tongue between his teeth, staring fixedly at the rapidly growing ship, which reeled as it powered through the sea. The whooshing howl of its machinery grew. A smoky braid twined itself into the clear Antarctic air. Men were gathering on the upper deck, clustering in yellow slickers along the rail.

And now, looking up, Sara understood the reason for the thick, strangely rough strand of dark wire at the leading edge of the forward shroud. That Madsen had warned her to keep her hands away from. She caught her breath at the audacity of the plan. And the danger.

The steel hull rose high above *Anemone*'s deck. The huge roaring bow wave that swept out from it pitched them as they cut through. But Madsen kept the throttles slammed forward, turbines howling. She crouched, gripping the winch as the slanting stay crept up on the taut harpoon line, drawn ruler-straight from the squat gun to the flurrying, speeding whale.

But just as the cutter was about to touch it, the fleeing whale surged, breaking the surface to the left. The line slacked, drooping into a catenary. *Anemone* rose, then plunged downward.

She shook along her whole length, quivering as the forward stay, the main bracing of the mast, bent inward, tensioning the mast like a drawn bow.

Then, quite suddenly, the stay snapped. It parted in a flurry of singing wire-ends, aluminum tubing, and suddenly released Kevlar as the whole jib- and jib-furling assembly exploded. The mast sprang back upright with a note like a plucked string, but octaves deeper, shaking the boat from stem to stern and whipping Eddi's head forward and back as she struggled to unstrap herself. Looking up, Madsen flung up an arm as the mast tottered. "Look out!" Dorée screamed, ducking for the companionway. Sara too crouched, unable to move as the mast vibrated above them, hesitated, then began to topple.

But not completely. It snagged, quivering, as if caught by some invisible force. In fact, she couldn't quite see why it hadn't kept toppling backward, to crash down on their heads.

Then she understood, just as Madsen cut the throttles and reached for the mainsail halyard. Before he could trip it she was on him. "No! That's all that's holding it up! The mainsail, pushing forward!"

"Oh, shit—you're right." His face bleached as he realized what he'd almost done. He shoved her out of the cockpit. "Get forward. Do something!"

Not a very specific order, but she grabbed Eddi as the videographer finally freed herself. They slipped and scrabbled on all fours along the rocking deck as the jib raved and thundered above their bent backs. The clew caught her a slam on the head that if not for the helmet would have knocked her silly. At the same moment a jet of water crashed down, searching the forecastle, then steadying on Eddi. It slammed her to her belly and skidded her into the chainplates, where she clung helplessly as the fire hose battered her.

The jet lifted, swept forward. Sara dropped prone and got a grip on her shipmate's plait and hauled her bodily inboard as *Anemone* staggered back into the creaming wake of the kill ship. She stared down for an infinite second into light pearl varied with green and darker green, and a pure white where it clashed with itself and surfaced, like boiling, liquid glass. But where it roiled and foamed to the left of the wake, behind the fleeing whale, that froth was tinged crimson. Above them sailors shook their fists and called imprecations in Japanese. One reared back and pitched, and a small object left his fist and turned end over end, suddenly exploding with a loud crack and flash and a puff of smoke.

"We have to drop the jib," Eddi panted, lying full length beside her. "Drop it and use the halyard. Tie it to something." Sara, looking up, saw she was right. The whole immense jib was flailing and beating with superhuman power as *Anemone* slowed, turning her rump to the wind.

As she reached up and grabbed one of the darting, shaking sheets her shoulder was nearly yanked out of its socket, but she held on and Eddi grabbed it too, and they worked their way forward, dragging and gathering the flailing fabric down to the deck inch by inch, then yard by yard.

The engines whined again, and spray burst over the cockpit. Lars was backing down, bulldozing *Anemone*'s flat chisel of a stern into the oncoming seas, putting just that much more wind pressure on the tottering mast. Then they were on their feet, hauling the slick sodden sail to their breasts. They stuffed it into the open hatch, where Mick gathered folds in as fast as they could shove them.

The heavy stainless halyard shackle came down at last into Sara's hands. She pulled the lanyarded pin to snap it open, fought it up to the bow, and snapped it into the bullnose just before her hands gave out and she slid back gasping, numb, beaten, bruised. Her fingers left bloody smears on the thick braided line, the icy white deck. Tehiyah and Hideyashi were still hauling, the winch clattering through the wind and the crash of the seas. The halyard drew taut between masthead and bow, and Sara sobbed, wheezing, as the mast ceased its drunken sway and stiffened once more into its wonted vertical.

"Sara, good work." Hideyashi gave her an admiring smile. Madsen slapped her shoulder, and she winced. He ruddered the bow around into the wind. *Anemone* coasted to a halt, idling, rolling as she picked up the chop.

"You were wonderful," Dorée said, teeth gleaming. Then those thick glorious eyebrows gathered into a frown. "Oh—you're bleeding!"

"Yes, my hands—"

"No. Your leg. Wait—let me unzip this."

Sara looked down to see a jagged cut welling bright blood from her upper thigh. Dorée hooked a finger through a tear in her suit. "What in the world did this?"

"I don't remember. Everything was so confused—"

"They threw a firecracker," Eddi said.

"Not a firecracker," Lars said, face hard. "Some kind of grenade."

Tehiyah glared at the ships. "We didn't hurt them. We were—we were nonviolent."

"Sometimes that only gets you so far," the new captain muttered.

Sara bent for a closer look. It stung, but didn't look like anything a Band-Aid wouldn't cover. "I'm all right. Really. Let's—we need to stop them. They're still—"

"Still killing," Eddi finished for her, and stood. "She's right, Lars. We've got to fuck up this murdering shit. Or die trying."

Madsen glanced aloft, then across the water to where *Number 3* had slowed, winching in the line. The minke, exhausted, wallowed at its end. Once more the puny crack of rifle shots echoed from the distant bergs. "All right," he said, and pushed the throttles forward again.

As *Anemone* surged once more Sara caught an undulation on the water some distance away. It was difficult to make out and she shielded her gaze. Close together rolled several brownish, irregular, lumpy shapes, like immense, half-awash driftlogs. The seas seethed about one end, which rose and then fell, rose and fell. Then from the midst of it jutted a queerly sideways jet that flamed in the dusklight like red fire.

"Sperm whale," Hideyashi said, lowering binoculars. "He's been there awhile. Just lying off." He made as if to pass them to her, but she waved them away.

"I should bandage that," Auer said, looking at Sara's thigh.

"Let it bleed, Eddi. It'll clot soon enough." She followed Madsen's anxious eye aloft again. "Will it hold, Lars?"

"I don't know. We ought to get another line on it."

"Then let's do it," she snapped. "Hy, give me a hand? We'll take the other halyard forward too. That'll give us two lines bracing it. Will that be enough, Lars?"

"We might need more," he said, still looking aloft. Then pulled her toward the wheel. "But you've done enough hard labor. Steer; I'll go up. Aim for the factory ship. If we can get ahead of them and toss some tear gas aboard, we might still do some damage."

When she stepped into his place and looked over the bow she saw that indeed the factory ship was closing. Still a couple of miles distant, but it was bow-on and a white mustache showed at its stem. Sara did a careful check all around the compass and advanced the throttle. Then a little more, aiming midway between where the larger ship was coming on, and where the still-hove-to *Maru Number 3* was winching the bloody minke from the sea. Tiny men bustled about, lashing its tail to the rail with rust-colored canvas straps as the kill ship leaned to its weight.

"We need to escalate," Dorée said, beside her.

"Escalate to what?"

"I don't know. But they're throwing grenades—we've got to push back. Not let them drive us off. If we had something like a laser, to blind them—"

"*Blinding* people, Tehiyah—?"

"Oh, not permanently! Just to dazzle them for a few minutes. So they couldn't see to aim the harpoons."

Sara was about to ask *but then what will* they *escalate to* when a Jacuzzi-burst of lime and cream foamed from *Siryu*'s screws. It began to move ahead, dragging the dead minke. The power of the kill ship's engines must be immense; it was many times the mass and height of *Anemone*, of steel, not composite, but it was faster and just as maneuverable.

Then she looked ahead, and her fingers tightened on the smooth stainless wheel. "Lars—*look*."

"No," Eddi murmured, beside her.

Some quarter mile ahead of the swiftly accelerating, queerly pointed bow, two fins sickled the disturbed sea. Two spouts leaped shredding into iridescent mist. One was larger; the other, smaller, so close beside the first as nearly to be touching. They vanished for seconds, then reemerged a hundred yards farther on, fleeing the oncoming hunter. But that vessel was moving ever more rapidly. Sara cursed as she saw it was overtaking the creatures that fled, surfacing and submerging, but with ever shorter periods between disappearances. "Lars! I need to speed up—"

"Not now," he shouted back. He and Kimura were precariously counterbalanced ten feet up the mast, wrestling a wire rope toward the crosstrees. "Keep her steady. No faster than this."

When she looked forward again she nearly wrenched the wheel over. Something heaved and rolled just beneath the surface a hundred yards ahead. Then it spouted, and that crooked, single, leaned-over blow told her what it was.

An immense, squared-off bulk, far larger than the more streamlined minkes, was heading across her bow, toward the kill ship and the mother-calf pair it was pursuing. She clung to the wheel, disbelieving. "Eddi?" she croaked, and turned to see the videographer already zooming in, the camera lens flashing as it pointed nearly into the low ruddy sun. "Hideyashi! Do you see that?" But the Japanese was trying to toss the heavy shackled end of the wire rope over the crosstrees above his head.

"Turn away from the wind," Madsen shouted, shading his eyes up at Hy's struggle. "Put your stern to the seas." She put the helm over obediently, but kept glancing back to where the whale had lifted its tail, then slid under in a swirling vortex. Only then did she put its creamy yellowish hue together with the one they'd seen earlier.

But no. That had been days ago, hundreds of miles away. This couldn't be the same individual.

"Isn't that the same one we saw before?" Eddi asked around the camera. "The first time we saw whales? The one I named Cappuccino?"

Sara shook her head. "I don't see how, Eddi—"

"That was a loner too. A fucking big 'un. With sort of a shredded-looking tail, too. Just like that."

She didn't answer. She hadn't noticed any shredded tail, either on the previous whale or this one. Though as it had raised its flukes to dive, one *might* have seemed slightly ragged.

A chorus of yells. The wire had circled the mast above the spreaders and the men were running the bitter end forward. She brought the bow back to where she thought it ought to be, but the gray-and-black bulk of the factory vessel was nearer, a looming presence against the shining lavender and blue shadows of the berg. Heavy smoke jutted from its stacks, and an industrial clanking rang across the water.

When she looked back at the kill ship she blinked. Something huge ranged alongside it, bulging the water. It traveled at incredible speed, straight for the queerly curved prow. "Lars!" she yelled. "Hy! Look at *Number 3!*"

"It's turning away," Auer breathed, beside her. Sara saw this was so; as she watched, the recurved prow wavered and began to foreshorten as the ship refused the imminent impact of that onrushing mass. A spout erupted near the kill ship; the sea burst apart as the whale lifted a blunt monolithic head, then plunged again.

"Oh no," the videographer breathed. "It's not going to—"

"Ram them?" She could hardly breathe, standing on tiptoes at the wheel. "I don't—I don't *think* so—"

A puff of smoke, and a detonation rolled across the roiling sea. A black line drew straight against sky and ice, and ended at the onrushing tons.

Eddi screamed. The camera jerked, but came back on target. Sara went rigid, unable to comprehend. Then found it all too easy. Protected or not, a sperm whale represented enormous profit. So much bigger than the minkes. So many more tons of meat, plus sperm oil, precious lubricants. Yes, they were witnesses. Could testify, but in what court? The whalers had shown how well they'd insulated themselves, in layers of public apathy, political connection, national self-interest.

"Get up on step, Sara. Head over. We'll get footage, anyway." Madsen came aft, wiping grease off on his suit. He looked as shaken as she felt, even more bitterly, helplessly angry.

Then Tehiyah said, clinging to a shroud and pointing ahead, "What are they doing?"

Sara snatched the binoculars as she pushed both throttles to full power. The turbines wound up as she searched. "What? What?"

Auer said, "I saw its tail come up. So big . . . then it toppled over, over the line. . . . It went taut . . . then it snapped. Just—snapped."

The circle of the glasses steadied for a second, and Sara glimpsed men gathered around a line that hung limp, its frayed, ragged end swinging free a fathom above the sea. Cheers rang out from the accelerating sailboat, but immediately quenched as the kill ship swung back to its original course, picking up speed once again after the fleeing mother and calf.

Lars told her to forget *Number 3*, to steer for the oncoming factory. It looked immense now, and she swung the wheel over with real trepidation. These people were ready to harpoon sperm whales in the presence of witnesses. Might it not be convenient for those witnesses to disappear, ground under by "accident" beneath the overhanging bows of the oncoming ship? But *Anemone* rode smoothly as a speedboat now, curving sinuously as any water snake as Sara maneuvered to avoid a rocking floe. The men and Tehiyah busied themselves on the starboard side, flemishing out the mooring lines. "We'll get gas on her forecastle, blind the pilothouse crew," Bodine yelled back. "Then fuck up her props. Cripple her, and she can't follow the killers to process the meat. Get in close!"

The factory ship grew rapidly, but Sara saw she'd misjudged its speed; it was drawing ahead; she was coming in on its quarter, not its bow. A low-hanging curtain of wet-smelling fog blew over them. When they emerged it was much closer. She came left to follow it, and a massive, sloped ramp, like something down which one would drive a tractor-trailer, came into view. It gleamed with what she realized after a moment was blood. Its metallic stink rode the wind. A minke was being winched up into the cavernous maw. From above the slowly inching carcass scuppers vomited pure red back into the sea.

They all fell silent. Except for Eddi, who sobbed as she filmed. Even Dorée was speechless, staring up at black ramparts like an evil keep they had no hope of breaching. The very wake behind the thing tumbled carmine, and the ship emanated a terrible miasma of decay and rotten meat and feces steeped and layer-caked into a dreadful dense effluvium. The old slavers must have trailed such a stench, so honest sailors could smell them miles downwind.

Tehiyah turned away, choking into the sleeve of her mustang suit. "It's horrible . . . you can smell the death. If only we could record this smell for you too. It hangs over the ocean, so thick it seems nothing can live that breathes it for long."

"Along the port side," Madsen snapped at Sara from where he rove their mooring lines into one of the blue fenders she'd last seen hanging off *Anemone*'s side at Ushuaia. "Get a hundred yards ahead. Then come hard right and cut 'cross her bow."

"That'll be dangerous, Lars. Do we have to—"

"They'll turn to avoid. We've got to drop it right under her forefoot. If you can't do it—"

"I'll do it," she snapped, and bumped the throttles to make sure they were all the way forward. The unaltered keen of the turbines told her they were.

Forward, under the massive bulwarks less than a hundred yards away. "Closer!" Madsen yelled. She bit her lip and edged the rudder over. Eighty yards. Seventy.

Fifty. Then even closer, until the roar of the bow wave was deafening. As was the hum and roar of the massive structure rushing alongside them, towering over them. From far above the white plumes of fire hoses probed out and down. She cringed, anticipating the blow, until she saw that, this close, the nozzles could not angle down far enough to bear. She laughed aloud. Her self seemed to inhabit another realm now, or to float detached from this world by one of the tiny curled dimensions string theory posited.

"Close enough. Watch for the suck," Madsen yelled. She felt it, like gravity from a heavy star, a yearning between the rushing hulls that fought her for control of the wheel.

From behind her, Dorée screamed.

When Sara looked around a massive bluegray scimitar was lifted above her head. For a moment she froze, unable to grasp what it was, or what the seething roar of white at its base meant. Then she knew.

It was the massive curved bow of the kill ship, cutting in at top speed behind them and the much larger factory vessel. For an instant she tried to believe it would pass between them. But the killer was coming directly up *Anemone*'s wake. It would be on them in seconds. That thirty-foot-high mass of rust-streaked steel would power over the spot where she stood. Angled metal would trample, tear apart the fragile fabric of the sailboat's stern. Her throat closed. Her breath went solid.

"Sheer away," Madsen screamed, from where he stood clinging to the stay, looking back and up at the same imminent doom. "Sheer off!" But her own terrified brain had already come to the same conclusion, and she spun the wheel hard. The boat careened violently as the stern skated around. For endless seconds permeated with the consciousness of impending death she watched it approach the rushing black hull of the factory ship, regretting too late that when you turned the wheel on a boat—unlike a car, where the front wheels pivoted and the trunk followed—the stern pivoted around the bow, and only then pushed it onto the new course.

Which meant they were now broadside to the oncoming blade. The sea roared as the bow tore it apart, boiled it white, and creamed it out to either side. From above men aimed what she only belatedly realized were rifles down at them. But this hardly mattered. The inexorably advancing stem was going to split them apart exactly where she stood.

The Dane seized the wheel around her cramped-solid hands and pushed it over still further. Just as that massive blade met the racing boat's hull, sliding like a huge blunt chisel along their port side, flexing it inward, some invisible pressure wave just ahead of the oncoming stem seemed to lift and shove her off. The Dewoitine seemed to twist herself almost consciously away from oncoming destruction, her stern rising, throwing them all forward, then slewing hard around as the rusty steel rushed past, loud as a locomotive.

When Sara lifted her gaze from death passing just feet away, it locked with the sardonic gaze of the same blunt-faced, grizzled Japanese she'd glimpsed there before. He gazed down from the bridge wing like some Olympian god, and as she stared, raised a single finger.

Before she could react Captain Crunch was past. Rocking, heading in the opposite direction now, *Anemone* rolled free. From the port bow Hideyashi, back arched to look upward, shouted something at the impassive men who lined the lifelines. For a moment her ear struggled to wring sense from the syllables; but it was not in English. The crewmen recoiled as if scalded. An older man spat and turned his back; a younger one, cheeks scarlet, shook a fist at Kimura as the killer rapidly receded, shadowing the much larger factory, which had not altered its course at all during the entire incident.

"What'd you say to them?" Bodine yelled. "Boy, that sure pulled their chain."

"A haiku. By Soseki Natsume. We all must learn it in school."

"A *haiku*?" Eddi gaped. "You mean—"

"A short poem, about honoring nature. This one"—he paused, hanging off the lifeline as the boat rocked uneasily in the departing wakes, then translated,

"Over the wintry
forest, winds howl in rage
with no leaves to blow."

Bodine blew a raspberry. "Poetry ain't going to stop these assholes." But his tone held grudging admiration.

Lars stepped back from the wheel as Sara's throat finally unlocked. She gagged out an acid mouthful straight from her stomach. She spat it drooling over the side, then turned on him. "You idiot. They almost killed us!"

He didn't answer. Just looked past her to where Bodine had vanished, ducking down into the forepeak. He jerked around fast, though, when she grabbed his earlobe and pinched. Blue eyes blazed; he struck her hand away. "What are you doing? That hurt."

"As much as if we were Cuisinarted under that ship? These people are serious, Lars. They'd be perfectly happy to kill us." She coughed up another burning mouthful of reflux and spat it between her boots as she wrestled the wheel, trying to keep the mast from whipping as they rolled on the surge. "I saw Nakame again as they passed. He gave us the finger, like 'you fools.'"

"So what. We're as determined as they are."

"They're not backing down. Not from anything the few of us can bring to bear."

"That may not be so," he muttered, looking after the ships that were still steadily moving away. Then reached over her. "Give me the wheel."

"I've got it."

"I said, *give me the wheel*." He hip-blocked her abruptly. Their bulky suits cushioned the impact, but the blow was still so unexpected she half fell across the cockpit locker. He bent, cranking the wheel left until the bow pointed again along the emerald-and-cream highway that roiled and steamed where the ships had pressed it down, and shoved the throttles forward again.

She started to get up, then sagged back as the companionway hatch slammed open from below.

A blunt sausage covered in rough green fabric pushed out like some obscene turd. It thumped down onto the cockpit sole, followed by a legless Bodine. The ex-soldier maneuvered with his arms more swiftly and gracefully than he could have dragging the metal-and-plastic encumbrances of artificial limbs. He positioned himself on the opposite seat, unsnapped the duffel, and began hauling things out. Sara drew a shocked breath.

"Oh no," Eddi said, from up where she had been filming.

"Set up to port," Madsen said urgently, nudging the throttle to make sure it was at full ahead. From the storm of the engines, the white jet of water from beneath the stern, they were all out already. "I'll go up the starboard side."

"The killer? Or the factory?" Bodine was fitting parts together, assembling a drab green tube a little larger than something one would mail a poster in. As Sara watched, braced against the turtleback, speechless, he telescoped it apart. Then lay forward over the cockpit coaming and settled it over his right shoulder. With his right hand he pulled down a short handle; a spring-loaded sight flipped out.

"What *is* that thing?"

"Move back, Sara. Eddi, stay up there. You don't want to be behind him when this goes off."

"But *what is it*?" She felt like the ball in a pachinko machine, ricocheted from emotion to emotion too rapidly to register them, still less respond. "Some kind of weapon? You didn't tell us about this. Mick—what the *fuck* are you doing?"

"Two hundred," Bodine murmured around the tube. "We'll need to be a lot closer for a right-angle impact."

"I'm all out. We're gaining."

She clung tight, caught between outrage and terror. *Anemone* hit another wave system from one of the ships, maybe even an old one from the second killer, now a mile off and dimly outlined in the fading light, wheeling back to rejoin the others. Who were still steaming at full speed, still drawn close together, though as she watched the smaller ship began to drop back slightly.

A smoky haze rolled over them, and she coughed. Not just engine smoke, but something evil. Freighted with death and congealed blood, rot and corruption; like, she imagined, what a death camp must have smelled like.

On the ramp of the factory ship, three crewmen were working their way down toward where the wake burbled. They were pushing what she first thought were thick glistening red rubber mats that undulated obscenely as they tumbled over one another. With a final flourish the workers shoveled them into the sea. Then they were passing down *Anemone*'s side: scarlet and purple coils of intestines, veined with bright yellow fat; distended purple and blue organs. Already foot-long silver fish were darting in through curling tendrils of blood to nip and tear, every fin and scale and greedy onyx eye perfectly distinct in the clear green.

She gagged. Life from death, death from life. For a moment that seemed longer than it probably was she wondered at them. Wriggling and tearing, jerking at the unexpected banquet with the force of their whole bodies, they bolted down ragged chunks with a shaking, ravenous, oblivious hunger that fascinated even as it disgusted.

Fans of white grew above the ramp. They waved slowly, like the defensive stinging tendrils of an exotic invertebrate. *Anemone* was sliding over the smooth water of the ships' wakes with a whining hiss, barely rolling as she skated. Sara tried to muster her anger. Lars and Mick had never told her they intended to do this. But now she too felt the antediluvian excitement of the chase. It made her hands clench, her eyesight sharpen, her breath pump fast and shallow. The world collapsed to this narrowing strip of sea. To their prey: mammothine, malevolent, beginning a ponderous turn away as they bounded in to snap at its tendons. "Guys—don't do this. You never told us—"

"A hundred meters," Bodine shouted.

"At the waterline. Pick your spot."

"Forward of the propeller guard. The engine room?"

"Sounds good to me," Madsen said.

The soldier curled into the extended tube. Its open end rose and fell as they closed. Sara saw where he was sighting. Just ahead of the turbulence at the stern; low on the hull, a cagelike contrivance of welded pipe.

She coughed involuntarily, still tasting the acid afterscrape in her throat, the pickle sourness. And something in that taste, like a bite of rancid apple, returned her to the knowledge of herself. Her arms and legs might still feel as if they weren't her own. But her mind—her conscience—was. She reached forward, arm outstretched. "Stop! You can't—"

Solid fire burst at that moment from the rear of the tube, changing instantly to a cloud of whitish-yellow airborne powder so hot and choking the first breath overwhelmed her with a cloy of burned rubber, chalk, burned insulation, overheated brakes. Within this fog she stumbled over Bodine and they fell, grappling like wrestlers, yet cushioned by their suits and the gritty sole of the cockpit. The tube, smoking from both ends, thunked down and spun into a corner. "Turn away. Turn away!" Bodine shouted hoarsely past her. Madsen yelled back that he already had.

"D'I hit it? Couldn't see, this stupid bitch knocked me down—"

"Straight and true, my friend. Straight and true. Not a big explosion—"

"It's a shaped charge. Penetrates, then sprays molten metal."

The cloud cleared, falling away as *Anemone*, skimming in a huge circle, moved free. The wind took it off, slowly thinning at the edges, a strange yellow-white against the blue-white and rose-white of ice, the green-white of cold sea. Hideyashi tumbled into the cockpit with them, Eddi a scuffling step behind. Her face was pale as new snow. Her teeth chattered. "You need to get below," Madsen told her. "Get warmed up."

"Fuck that," she gasped. "Nobody said you were going to *shoot* at them. This is a nonviolent organization!"

"Greenpeace is nonviolent," Bodine said, picking up the tube, examining it, then tossing it overboard. It sank immediately. "Sea Shepherd'll bust up equipment, but they won't hurt people. And does it help? Does it? Anyhow, you call what *they're* doing out here nonviolent?"

"No. No, but we're not them. The Japanese, I mean."

Bodine heaved a sigh. "You got an opinion too, Hy?"

Kimura looked shocked too, but maybe not as much. "I did not know you were going to do a thing like this."

"Would you still have jumped ship if you had?"

He looked from one man to the other, but did not answer.

Bodine shrugged and bent to the duffel again. Was pulling out another tube when Sara slammed her boot down on it. "No more, Mick."

"Take your fucking boot off my hand, Sara."

"I will if you put that away. Eddi? Hy?"

"She's right, guys. This stops now." Auer beat at herself with stiff arms, breath panting out in white puffs. "No more."

"Coming up again," Madsen said, above them. When Sara looked up from where Bodine was still bent, hand pinned, she saw they'd completed a great circle and were coming up behind the factory ship again. From which, when she shaded her eyes, a plume of smoke was rising, along with the pulsating warble of an electronic alarm.

Dorée hadn't moved from her stance on the bow during the attack. The actress clung there still, one hand shading her eyes as she stared ahead, the other wrapped around the jury-rigged braid of nylon and wire that now held up the mast. "Tehiyah!" Eddi yelled. She waved, but didn't turn.

"This isn't a voting situation." Bodine looked up. "Let me go, Sara. I'm warning you."

"*Number Three*'s dropping aft," Madsen warned at the same moment. Past Tehiyah's erect slim silhouette Sara saw the killer leaning into a turn, positioning itself between them and the massive ship from which smoke was now coming up more strongly, black and thick as blood in the water. "Watch out, Mick. That's Crunch, on the bridge."

Eddi turned back as Bodine bowed, almost politely, and head-butted Sara in the midriff. As she staggered back he pulled his hand from under her boot and a second tube out of the duffel. He rolled over prone, into the same position as before, and slotted the tube into firing configuration with a cheap-sounding clack. His face was flushed and he moved in a different way, not longer slumped or simian but tensed, graceful, nestling into the weapon as if into an embrace long missed. "Target: kill ship. We'll put this one into her bridge."

"Mick, *no.*" She threw herself at him, but a hard hand grabbed her shoulder and dragged her back. Madsen threw her down. When she tried to get up he shoved her down again with a boot on her rump. The wheel creaked as the bow steadied on the kill ship, now nearing rapidly as they overtook.

Auer kicked his leg off Sara and hauled her up. Past her along the killer's rail Sara saw a solid line of yellow-slickered men flourishing objects, shaking their fists, and from the deck above the plumes of fire hoses swaying this way and that. Bodine raised the muzzle slightly, settling it on a stocky figure which stood alone on the outthrust wing of the other ship, high above the sea.

From the kill ship, a small flash, a tiny burst of smoke whipped away instantly by the wind. Then another, a few feet forward of the first. In the water between the racing vessels white bursts of foam fountained up. The yellow slickers scattered, leaving only the shooters at the rail.

"They've got rifles," Dorée screamed back. "Guns! They're shooting at us!"

"Please. Don't do this." Sara braced herself to lunge again, but once more a hand dragged her back. She sat down hard on the bench seat.

"Mick?" Madsen said, from the wheel. Another duality of pops; two more fountains of white ripped open the jade-green sea. *Anemone* raced toward them, swept over them; the opening circles on the translucent green vanished beneath her outstretched stem.

Bodine yelled, "Warning shots. They're not aiming at us.—Film this, Eddi. Auer! *Film this*!"

"Those are the guns they kill the whales with," Tehiyah shouted.

"Keep closing, Lars. Keep closing."

As Eddi reluctantly lifted her camera Sara lunged. When Madsen grabbed for her again she ducked under his hand and kicked out. Her heavy sea boot caught the tube and it flew over the side, tumbling end over end, hit the bow wave, and vanished. At the same moment Eddi gave a full-throated scream. When Sara turned, her shaking camera was pointed forward. "Tehiyah!" she shouted again.

On the bow, a suited figure sagged from the stay.

"Oh God," Madsen said. "Not—"

Sara pushed past them and clambered over the turtleback onto the long flat tapered wedge forward of the mast. Her boots slipped and she almost fell, but recovered and got to the bow just as Dorée's arm slipped free and she slumped over the pulpit.

Sara eased her down. When she saw the blood, she rolled her onto her side. Dorée's eyelids fluttered; she breathed in shallow gasps. Sara unzipped and yanked the suit down, pulled the sweater up, reached for her knife. The bra fell away, revealing Tehiyah's chest.

And a wound that pumped bright scarlet in spurting arterial jets. This blood, which felt extremely hot, ran over her fingers, steaming, and soaked the actress's long tangled black hair. She shouted, "The kit. Bring the first-aid kit!"

Dorée opened the lionine eyes that had fascinated millions and looked into the sky. They took on a glossy shine. Her lips moved, but formed no word Sara could decipher.

Then she closed them, and ceased breathing. That quickly, and, it seemed, peacefully, though a single, questioning frown line remained.

Eddi and Hideyashi knelt. Auer said, "CPR?"

"I'm on it." Sara cleared the airway and positioned the actress's head, then lowered her face to Tehiyah's.

The lips beneath hers were still warm. They seemed to quiver, though perhaps she imagined this. She breathed into them, raised her face for a breath, and lowered it again. Beneath hers the full lips quivered again, very faintly. Then stilled.

Auer leaned her locked fists into Dorée's sternum. The body bucked and a new pulse of blood jetted, but more slowly than when it had been driven by the heart's force. Hideyashi stood over them, swaying, moaning. Sara lifted her head between breaths and saw *Anemone* had turned away, was headed now, at low speed, away from the ships.

Bodine came crawling along the deck, scuttling crablike from stanchion to stanchion. "Is she okay?"

"She's *dead*, Mick." Auer sat back on her heels, wiping her hands on her suit. The smears looked like a child's first attempt at finger painting. "They shot her in the heart."

"I do not think they were aiming at us," Kimura said, wringing his hands. "They were pointing the guns into the water. That seemed very clear to me."

"Ricochet," Bodine said. "But even a ricochet, from a high-velocity bullet . . ." He frowned, seemed about to add more information, but Sara's look must have stopped him. He coughed and dragged himself upright. "Can one of you open that hatch? I'll get down below, then we can—"

"No. Leave her," Sara said, surprising herself as a coherent thought finally dislodged itself from the icejam. "She'll be better off up here. Well? Are you happy now? Satisfied? I tried to stop you, you assholes."

They said nothing, and she turned away. Madsen looked dazed. Eddi, tears streaking her cheeks, went aft. She came back with the camera. The lens stared here and there, recording, as Sara arranged Dorée's clothing, wiped up blood with handfuls of snow, rezipped her suit. Auer resnapped the fasteners of the life preserver, and made up Tchiyah's safety line into a neat coil.

Engines barely audible, *Anemone* rose and fell through a quieting sea. Nothing disturbed its heaving, glossy, faintly oily-looking surface. In the distance, the departing ships were specks in a roseate mist as the sun declined, once again. Not to set, but only to half-light a shadowy underworld of eternal twilight.

16

Snow and Wind

They pitched into a switching wind that pried up the greasy sea in long swells. Bergs, white on white in the falling snow, had closed between them and the fleet, which had stood off to the eastward. The snow had resumed after they departed the killing grounds. It fell ceaselessly through the dusk, so there were no stars. A subdued Madsen had directed the careful hoist of the main, fully reefed, then shut the engines down. Sara steered from the dome, though its plastic was scratched now and hard to see through.

But she could make out the tarp-wrapped bundle lashed to the lifelines. They'd discussed what to do with Tehiyah's body. This decision was unanimous. They had to take her home. Otherwise, no one would believe she'd died from a whaler's bullet. That settled, there was only one place for the remains. Out in the weather, where the freezing temperatures and dehydrating wind would slow decomposition. They'd laid her along the gunwale and lashed her to the chainplates, but that evening Sara had noticed spray running off the tarp. Too dark by then to do anything, but she'd put it aside to address when the light came again.

The radar was gone; the screen blank. The wiping away of the stay and near collapse of the mast had sheared off the antenna housing. Sara didn't want to talk to anyone, interact with anyone, do anything but grip the wheel like a human autopilot. *Anemone* was her body; matching the compass was all she required of her mind.

Without direction, without order, she'd gradually brought their course around to north, then northeast, threading amid drifting bergs. At last, when it grew too dim to see, she'd sheeted the main out and let the boat drift to a stop, lifting and falling to the swell. The others must have noticed, but no one said anything. She braced her knees against the dashboard and dozed, waking only now and again to scan the dark horizon.

As the light returned the smell of coffee perked the air. Bodine tottered aft and sat at the salon table. Pans clattered in the galley as Hideyashi, who seemed to be growing into the job of short-order cook, fried cheese-and-onion omelets.

Suddenly she was very hungry. Dru and Tehiyah had died. So be it. The mission of those who remained was simple: to make it home. She made a last inspection of the falling snow, salmon-pink in the direction of the sun, and climbed down. Shook her legs out, splashed her face, combed and pinned up her snarled hair. It was greasy and the ends were split, but who cared.

"Milk?" The Japanese offered canned Nestlé. "The water system has frozen. I had to melt ice with the stove to make coffee."

"Thanks, Hy."

Madsen came in from aft and slid into the place Dru Perrault had once occupied. He'd shaved carefully around his beard, making a goatee, and his blond hair was tied back. He moved silverware around, making each piece parallel to each other one. It seemed strange to be able to do this, but the motion of the boat was so gentle that the forks and knives did not even shift. She caught a whiff of aftershave. He nodded, giving her an ingratiating smile. She nodded back, but didn't feel like smiling. Not after basically having been ignored and beaten into submission the day before, and being made an accessory to an armed attack.

"Ice heavy, Sara?"

"We're in an open patch. But I still had to stay alert."

"We're hove to? Safe?"

"Or I wouldn't be down here, Lars. Would I?" she said savagely. "We need to do something about Tehiyah. She's getting wet."

His mouth tightened. He turned to Bodine. "We also need to get a message out. Tehiyah Dorée dead of a whaler's bullet—that's going to make news all over the world." He must have caught some warning in her face, or maybe Eddi's, because he added, "I mean—does that sound callous? It's what she would have wanted. And you know it."

"Maybe," Sara mumbled. "Probably." What did it matter now?

"That's gonna be tough. We lost the shortwave antenna, along with the radar. And we're way out of phone range." Bodine smacked his lips as Kimura slid an omelet onto his plate. Cut into it, and mumbled around the first mouthful, "I can receive, though. Getting a lot of traffic from the fleet. Hy, maybe you can come translate, after we eat."

"After we take care of Tehiyah," Sara said.

"That can wait. No hurry there."

"No, it can't. We'll do it now."

All three men looked at her. "Okay," Madsen muttered at last.

After breakfast she and Eddi and Hideyashi beat the ice off the mainsail and cleared the compacted snow out of the tracks. Then they gathered on the foredeck. It wasn't snowing at the moment, but a black mist that was probably a coming squall stretched from broad on their left hand all the way off to the horizon, inchoate and somehow more threatening than a mere storm should be. All around the rollers coursed, endless, devoid. Their soullessness struck her through with something deeper than terror. "There was spray last night," she said, coughing into her glove as the cold bit her lungs and looking down at the glistening dew on the rough canvas. "It'll freeze, then thaw, freeze and then thaw. That's not going to be good for . . . long-term preservation."

"We must put her below, then," Kimura said.

"Can't, Hy. Granted, it's not that much warmer down there. But she'll still start to . . . rot."

She looked around again, noticing only then that the helmsman's dome was empty. Yet the wake stretched straight. Lars must have put the self-steerer back on. Whoever was on duty was still supposed to keep lookout, but he must have figured they'd keep an eye out while they were on deck. Above them the makeshift forward stay vibrated as *Anemone* plunged and reared, reminding her of a painting she'd seen once somewhere, a ship too small for the seas, a grim cape towering behind it into ominous clouds. The wind was stronger; the seas were growing, whitecaps breaking here and there between them and the still-ghostly horizon. One dead ahead caught her eye and for a second she tensed—*ice?*—but then it disappeared.

"Tie her to the mast?" Eddi was saying.

Sara sighed and looked up. The main snapped and bellied, reefed, but still catching each gust. "I don't know. That might jam something? If we've got to get that sail down fast—"

"Okay, then up forward." Auer pointed.

They looked back and forth. "That is where she'd want to be," Hy said. "Leading us home."

No further discussion seemed necessary. They stood her upright, the tightly wrapped body stiff and unresponsive as a wooden figurehead, and lashed her to the stay. By the waist, then by the feet. Spray kept flying up from the port side as they worked, and by the time they were done the first thin glaze was silver-white.

When they stepped back Dorée was in roughly the same posture as when the bullet had struck her down. Sara found that fitting. As if still defiant, even in death. "We loved you, Tehiyah," Eddi said softly, then lost her footing and began to slide. Sara grabbed her, but started to go too, soles gaining no grip on the rapidly accreting snow. She threw out a hand; locked arms with Kimura. His other arm gripped the port lifeline, and snapped them all up short like a child's game of crack the whip.

"We better get back below," Sara said. But she looked back once more, as they dropped down the forehatch. The mummied bundle stood erect, nodding slightly as the bow dipped and then heaved, slowly being covered, shrouded, encapsulated by the solidifying sea.

The salon was empty. They found both men in the forepeak, scowling as they listened to excited chatter from a speaker. "Hy, come listen to this," Madsen said. "What's going on?"

The Japanese cocked his head as gear swayed and stirred around them in the narrow tunnel. "The factory ship. It has caught fire."

"Really," Auer said from the doorway. She rubbed her arms. "From whatever it was you shot at them?"

Madsen said, "They don't say."

"I thought you said the radio was broken," Sara pointed out.

"The antenna, not the radio," Lars snapped. "He's got a stub up. We can't transmit, but we can receive."

"Just a sec." Bodine turned up the speaker. This transmission was in English. "*Maritime New Zealand, this is* Ishinomaki Maru. *We have two casualties from smoke inhalation. We will advise again in two hours, advise again in two hours this frequency.* Ishinomaki Maru, *out.*"

"These are not safe ships," Kimura said. "Very unregulated. There were two fires on our way down from Japan. There are many accidents, with the machinery. It may not have been—us."

"We put it right into their engine room," Bodine noted. "If we hit a fuel tank, or even just a fuel line, that'd sure as hell start a fire."

Sara knelt on a coil of line, feeling lightheaded. Then almost panicked; who was on lookout? What if they hit ice? But when she gazed back along the twisting length of the forepeak she glimpsed Auer's legs ascending into the dome.

"Well, we wanted to fuck them up," Madsen said. "Are they still whaling? Or are they headed for port? Japan? New Zealand? Australia?"

"That I am not sure of," Kimura said. "I heard no one say they were doing anything other than fighting the fire. It sounds like the kill ships are nearby the *Ishinomaki*."

"The transmissions are fading," Bodine said.

"We could still pursue," Madsen said. "Replace the forward stay, and—"

"Oh, for God's sake," said Sara. "Dru and Tehiyah—haven't we paid enough? Eddi thinks so. Hy too. Hy?"

"I think it would probably be wise to call an end to your expedition," Kimura said, looking down. "But I do not really have a—"

Sara lost her patience. "Oh, for—! You're a grown-up. You're got as much of a vote as any of us."

Bodine looked resigned. Spread his hands. "I guess the girls have got it right this time, Lars. If we didn't have all this damage . . . maybe. But we do. So, yeah—time for a strategic retreat."

Sara blinked, taken aback. She'd expected him to agree with Madsen, as he had every time so far. "Well—about damn time. Okay. Northeast. That's the course for Australia—isn't it?" No one answered. "Lars? So?"

"That might not be possible," he said, after a moment.

She frowned. "What's that supposed to mean?"

"The stay. We can run before the wind, because that presses forward on the mast. But the farther north we head up, with the wind the way it is, the more strain we put on that jury-rigged shit." He shrugged. "I'm not sure how to address that. But there it is. We sure don't want the mast to come down. Right now, we're probably safe. If the wind changes—"

"So meanwhile, we just sail east?" Sara put in.

"Got a better idea?"

"Drop the sails. Run the engines."

"Not enough fuel. Land's thousands of miles away."

"But we can run north, out of the ice. We might see a freighter, or a military ship. Get help repairing the keel, the mast, the radio."

"The antenna," Mick corrected absent-mindedly, glued to the earphones again.

Sara shrugged him off. "So we're going back? On the motor?"

"I guess," Lars said. She looked at him a moment longer, then reached for a handhold and pulled herself to her feet. Staggered aft, barking her shin on the jamb, and passed the decision up to Eddi. Shortly after, the motor coughed, but didn't start. Coughed again, a shaky, disgruntled noise. But no reassuring purr came, much less the banshee howl. They exchanged looks.

"It's not catching," Auer called down.

"Did you set the throttle to Start?" Madsen yelled back.

"Yeah."

"It should crank right up," Bodine said. Then got a funny look. "Or, wait a minute—"

"The strainers." Sara gripped her forehead. "Oh, fuck. Remember, they froze—"

The starter ground again and they both shouted, "Stop. Stop!"

"It's not like starting a car," Sara added. "We need to go back there and see what's wrong. Mick . . ."

Bodine winced. Started to hoist himself, then winced again. Sweat broke on his forehead. "You all right?" Madsen asked him.

"Could use . . . a hand." He snorted. "Or better yet, two fucking legs." He grimaced as he lurched up. Sara walked behind him, and waited as he let himself down the half ladder into the engine room.

This time it took even longer to get the ice chipped and melted out of the strainer and the hoses. There were actually two strainers, one for each engine, but Bodine said once one was running the space would warm up enough to melt the ice in the other. Still, it meant hours of lying on a freezing deck, taking turns chipping until their hands bled and their faces stung from flying chips.

She said, "You know, if we'd put antifreeze or alcohol or something in these, after we shut down, they wouldn't be frozen like this."

"Yeah, if one of us had remembered. After Tehiyah—"

"I'm only saying."

They lay full length, facing each other as he chipped away. He kept avoiding her eyes. At last, as if making a decision, he sighed. "All right, Sara."

"All right, what?"

"You're mad at me. Guess you have a right to be, but—"

"Fucking correct, I do. Keeping secrets. Treating Eddi and me like children. Then head-butting me. Not to mention, firing some kind of illegal weapon—"

The hammer clanged. "I butted you because you were stomping on my hand," he reminded her. "And those whalers had already tried to kill us. Run us down. And damn near succeeded. Or did you forget that?"

They glared at each other, but she had to admit, he was right about the whalers. She shuddered. The sheer terror of those moments when the prow had loomed over her, and she'd expected to die . . . Maybe it *was* war. Violence for violence. This man had given his legs in battle. She couldn't call him a coward, or someone who evaded the consequences of his beliefs.

"But for what it's worth," he muttered, looking past her, "I'm sorry I dragged you into it. And about Tehiyah. I didn't intend that."

She drew a deep breath, suddenly shaky, as if her feelings were only now catching up to everything that had happened. Who the fuck was she to point fingers and act sanctimonious? The disgraced Dr. Pollard. The failure. The outcast. "Well. As long as we're apologizing. That time, up in the forepeak—"

He let the hammer sag, and looked away. "Don't worry about it."

"I just wanted to say. It wasn't what you think. Not—your legs."

His gaze came back. Dwelt on her face. "No?"

"No."

"Then what?"

"I had some silly notion it would be . . . unprofessional." A sharp corner of the engine was digging into her back; she wriggled away. The cold air was still and icy down here, and the sea sounded very close, sloshing beneath the thin hull only inches below. She took a deep breath. "But I was wrong. What did Quill used to say? 'South of sixty, there's no law'?"

"Actually, the saying is, 'no God.'"

"Uh-huh. So . . . what I wanted to say is . . . I was wrong."

His mouth was sour on hers. His breath was not so great and his stubble grated on her skin. But none of this stilled the hunger to feel someone's arms around her, or to keep kissing him. And she probably smelled just as bad.

But you didn't have to smell great to want a man.

She glanced back once, up the ladderway, to make sure no one was coming. Then stripped off jacket and sweater and bra. His gaze followed the swing of her breasts as he unzipped his own clothes, then cursed as he couldn't get his pants off.

"Turn over, on your back," she told him, and straddled him, shivering, naked legs and shoulders instantly goosefleshed in the frigid air, yet with an interior heat igniting. She left her boots on and pushed her pants down onto them, careful not to dislodge the scab on her thigh, so that when she knelt her knees weren't on the cold deck but on the folds of cloth. Their smells mingled, and she bent to his cock springing up from a nest of kinky black hair but before she took it into her mouth decided against it and just brushed it lightly with her cheek.

She forked her body over him and guided him in, to a place that was exactly where she'd wanted someone for so long, and gasped and arched her back. Then whispered "Fuck" as the back of her head slammed into an arch of hollow steel tubing.

He half rolled and they crawled and pushed deeper into the embrace of the engine and the muffler and heavy thick black rubber hoses strapped with shining stainless connectors and extruded metal tubes bent and twisted in among one another. Here they were boxed in on all sides but she had room to straighten. She reached up to grasp an icy cold thick stem of metal with both hands. She used that leverage to lift and then plunge, him grunting beneath her, his face turning blotchy and red. An iron stem seemed to be reciprocating inside her, hard and thick but hot instead of icy cold. For a few seconds it felt like a hard yoga workout. Then the pleasure fired like electricity deep in her belly, and he reached up and grasped her breasts. She arched her back and opened her mouth and he closed his eyes and bared his teeth and they hung there, welded like hot-running machines, as the energy and lust they'd brought out of the sea so long before came again into both of them and they moved together, together, straining at the boundaries of self and space.

She lifted herself and collapsed beside him. Suddenly she was cold again, and her knees hurt where she'd knelt, and soreness chafed her thighs. But she didn't care. He pulled her sweater down and covered her with his arm. "Incredible," he said into her ear, and for a few minutes they snuggled, drowsy, spent. Until her legs began to cramp. So at last they moved apart, rearranged themselves. She crept out from between the engines and searched around on the deck and found the hammer and the screwdriver they'd been using to chisel out the ice and set to work again.

But when they tried the engine again it still didn't start. This time Bodine traced the line and found more ice in the hoses to the saltwater cooling pump. He took off the connectors, leaving the through-hull closed, and she carried the heavy black hose up into the galley. Her legs were still quivering as she poured the boiling water Hy had going for the dinner spaghetti into it. Meanwhile he took the pump apart and blowtorched the ice out. When they reinstalled the hose and pump the engine turned over and kept running. A weak cheer rang out in the salon as Eddi brought the wheel around. The thrum wormed through the hull. Madsen said to keep it down to a thousand rpm, to stretch their fuel. But they were headed north.

"Next stop, Capetown. But we're taking on a lot of ice," he added, peering out through the portlight. "That sleet's freezing. We should probably knock some off before it gets dark."

"We have to do that now?" Eddi called from the dome. She'd been steering for hours, but refused every time Sara offered to take a turn.

"You know how Jamie used to nag us to not let it build up. Said we could turn over. And then, if you go in the water—"

"Helpless in sixty seconds."

"Dead in five minutes."

Kimura looked from one to the other as they doubled, howling. Sara wiped laugh-tears and sniffled. Suddenly she felt giggly. Maybe it was getting laid after so long, or maybe, more likely, it was just being headed home.

Home . . . there was a little science center on Nantucket. It was named after Maria Mitchell, the first female American astronomer. Maybe she could teach there. With her degree, it would be a step down. Maybe a couple of steps. But she could get an apartment. Take fourth-graders out to the Moors to bird-watch.

For a moment something like a question, or even like a vision, hung between her and the sea: Mick Bodine working his way up a handrail toward the door of a cottage in Coatue, or maybe Madaket. There might be something like contentment. Stalking the marshes again, in the winter silence—

She shook herself. What was she thinking? They might not make it back. Even if they did, they'd probably be looking at criminal charges. Piracy. A jail sentence. They were so far beyond the pale it was ridiculous to think of any life after this.

Lars handed her one of the baseball bats. It was dented, beaten up, they'd used them so often and so abusively. She took a swing, grinning at Kimura's boggled expression. "You too," she told him, and jaundiced daylight slid in slanting as they pulled on their suits and the companionway hatch slammed open.

Topside the light was machined steel. A bank of clouds lay on the starboard hand, solid as icebergs. The sleet had stopped but she guessed only for the moment. A squall trailed its skirts into the sea. *Anemone* rolled. The halyards clanged. The mast creaked. Ice fell from aloft, clattering on the icy decks. Sara looked away from the bundle strapped to the forward stay. Tehiyah was going home too, but not as she'd probably hoped: in triumph, to television specials and celebrity fund-raisers.

She clipped on her safety line, made sure Hy's was on too. Then led him forward, stepping carefully as Lars began flailing at the boom. "Like this," she told Kimura, and wound up and took a solid whack at the inches of rime atop the coach roof. The pale carapace resisted, but gradually cracks spiderwebbed it. At her third swing it burst apart like dropped crystal. She kicked it over the side. The green sea walked past, bubbles whirling in their wake. She squatted and hammered with the butt of the bat until the ice split and clattered apart like supercooled diamonds. Kimura's first clumsy swing glanced off without making a scratch. "Didn't you have to do this on the whaler?" she asked him, sitting back on her heels.

"No. We had steam lances."

"How nice. Well, here we have to, every couple days. I guess until we get far enough north." She shivered, visualizing how cold it would be here in another month. She'd always remember this sere beauty. But even more, this sea's paralyzing terror. It was a place apart, inviolable, touched by man but not yet tamed. She didn't condone what Mick and Lars had done. But now she understood it. If the whales could be saved, perhaps there was hope.

They worked forward, whacking and cracking until the ice delaminated and slid overboard in pearlescent sheets. Kimura whooped and struck a samurai pose, then flailed at the lifelines, knocking off frosted tubes that shattered like glass straws. She worked until her arms were leaden, then rested, feeling a looseness, a trickle between her thighs, as she squatted on her haunches.

The squall brushed over them and snow began to fall, heavy wet flakes that cut off vision. She got up and tapped ice off the shrouded form lashed to the forward brace, loosening the silvery shell until it crashed to the deck. The snow whirled down, speckling the sea with millions of dimples that spread with a hiss so faint it could barely be heard above the motor's hum, the ripple as the prow parted the dull green.

She kicked the ice from the corpse over the bow and was turning when she half glimpsed something far off behind them, only dimly visible in the falling snow. She shaded her eyes and looked again, blinking flakes from her lashes. Another barely distinguishable glimpse of some disturbance against the unillumined sea. A small boat? She edged aft, clearing her safety line as she went, peering in that direction. But she didn't see it again. If it had been there at all.

"Looking for something?" Lars was hanging off the stern, suit unfastened, one arm around the after stay. Obviously pissing, though his lower body was turned away. From next to him Mick looked up from the cockpit seat.

"You're going to freeze that thing off."

"Yeah, it wasn't such a good idea. Instant frostbite." He shook and tucked.

"See something?" Mick said. He kept looking at her, as if he'd never really seen her before. A smile lurked in his eyes. She smoothed her hair and looked aside. For just a moment, she saw the cottage again. The winter marsh behind it, reeds and cattails blowing in the wind, and in the distance, the far distance, the surf white as an old woman's hair toward Smith's Point.

"Thought I did. Like an inflatable."

The Dane said, "Out here? Hundreds of miles from anything?" He looked at the wheel, which was unattended; Auer was still steering from the enclosed station. "I'll take my trick up here. It's snowing and the radar's out; I can see better than from the dome."

"I'll take it, since I'm up here," Bodine said. "Been a while since I've steered."

When she looked back again the snowy curtain wavered. For a moment she saw the sea clear; black jagged waves; utterly empty, save for the vee of their wake. Void, like the thousands of miles all around.

She tried not to think of how casually this icy sea had eaten Perrault. Her breath caught in her throat; a band of dread oppressed her chest, tightening around her lungs. She coughed. Courage, she thought. "Just my imagination, I guess."

She slid open the companionway hatch, and set a boot on the first step. Then glanced aft as she started to lower herself down the ladder.

And froze, throat locked. From the blowing snow and mist and twisting steam from the exhaust, something unimaginable was taking shape.

17

The Rogue

The yell had barely left her throat, pulling everyone in the cockpit around, when the whale crashed into the sloping stern, jerking them off their feet and tumbling them over one another. Madsen grabbed the wheel. Kimura slammed down into the winch, yelping as something snapped audibly. Sara lost her balance, flailing in the companionway, then toppling over the coaming. Only at the last moment did she catch herself as the blunt head, bigger than a tractor-trailer, descended on the dinghy and its ramp with a shearing crunch that shook the whole boat.

It hung there, to the accompaniment of the grating slide of shattered ice and the discordant twang of rigging like a harp being crushed in a garbage compactor, and the groaning crackle of a hull under unendurable stress. As the stern was forced down, green water flooded up, boiling along the slanted counter. Ice shattered and flew as the deck warped beneath the terrific downward weight of the coffee-colored mass.

She clung astonished. This close, staring up, she registered strange traceries on that parchment-colored integument, as if urban gangs had gouged graffiti into it year after year until it became a palimpsest of uninterpretable images. No gleam of gold diatoms this time. That is, if it was the same whale. Yet there couldn't be two this color, this size. Purplish eruptions big as her fists dotted it, as if crab-sized chiggers had burrowed beneath the skin. The whole gigantic forehead, the size of a two-story house, was hung with shredding skin as if from a bad sunburn. No eyes were visible; the orbs were so far around and below that from her vantage point the creature looked blind. Nor could she see a mouth, so far was it slung below the gigantic head.

With a massive low snort a choking spray that smelled like a combination of rotten fish and a freshly fertilized field blew over them. Madsen had seized a boat hook and was darting it at the monster again and again. The blunt tip bounced back without making the slightest impression. But gradually the thing slid aft, or else the boat was skidding out from under it, hull shrieking. But some projection, or perhaps the burst and torn-apart inflatable, caught or dragged, not letting it go cleanly, and *Anemone* reared farther, dragged down by the stern as in the cabin gear left shelves and lockers with a roaring clatter.

Sara had to grab the jambs of the companionway so as not to fall. Below her in the tilted cockpit a bloodlessly detached leg tobogganed down the ramp. A turbulent foam frothed where the screw-wash met the gigantic bulk that lay pressing down the rearmost projection of the boat, now many feet under water. For a moment she could not credit her eyes. Then a body followed, hands outflung, clawing at polished fiberglass, and she gasped.

It was Bodine, shouting hoarsely as he went.

She lunged, hand outstretched. "Mick!" she screamed. But without looking back, he vanished into the boiling whirlpool.

The whale slipped free and with an enormous rolling turmoil submerged. When the sea crashed back the animal was still visible, submerged, wavering. Then it sank away, receding, leaving *Anemone* quivering all over with the sudden release. For a moment Sara glimpsed a human form beneath the seethe, stroking desperately upward. Then it too sank away, fading; became indistinct, and vanished.

The boat pitched back upright, shaking off the sea, though the stern was bent awkwardly and splintered edges showed like torn burlap where the high-strength composite had cracked and only partially sprung back into place. From them long skeins of shed skin trailed like snagged veils. The rigging groaned. Ice clattered down, shattering like chandeliers in an earthquake all around her. Where whale and man had vanished a turbulent whirlpool of silvery-green sea boiled, then drifted astern as the screw bit in again and the boat resumed its forward progress.

She scrambled out of the hatchway and seized the wheel, pushing Lars aside. Whipped it over to port, shouting into the hatchway, "Eddi! Give me the controls!"

"Holy fuck," Lars said, trembling, white-faced, bracing himself with one arm. He'd nearly gone down the sloping stern too. Kimura lay where he'd fallen, holding his side.

"Mick's down there. Get a line. Get a life preserver!"

"D'you see him? Where is he?"

"In that boil. To your left. There. He'll come up. When he does, hit him with that throw line."

"Open the locker," Madsen snapped. "Hy? Move!" Kimura started. He reached in and came up with a hank of orange line and a throw ring. Sara kept the rudder over, gaze nailed to where Bodine had gone down. The bow came round so slowly that she started to advance the throttle, but then dropped her hand. If they went too fast she'd overshoot. *Helpless in sixty seconds* kept going through her mind. Fully thirty had to have gone by already. She stood on tiptoe. Was that a head, bobbing in the dissipating foam? or the peak of a wave?

"Hy, get up on the coach roof. Do you see him? Do you see?"

"My ribs," Kimura panted, bent where he sat. Sweat dripped off his brows. His fingers dug into his side, relaxed, spasmed again. He gathered himself, face contorted, and crawled like a stepped-on crab up onto the coach roof. Shaded his eyes. "I . . . see something," he began.

Sara brought the rudder back to centerline, aiming at the fading patch that rocked fifty yards ahead. "Where? Where is he? Point, Hy. Point."

The Japanese stretched out a shaking arm. Following it, she was drawn not to where Bodine had disappeared, but off to the right. Where the sea broke over what looked like tan rocks. A crooked, sideways jet burst like a geyser, broke into mist, and drifted raining across the back of a swell.

"*Pis og lort.* It's coming again," Madsen cursed, as if he didn't believe what he was seeing. He bent to a forward locker divided from the rest, unsnapped a latch, and hauled it up.

Sara jerked her eyes off the oncoming monster and searched again where the sea was now gentling, smoothing. They purred up on it and she reached for the throttle, intending to stop, but Madsen's glove overrode hers and pushed it all the way forward. She rounded on him. "Mick's still down there!"

"He's not coming up. It's been too long."

"No! We've got to be here when he—"

"He's dead—"

They were screaming in each other's face when Eddi swarmed up the companionway and thrust herself between them. She stared to starboard. "Oh Christ," she moaned. "Look."

The very sea bulged, driven before the massive ondriving head as if by the bow of a great ship. The same thought must have hit all three of them at the same time, for they grasped the wheel together and hauled it over. *Anemone*'s bow swung toward the oncoming beast, but so damned slowly. Lars hit the button for the second engine. It coughed into life and he pushed the gear lever forward. The boat came around faster. Until it was aimed head to head, and boat and animal drove toward each other across a slick jostling sea.

"Shoot this at it," Lars shouted, and handed her an object in tangerine plastic that only belatedly did she recognize was a flare pistol. "It's cocked."

She leveled it across the coach roof and pulled the trigger. A ball of scarlet flame cracked out, bright in the gray light and the falling snow. It drew a short arc and met the oncoming head, spattering bright sparks, and glanced off and down into the sea. Still burning, it sank, rays shimmering up to refract in a slowly fading glimmer. But the whale drove on.

It had not altered its course at all, had not even seemed to notice it. At the last possible moment Madsen spun the wheel left.

They met with a crash that knocked them all off their feet and set the mast jangling again.

But the boat's smooth flank seemed to yield, absorbing the blow. The whale dragged down their side, its spout jetting again to drench them all with a stinking exhalation. For a moment she thought they'd avoided a direct collision. But then something hard crashed against the hull. A crunch ran up her bones into the very tympana of her ears, as if her own body were being torn apart. And as the scribbled waxy-yellow bulk, scored with livid signs, passed by again, she glimpsed something hanging from its flank, long as a man's body, trailed by many fathoms of bright orange line striped at intervals with black. From his clinging perch, one arm hugging the mast, Kimura yelled, "Harpoon. One of our—one of *their* harpoons."

"The fleet's?" Madsen shouted.

The Japanese nodded hard. "From *Number* 3. They use that line."

The whale had half rolled as it slid aft. Now, for the second time, she looked directly down into its eye. Only for a fraction of a second, though, as her gaze dropped to a splitting-wedge of jaw, long as a stretch limousine, that gaped to expose yellow pointed teeth many inches long.

Then it was gone again, in a welter of foam. The lift and drop of a massive tail sent solid sea cascading over them, drenching them all.

With a spasmodic, rejecting gesture a panting Madsen pushed both throttles all the way forward and spun the wheel centerline, pointing between two small floes several hundred yards ahead. "Shit, shit," he mumbled. The engines rose in pitch. Yet something was wrong with the notes, as if one warred with the other, discordant, grinding. A shudder worked its way up the steering pedestal, plucking the after shroud to a shimmy. A thunderclap came from astern, echoing over the water and back off the ice. The mast swayed and creaked. From beneath came that same cracking groan they'd heard earlier in the voyage.

"Oh fuck, the keel," Eddi said, clinging to the winch and looking astern, where the whale had submerged again. The thunder, Sara realized, must have been its tail striking the sea as it sounded.

She whirled, staring. "Where are you going? Mick—he's still back there—"

"He's dead, Sara. He never came up."

Eddi's arms wrapped her as if she thought she might go over the side after him. She shuddered, looking down at the cold sea sliding past as *Anemone* accelerated. But slowly, with a deep shudder like her own.

"She's not getting on step," Madsen yelled. "I've got rpm, but something's wrong."

Auer hugged her closer, and water squelched and ran down between them. "Hy, you better get down from there," she shouted. "Can you get down?"

"My side. I think I broke something."

"Sara, can you help me get him down?"

"I need a lookout. In case that thing comes back."

"Yeah. Yeah. I'll be right back up." She forced herself to move. They got the sobbing man into the cockpit, then down into the salon. They laid him in a bunk. When she stepped back Sara heard a splash. She looked down and flinched. The water around her boots was an inch deep.

When they poked their heads topside again the engines were howling, the stern was shaking, and the masttop was quivering in large circles against charcoal clouds from which snow was still dropping. Madsen kept adjusting the throttles and frowning. He shouted, above the yowl of engines and the whine of the wind, "How's he doing?"

"In pain. A broken rib?"

"I think we left it behind. It can't keep up, not at this speed. But there's something wrong."

"Sounds like it," Auer said. "And we're taking water below."

Lars blanched. "Water? How fast? How much?"

"About an inch on the salon floor." Sara kept swallowing, trying not to think about Mick tobogganing past, just out of her reach, or the thing that had attacked them. "When it hit us? Maybe it knocked something loose. Like the keel."

"That wire Dru and Jamie rigged," Eddi said.

"I need to check it." He looked around the horizon, then back where they'd come from. The sea surged in the gathering darkness. Snow whirled into their faces. "Eddi, can you take it?"

"Up here? It's fucking freezing, with this wind—"

"Afraid so. No radar. Use the binoculars. Look for white patches. But keep going. As fast as you can without shaking her to pieces."

"We're burning a lot of fuel," Sara pointed out.

"I just want to leave that thing astern." Madsen relinquished the wheel. "Okay, I'm going below."

In the salon Sara squatted beside him as he pulled the access plates off the keel well and inspected the pivots. Hy kept groaning in the bunk but there was nothing she could do for him until they figured out where the leak was coming from. Finally the Dane clambered out. He said harshly, "The pins, all right. Sheared through their sockets."

"But it's only an inch deep, and it hasn't come up any."

"That's because it runs aft and down into the bilge, and the pumps in the engine compartment pump it out. As long as they're running, we're okay. When they stop, we sink."

"Oh shit."

"Uh-huh." Oil and bilge-muck smeared his cheeks. He looked gaunt and exhausted. "It didn't seem like anything could kill Mick," he muttered. "He got through the war. Coped with everything." He glanced at her. "At one point I thought the two of you—"

"Is there any way we can slow down the leak?" she asked. Not wanting to talk about the other.

"Not that I can see. We're lucky it didn't tear out of the hull. Then we'd just turn over and go down." He rubbed his cheek, glancing to where the Japanese moaned. "Can you do something for him? I'm going to check the shafts. See if that's where all that vibration's coming from."

When he went aft she pulled a chair to the bunk. "Any better, Hy?"

"Every time I breathe, hurts."

"Are you spitting up blood?" She had a vague memory, something about broken ribs puncturing the lungs. "Let me get the first-aid book."

"I very need something for this pain," he said. "This is really hurts."

The book wasn't very helpful. Wrapping or bandaging wouldn't help. Painkillers would help him breathe, that was about all. She selected some and took them to him. "Water," he croaked.

"The system's still frozen. I'm melting ice for tea. Can you get them down dry?" He made a face but swallowed and lay back, stiffening with each breath. She put her face in her hands. She ought to cry, oughtn't she? But they hadn't really been in love. Had they?

"Are you all right, Sara?" Hy peered at her like a sick cat.

"I'm just so very tired. And scared." She shook herself and lifted her head. "I understand why it's angry. After all. What I don't understand is why it's displaying this agonistic behavior toward *us.* We were trying to *stop* the killing."

He passed a hand over a sweating forehead. "Perhaps it has confused us with the whalers."

"It's the only explanation I can think of. Did you see the harpoon?"

"I saw it." Kimura shifted and flinched again. Breathed hard. "Oh. That does not feel good. Like harpoon in *my* side. But the strange thing is, they are not designed to do that."

"To do what?"

"To stick in like that. I don't know the right word—but there are explosives in the head. A bomb? It explodes inside, to kill. This one did not go off, or the animal would not be alive. An explosion inside will kill any whale." He hesitated. "That is why I am not sure this is a whale."

For a second she wasn't sure she'd heard right. "What—what are you saying? That it *isn't* a whale? I *saw* it. What the hell *else* can it be?"

"No, no—you are right. It is what it is. A sperm whale. Male, most likely, from the size. It witnessed the attack on the pod—"

"On its mate, maybe? Maybe that was its calf—"

"Those were minkes, not sperm, Sara. Also sperm pods do not come down to the Antarctic. Only the males."

"Oh. Right." She was still puzzling over what he'd said, though. "You didn't hit your head, did you? When you got knocked down?"

"No."

"No bumps, lacerations? Blood from your scalp?"

He shook his head. "What is your feeling? You are the animal behaviorist, after all."

Behind them the engine-hum dropped a note, then another. A disquieting vibration laced it, setting up a sympathetic buzzing somewhere in the galley. She tried to think objectively, but it seemed harder than usual. "Well—I hadn't really had time to think about it. In chimps—I guess, more generally, in primates—we see agonistic behavior mainly either in dominance relationships, or in territorial defense. In fact, they meet Vehrenkamp's—uh, criteria for despotic dominance. But—*whales*?" She waved her hands, as if she were back in the classroom, and just that gesture made the words come more easily. "If they *have* social hierarchies, there's got to be some mechanism for intimidating conspecifics. To assert dominance status, and access to sexually receptive females. I could see a butting behavior stemming from sexual competition. Chimps also defend territory, to exploit scarce food resources, and cooperate to do so by violence—thus mimicking, or prefiguring, human tribal warfare. Um—but I can't see whales doing that."

He looked grave. "It's hard to conceive of. Based on what little I have seen, I would agree that it is unlikely."

"But there *is* a precedent for a rogue. Almost two centuries ago, now—"

"Mocha Dick," Kimura said.

Despite herself a chill tensed her shoulders. She sat back, trying to force the behavior they'd just observed into some methodological framework. Could this animal really be aggressive, malevolent, murderous? Like the legendary beast?

The old frame house still stood on Center Street, only a block or two from the restaurants and bike rental stands and T-shirt shops of Nantucket harbor. Her family had lost it long ago; the last time she'd been to the island, it had been a fancy art gallery, with a candy shop next door.

A plaque at street level said it had been owned by Captain George Pollard, Jr.; that Herman Melville had spoken to him, and that Pollard's true story had been the basis for the famous novel.

But in fact, Melville had not met the old man until long after the book had been published. Pollard had gotten another captaincy after the sinking of the *Essex*, despite the lurid tales of castaways and cannibalism. But he'd lost that ship as well, and two strikes were enough for the canny shipowners whose mansions still stood along maple-shaded streets. Pitied by the townspeople, Pollard had finally been given the sinecure of a night watchman.

But Melville had read about the disaster, or heard a garbled sea-version during his own voyages. He'd changed the name, and perhaps the beast's color—although most sources said the name "Mocha" had actually referred to Mocha Island, off Chile—to Moby Dick, the White Whale. Now she wondered what might have led to that long-ago maritime disaster. Could the same events recur after two long centuries? Could a difference in color between one creature and its fellows, the very whiteness of the whale itself, lead to rejection, thence to self-awareness, and at last, to violence? Was she perhaps reading her own feelings into this creature's? Or did she even need a reductive explanation?

"You're very quiet," Kimura murmured.

"I'm thinking."

"About your hypothesis? Damage to spindle neurons?"

"Right now, I'm wondering if that's even necessary."

"How do you mean?"

She spread her hands. "Well, try to look at this from the animal's point of view. It's probably seen this slaughter, this predation, going on for its whole life. This . . . mass murder. Then it sees the bloodshed once more, up close, and snaps. Like a psychotic break.

"Or maybe not even that. I mean, what would *we* do if aliens began harvesting us as food? Generation after generation? Maybe attack *is* the only rational response." She halted, hands outstretched, as she remembered her own lab, and Arminius's menaced snarl. The last time she'd seen him, before the intern had gone in to work with him. She'd dismissed it as morning grouchiness, maybe hunger. Dismissed it . . . to her everlasting regret.

Madsen came back, wiping his hands on a paper towel he wadded and threw aside. He blew out, looking tired, avoiding their questioning looks. "The pumps are clear. But they won't run long without charge from the generators. And something's still wrong. A lot of vibration. Either the props are damaged, or the shafts got wrenched out of line when that thing slammed into the stern."

Sara looked down at the ripples that ran to and fro, lapping at her boots. "Can we keep running the engines?"

"Not for much longer. The mounting bolts are starting to pull out. I told Eddi to run slower, bring the rpm down." He jerked the silly dog-faced cap off and scratched tousled dark blond hair, and Sara saw that before many more years he'd begin to bald. "I'm not—I don't know as much about all that as Dru and Jamie did. Or even Mick."

"But we have to keep one going, right? To pump?"

"Until we run out of fuel, anyway. We'll just have to make as much distance toward Melbourne as we can." He caught her quizzical look. "Yeah—Australia. With damaged shafts and the mast the way it is, we can't make Cape Town. So that's our only hope now. Or maybe Tasmania—that'd be a few hundred miles closer."

Kimura winced as the boat leaned. Eddi must be avoiding ice. He lifted a hand. "Yeah?" Madsen said.

"It may not be smart to keep engine on."

"What do you mean?"

"The longer you run, the more damage. We will need it if there is another storm. Also, the sound will tell it where we are."

"It?" The Dane blinked, then understood. "Will tell *it* where we are? Yeah, I guess so, maybe. Wait a minute. It didn't attack us, until we were running the engines. Before that, we were sailing."

"And when we were with the fleet, we were running on the motors," Sara said.

Madsen kicked at the water sloshing back and forth. "But if we shut down, we lose the bilge pumps."

"But if it's following us . . . Hy, how fast can a sperm whale swim?"

Kimura said, "*Physeter macrocephalus* can make up to forty kilometers an hour when he is being chased. But not for long periods. Maybe half that, over distance."

"What's that in knots?" She'd never been good at converting.

"It would be about forty miles an hour, to sprint. Maybe fifteen or twenty, to keep going?"

Madsen grimaced. "Jesus. I thought we'd be getting some distance on him. But maybe not."

"What else can you tell us?" Sara asked the Japanese, suddenly conscious that they weren't making the best use of the closest thing to a whale expert aboard.

Kimura settled himself in the bunk; his voice grew precise, almost pedantic. "Well, this one is middle-aged. Forty to sixty years old. From the size, and the fact he, it, travels alone—the younger bulls pod in age groups; they only become solitary later."

They were interrupted by a louder racket aft, a teeth-edging clatter added to the already noisy engine vibration. "Something else let go," Madsen observed gloomily. "I'd better go look."

The companionway clacked back, revealing a square of near black. Snow eddied down in whirls before falling into the sloshing water and vanishing. It seemed to be coming down much more heavily than when she'd been on deck. "Hey! I'm freezing my ass off up here," Auer yelled. "How about somebody else takes a freakin' turn?"

"Just a sec, Eddi." She made herself add, "I'll come up. But we're trying to decide what to do."

"Well, make it fast. Please."

A minute or two later, without warning, the engines shut down. First one, shaking the whole boat with a resounding series of knocks, then the other. The salon went quiet. The buzzing in the galley died. When he came back Madsen said, "Well, that's it. They're tearing out of the mountings and seizing up."

"Maybe it's best," Kimura said. "With the whale, I mean."

"Maybe, but we've still got this leak." Madsen kicked up spray. "We can run the small pump for a while, it's electric, but once the battery dies . . ."

"Let's make sure we've gotten away from that thing," Sara said, getting up. Reluctantly, she pulled her mustang suit down from where she'd hung it to drip. It stank of mildew. As she thrust her legs in she smelled sweat and sex too. Don't think of him. He was gone, along with Dru and Tehiyah. They'd be hard put to make it to safety themselves, the way the Dewoitine was coming apart around them. She didn't want to go topside again. Once she got home, she'd never go to sea again. Just the ferry, back and forth to Hyannis. "Uh, Lars, what sails we want up?"

"We should be okay with the main. I hope. Just keep both reefs in it."

"That won't give us much speed." She moved toward the companionway, grabbing a scarlet scarf to wrap around her face. Tehiyah's? Well, she wouldn't be needing it anymore. The most unsettling thing now was watching Lars's confidence erode. Who'd been senior in his and Bodine's partnership? She'd thought it was the Dane. But maybe not.

"If he can't hear us, we won't need speed," the Japanese said. "We can dodge away and he will not find us. And maybe I can see if he is back there. With the equipment Mr. Bodine had." He started to struggle up, but stopped at a sitting position, holding his side with eyelids squinched closed. "Is there more of pills? And you said, tea?"

"I'll get it." Lars blinked and stood. "Go on, give Eddi a break. I'm going to get a GPS position. I'll come up in an hour. Three left fit to crew. An hour on, two hours off?"

"Sounds like a plan," she said, coughing as a chill shook her. She really didn't want to go out into the snow. Into the wind. Up on deck, exposed.

"We'll get out of this, Sara." He tried a grin.

"Yeah. Sure we will." She gave the groaning Kimura a quick pat, squeezed Madsen's arm, and headed up.

18

The Night and the Darkness

The snow blew past in wavering curtains, so thick at times she couldn't see fifty yards. At other moments a caricature of the moon sped through cloud-wrack, an uncanny doppelgänger of the dimmed-out, low-lying sun. Above her the wind genny clattered away, vibrating in the gusts.

She stood braced into the wind-cheating upward flip of the coach-roof, glasses laid across it, every fiber shuddering, face and fingers unfeeling as ancient marble. The wind streamed through the shrouds with a discordant hum. The main, reefed down, strained taut as the boat heaved upward, then fought like a captured demon when she sank. Sara kept aiming the binoculars aft, searching their wake, but was afraid to spend long with her back to the bow.

With good reason. An hour past midnight a pale ghost glimmered ahead. She stepped aft, disengaged the self-steerer, and took the wheel. The berg rose above her on a dark wave, burning white in the queer eclipse-like semidarkness, then sank away. She sketched a dodge north-east, then turned east again. When the twilight vibrated unbroken ahead once more she hooked the steerer up again and resumed her post.

Moon and sun waned amid the speeding clouds. For long periods they disappeared entirely, leaving her submerged in a weird objectless dusk so disorienting she had to beat her sides with her arms to reassure herself she was awake, or even alive. But then they emerged again, feeble and flickering, distant candles, but there, riding with her on her flight through a desolation that seemed more than ever hostile to any life but that which moved hidden far beneath. From below came sporadic hammering and clanking. Madsen or Eddi trying to fix something. She stamped wooden feet in frozen boots. Snow built epaulets on her shoulders, coated her mask. The cold grew more intense, and she began to shake. She shook for a long time. Then, very gradually, the shudders eased off.

Sometime later the companionway hatch banged open. She tried to back away and stumbled, only just catching herself before her face smashed into the wheel.

A bulky worm heaved itself from the dimly lit square. The square vanished with a thump, and the figure straightened to a half bow. "You all right?" Madsen muttered, as if through heavy cloth. In the gray obscurity he had no face, only a blank oval with the merest suggestion of goggles.

"Yeah. F-frozen though, though."

"Much ice?"

"Now and then. Might be smaller pieces I can't see. We scraped one a while ago."

"Yeah, I heard."

"What were you doing down there?"

"Trying to brace the starboard side. Some of the frames are broken."

"The keel?"

"Nothing we can do about that until we get to calmer water. What I'm really afraid of—" His head bent; he peered around. "Huh. Seas are bigger."

"Yeah, they're kicking up again. What is it you're really afraid of?"

"We're taking water through the starboard buoyancy tank. The one that's supposed to be airtight. Hey." He squinted. "What happened to Tehiyah?"

Sara frowned, glancing toward the bow. A rift in the snowfall showed flapping canvas. The cold fingers of the wind had partially unwrapped the body. The head rose defiantly erect. Frozen solid, of course, but no doubt still as beautiful as ever. An ice sculpture. A grisly figurehead. She started to answer, but found no words to acknowledge the horror and fatigue. Instead she murmured, "The moon's going down."

"I'll sheet out. I don't see how the thing could still be following us. But we need to keep that water down. I told Eddi to turn in. She'll be on deck next. Can you bail? For maybe half an hour?"

Bail, she thought. Haul water, after freezing up here? Anger tried to take her, then fell away. She doubted she'd ever feel emotion again. She felt him squeeze her shoulder, and nodded apathetically. Then bent to slide the door back. Leaving Lars upright in the dusk, swaying with the roll, the boom surging against its restraints as the wind danced with castanets beneath the bitter moon.

Belowdecks a single light burned all the way forward. A feminine snore sawed from Eddi's cubicle. Sara stripped off boots and propped them upside down on the drain mat. Stripped off her suit. It crackled with ice as she beat at it. She leaned against the bulkhead and breathed slowly, closing her eyes. Fuck bailing. She was turning in. But as she took her first step aft she cursed wildly as her stockinged foot plunged into inches of freezing water.

She put her boots back on, went into the galley, and found the square brown bottle. She lifted it, murmuring, "To you, Tehiyah. Mick. Dru." The rum ignited in her throat. She shuddered. Hunger stirred at last. She rooted out a can of corned beef from some previous voyage and forked the frozen fat and forbidden red meat out of the sharp tin into her mouth, shuddering as warmth slowly pulsed out from her marrow into fingers and feet once again.

Then, reluctantly, she searched for the bailer. For aeons in the sloshing, frigid dimness she lifted bucket after bucket from boot height in the open bilge to waist level, wading across the width of the salon, and dumping it in the galley sink. Then trudged back for another, over and over, like Sisyphus.

When she could not lift her arms again, when her hands crimped into spasmed claws from the drag of the wire bail, she hung the bucket at last and waded toward the light. As she neared, it became a glimmer at the end of a long tunnel.

Deep within the forepeak someone bent over the keyboard. A screen flickered. She clung to the hatchway, fear harrowing her spine. Then he lifted his head and she saw it was not Bodine's ghost but rather Hy. Kimura peered into what must be to him utter darkness. She hesitated, then ducked inside and walked bent through the shifting of lines and tackle until she crouched beside him.

"What are you doing?"

"Listening," he whispered. Very carefully, he lifted the headphones, hissing as his torso twisted, and fitted them to her ears.

She closed her eyes. A distant shushing, a subdued susurration almost below the level of hearing. It swelled and waned like surf on a faraway strand.

"What is it?"

"Listen closely."

She did; to that unsettling, uncanny rush and ebb like a tide rustling a million crepitating potato chips along the ocean floor. Her lips parted. For a moment she wondered how deep it was here, how many fathoms down the black ocean reached to meet lightless rock. The Japanese frowned at the screen and fingernailed a dial.

Then she heard it. A staccato clatter, far away, succeeded by a slow deep sequence of tones or notes unlike anything she'd heard from the humpbacks. It died away echoing into deeps vast as interplanetary space, reverberating, growing fainter and fainter, lower and lower.

"What is that?" she whispered, suppressing a shiver.

"The first clicks, they are what we call a 'coda.' It is the whale identifying itself."

"The 5R. Mick said—he told me about it."

"I think it is the one that attacked us. From the way Mick described its call. He said he also recorded it. But I can't access. The files are password-protected."

She bent her fingers back one by one, wiggling them. As soon as she let go they curled into a fist again. "And then . . . ?"

He pushed back from the keyboard, the smooth face creased with worry. Winced, and rubbed his side. "The rest of its call? It is not one I have heard or read of."

"Who's it calling to?"

"That too I do not know. But I hear no answer."

She shivered again. Someday the last whale in the sea would call like that, to generations passed away, a whole world erased. "Can you, um, speculate?"

He looked away, frowning. "That is not a very scientific thing to do."

She suppressed a sigh. "Try it, Hy. Take a flier."

A spoke of light shimmered. He put it on the speaker, and they listened again: the clicking introduction, then the lingering, echoing whistle, rising and falling, drawn out, trailing off at last into that uneasy continuing breath of the sea.

"If I were to guess . . . it might be something like a hunting call. Or even a . . . battle chant."

She sat appalled. Finally managed, "Are you serious?"

"Why not?" He turned a blazing gaze on her. "A strange repeated call no one has heard or recorded. It has been hunting us. Isn't that so?"

". . . I guess so."

He shrugged. "Or perhaps something like a death song? To assert that positively, no, I could not. But you asked me to speculate."

She shuddered, imagining the beast searching through the deeps, listening for the engine-mutter of its prey. Sorting through the grinding of ice and the crash of wind-driven waves for their telltale spoor. Tuning through the crash and whisper of the sea for them, as Bodine had tuned through it for those he sought. If that was what it had homed in on before, and not simply the echo of their air-filled hull, or the humming whisper of their lute-stringed keel through the water. "So it's still tracking us?" she whispered.

"It is far astern now, I think." He ratcheted a geared knob and watched the display; ratcheted a few more degrees. Only a faint radiance flickered, a spoke bent upward here and there, then died away.

"How far?"

"That I can't tell. Only the bearing. That is all the equipment can give." He hesitated, then added, "It is still back there. Calling. That is all I can say with certainty."

She sat back on her heels, boots squishing, feet icy once more. The liquor glow had ebbed. The chill was creeping back. Her heart seemed to pump reluctantly, laboring to push some fluid thicker than blood. Like a whale's, slow and tremendous, counting off life against some timescale longer than a human's.

"And if it catches up?" she whispered.

"Then we die," Kimura whispered back. As if, she thought, it could hear them if they spoke aloud.

The call came again, eerie, tremulous, the frequency shifted by the electronics to a sound they could register with their feeble, narrow human senses. While all around them passed other sounds they could not hear, messages they did not even suspect, in what to them was only the night and the darkness.

"We ought to have some kind of plan. What we should do, if it does." She cast about for any possibility, and found so little. Abandon *Black Anemone* for a floe? Slow but sure death. Find the whaling fleet again, throw themselves on their mercy? Even if they were so inclined, that fleet lay hundreds of miles astern.

No. Hideyashi was right. If the creature found them again, they'd all die. She hugged herself, seeing the inrushing water, feeling the final embrace of that bitter sea. Even if it didn't return, the damage it had already done might finish them. *Bail*, Lars had told her. Without the engines, the wind genny could provide only so much power. "Maybe you'd better turn this off," she told him. "Conserve electricity."

"Well, you know, we are learning something."

"We are? What exactly are we learning here, Hy? And will it really matter, in the end?"

She waited for an answer, but he just breathed hard and clutched his side.

She was getting up to go aft when he murmured, "There is perhaps another possibility."

"What?"

He looked away. "Oh, it is nothing. Forget I said it."

This was the second time he'd done this. A wave of fatigued rage rose again, sharper now than during the bout topside with Lars. She gripped his neck and said fiercely, "*What,* Hy? Don't fucking *tease* me. Spit it out."

He murmured, face still turned away, "I was just thinking. It might be possible this is not a whale."

She shook him, eliciting a squeak of pain. "Then *what is it*?" Then dropped her hands. "Sorry. I didn't mean to—but you're testing my patience. We're about to die, maybe, and you—"

He hesitated again, but must have caught the look in her eye. He hurriedly said, still not meeting her gaze, "It might be a *kami*."

"A *kami.* Is that a Japanese word? Wait. You used it before. What is it, again?"

He worked his tongue around, obviously sorry he'd brought it up. "Oh, well, it is from Japanese . . . religion. Or no, folklore. In English it would be a god, or a demon . . . or maybe a spirit . . . but not exactly any of those."

She wasn't sure she was hearing this right. "What are you saying? That it's a supernatural being? Hy, I thought—"

"I know, I know." His hands fluttered up like startled moths at the same time a hollow scrape began up forward. They both froze. The scrape grew louder, drawing aft, accompanied by thumps and shudders. Someone, probably Madsen, had driven wooden wedges into gaps between the frames and the composite skin. That thin membrane vibrated ominously to a renewed cracking and scraping. Then subsided, as whatever they'd hit drifted free. This time.

When she looked back he was wiping his forehead. Who could sweat, in this cold? She said cruelly, "Are you *okay*, Hy? Because saying this thing is some kind of fucking spirit, well, that's pretty far out there. Especially for a *neuroanatomist*."

To her surprise he didn't look ashamed. "Well, you know, the words do not translate exactly in the way you use them in the West." He took a breath. "A wise priest once said, 'One should not bring logic to any discussion of Shinto.' In our culture, that other world is not separate from ours. It *is* ours. Right here with us, always."

She remembered then: His father was a priest. Maybe, under enough stress, everybody reverted to childlike beliefs, childish behaviors. She hadn't thought he was that far gone. So she said only, "Okay, I guess that's a . . . hypothesis. But how would you test it? And what would it mean? About the whale, that is."

"Oh, it actually might make sense." He looked almost eager. "You see, Shinto holds that anything we feel but cannot grasp, anything very powerful or very beautiful or that we human beings cannot understand—that can be *kami*. It does not have to be what you Westerners would call 'gods.'"

"Hy. This whale is powerful. Maybe even smart. But it's not some underwater ghost, or visitor from the spirit world. It's just a very violent rogue male, that's decided we're—"

He shook his head. "But you see, *kami* can appear as animals. Can have both a merciful and a violent nature. If the manifestation is violent, this means the human and the spirit world are out of balance."

She snorted. "And what's that mean? And how do we bring them back 'in balance'?"

"To that, the answer is simple. Any priest will tell you that. We will have to placate it in some way."

She started to laugh, but stopped. Crazy, yet . . . hadn't she felt something uncanny about it too?

No. No! This whole discussion was ridiculous. She must be even more tired than she'd thought, maybe even a little drunk. She turned to leave, but found a dark shape blotting out the exit. She tensed.

"It's just a whale," Eddi Auer said from the doorway. She sounded exhausted, not like someone just awakened from a refreshing sleep. Her voice dragged. "Just a huge whale. And it's hurt, so it's calling. Is this water on the floor deeper? It feels deeper. And are we leaning over to starboard?"

"We need to keep bailing," Sara said, though her forearms spasmed painfully as she said it. "I put in half an hour. Maybe that's not enough."

"You think that's what its vocalization means, Eddi?" Kimura said. "It is calling for help?"

"That's what it's saying. It's wounded. You saw that harpoon. But I guess no one's answering."

"Sperms are fairly rare in icy waters," the Japanese said. "Though they have been reported. I was surprised to see it here, myself."

"If there was some way to help it—"

"*Help* it?" Sara couldn't restrain a sardonic laugh. "It tried to sink us!"

Eddi said stubbornly, "Or maybe it was just trying to rub the harpoon off. Did you ever think of that?"

Sara and Kimura looked at each other as Auer went on. "If we could do something for it, maybe get that harpoon out, it'd realize we're different from the whalers. And isn't that what we're out here for? To help them?"

Sara raked her hands through her hair, feeling like pulling it out, roots and all. It was dirty and sticky, but she didn't give a damn how it—or she—looked just now. "Well, these are interesting theories. That it's some kind of vengeful spirit. Or a poor wounded lion, looking for a mouse to pull the thorn from its paw. But with any luck, we'll be in Australia in a few days. Eddi, you on your way up?"

"It's gonna be my turn soon. Shouldn't you be in your bunk? You don't look so good."

"I guess so." But she didn't feel sleepy, just terribly tired. The fatty beef churned in her stomach. "I guess . . . guess I'll lie down. Yeah." She shook her head once more, marveling at the human capacity for delusion. Then stumbled out.

When Eddi roused her she sat bolt upright from a horrible dream she instantly wished she was back in. The interior was pitch-dark, creaking. She stared at Auer's face outlined by a flashlight. "What time is it?"

"You looked like you needed the sleep. Come on, Sara. We're not going that fast, but we need a lookout on deck."

"Ice?"

"None for the last hour. Maybe we're out of it. The snow's letting up too. Need a hand?"

"No. No, I'm all right. I'm getting up."

The flash winked out. She groped into her suit and found her boots floating. This woke her the rest of the way. Her cubicle had been dry when she'd crawled into her bunk. The clatter of the bucket in the salon was succeeded by Eddi's curses.

Topside the sky was only faintly lighter than when she'd gone below, but only a little snow whispered across her face mask or scratched at her goggles. The seas still bulged astern, marching after them through a light haze. The moon was gone. She missed its pale vigil, but turned the illumination up on the instruments to give the illusion of company.

The sun never quite set, but that didn't mean it was day. The waves rolled black against gray. They seemed to curve upward, so that *Anemone* sailed at the bottom of a well. Very gradually the zenith lightened to a toneless pewter against which the masthead and sail were curving shadows. The snow was definitely lifting.

All at once, very suddenly, a fissure of opaline light cracked apart and there was the sun. She blinked as its rays lanced deep into the peaked waves, igniting a painful blue at their thin crests while they still remained black as obsidian in their hearts. They passed by, sizzling as they toppled, and she reflected dully how fearsome they would have seemed to her once. *Anemone* did seem less lively. Still lifting to each wave, but reeling as she did so, and always with that nagging inclination to starboard. Sara looked forward. The wrapped bundle lashed up there had its boots almost in the water. The tarp had unwrapped even more during the night. It flapped and cracked as the wind toyed with it, streaming it out over the sea. God, she had to fix that . . . had meant to do so before, but . . .

She turned and craned aft, searching each peak as it rose, rolled forward, shining indigo, then grass-green, and at last a brilliant priceless malachite veined with quartz as it surged past, breaking with a milky spatter against the quarter. The boom creaked as they rolled. Moving with tired deliberation, staggering, she stepped up on the cockpit seat and from there to the top of the coachroof. She balanced the binoculars on gloved fingertips to search long and earnestly the path the broad stern impressed into the heaving sea. From one quarter of the horizon to the other, then, slowly, back again. And at last lowered the glasses, blinking as cornflower afterimages pulsed and subdivided behind her retinas.

They were alone. Save for, far to the west, an inchoate shadow that might be fog. The rest of the horizon was distinct, with scattered clouds sailing past at no great altitude. But no spout had disturbed the undulating surface. No wave had broken on anything resembling a reef of pale coral.

The hatch slid back with a clack. Madsen's bare head emerged like a turtle's. He squinted pouched, swollen eyes at the low orb of the sun. His first words were, "We're taking more water."

She stared, sagging. He added, "But we made sixty miles last night."

"That's good, right?"

"I'm no navigator, but we're headed in the right direction." He sighed and heaved himself up. Searched around. "Any sign of—of it?"

She shook her head. "And the ice—haven't seen any since dawn. Are we out of it?"

"Not according to the chart, but I'm getting the impression that chart's just a guess. Especially this far east."

She wasn't sure she wanted to hear the answer to her next question. "How far is it to, um, Australia, anyway, Lars?"

He looked away. "About four thousand miles."

Holy crap, she thought, but didn't allow her lips to shape the words. "Nothing closer?"

He explained that two or three small groups or individual islands dotted the Southern Indian Ocean, but they were uninhabitable. "Landing there this close to the end of the season—well, we'd be better off running downwind all the way to Tasmania. Yeah, it's a long way. But nine or ten knots, that's a thousand miles every four days."

"So sixteen days, we'll be there."

"If we can stay afloat." He pulled himself the rest of the way up. "But the water's getting ahead of us now. Have to go to full-time bailing. Eddi's down there now—"

"Lars . . . there are only three of us who can steer and bail. I don't think we can do that nonstop for sixteen days."

"Then we've no other choice but to start the engine."

She couldn't suppress a shiver. She didn't want to even voice what Hy had told her, his guess about what had lured the whale to them. "You said it was shaking the boat apart."

"No, I said *running the props* was shaking the boat apart. We can idle one engine. Just use it to run the pump. That'll stretch our fuel too." He blew out again and searched the western horizon once more. She turned too, looking past the racketing genny and the searching slanted finger of the steering vane to trace their wake back over the smoothly rolling hills that darkened from olive to indigo as clouds moved between them and the sun. A single albatross balanced far above, as if Nature herself were monitoring this trespasser on her final keep. He added, "So the real question is whether it's still after us."

She shuddered. The sunlight helped, but the wind was still biting cold. The short Antarctic summer was drawing to an end. What would the temperature fall to in another two weeks? "Uh, what's Hy say?"

"Those weird calls he was hearing? He lost them."

"That's good."

He put his hands on her shoulders. "You need to get below. Don't bail just yet. We'll figure something out. Get some sleep, Sara. I've got the watch."

She wanted to believe his confident tone was based on more than wish. But, too tired to respond, she just nodded. And was bending to the companionway when a black head bobbed up, its crown narrowly missing striking her in the teeth. Kimura, some awkward burden cradled in one crooked arm, so that he was coming up one slow step at a time, crabbed sideways, sheltering whatever it was he carried. He winced at each step, favoring his side. She sagged to the bench seat, mind empty. Just a pair of eyes, watching whatever happened next.

"Good morning."

"Hy, what you got there?" Madsen looked up from the self-steering mechanism. "Brought us up a snack?"

"It is not for you." The Japanese moved without haste. He was freshly shaven and his hair looked shorter than the night before. A white hand towel, neatly folded into a band, was tied across his forehead. With careful deliberate motions he laid out objects on the seat. A dish of cooked rice. Two sardines, arranged on a saucer with consummate artistry. A small raft nailed, no, lashed together, of the spare timber—"dunnage," Quill had called it—stowed in one of the forward lockers for repairs. On it sat the lower half of a gallon bleach bottle, the white plastic cut into a makeshift chair or throne. More complexly knotted string fixed this to the raft. The last object Kimura produced was the rum bottle, still a third full. He placed it carefully in its carved, braided receptacle.

"Uh, what's this?" Madsen said, looking taken aback.

"A placating ritual." Hy rearranged the bottle as if to find some slightly more aesthetically pleasing aspect that to her looked exactly the same. "I will be the *ujiko.* The officiant."

Lars turned to look at Sara quizzically. She blinked back dully, not really caring.

Kimura said gravely, "I explained this to Sara last night. In some way, we have defiled the order of things. Or perhaps it is humanity as a whole that has disturbed this proper order. Who did it does not really matter. Only that it needs to be set right. We must rebalance our relationship to the sacred world. That is the world from which the being that has been pursuing us comes."

"It's Shinto," Sara mumbled. "His father's a priest, back in Japan."

"Hmm. I guess I get it," Madsen said. More equably than she might have expected. "Sooo . . . anything you want us to do?"

"That is essential to the ritual, yes. I will ask for your participation in a moment." He lifted the raft in both hands, avoiding their eyes, and carried it aft and set it atop the ramp leading down into the burble of melted green they trailed through the embroidered sea. From inside his suit he produced a yellow pencil. Thin lightning-shaped strips of white paper were stapled to it. "The purification," he said. Lifting it in both hands, he waved it streaming in the wind, over their heads, over the stern, the wheel, and the raft.

He lowered the wand and pushed the pencil point into a gap on top of the binnacle. Paused, head bowed, then turned to face the wake.

He lifted his arms, and with a solemn face intoned several sentences in Japanese. He spoke reverently and with obvious awe, gaze lifted to the waves that hulked all around. Then lifted the little woven raft by one end and let it go. It slid down the slanted fiberglass and bumped over a crack where the whale had fractured the hull.

To Sara's surprise it did not capsize, but sideslipped delicately into the wake. A cloud passed away from the sun. The little craft fell astern, bobbing and whirling in the smoothed turquoise and silver. As it shrank he raised his arms and spoke again, in the same somber tones.

"So what was that all about?" Madsen said when he stopped.

"The invocation. And the offering."

"Who are you praying to?" Sara asked him. "The whale?"

"If it is a *kami*, yes. 'To the great whale: I apologize for our errors and wrongdoing, that which we have done, whether knowingly or not, against the fitness of things. I offer you these gifts in apology and reverence, and ask that we be purged of defilement and the world be restored to its rightness.' That is my *norito*: the words I addressed to him. In brief." He lowered his head. "Now, we all make a circular progression."

"A what?" Madsen frowned.

"A circular progression. All together. It is important that all who witness, participate. And that we make the perfect form, the form of the universe completed. Can we turn the boat in a circle?"

The Dane shook his head. "Not without stressing the shit out of that forestay."

"Then we will progress ourselves. Can you help? Join me?"

Sara said, "Uh—don't take this the wrong way, Hy, but I don't believe this kind of thing has the slightest influence on reality." Then was instantly sorry. Who was she to ridicule, if a ritual gave him comfort?

But her objection didn't seem to offend him. In fact, he smiled, as if at an uncomprehending three-year-old. "Shinto does not require belief," he said, watching the paper streamers flicker in the wind. "It is not important what we believe. What matters is what we do. Will you do this with me?"

"All right," she said. Then, feeling a little ridiculous, followed him in a tight circle around *Anemone*'s helm pedestal. Madsen hesitated, then trailed them, muttering something inaudible.

When they'd made a complete circuit, Kimura said, "Now we bow. All together. Toward the wake." He demonstrated, hands together, a pained grimace crossing his face. She and Madsen bowed awkwardly too as *Anemone* rose on a crest, and the sun washed over the sea in spangles like a sudden spray of etiolated gold, and the albatross declined, descended, until it hovered fifty yards up, great wings outstretched over the tiny rocking raft as it rose one last time at the crest of a far-off wave, then vanished from their sight.

A silence succeeded, broken only by a clank and a muffled curse as down below Eddi's bucket collided with something.

Madsen cleared his throat. He checked the gearshift lever. Made sure it was in neutral. Then bent, and pressed the button. A muffled cough below; the oily taint of diesel; a whiff of white fume blowing over them, then scudding off over the sea, coiling and uncoiling. Hardly dissipating at all as it too was borne away by the clear hard wind.

19

The Sacrifice

She went below and lay in her bunk but the unsteady beat of the diesel, now stronger, now fainter, would not let her sleep. She could not help wondering if something else also listened, miles distant, fathoms down. But they'd been sailing for nearly a whole day since they'd seen it last, first dodging amid the ice, then running fair in the open sea. Sixty miles last night; at least a hundred since the thing had body-slammed them. Surely distance would screen their signature amid the constant crowd noise of the sea.

At last she got up and went aft. Auer snored behind her curtain. The water she waded through was no shallower than it had been when she came off watch. But it wasn't any deeper, either.

Suddenly ravenous, she found crackers and jam and made herself a plateful in the galley, looking out the portlight at the sea surging only inches below the greasy salt-streaked glass. The food seemed insubstantial, as if her body were a furnace that demanded fat and meat, but she stoked it with grape jelly and saltines until she could eat no more. Perhaps later she could make something more substantial. It did seem like a long time since they'd sat down to a real meal. Baked yams. Beans and rice. She dropped to the damp mildew-smelling banquette and leaned back, blinking at the black streaks on the overhead.

She woke after some interminable time and had to pee. The engine noise was louder as she squatted in the head. She turned a tap, then remembered: frozen. She cleaned up with hand sanitizer and toilet paper. Wiped down the commode seat, which needed it. Remembering guiltily how Quill had driven them to keep things clean. They'd have to start paying attention again. Once they had time to do more than steer and bail.

The slow clump of steps on the companionway ladder. She opened the door of the head to see a stooped Madsen looking toward Auer's curtain. "She asleep?"

"Sounds like it."

"I hate to wake her. Can you take it awhile? I want to check that pump. We're still on zero eight zero."

"Sure." She got back into her suit, wound Tehiyah's scarf around her jaw, and found her goggles.

The day was grayer now. No sun in sight. Thick clouds frosted the sky from one horizon to the other like black icing. She checked the sails, then the compass. Adjusted the self-steerer. She wasn't on deck for more than ten minutes when the first flakes drove down, skidding and zigzagging over a slaty, lumpy sea to crash and be instantly absorbed. When she looked back the sea behind was weathered tar. Their faithful albatross had left them; it no longer hovered like some benediction or curse. She stood at the wheel, looking at the wrapped shape on the bow. Each time the boat sagged off, Dorée seemed to be walking across the sea.

She yawned, and gradually the hollowed waves became long dunes rising from shining sand where lilliputian plovers darted back and forth, tiny legs clicking smartly as windup toys. Above stretched the wind-scalloped curves of Smith's Point, dotted with poverty grass and the tiny dancing pink flowers of searocket. And above them, the bent low wind-twisted bonsai shapes of pitch pines and scrub oaks.

The cottage stood above a salt pond on sturdy pilings black with age. It had been built of driftwood, planks swept overboard and blown ashore, bits of long-wrecked ships. A rocker, white paint flaking, nodded on the porch, pushed by the wind that howled without cease, sandpapering the world to a satin finish and bleaching every color to its ghost. A flame-light glowed in a window high above the marsh. She trudged toward the glow but it did not come nearer. Instead the world grew darker, the sky more threatening. Saltbushes thrashed in the wind, and the clouds raced as if fleeing Armageddon. Someone was waiting in there. Someone she'd once known. For a moment she almost glimpsed him, or perhaps her, though the antique wavy glass, half lit by that flickering flame. Then it shrank, vanished, and she kept slogging upward, but now the cottage was even farther away than when she'd first come up from the beach where the plovers and sanderlings still skittered, spindly legs clicking like clockwork. . . .

Madsen bulled through the half-closed hatchway, shouldering it aside. Something cracked sharply. "Pump's working. You awake? Maybe you better go back below."

She roused herself and twisted her ear. The pain obliterated dunes, cottage, the waving cattails. "Tehiyah's unwrapping," she said. "I'm going forward to fix her."

"Keep your line clipped." He wedged himself against the genny mast and sank into his own somber study of the sea.

The waves heaved. She snapped the carabiner and began working forward. The deck was worn and here and there cracks showed in the gelcoat where they'd beaten the ice off. There was little now except where it had lodged in crannies, but the snow was coming down harder, blowing past in big flakes in a steady river that tickled her cheeks under the goggles.

She got to the bow and hauled herself erect. Dorée gazed unflinchingly ahead, slender neck encrusted with a white rime of salt. Her eyes were open. This seemed strange, as Sara could have sworn they'd been closed when they'd tied off the tarp. She tried to reclose them, but the lids were frozen solid to the eyeballs. With one elbow around the stay, she hauled in the flapping tarp, wrapped it tight again, and tied it off. Then dropped to hands and knees and crept aft.

She was halfway back when she glimpsed something in the hazy sea astern. A crack in the ocean, through which knobby protuberances showed. Then a wave broke over them, veiling them with trailing spray mixed with falling snow.

"Lars!" She pointed and Madsen, at the wheel, turned quickly and looked back, but when he did there was only a scar on the sea and nothing more and that too vanished as flakes blanched the roiling gray. He stayed twisted, eyes shaded with a glove, as she struggled forward. Then something caught and snatched her back, and she jerked at it, panicky, until she realized it was only her safety line, snagged on a sheave.

"Thought I saw something," she panted, swinging her legs down into the cockpit. "Out in the fog. Over there."

She pointed again and he pulled the binoculars from their waterproof stowage and swept them over the sea. She stood indecisive in the blowing flurries, then bent to the companionway. "Eddi! Hy! Get your suits, and get up here!" she yelled.

The whale came in from dead abeam, pushing up a black fold of weltering sea like the cowcatcher of some old-time locomotive. He materialized from the snow-mist out of which the flakes blew ever thicker, driving parallel to the wavecrests until they reached up and pulled them down. Sara watched him come, the huge vertical forehead only partially visible behind the swell he was pushing. Then bent again and screamed down, "*Get up here! Now!*"

Anemone lifted as the bulge in the sea neared, but not fast enough. When the whale hit she folded around the impact like a hollow vibrating tube. The jury-rigged forward stay snapped instantly. The whale kept coming, bulldozering them, a boil of sea white behind it. She saw the tail down there, whipping up and down with unbelievable rapidity for its size. The boat careened over and began to slide through the water sideways.

Her ears seemed to turn off then. Madsen's mouth was open, yelling, but no words emerged. Gear was falling from aloft. The noise must have been terrific, but she didn't hear it. The mast toppled, toward them, veering aside only at the last moment to crash down beside the cockpit. Then it too, still attached by a crazy snarled mass of steel and nylon rigging, was being shoved through the water by a frenzied power as the whale nodded its way through the seething sea, leaving a foamed highway twenty yards wide behind it.

At the companionway, the pale oval of Eddi's features. Her gaze sought Sara's, then slipped aside as she fell back down the ladder.

Then sound came back. The clatter and crash from below. The tail emerged from the sea, pointed flukes notched deep, and slammed down flat with the doom-crack of a close strike of lightning. The livid sea rolled back almost biblically, opening like thick lips, then reversing itself and surging back in, filling a sudden vacancy where a vast sand-colored mass had just submerged.

Anemone screamed and rolled back upright, quivering along her whole length. The snarled cordage and wire and aluminum and sailcloth that lay tangled and heavy along her whole starboard side grated on her deck. She groaned to port, then to starboard, but her rolls were different now. Shorter. Quicker.

Quill's red toolbox was flung up, followed by Eddi Auer, the videocamera slung around her neck. Kimura was close behind. Both were in the bright red mustang suits, but neither had gloves on. Eddi looked over the side and whistled. "Shit. It finally came down."

"The whale rammed us again," Sara told her. "It knocked the mast down."

"Oh, holy King Jesus. Where is it?"

"I don't know," Madsen said, head whipping anxiously around, the boat hook brandished like a spear. The waves surged and dropped away, blue and black, looking as if they were coated with granular grease. Snow blew out of the mist. He must have realized how ridiculous it was as a weapon, because he lowered the pole and set it aside. His face was strained. "But it'll probably be back."

"So what do we do?" Eddi said.

He shrugged, looking around. White sclera gleamed at the margins of blue irises. "What *can* we do? Other than wait."

Sara said, "Eddi, are we leaking more below?"

"I don't know. I smelled fuel, though."

"We ought to check, Lars."

He didn't answer. Just stared off to where the snow was blowing. *Anemone* heaved on a long-backed sea, then sagged. The mast grated, dragging a few more feet overboard.

"Hadn't we better cut that loose?" the Japanese suggested.

"There it is." Lars didn't point, or turn toward it. Just kept looking off to starboard. As one, they turned in the same direction.

The blowing snow made everything inchoate, softened, seen through petroleum jelly smeared over a lens. The whale rode up within a swell as if cast into it, like some enormous antediluvian insect sealed into gray-green amber. The gigantic squared-off head lay half turned toward them, one paddle-shaped flipper tilting this way and that to keep the whole mass floating miraculously motionless within the surge. It was anything but white. Dark seams ran though it, like mineral-laced travertine. Strange bumps and callosities speckled it, those, too, contrasting with what seemed to be its proper integument. Yet its unnatural paleness, suspended against the dark sea, filled her with all the terror Melville had ascribed to it. As the crest rolled away over it that crooked spout jetted, became mist, smoking in the wind, and blew away to leeward with the falling snow.

"What's it *doing*?" Auer breathed, voice shaking. "Is it *watching* us?"

Kimura moaned aloud. When Sara glanced his way he was hauling himself atop the cockpit seat, steadying his ascent with a hand on the helm pedestal. He let go and swayed with the boat's jerky roll. He made an obeisance left, right, to the left again. Pain crossed his face each time, but he bowed very low.

Straightening, he removed a Baggie from his pocket, tore it open, and scattered it about the cockpit. A few grains hit her face, and she tasted salt. He clapped his hands, bowed again to the whale, and raised his hands. Loudly, he began what she assumed was another invocation.

"Lars?" Sara said. He didn't respond and she tugged at his arm. "*Lars!*"

"I don't know what to do," he muttered. "God damn it. God *damn* it! After all we risked for them—"

"Can we use the engines? Get away?"

"I smelled fuel," Eddi said again. "I don't think we even want to—"

"We've got to do *something*," Sara said, but more to herself. Waves of dizziness were sweeping up from her feet, prickling her face, which burned as if it had been thrust into a furnace. At the same time her mind seemed to float free, regarding them and herself as if from some enormous distance.

The swell receded and the immense bulk, perhaps sixty yards away and longer than the boat, dropped with it, with incredible grace. The snow thinned and for a second or two she saw the whale quite clearly. It was arching its back in a strange way, the finless deformed-looking hump flexing until it pierced the roof of the sea. Kimura's voice rose, droning on, sentence after sentence. For a moment she wondered: What is going on? Is this truly some sort of communication? Then the tail rose, immense, dripping, the sea running off it in creeks. When it dropped again the crash rolled like artillery.

"See that? He's trying to shake the harpoon out," Auer breathed, beside her.

Sara turned to see the aimed camera. The ruby filming light. Eddi's knees were shaking, but her hands were free of the slightest tremor. When she looked back at the creamy-colored mountain that rode the swells Sara made out the shaft and the attached line dangling from its side, above the small lateral fin. The eye must be forward of it, but she couldn't make that out.

"It's waiting," Eddi breathed. She crouched, gasping for breath.

"Eddi, what's wrong?"

"It's *waiting for us to help it*." She dropped the camera and hugged her belly, as if slugged in the stomach. Then, with an abrupt gesture, unlooped the webbed strap and thrust it into Sara's hands. "Here. It's recording."

"Eddi—hold on. What are you—"

But Auer was already climbing the sagging mass of fabric and wire and boom. Picking her way carefully but rapidly, dancing across that shifting mass like a tightrope walker. Kimura lowered his hands and stopped in midsentence. Madsen shouted hoarsely. Sara stood frozen. Then, without thought, lifted the camera.

Its screen framed something white against a darker ground. It took a moment before she understood it was a splash. From it a reddish form surged up and struck out in a clumsy crawl.

"Eddi!" she screamed, lowering the camera. A swell rolled past *Anemone*, obliterating the swimmer, rolling completely over her. Yet she emerged again. Short blond hair flew as she shook her head, raising it to look to where the whale lay off, flippers slowly flexing. It had turned slightly, so that its head was closer to the boat, but still did not seem to be moving from its station. Eddi looked back, then forward again; as if gauging the distance remaining to her, or perhaps reconsidering the wisdom of her act.

When she resumed swimming Kimura clapped three times. He bowed left, right, left again. Then resumed praying, in a higher note than before, in a tense rapid monotone. Slowly, Sara raised the camera again. Remembering only then how Eddi hadn't dared to approach the right whales in the icy embayment. That seamed scar serpenting up her body, disguised by the writhe of tattoo—

Auer sank, submerged by a swell, then rose again on a crest. She'd almost reached the whale, which seemed to be waiting for her. Or was it simply lying to, resting? The great flukes started to lift, then sank back. It lay half tilted over, right side uppermost, the haft of the black shaft buried in its flank swizzling the surface with ripples of foam.

Eddi vanished, then came up again. Closer. Almost there. Sara shuddered. Even in the insulated suit, the cold water had to be paralyzing. Freezing a swimmer's breath, numbing legs and arms and face. Already Auer moved more slowly, lifting her arms clumsily.

The immense tail stirred upward, then once again relaxed. The spout jetted and drifted away. The snow fell. The Dewoitine creaked and swayed as part of the fallen rigging slid off into the water and began hammering the hull at the end of its shroud wires.

The whale rolled, but kept its position relative to the boat. Auer was moving very deliberately now. An arm came up, lingered in the air, then sank. Seconds later, the other rose. But she was still forging forward. Only a few yards to go.

The animal rolled upward, then down. Sara could swear it was watching the approaching swimmer, though she still could not make out its eye, which must spend most of its time beneath the surface. Could it see her?

Hy tore apart another packet. Offering the salt in his outstretched hand, he called in English, "This we offer in purification and regret. Is there another sacrifice we can make? One more pleasing to you?"

By a great effort of will Sara concentrated on the little square of image the camera framed. In it a figure floated outstretched, one arm reaching for the dangling harpoon. The whale lay without stirring, head turned slightly in her direction. As if regarding her. As if considering. "God," she muttered, the camera shaking in her hands so the picture jerked. "God. God. *Eddi.*"

With a delicacy so precise it looked almost like laziness, the whale stirred. It pivoted along its length, and the head moved with great majesty and deliberateness around toward its flank. It dipped beneath the surface as the back bent. Then rose again, dragging a dropped length of bone and flesh into view, the lower surface studded with long pointed yellow cones.

With a single leisurely sweep of its lower jaw, the whale bit Eddi in half.

The camera jumped in Sara's hands. She heard herself screaming as the upper half of Auer's body floated upward, spinning, mouth a round blackness, gazing back toward them, one hand raised, fingers splayed as if in unutterable agony. The stroke had stripped off part of her suit, and on the uplifted arm and shoulder Sara could make out the dark intaglio of creatures against shockingly white skin. Then the blond head tilted back, and went down into a welling cloudy pool of whirling pink. The tips of upraised white stiffened fingers were the last part of her to leave the light.

"Eddi!" she screamed. The camera dropped from unfeeling fingers, but recoiled before it hit the deck, restrained by the strap. Madsen was bellowing hoarsely, twisting the wheel, though it had no effect. Kimura stood in appalled silence, staring toward where the beast had slowly sunk from sight. A scrap of red fabric floated, then spiraled down. It glimmered beneath the surface, then grew obscure. Until the sea surged empty save for whirls of rocking foam. *Anemone* rose on a wave, then dropped away, and the burdening hamper scraped and slid. Something knocked the hull from beneath with the insistent thud of a battering ram.

Looking over the side, Sara saw a pale patch ghostly deep beneath the surface. The size of a handkerchief, perhaps. But as she stared down through the greasy snow-speckled surface the shape grew, swelled, neared, until she gave a choked gasp and stumbled back.

The whale burst from below with enormous force, blasting the sea open. The head emerged for many yards, lofting upward to cleave the snowy air, turning about its axis as it rose, rose; then fell back again with a crash of green water that rolled over the cockpit and knocked them all to hands and knees. Kimura somersaulted forward. His head hit a locker with a sickening thunk. Madsen crouched, clinging to the wheel. Sara found herself on the cockpit sole, panting, fingers digging into the worn teak gridwork on which her boots had grated for so many watch-worn hours.

When some seconds had passed and she was still alive, she pushed herself up, slowly, fearfully. Then came to her feet as Kimura gibbered in Japanese, rolling a bloodied visage from side to side.

Alongside the wallowing boat a gigantic mass slowly stirred. She leaned over to look down at it.

Down, into the monster's eye.

Far smaller than it ought to be, that orb stared unblinking up. A film seemed to lie over it, but the soul that peered upward through it penetrated into hers. It was not empty, like a shark's, whose blank eye conveyed naked hunger and nothing more. For an endless moment she met it; inhuman, yet intelligent; a recognizing gaze that clearly registered her own presence as a sentient being. Yet it communicated no sympathy, nor any indication of kinship. She shuddered.

A lid slowly drew down over that eye, and it grew dim. The whole immense furrowed stained mass was slowly sinking away, the sea's gray-green filtering between them. Then it was gone, a mammoth specter retreating once more into obscurity, the deep. Only then, with a sob, was her aching throat suddenly released to breathe again, the frigid air searing her trachea, her whole body shaking.

That single glance, cast up from only feet away, had seemed to convey some message. But who could say what? All she could retain was what she'd felt, looking down into it. A focused hatred, an unbending, unending, utterly determined wrath. As if the gigantic animal had spoken aloud.

You are next. But not right away. I want you to suffer, to fear me, first.

Then I will kill you all.

20

The Chase—Third Day

They stood and lay about the cockpit for long minutes. No one spoke, save for Kimura's moaning. At last Sara took a breath that reached down to her loins. She forced resolve into her voice, though pee was trickling hotly down her thighs under the suit. "Is it gone?" she murmured.

No answer came. She looked overside again, dreading the cold regard of that all-seeing eye; yet met this time only the murky, wind-churned depths, streamed through with tiny organisms, small shimmering oval jellies, blissfully ignorant of either existence or death. She staggered aft and peered over with the same result. Save that *Anemone*'s slanted stern was now plunging in and out as she pitched, penetrating the surface more deeply than ever before. An oily stain coruscated, smoothing the cat's-paws the wind left even in the lee of the hull.

She lurched to the other side, to regard the soft patter of the snow, the rippled crest of a comber as it birthed from the mist and swept toward them, dimpled and veined like hardened obsidian. She stared out for long minutes, shaking. Was this how Captain George Pollard had felt, all those years before, after that first blow from the maddened beast that had attacked his ship? Waiting for it to return, and finish the job once and for all?

But the minutes throbbed past, and the dark seas swept out from the fog and vanished back into it; and it did not reappear.

When she shook Madsen, slumped by the pedestal, he flinched away, then shuddered before looking up. "Yeah. Yeah," he muttered.

"Take these," she said, and thrust bolt cutters into his gloves. Rooted in the toolbox and came up with a hacksaw. When she tapped Kimura's shoulder with this he opened his eyes and blinked at it through matted hair and clotted blood. "My head . . ."

"Scalp cuts, Hy. You'll live." She hated the contempt in her voice. But a woman's scorn could make men act. It seemed to now, for they stirred and rose, gripped their tools, and advanced on the wreckage that lay grinding alongside. Madsen angled the handles of the cutters. Hardened steel jaws snapped through a stay, and he moved to the next. Kimura said, "Help me here, please." They both heaved on a mass of metal, then again, harder, until it screeched and slid off, leaving a ragged scar deep in the gunwale, and sank glimmering away, turning end over end as it departed the light.

When they were well at work she handed herself below. The salon was wrecked. Everything from drawers and lockers lay heaped in piles, shattered or broken. To her left water spurted in thin sheets through a crack that ran from the overhead to the cabin sole each time the boat rolled. The galley was if anything worse; even the dish racks were gone, wrenched from the bulkheads by the weight of what they held and smashed to flinders. Glass crunched underfoot, beneath water already a foot deep. She lifted her head and sniffed. An unmistakable petroleum cloy packed the air, more solidly as she moved aft. She cracked the door of her own cabin, Quill's old stateroom; glanced in; eased it closed, sighing.

Madsen pushed by in the passageway. She started to follow, then stopped. She wanted to run topside. Not linger in this shadowy, creaking Hades. The monster could return at any moment. She couldn't shake the dread that single look had imparted. No pity, no fellow feeling, had gleamed from that condemning orb. Only an implacable hatred.

She picked up a settee cushion, which ran water. Dropped it and wandered to the foot of the companionway and stood clinging, head twisted to study the sea jetting in those thin delicate laminations. It was coming in through three cracks, spaced at roughly similar intervals along the port side. Where the ribs had punched through the skin, no doubt. Her breath glowed in the cold air. A shiver racked her from spine to fingertips. Her feet were ice. The water rolled and sloshed, the sound not loud, but intensely disquieting.

Madsen came out wiping his hands on a rag. A dark smear sullied the hound-cap's white muzzle. "Fuel line," he said, sounding relieved. "Leaked a few gallons, but I got it cut off. We can forget about the engines. But I don't think we'll burn."

"I guess that's good news." She glanced at Eddi's cubby. The blue curtain had been torn in two and hung sagging, half off its rings.

She jerked her gaze away as he added, "We're taking water fast. We better start thinking about what to do when this thing sinks out from under us."

"Sinks from . . . but what *can* we do? The inflatable, it went down when the whale . . ." Suddenly she couldn't finish a sentence.

"We have that emergency raft baled up forward. Have to drag it back and check it out."

She felt hope for a moment, then remembered: The nearest downwind land was four thousand miles distant. "Three people in an unheated raft aren't going to make it to Australia, Lars. Can we send an SOS somehow?"

"The best I can do is try the handheld. But it's short-range. And needless to say, there aren't many ships way down here."

"Then we have to stay afloat."

"Oh yeah? Well, suggestions are welcome."

His tone was dismissive. Suddenly she'd had enough. "*You* got us into this. We wanted to turn back. Eddi and I *voted* to, after Dru died. But you and Mick insisted. And now look at us."

"Oh, yes. Look at us."

Was she reading this wrong, or was that contempt in his voice? "What the *fuck*, Lars? What's with the attitude? I'm pointing out that we wouldn't be trapped here on a sinking boat if you hadn't decided you knew better than everybody else. It's *your* fucking arrogance—"

"Correct me if I'm wrong. But didn't we come down here for a reason?"

This time there was no doubt; he was sneering at her. Leaning against the bulkhead, arms crossed. She said, "Yeah. We did. But we haven't made much of an impact."

"We attacked the fleet. Pretty effectively, I think. We struck a hard blow."

"We barely scratched them! They're still down there. Still killing whales. All we've managed to do is mightily piss off one of them. Of the whales, I mean."

"Oh. So you think it's a whale, now? Not a spirit?"

She slapped him. It felt so very good she almost did it again, but faded on the backswing. He sucked a breath and looked so dazed she relented. "You deserved that," she muttered. "But maybe I—overreacted. Sorry."

He didn't answer. Just slung the rag across the cabin, and went forward. He called over a shoulder, "I'm going to try to slow these leaks down. If you see that—*thing*—again, how about letting me know."

"I said I'm sorry," she called after him. But he didn't look back.

On deck again she snugged up her suit zipper. *Anemone* was rolling, but not as hard as during real storms. The wind seemed stronger now that they weren't making headway, though it sounded weird without the whine of the rigging. But the snow had stopped while she was below. It lay piled in every corner and against every fitting, drifts streaming away on the lee side of each winch and chainplate. The sky was gray or maybe white, a color without hue. Without form, either, like looking straight up into fog.

Hideyashi sat with head in hands on the cockpit bench, knees sprawled. He was shaking. "Hy, get out of this wind," she said. "We've got to conserve body heat."

Without looking at her he muttered, "It does not matter. I did not have *kokoro*."

"And what is that?" she said, suddenly very tired. A ripple on an oncoming wave nearly stopped her heart. But it was not what she feared.

"The purity of heart which allows one to connect with the *kami*. I know now I do not have it."

"Well, Hy, if any of us did, I'm sure it would be you."

He murmured to his boots, "Or else, the sin we have committed is too great to apologize for. Nature has turned on us and now she will destroy us."

"This is Shinto you're talking again?" She kept feeling as if someone were watching her, staring at her from behind. But no matter how quickly she turned, the granite rollers were vacant. The boat had turned slightly away from the oncoming seas and now lurched more heavily, surging abruptly from side to side as the crests hissed past. A brighter patch glowed through the white. She lifted her face to it. Was it her imagination, or did a tiny bloom of warmth play on her cheeks? She felt naked without mast and sail between her and the sky.

She lowered her gaze to a bundle recumbent on the forward deck, tangled in the fallen stays. The snow dusted it, making it seem like a deformed part of the hull itself. "Keep an eye out for me. I'm going forward."

Clipped to the sagging jackline, she crept around the coach house on the port side. Here there was no fallen cordage, only slick snow-ice her soles got hardly any purchase on. She went down twice working her way forward. On the second fall pain jarred through a wrist, and she cursed and scrabbled forward as the hull canted, hesitated, canted again.

"Tehiyah," she murmured, resting stretched out beside the bundle. The rime covered it in a translucent crust like spun sugar. A fairy-tale shroud. The fallen lines had wrapped around the body. She had to work for some time with numb fingers to strip them away. She cut shorter lengths and knitted the tarped body to the stanchions of the bow pulpit. Her brain seemed even deader than usual and she couldn't recall any knots other than the ones to tie her shoes with, so that's what she used.

She made them tight, but couldn't say she had much confidence in her work.

"Shinto is only recognizing what is," Kimura said when she slid back into the cockpit. "Don't you feel it?"

She lowered her head slowly. Hugged herself. Okay, maybe she did. Or maybe it seemed more important, just now, to find some way to keep on living, rather than worry about Nature. At the moment it was Nature that was trying to kill them, after all.

"Eddi had it," the Japanese said miserably. He probed his side. "Ahh . . . I can feel them grinding. The broken ends."

"What'd you say about . . . ?" She started awake, back from a dream of a beach, of waves rolling in out of fog.

"I said, Eddi—she had *kokoro*. And great courage. I asked if there was another sacrifice that would be more pleasing. But I did not mean her. She offered herself."

"Good grief," she said, drawing back to stare. "Are you serious? Is that what you think?"

"Of course. That is why it departed, and has not returned. Why else?"

Madsen's sudden appearance in the companionway hatch made her gasp. He was rubbing reddened eyes, and the blond goatee was matted with grease. "I got some rags in the worst leaks. But it's still rising."

She cleared her throat. Finish your sentences, Sara. "What's the plan here . . . Lars? We don't have sails. Don't have engines."

"Plan? Stay afloat as long as we can, I guess. I checked Dru's charts. We'll drift downwind at three or four knots. The current goes east at this latitude, too. If we can stay on top of the waves, we'll get there. There's more ship traffic closer to Australia. Somebody will see us. Eventually."

"Do we have enough food?" Kimura asked.

"Only three of us now. Food's not our problem," Sara told him. "But if we sink?"

"Then it's the raft. But our chances won't be as . . . they won't be good then." He looked away. "Anyway. That means we all have to hand-pump and bail. Two at a time. One sleeps."

"My ribs are broken."

"Sorry. You too."

"There isn't any way at all we can run the electric?" She looked up at the genny, which was still, miraculously, spinning away, pointed into the wind. The falling mast must have just missed it. "We still have power, don't we?"

"That pump draws a lot of amps. Maybe for an hour or two a day, if we let it build up." He took a deep breath. His gaze, she noticed, could not stop roaming the waves that towered all around. "So, Hy, what do you think? As our whale expert. Is it coming back?"

The younger man shrugged. "I did not have *kokoro*," he said again, but not as loudly as he'd said it to her. "Not like Eddi."

"What did you say?" the Dane said sharply.

Kimura shook himself. "I am sorry. I was discouraged, and lost heart. We must struggle to survive. But that is true of all living things, is it not? The great Darwin's insight."

Lars frowned. "How about a straight answer?"

"I cannot give you that. I do not know what motivates this creature." He sighed. "Perhaps it thinks it has wounded us enough. Perhaps it was satisfied with Eddi. I see no other reason it would have stopped attacking."

"Mocha Dick," Sara mumbled. They flinched and glanced at her. "The whale in the 1820s that attacked whaleships. We talked about it, Hy, remember? It rammed the *Essex* twice. If this one's obeying the same instinctual drives, two attacks might be enough."

Madsen dug fingers into his mouth as if feeling for missing teeth. Finally he said, "Instinctual drives?"

"It's still just an animal, Lars. No matter what supernatural motivations Hy's come up with."

"A damn ungrateful one," Madsen said. "We come down here to help. It attacks *us*—"

Kimura just smiled sadly. "*Kokoro*," he murmured, so softly it could have been meant only for himself.

"All right, then," the Dane said. "I'll pump first. Sara, can you come bail?"

She sat for a moment longer. Then took a deep breath, and staggered to her feet.

They pumped and bailed through the day. The suck-suck, gush-gush of the hand pump clacked from the engine room. She dragged between salon and galley, dipping the bucket into the never-ending spring of the keel well, always fresh and always full, and lugging it into the galley to dump down the sink. An hour of this left her too exhausted to stand. Her hands cramped into lobster claws. The inside of her forearms ached fiercely. Meanwhile the water had risen at least two inches. She didn't want to think how little time this meant they had left.

Though immersed in icy water, her feet felt as if they were on fire. Finally she set the bucket down and sat and pulled her boots off. She peeled her socks down, unable to remember the last time she'd changed them.

She stared at sloughing ulcers. Her toes were red and inflamed. Blisters had broken and were weeping.

"Sara. Sara!"

"What!" she screamed.

"Back here."

When she got there, feet stamped back naked into the wet boots, Madsen was lying in his back in several inches of water, cursing and working over his head under one of the engines. "I think I have frostbite," she told him. "On my feet."

"What color are they?"

"What?"

"Your feet. Your toes."

"Red. Infected."

"Probably just chilblains. If they were black, I'd say frostbite." He peered up into the recesses of the engine, and despite herself she looked at the wedge of deck where she and Mick Bodine had lain. "I fixed the fuel line, but it still won't start."

"Are we sure we *want* to start it? Remember, you know . . ." She sagged to a perch on the step. Started to scratch between her toes, but stopped herself.

"How much progress did you make bailing by hand?" He picked up a wrench and began tinkering it into place.

"It's even higher than . . . okay. I get it." She hugged herself, watching the smoke of her breath curl in the icy air. She wanted to believe he could get it started, but fear made her hope desperately he couldn't.

"Sorry I was an ass," he muttered from beneath the engine.

"That's all right. I lost my temper." She took a few deep breaths.

"We haven't gotten along on this cruise. I guess it's mainly my fault." He lay silent, then added, "The voyage hasn't turned out so well. I know that. But it's not the last mission we'll send out, you know."

She opened her mouth, but good judgment intervened and all she said was, "Want me to pump now?"

"If you can. I'm not sure a pail doesn't get the water out faster."

She held up a claw. "I can't lift one anymore."

"Then pump," he snapped. The wrench slipped with a bang and he sucked at a bleeding knuckle. "Fuck. *Fuck!*"

Kimura took a turn bailing, but he was very slow and complained incessantly: his chest, his ribs, and so forth. At last he said he couldn't anymore, but would make something hot for dinner. Madsen reluctantly agreed.

Toward dusk they gathered in the salon. The water inside was over a foot deep now. It rolled past in waves. Sometimes she caught glimpses of extremely small zebras on surfboards riding the breaks. She assumed these were hallucinations. The electric pump hummed busily aft, but Madsen had warned they didn't have enough power left to run it for long. Her hands kept spasming, as if she were still bailing. She sagged over the table, then snapped upright as a lit candle, a mug of hot tea, and a plate of rice and steaming-hot stir-fried peppers, onions, and some kind of white meat materialized.

"Oh, man," Madsen said. "This looks fucking great, Hy. Where'd you find all this stuff?"

"Bottom of the freezer. You have to eat it up now, it's not going to keep."

"We can't keep stuff frozen in the fucking Antarctic?"

No one answered. Sara was stuffing herself. The rice tasted different the way Hideyashi made it. She wondered how, then didn't care. Just filling her mouth with hot food seemed to make everything better. Even the ache in her back and arms ebbed as she swallowed.

Their self-anointed captain laid the GPS on the table. "We're still only getting two satellites, but the good news is we're making four knots downwind. A hundred miles a day."

"Forty days," Sara said. "And forty nights."

"I was thinking. The reason we couldn't transmit on the radio is, we lost the antenna."

"Did you try the handheld? Like you said?"

"Yeah, for an hour. Giving a Mayday and our position over and over. No answer. But if I can find some way to get another antenna up—a kite, maybe—we could broadcast shortwave."

"A kite?" she said. But anything was worth trying. "Uh, sure—maybe. But hadn't we better stop this water rising first?" He seemed to want to spend more time tinkering with the engine than bailing.

Lars nodded halfheartedly. "I just don't see how we can do that without restarting an engine. The wind genny doesn't give us much, and you can see we're losing ground, as far as the bailing goes."

"But you said you can't start it."

He blinked slowly. "I haven't given up yet."

"Would anyone like more?" Hy said from the galley. They held their plates out and he heaped them full again.

That night she rigged a line to keep her back from truly breaking. It ran across the cabin into the galley with a pulley she'd found under one of the lockers. No longer did she have to dip the pail far down into the keel well to fill it. The water eddied just below her knees now, flashing in the lanternglow that was the only light they had. All she had to do was pull it down, tip it to fill, then run it along dangling into the galley. She could lift only about half a pailful this way, but it went so much faster she had to be coming out ahead.

As long as she didn't stop, the water stayed where it was. If she sat down to rest, soaking feet dangling in freezing water, it gained on her. Her feet no longer itched. In fact, she couldn't feel them at all. She floundered about banging into things as the boat rolled.

Occasionally, bending to fill the bucket, she seemed to hear, or maybe feel, a faint clicking that carried up through the hull.

Toward midnight the water made a sudden rush. In less than an hour it rose from below her knees to just above them. She went forward and found Hy in his bunk. He moved slowly even when she screamed at him, but at last crept out and joined her, wielding the spaghetti pot. They battled for another hour as she passed into a daze from which she returned only now and again, usually panting folded over the sink, watching a pailful of bilge swirl down. It really did go the other way in the Southern Hemisphere. For some reason that seemed deeply significant.

Anemone swayed far over to one side, and the water swept that way too. She lay over for a long time, drifting in a logy way. Then suddenly flipped, and all the water rushed to the other side. This made it harder to judge the depth, but Sara marked it on the bulkhead with a pencil.

Finally, wading through the water, she tripped and fell full length into it. It was freezing but didn't feel cold. She lay relaxed as a starfish before the fire penetrated and she screamed bubbles into the cold sea. She staggered up again, sobbing, just as the boat creaked ominously.

The roll started fast. She grabbed a handhold, expecting it to stop, but it didn't. The boat just kept on going over, farther and farther, and the water went to that side and it rolled even faster. The lantern tipped and fell and went out. Kimura cried out in Japanese. His pan clattered and splashed in the dark. She skidded downhill and caught the corner of the nav table in her solar plexus. Stars flashed.

Madsen came awake instantly when she shook him. "We're going to turn over," she yelled, right into his ear. "We almost did. Just then. Lars, *wake up*!"

Madsen stood in the slanting salon, staring in the glancing too-white beams of their flashlights at the sea that had shoaled up to starboard, covering the nav station. And the radio, she suddenly realized. That horror, the loss of even the possibility of calling for help, was only a small addition to the fear she felt now, clinging as the boat bucked and the sea within rolled like the dark sea without. "We're going to turn over," she said again. "Capsize and go down. Lars. The raft?"

"Up forward," he said, but when she shone the beam that way the water was already above the hatch to the forepeak. The whole boat echoed and protested as it rolled, nose down, stern slanting up, and the bitter cold gripped her thighs and belly.

"Hy?" he shouted.

The curtain to Kimura's cubicle stirred. He was back in the upper bunk, still above the glimmering surface.

Abruptly Sara saw flame. She waded forward. "You were supposed to be bailing, you asshole!"

"I was tired. And there's no point."

"No *point*? We'll die!"

"We are going to anyway. Why should I do so with my hands bleeding?" He yawned in their conjoined beams. She couldn't decide what this was: resignation? Realism? Utter fatigue? Terminal apathy?

She could sympathize. But she wasn't going to give up. "We've got to get that emergency raft ready," she told the tall man beside her.

"I don't think that's the answer, Sara. We'll just die out there instead of in here."

"So you're saying it's hopeless too?"

"I can work on the engine more. Try to start it again. The water's not as high back there. I'm starting to think there must be air in the lines. Get it out somehow, I might get one started. Then we could run the pump."

She was about to say No, don't, but instead muttered, "If you can. Do it."

"And you'll bail?"

"Oh, yes. We'll both bail," she said grimly, and waded forward, fixing the beam of her light on the sallow slack face that blinked slowly from the upper bunk.

They bailed, though it made no difference she could see. She didn't need to push the bucket back and forth now, which was good, because the deck was too steep now to climb. She just bent, filled it, and poured it into the sink. Now and then the water sloshed up and into the sink all on its own, it was getting that deep. At first this encouraged her, until it started vomiting back up. Then she understood. The drain too was underwater and the sink at the waterline. Which was not good. Not good at all.

All this went on in the near dark and freezing cold, with Kimura wheezing unwillingly beside her. She lifted three buckets to his one. Her back passed through agony to numbness to renewed agony. Her fingers burned, and the tips of her ears. She couldn't feel her legs at all.

At last he lowered his container and slumped. She ignored this for a while, hauling up bucket after bucket. Then sucked a breath, about to scream at him, when a whoosh surrounded them all. *Anemone* gracefully inclined, like a kneeling elephant, and went hard over to starboard. The water flooded up and covered her, so shocking, burning cold it felt somehow glutinous. She let go of the sink and drifted, expecting to die.

She came up sputtering and flailing. About her the boat was rocking, seeking some new equilibrium or preparing for some new overturn. Then something twanged outside, the sound ringing through the water like the snap of a guitar string.

Anemone staggered. Wavered. And slowly settled back. Not to an even keel or anything like it, but to a less extreme angle. The hissing all around came again, and she rocked gently as a babe in a nanny's arms.

A grinding from aft was succeeded by a burring like a drill at low speed vibrating against loose metal. It died away, followed by hollow clicks and Danish curses.

Kimura was splashing and floundering off toward the companionway.

She hung back, then decided she'd better follow. If they went down, the only exits would be underwater.

They reached the ladder, which now led up at an angle like the steps from a hotel pool, together. The hatch cover slid back, and past his head she saw the starless gray of Antarctic half-night and felt the chilling blast of the wind. The boat sagged. More things fell from the shelves, splashing now instead of shattering. Strange, she'd have thought everything that could fall had already come down. They had to get out, *now*—

With a grinding whine the engine fired. It hacked and whined and snorted and fired again. The starter slowed, then speeded up, as if whoever was on the button had decided to stake every amp in the battery on one last effort to turn it over. It fired and whined and whined and fired.

It caught in a jarring discordant clatter that filled the salon. Choking smoke eddied from aft. She sneezed and retched. Her heart seemed to vibrate between joy and terror in seconds-long alterations. She wanted both to weep and to laugh an insane chortle, but only crouched in the water, elbows on her knees, and shuddered.

In the engine room Madsen danced like a drunken bear, boots splashing. He grabbed and whirled her and for a moment she caught his glee and grinned and threw back her hair. Then released him and staggered back, caroming off throbbing steel that filled the space with a deafening roar. "I'm running full out, to recharge," he yelled into her ear. "And run the pumps, too. If we can get the bilge dry we can fix the leaks. Then rig an antenna."

"The radio was underwater."

"Yeah, but everything aboard's supposed to be waterproof. Dru always said that. First-class equipment." He seized her again and they whirled in a tarantella that ended only when she pushed herself away and staggered to the step and sat down, panting, clutching her face with fingers that burned as if they had been dipped in molten lead.

They weren't dead. Not yet.

They might even still make it home.

She woke to a slightly brighter sky through the portlight. The engine was still running and *Anemone*, or the mastless wreck she'd become, was rolling wildly. Sara shuddered in the bunk—her old one, Quill's was too far from any exit—and slid out.

She shivered again in the moldy cold as she pulled on wet clothes that stank, thrust numb feet back into boots soled with ice. But when she dropped to the deck there was no splash. When she pulled the curtain aside only two or three inches of sea filmed the deck and rolled in gleaming sheets over itself. She took slow breaths, afraid she was going to wake from a reassuring dream. But the growl of her stomach told her this was reality.

She opened the freezer, but all that met her was the stink of rotting food. She held her breath, dug deep, and found a slab of still partially frozen tofu. She tore pieces off with her teeth, holding it in both hands, swallowing even as she gagged on the cilantro marinade. For a moment she seemed to glimpse herself from above, freezing, ulcerated, crouching like a cave dweller. She closed her eyes and tore off another ice-gritty mouthful.

Kimura joined her. He looked mournful and ill and the way he stared at her made her feel even more like a barbarian. "I will make hot tea for us," he said.

"That'd be good. Lars up yet?"

"I don't think he went to sleep."

A stir at the engine room door, and Madsen staggered out. His weeping eyes were rimmed with scarlet. Beneath a mask of grease and soot curved a tentative smile. He said hoarsely, "We might be able to jack one of the shafts back in place. Get one of the propellers going again."

A shuddering thud ran through the hull. They looked at each other. "Ice?" Kimura ventured.

She suddenly straightened, visions of white walls and sharp pinnacles running through her brain. How long since anyone had been topside? She dragged herself to the dome. Peered out through the scratched plastic, half crusted with frozen snow.

"Might be a berg way off. Maybe a couple miles. But I can't see alongside."

"I'll go." Lars wiped his hands on a rag, zipped his suit, and climbed the ladder. Halfway back he turned and said, "That tea sounds good."

The bump came again, but it didn't sound like ice. She frowned and craned up in her seat, trying to see over the side. No luck. The sky was overcast, as usual. The seas moved past in the same relentless succession. Birds wheeled over a disturbance on the surface, far off.

When she climbed down Kimura handed her a mug. The hot sweet liquid went down like grace itself and she gulped it all, not caring as she scorched her tongue. "More, please?"

"I boiled only a little water, so it would not take long. I will take some up to Lars." He balanced another mug toward the companionway. She hesitated, looking at the blue flame on the stove. She bent over it, inhaling the eddying fumes, turning her face from side to side to bathe each cheek in the rising heat. How could anyone ever complain of being *too hot*?

Then she followed him.

The wind blustered, gusting and then falling away. She clung to the cockpit coaming, knees so weak she swayed. The raw bean paste wasn't sitting well. She'd always loathed cilantro. Madsen was huddled atop the coachroof, staring over the side. She looked over, following his gaze, and all thought ceased.

The whale lay alongside, longer than the boat. Its massive back seemed to undulate, like a Dijon-colored mudbank, as the crests passed, lifting it a portion of a second after the hull, then letting them both down. As she watched the nostril opened and the spout jetted with a rushing hiss like a tractor-trailer releasing its brakes, spraying water and steam many feet into the air. It blew over them, bringing the nauseating now-familiar smell of decay, spoiled fish, and the sea. The aperture gaped again as the thing inhaled. The tail stirred in the water, yet did not rise. The massive bulk drifted slowly in to meet the hull with that same soft, yielding thud she'd felt from inside. The bilge pump hummed and a stream spurted from the side and played over the thing's flank.

"It's not ice," Madsen muttered. He grinned at her through the mask of grease and soot. Crystal blue eyes glittered madly. "Not ice."

"Oh God. Lars."

"It's the motor. Every time we run the motor."

"Can you shut it off? Maybe then . . ."

This seemed to strike him as a novel idea. He lifted his head.

As he did so the mass alongside rolled along its length, and the eye, the same one she'd met twice before, rotated up into view. She stared down but that dark orb did not meet her gaze. It seemed to be following Madsen as he crept aft on all fours and swung down into the companionway. The engine rose a note, knocked, quivered, and fell silent. The wind caught a rag of smoke and swept it over them.

In the silence the pump hummed again, the stream pulsed once more against the animal's side. The eye shifted to it, then squeezed closed.

With a lazy, graceful flick that massive tail stirred up whirlpools of olivine that lapped in little splashes against the hull. Sara crouched, watching it move off. She felt like howling, like cackling. "Go away," she screamed at it. "Leave us alone." She bent over the side and the raw protein came up in a rush, her stomach clenching like a drawn knot, caustic searing her throat, and she spat after the vomit into the sea, watching the thing plow through the water, waves breaking over it in little flurries of spray. Then a larger wave covered it. She stared, hope struggling against a weight that seemed to be crushing her heart.

"Fuck," Madsen said softly from the companionway.

It emerged from the wave with the huge head turned toward them. The tail came up. Then down.

With ponderous slowness it gathered speed, wrinkling up the sea like a pushed blanket until it seemed to be burrowing beneath it.

Anemone reeled at the impact, but also yielded, as if weary of the contest. A splintering and cracking came from forward. The whale had struck the starboard side this time, the undamaged side, two objects nearly the same size, but it was solid tons and the boat a mere bubble of overfatigued fiber and resin and thin wood cradling empty air. Sara watched the side cave in with utter detachment. Her hands tightened on the winch she clung to; that was all. A scream echoed from below. Kimura. "Hy. Hy!" she leaned to yell. "Are you all right?"

He was sobbing. "I am here. What is—"

"Get up on deck. The whale. It's back. Hurry!"

"I am—I am coming."

Madsen thrust past her, hustling himself down the companionway at the same time Kimura was trying to come up. "Lars—what are—"

"I'll stop it," he said over his shoulder. "Start the engine again. I'll stop it. For good, this time."

She hesitated, then bent to the starter. Still warm, the diesel cranked again immediately. But they still didn't have any way to make it turn the propeller. Or was that what he'd been working on down below? This glacial sequence of thoughts was interrupted as the whale slid away from the side. It sank slowly, as if stunned. But just as it vanished the tail rose, to just below the surface. The long dun-colored ghost slid forward, *beneath* the boat. A quiver ran through the hull, as if its back had brushed the downslung keel.

The sea herniated as if the whale had grown within it. Waves rolled out as it surged forth, breaching half its length before crashing back. As it leaped free she caught the prunelike wrinkles along the after part of its body, and, still dangling ahead of the fluke, the still-embedded harpoon. It waggled its head and half rolled, as if nearsightedly seeking them. Lay for a minute or two, then began swimming again.

"It is coming once more," Kimura remarked. Standing at the edge of the cockpit, he clapped his hands twice, halfheartedly, then let them drop. For a moment she wondered if he'd had some idea of sacrificing himself, as he thought Eddi had done. But he only watched, stretching out one hand to brace himself as *Anemone* leaned to starboard. They were taking water again, that was clear. After all the bailing, all the patching, they were still going down. Regardless of what the oncoming beast did now, it had sealed their fate. It swam faster, aiming this time for their port side, which it had damaged before. This time it would crash through, and down they'd go.

The forward hatch hinged up. Madsen's silly cap bobbed up, and both arms braced and drew his long body out onto the foredeck. A long handbag dangled from his shoulder. No, not a handbag. A case.

Lying quickly down full length on the snow-covered foredeck, he withdrew another launcher. He telescoped it apart and put one end over his shoulder. "Turn away," he shouted back.

She understood then, and bent to put the engine into gear. The whole stern began to shake, the shudder quickly growing so violent she had to cling to the pedestal. She put the rudder hard over and *Anemone* began to move, sagging away to starboard, slowly sinking. But wheeling, angling her bow away from the rapidly closing animal.

The whale was at speed now, the spout jetting at intervals like the stack of a steam locomotive. A crest burst and it crashed through, exploding a massive breach in that watery wall, then blasting out of it, head lifting and dropping as it pitched to the unimaginable power of that massively pistoning tail.

She raised her eyes to a figure on the coachroof. Kimura was bowing, hands together, to the approaching beast. He unclasped his hands and scattered something over the boat. Crystal granules of salt flew on the wind like tiny diamonds. Sara stood riveted, hands braced on the hard-over wheel, as *Anemone* shook. Green water lapped up over her pointed bow, as if she were bent on diving, like a submarine. The engine-pitch dropped, as if laboring under terrific load.

A flash of fire from the foredeck yanked her gaze back. The flame darted out across the sea and plunged into the whale's flank slightly ahead of the harpoon. A muffled bang echoed on the wind. For a moment the whale did not falter, only kept plunging ahead. Then, a fraction of a second after the first, came a second detonation, like a stick of dynamite damped under many feet of sand.

The whale's head lifted and blood exploded from its side. Yet its momentum carried it onward, the sea rolling away in front, and once again *Anemone* vibrated to the shock of many tons driven at furious speed. Sara crouched, desperately wrapping her arms around the pedestal to the sound of tearing carbon fiber and snapping ribs as the boat tilted back. Even the sinking bow came rearing up out of the sea. She caught a man's form sliding back and down off the canted foredeck, the still-smoking tube rolling away. At the last moment one arm snagged a line on the tarp-bound bundle lashed to the side. But the line came away, unraveling, and he slid under the lower lifeline and shot out into the roiling sea.

The boat hesitated, forced over so far the gunwale was buried deep. Then, to a ripping and snapping, as if suddenly released, she rolled back. Bobbed higher, as if released from some heavy burden carried too long.

The sperm's massive head lay half within the hull, which rolled and pitched about it with a grinding frisson. Blood poured from an open crater near one flipper as if fire-pumped. Pieces of white hull composite and dark wood bobbed out on boiling water, then were sucked back in. The great tail vibrated, then flexed upward slowly, as if drawn on invisible cables. It hesitated. Tensed. Then smacked down with a blow that sent the red-stained sea shattering apart, sending bloody spray over Sara as she cowered, covering her ears.

A head surrounded by a floating whirl of long blond hair came up screaming just under the counter. Beside it floated a silly cap with sad hound-dog eyes. Head and hat whirled in a complete turn. Bare hands white as marble thrashed at the icy sea.

Then the thrashing slowed. Lars's gaze sought hers, held it for perhaps a second; then slid off. The chin lowered deliberately, as if praying, into a welter of bubbles. And sank. The uplifted hands still stroked feebly, agitating the surface for some seconds, until the sea smoothed again, sealing itself on the glassy backside of a comber.

Slowly, *Black Anemone* began to capsize. The whale's tail flexed again. It dropped beneath the water, and the flipper jerked. Its head emerged, foot by foot, and then the monster floated free of the hole in the boat's side in a gush of water and debris like a monstrous birth.

As the big Dewoitine corkscrewed herself down into the green sea Sara let go of the wheel and scrambled backward. The backs of her legs struck the coaming at the rear of the cockpit and she went over. Her head hit something hard and she grabbed to stop herself but too late. She was sliding and then she was underwater, the cold green all around filling her mouth with an explosive unimaginable cold that drove fiery needles deep into every centimeter of exposed skin.

When she fought her way back to the surface a strange long red mass rolled uneasily on the sea. Some yards distant Hideyashi was fighting desperately beneath a heap of lines from the dumped-open cockpit lockers. He thrashed and clawed, but the heavy wet nylon kept dragging him down. At last, still struggling, he too sank, leaving only a heaving mass of blue and white cordage.

Something in that silent vanishing energized her. She furiously worked arms and legs, floating back from the russet curvature she now recognized as *Anemone*'s broad bottom, exposed obscenely to the rushing clouds. A blackgreen rime of weedy growth fringed the trailing edge of the now-vertical rudder, elevated high above her like some skyward-reaching pylon. There was no keel. It had wrenched out at last.

The cold was crushing her lungs. She stopped swimming a few yards away, and drifted, watching. At least the air in the mustang suit was buoying her up.

A clicking that seemed to penetrate her came through the water. It waned, then grew again. Grew into pain, and she cried out strangling through the water in her mouth. A turbulence like a waterfall rushed closer.

A gigantic form rose from the sea, streaming white water from puckered flanks. The whale blew in midair, but now black blood vomited from the blowhole. Its judging eye was squeezed closed. It fell from midair full on the capsized boat, filling the sea with a bursting crackle and sending a massive wall of water back into her face that tumbled her over and over like the backwash of a heavy surf.

21

The Shroud of the Sea

When she opened her eyes again a pearly opalescence filled her vision. She lay on her back, arms outstretched. Was her body gone? She couldn't feel it.

Then her gaze locked on a bird slanting far above, and the opaline light became clouds, writhing and re-forming as they drove rapidly from one wall of her vision to the other. As they did, more spilled over a horizon that as she turned her head seemed far too close, jagged and foam-topped. A wave lifted her, covering her face so she choked and coughed, then rolled away.

She turned on her belly and tried to swim but her arms were teak balks. They swung from the shoulders but she could not feel her hands or even her elbows.

When she lifted her head she floated alone on a dusky sea across which bits of white and brown were scattered as if dropped from a height. Shattered bits of foam hull coring, of soaked-through cardboard, bobbed here and there. Astonishingly little, though, and she could only conclude that most of what the boat carried had gone down with it.

The whale. She glanced around, suddenly stabbed by fear, but there was no sign of it. The rocket must have triggered the explosive in the harpoon too. Yet it had still lived for minutes afterward. Long enough to finish what it had begun, days before.

The flotsam rocked on long billows. Only four thousand miles to safety. She nearly laughed. She too was only floating debris. The last survivor. But not for long. Already the cold was creeping into her brain, slowing thoughts to molasses. The mustang suit would give her a little longer, but soon her core temperature would fall. The sea would suck out her heat, and give her peace in exchange. She'd fall apart and dissolve like sodden cardboard. She blinked something sharp from her eyes. She'd lost her goggles somehow, and her glasses, too, torn off by the wave-surge as the whale had breached for the last time.

But she had time for a last look around with those freezing eyes. At an old, old sight, yet somehow young; not changed a wink since she'd first glimpsed it as a little girl from the sand hills of Nantucket. Such a heartless immensity! A wave lifted her like God's hand, and from its crest she marveled at a white mass shining dully in the leaden light. A berg, far away. For a moment she hallucinated swimming to it. She stretched an arm, then let it subside. Smiled, and the fantasy flickered away.

A trough dropped her but the next wave lifted something dark a few yards away. It rolled uneasily, trailing a line. She eyed it with dull curiosity. Then breaststroked slowly toward it. Her arms barely moved. She went under and had to struggle up to the surface again. She was growing heavier. So heavy it was hard to stay afloat.

The second time she went down, surrounded by the serene translucent green she'd soon be part of, she looked yearningly up at the slowly receding, rocking, silvery surface. Perhaps she should just open her mouth. That at least was left: to choose death; and for an instant she relished that possibility, thrilled to the last exercise of will before whatever had moved and desired and called itself Sara Pollard returned to nonexistence. Merely to part her lips . . .

But she didn't want to drown. Everyone said dying of the cold was almost pleasant. So she fought her way to the air once more, knowing this was the last time she'd have the strength to do so. Reached out, and snagged a novocained claw in the tarp-wrapped bundle that rolled in the long swell.

Part of Dorée's exposure suit and life preserver was still visible beneath a corner that had come unwrapped again. Sara couldn't see the dead woman's face. She reached out to turn the tarpaulin back a little more, for company, than let her glove drop again. She didn't need to see her. They'd float together for a little while, that was all. She worked an arm through the lashing, sobbing, and finally got it through up to the elbow. Then she could relax. Stop fighting. Just drift. Drift and look out as thoughts oozed ever more slowly through her freezing brain.

Part of the sea. Part of Nature again. But had she ever really not been? And was all that immensity truly heartless? Maybe that was only her own error, her own blindness or conceit.

Her vision softened. She looked out across the beach to a light in a window. She knew that glowing square. It was the cottage she'd seen before. Now the shutters were thrown back and a welcoming flame glimmered and swayed. A kerosene light, like the one . . .

The one in her grandmother's house, out on the dunes. She remembered now how her mother's hand had enclosed her much smaller one. The sand had been gritty in her swimsuit. How she'd cried. She'd never thought of it since. But there the memory was, buried so long but still shining like dug-up gold.

Her heart beat, then beat again. Each time more weakly, as her blood congealed. As the world faded, she forced her eyes open for one last look.

She took the shape at first for a mirage, or a dream. A fragment of the sea that had separated from that sea to stand upright. Only when she'd closed her eyes, then opened them again, only when she saw it arching above her, blurry but there, present, real, and heard the voices calling down to her, did she believe it was the gray prow of ANS *Guerrico*, heading straight for her.

Epilogue

Los Angeles

The drama was done. Why then, she wondered, was she still here?

For the movie. Of course.

The press conference was at the Four Seasons. The lead actress had been joking with reporters that her six kids were bigger fans of her movies than she was. But this one, she predicted, would be different. She smoothed back long dark shining hair and curved those sensuous full lips and Sara could not help recalling how much Tehiyah had both scorned her and yearned to be her. And now the woman she'd envied most in the world would play her on the screen.

The director took the mike next. He leaned into it and his face fell into somber lines to convey *now we are in earnest*. "Seriously, this is an important film about a great woman and a cause she gave everything for. A wonderful actress gave her life to do something more important to her even than the cinema: defending the noblest creatures of the deep. *Eco Martyr*—the epic of the CPL's attack on the whaling fleet, and her heroic death—will be the most meaningful film of the year. Angelina, anything else?"

"Absolutely. I'm honored to be playing Tehiyah Dorée, and only hope she'll smile down on our efforts when the cameras start rolling."

Sara stood next to them on the platform, but did not speak. They'd all insisted she too was a "hero." Whatever that meant.

The Argentinian corvette that had picked her up had scoured the sea for other survivors. They'd found none, of course. But amid the floating life jackets and wreckage had bobbed Eddi's camera, buoyant in its waterproof housing. Captain Giordano said they'd picked up Madsen's distress calls, though Lars apparently hadn't been able to hear *Guerrico*'s replies on *Anemone*'s little handheld. The ship had homed in on the signal, but then he'd stopped transmitting, and they'd had to start a search.

She alone had survived to tell the tale. More than that: She had a book contract. An offer to narrate Eddi Auer's footage, as a PBS documentary. And a job as an adviser to this film, a "dramatization," "based on a true story."

More to the point, the Japanese had announced a voluntary halving of their quota for the next season, and would finally permit inspectors from the Whaling Commission aboard factory ships to certify the count.

It wasn't exactly what Mick and Lars had died for—nor, she guessed, Tehiyah and Eddi and Hideyashi and Dru—but it was a step forward. She herself had lost three fingers and the feeling in her hands and feet, but in view of what had happened to nearly everyone else who'd sailed from Ushuaia on the doomed *Black Anemone*, she'd won the lottery.

At center stage, the director introduced Jules-Louis Vergeigne. Dorée's former lover spoke for fifteen minutes about the CPL as bright-faced young volunteers passed out even brighter buttons with the League's logo and the legend *Earth to Japan: Whale Meat = Murder.* "We will never rest until we win," he ended. "As a token of that resolve, we have renamed the ship just chartered for next season's voyage. It will be christened . . . *Tehiyah Dorée*."

A burst of applause, in which everyone on the platform joined. When it died away Vergeigne leaned to the mike again. "And now, some brief remarks by Dr. Sara Pollard, the incredibly brave sole survivor of that fatal encounter with the whaling fleet that ended in Tehiyah's tragic death and the sinking of the antiwhaling cruiser *Black Anemone*."

She flinched. That wasn't what had happened, exactly. But she'd seen the advance script, and this wouldn't be the only change in the story. It's a movie, they kept saying. Roll with it. Take the money and run.

And that's exactly what she was doing, because they'd been perfectly clear: it would be made with or without her. Still, she didn't have to like it. And maybe someday, somehow, she'd find a way to tell the true story. The *whole* story.

The room quieted as she stepped forward. A buzz swept the audience as they noted the missing fingers, her clumsiness in grasping the mike. "I am so grateful to Angelina and Jules-Louis for honoring my good friend in this powerful way," she began. "We became so very close, all of us aboard *Anemone*. There was never any disagreement about our—our mission. Or the level of personal commitment it entailed from each of us. I will be proud to help make this film as authentic and exciting a re-creation of our voyage as I know Sebastian and John and everyone else wants it to be." She glanced at the director, who smiled and gestured; *Go on*.

She took a deep breath, and plunged ahead.

"I know you're here because of her and not me. And even Tehiyah wasn't really as big a star as she would've been, I think, if she'd lived. But I hope the film will convey something I came to realize while we were out there, freezing, tired, hurting, sick, afraid.

"All life is connected. In defending the great whales, we defend ourselves. In defending the earth, we defend our children's children. That's why this film will be so important. Those who died in the Antarctic wastes were the real heroes. I only hope . . . that we can do them justice."

She felt like throwing up, but they'd made her practice these "spontaneous remarks" over and over. There, she'd said them. She thrust the mike into someone's hands, she did not see just who, and pushed through to the stairs. A murmur rose, then trailed off. Heads swung away from Sara as the beautiful star took the mike again. Her honeyed words rose and laughter followed, cut off by the doors as they swung closed.

The young man who'd trailed her out joined her as she waited for the elevator. Her handler. She couldn't remember his name. "You're not staying for the party? Dr. Pollard?"

"What? Oh, no—no, I can't."

"Another commitment? You're not supposed to give any interviews, you know, until after—"

"They'll do better without me." She grinned as the door slid open. "The skeleton at the feast."

He made as if to come with her, but she halted him with a raised hand. "I'm kidding. Okay? I'll be back. I promise. Just need some air."

He looked doubtful, but stopped as the doors closed behind her.

Outside she stood for a long time bathed in the LA summer heat and car exhaust and the exhalation of air conditioners. Sweat prickled her skin. She plucked her shirt away, panting in sudden terror.

Around her human beings seethed like krill sensing a warming sea. They thronged the sidewalks and surged across the street. So many. So different. Their expressions worried, intent. Yet here and there . . . that lone man across the street . . . that woman at the wheel of the small car. Here and there, in passing visages, she saw the outcast, the beast. The rogue.

She no longer knew what that word meant. Only, perhaps, one who went solitary, perhaps even hated, but whose course was set by the compass of his own will. Those individuals wrote history.

But there was a larger stage, even, than human history.

Alone among the species of earth, one had gone rogue. Its hand, like Ishmael's, was raised against all others.

Lifting her head to soaring towers rearing into a darkening sky, she shuddered as if harrowed by an icy wind. Solitary, self-willed, self-obsessed, contemptuous of the past and careless of the future, Man himself was the rogue. But only for a time.

Only for a time.

Acknowledgments

Ex nihilo nihil fit. First of all thanks to the master, Herman Melville, in whose deep-graven wake—along with that of Joseph Conrad—all writers of the sea must sail. For this book I'm also indebted to J. C. Alonso, Robert P. Arthur, David Baxter, Ina Birch, Julia Blythe, Barbara Brown, Bonnie Culver, Lourdes Figueroa, Herb Gilliland, Adam Goldberger, Terra Layton, Terta Gillian Lewis, Kate Longley, Eric LoPresti, Pamela McGrady, Kate Ottaviano, Charle Ricci, Kathryn Parise, Naia Poyer, Matt Shear, Kenneth J. Silver, Bob White, Tom and Jean Wescott, Frances Anagnost Williams, and Georgina Winton, along with the following institutions: the Nantucket Atheneum, the Maria Mitchell Natural Science Museum, the Mariners' Museum in Newport News, the Provincetown Center for Coastal Studies, the Norman Mailer Writers Colony in Provincetown, the Nantucket Whaling Museum, the New Bedford Whaling Museum and Research Library, the Wilkes University Creative Writing Program, the Eastern Shore Public Library, and the Virginia Center for the Creative Arts, Mt. San Angelo.

Few novels stem from pure imagination. My discussions of humpback songs were informed by Mercado, Herman, and Pack in *Aquatic Mammals*, 2003. The description of sperm codas is from the papers of Ricardo Antunes, Luke Rendell, Hal Whitehead, Shane Gero, and Tyler Schulz. Descriptions of chimp behavior and primate research were largely from Muller and Mitani, 2005, and John Cohen's "Thinking Like a Chimpanzee" in the September 2010 issue of *Smithsonian*. The discussion of Von Economo neurons was written after perusing Ingrei Chen's "The Social Brain" in the June 2009 issue of the same magazine. Philip Hoare's magical *The Whale* has great descriptions of sperm whales in close-up, as does, of course, Melville. The tactics employed by the fictional CPL and their Japanese adversaries were informed by Peter Heller's *Whale Warriors* and the *Whale Wars* television series, plus U.S. Navy and IMO anti-boarding protocols and my own experiences in the Arctic and elsewhere both in large craft and under sail. John Nelson's *A Year in the Life of a Shinto Shrine* was useful for Hy Kimura's background. Other helpful works were Shapiro and Bjelke's *Time on Ice*, the Lonely Planet *Guide to Antarctica*, and Dan Beachy-Quick's poetic and haunting *A Whaler's Dictionary*, which I had the great pleasure of hearing him read from at the 2011 AWP conference in New York.

Let's emphasize that these were consulted for the purposes of *fiction*. I am *not* saying that anything in these references leads to the conclusions my characters reach or voice.

The translation of Soseki's haiku is widely quoted, but I have been unable to find any attribution for insertion of the original translator's name.

My most grateful thanks to George Witte, long-time editor and friend, with whom I've been discussing a reprise of the Mocha Dick legend for some years; to J. Michael Lennon, Wilkes University colleague, who also shared his thoughts on how to tell an old tale anew; and to Lenore Hart, anchor on lee shores, and my guiding star when skies are clear.

As always, all errors and deficiencies are my own.